M.K.R.LAMBERT

# *Scrungle Bungus & The Magic Fungus*

Alice
MEDIA

*First edition*

*Cover art by Kelsey Lambert*
*Advisor: Reece Lambert*
*Editing by Susan Young*

*This book was professionally typeset on Reedsy.*
*Find out more at reedsy.com*

*To Susi, Sis, Kelsey & Reece*
*Thank You.*

'I saw a cloud shaped like a cloud."

PEETLES

# Contents

# Foreword

This is a book with lots of words in it. Hope you enjoy it.

# *Preface*

**BE WARNED:**
**THIS IS NOT A CHILDREN'S BOOK.**

The book starts as a fairy tale and stays that way, to be honest. It does, however, deal with adult themes, is satirical at times, takes the piss out of the establishment, and blatant stupidity of the human race.

**There are bits of swearing throughout.**

Also, most of the words are from the English spelling, i.e., colour, labour, etc.

Hobgoblin Translations

Ya
[You:]
***pronoun***

1. From the English (you) used to refer to the person or people that the speaker is addressing: *What ya deein like?*

deein
['doing]
***noun***

1. From the English (doing) the activities in which a particular person engages: *What ya deein like?*

Gan

[go]

***verb***

1. From the English (Go) move from one place to another; travel: *Gan on get lost.*

Reet

[right]

***adjective***

1. From the English (right) forming adverbs and adjectives of time and place; travel: *Reet where's ya papers, like.*
2. Used for emphasis with adverbs and prepositions:

# Acknowledgments

Thanks to the constant UK roadwork that inspired a large section of this book, all the people who voted for Brexit, and Donald Trump, they are all a continuous source of inspiration.

There are a lot of vacuous individuals out there, and for the most part, in positions of power. I am constantly amazed by the human race and our ability to champion the ridiculous, inane, and pointless.

I would also like to thank the individual who dealt with my claim at Universal Credit; you will be thought of forever, by me as a complete and utter BASTARD.

# *Introduction*

THIS IS NOT A CHILDREN'S BOOK.

A bit is of swearing throughout.

# One

## Scrungle Bungus

Our story, like most good stories, starts up a tree. Not an everyday tree, but the only one of its kind, the Chanananananananana tree. This was its official name, but it sounded like you were freezing to death while falling down a well, so everyone shortened it to the Chana Tree.

Here, in its highest branches, an unusual creature called Scrungle Bungus had made a home. From the outside, it looked like the nest of an exceptionally large bird with an appreciation for medieval cantilevered turret design. Inside, there was a kitchen, a living room, a library, a small observatory, and a bedroom with an en-suite.

The scent of the Chana tree was of shoe polish and Thursday afternoons, which Scrungle liked very much. In the summer, the leaves of the Chana tree, a deep and beautiful purple, grew in a variety of different sizes. It didn't shed its leaves in winter; they just grew larger like enormous cabbage leaves, creating a blanket that kept all that lived in the tree cosily cocooned until spring.

The bark had the texture of smooth leather, cream in colour, which became a deeper beige as it neared the base. On the longest day of every fourth year, the tree would bear one fruit in the shape of an anvil, which was confusing for blacksmiths or scrap metal merchants.

Scrungle was a solitary creature and for the most part, content with how things were. He did feel lonely at times, but then he would find ways to amuse himself. Like putting things on hooks that were just out of reach. This was tricky as he was seven feet tall and his ceilings weren't that high.

A large portion of his time was spent reading. With no particular preference in genre, he would spend hours sitting in the high-backed wing chair, lost in an adventure, crime thriller, or mystery. It was Scrungle's way of learning about the larger world around him without actually having to go there. On occasion, he would sport a red crushed velvet smoking jacket while he sat and read. He didn't wear it often, as he didn't smoke.

When the weather was fine, he would walk around the little area where he lived, collecting mushrooms or finding sticks to throw out of the Chana tree when it became windy, as it felt like he was recycling and doing his bit for the environment.

He didn't have friends on the ground or neighbours; the one exception to this was the farmer, who owned the only farm for miles around. It was well away from Scrungle and the Chana tree, on the other side of the hill. In all the years Scrungle had lived in the Chana tree, the two had never spoken, just nodded at each other from a respectful distance. Then the farmer would shuffle slowly away, chewing on a hoof that used to be attached to a caribou. Scrungle was happy about this, as the farmer was usually high on cannabinoids and naked, except for a pair of hand-stitched moccasins, tied together with a piece of string, one green and the other yellow.

It was only in the evening that Scrungle would sometimes think he could do with a friend. Using his little telescope, Scrungle would gaze at the stars, making charts of the planets' positions. The enormity of the vast cosmos would make him feel profoundly small and insignificant. A simple longing to connect with another creature would come over him, to share in observing the sheer beauty and magnitude of the constellations—someone to talk to and, in doing so, feel less alone.

One day, just before the arrival of the first day of summer, Scrungle found himself feeling rather hungry. After building up an appetite spending the morning sorting through shoes that he had found while fishing in a pond for house bricks, it prompted him to opt for his usual meal of fungus. Scrungle had an extraordinary affinity for all types of fungi, and, unbeknownst to him, he was magically immune to the effects of fungus poisoning.

This was, in retrospect, fortunate, as it was the only thing his body would absorb.

There was one particularly special kind of fungus that was not for eating, as Scrungle used it to get in and out of the Chana tree. This magic fungus he kept in a special lidded clay jar, an amphora, in the kitchen. To use the magic mushrooms, he would just walk out to the branch that served as his front door, then simply snap one in two and throw it up over himself; it would explode into what Scrungle thought of as confetti fireworks, falling on his head and shoulders. As always, a light and floaty feeling would engulf him. Stepping off, he would gently glide to the ground below. To get back in, he would snap another magic mushroom in half (obviously having remembered to put one in his pocket before he decided to go out), flex at the knees, and with a bounce, Scrungle would float up.

He didn't wear clothes as such, only a top hat, and then only when he felt the need to impress. His body just made pockets when he needed them. The pockets had unknown depths that could accommodate a

large number of things without getting full.
The exception to this rule was the magic fungus. Over the years and through experimentation, he found that he couldn't put more than one of the special magic mushrooms in his pocket at any given time. Scrungle had tried to add a second, but the following glittering explosion had left him floating in the air for a good twenty minutes. This was confusing, as the long clay amphora in which he had found the fungi had been stuffed to the brim. However, it did have writing carved into the lid, which Scrungle surmised must be some form of spell or a use-by date. Either way, the stone jar did something to stop the fungus from self-detonating and creating an early new year.

Scrungle now stood on the creamy-coloured branch that served as his front door (or back door, depending on which way you decided to orientate yourself) and took a precautionary look around before going down to ground level, as you never knew who or what might be lurking. Nothing looked out of the ordinary, so back inside his home, he removed the lid of the large amphora and peered into its depths. To his utter dismay, there was only a single mushroom left.

"Oh dear." He said out loud.
Well, not really out loud, as he was telepathic and didn't have a mouth. It was an unusual kind of telepathy, as he couldn't literally read thoughts but could hear, see, feel, and interpret the meaning of the sounds, twitches, and movements that humans and creatures made. And, when Scrungle communicated back, it was into the mind of the creature he was conversing with in such a way that they could understand his meaning. Scrungle was oblivious to his power and how he could comprehend any form of communication. Being such a solitary creature, he assumed that everyone conversed this way. Standing now, looking into the nearly empty jar and thinking, Scrungle couldn't remember if he had ever refilled it.

The jar had been found many years ago when Scrungle and his

parents had all lived together in a huge wicker basket on the open grasslands near Splandoolie. They had taken a day trip to see an outcrop of rock on a nearby hillside that looked like the face of a depressed horse. The young Scrungle had been running in a field, pretending he was in the last throes of radiation poisoning when he had tripped. One of his stilt-like legs had caught the lid of a hastily buried clay jar. Some of the contents spilled out, breaking in two. Almost at once, the glittering, exploding fungus made him float up, then bob gently at head height. His parents had to tie a piece of string around his ankle, holding onto him like a balloon. Having no idea how long the floating would last, they started a sincere and earnest conversation, speculating that Scrungle would have to get a job as a wind chime or a weather sock when he grew up. Scrungle, on the other hand, was joyous and believed this was the best fungus he had ever found, pleading with his parents that he should keep it. This was after he had stopped all his floaty business and was firmly on the ground again. Eventually, they said yes, as long as he washed his hands.

"What to do?" He said out loud, in his head.

The idea of a ladder or rope jumped into his head, which he dismissed, as he was a terrible climber. Long legs that tapered down to a stubby point; no feet; long, thin arms with a hand that only had three fingers (and one of those doubled as a thumb).

Scrungle was also completely white, with a large, slightly flattened onion-shaped head, two round black eyes, and a drooping, rotund body that wobbled when he walked. On top of all this, there was his long, white nose, the kind you may find on a baby elephant without the nostril part. It kind of hung like a white sausage pendulum, which tended to get in the way while he played the violin. Not that he played the violin. He just thought it would so he didn't.

There was only one thing he could do, and that was to search for more of the magic fungus. Scrungle spent the rest of the morning filling his pockets with an odd assortment of things he thought he might need for an unspecified period of walking.

Once he felt he had finally packed into his pockets what he needed to pack, especially the now empty clay amphora jar and lid, Scrungle stood, taking one last look around his lovely, comfortable home, his telescope, his collection of peculiar-shaped chunks of coal, the rude vegetable compendium, the closet where he kept his smoking jacket, his books, and his reading chair.

Walking back to the branch and taking a deep breath, heart racing a little, he snapped the last of the magic fungus in two and threw it over his head. It exploded into fungus confetti, and a familiar floating feeling washed over him. Then he took a step off the tree branch as the last of the special fungus did its usual magic.

He descended at an even speed towards the ground. As his spindle-like legs touched down, a terrible thought washed over him. Standing and looking up, he felt a sense of dread. Maybe this was the last time he would ever be able to get back into his home, forever left to look at it longingly from afar. Had he just made a terrible mistake?

* * *

The day was warm, but not overly hot. Far away to Scrungle's left was a mountain range, hazy in the distance, its dark brown base blending into purple and dark blues, capped at the top with peaks of white, partly obscured by low clouds. To his right was a field of sweetcorn. The rustling sound of the leaves was carried over to Scrungle on a light breeze. The breeze got tired of carrying the rustling sound over and started carrying birdsong instead. Then it stopped its carrying entirely to lie down in the middle of the dirt track and have a nap.

Ambling along, feeling the grass on the stubby ends of his legs, he could see that straight ahead lay the King's Road. Scrungle had only been on the road once in his life when he was searching for his father. It was then that he saw the Chana tree for the first time, deciding it would be a lovely place to build a home and promptly giving up the search for his missing parent. Well, the home had already been built—turrets and all. Only after investigating a little closer did Scrungle realise it was abandoned, so he just sort of took it over.

As he drew nearer to the King's Road, he remembered that it was paved with solid flagstones and that some stones were made of flags. The stones made of flags weren't the best to walk on, as they had a damp and squishy feel from last night's rain.

With absolutely no idea which way to go, where to look, or how to get there. Scrungle turned and stood looking back at the Chana tree, admiring how beautiful it was, nestled in the little valley of the hills. Eventually, he turned away and stepped onto the King's Road. Setting off along it in a state of mild apprehension, he knew with unfettered certainty that the hunt for magic fungus had begun and that at some point he would need to fill in his life insurance documents.

Scrungle walked at a leisurely pace, stopping now and then to investigate fungus at the side of the road or an outcrop of fungi growing from a tree stump. He ate most of what he found, delighting in the different tastes he discovered. Some tasted like candy floss, some like toffee apples, and others like shepherd's pie. Then others might taste like broccoli, plastic, and sometimes industrial cleaner. There was no way to tell how it would taste just by looking. The most plain-looking toadstool could have an amazing flavor, while the most decorative fungi could taste like a wet paper towel or a speech from a politician.

The corn fields bordering the King's Road had soon given way to rows and rows of tall and elegant sunflowers, turning their heads to follow the sun. The field of bright yellow flowers kept Scrungle company until they abruptly ended, and the forest began with big, strong oaks, beeches, and sycamores to fill the gaps, and now and then, a larch for variety. The road had narrowed a little, and tufts of grass had sprung up in between some of the uneven flagstones. The tree leaves that shaded the road obscured the midday sun. A little trickle of a stream ran along the side of him as he walked.

He saw a particularly lovely-looking crop of fungi. The heads of the mushrooms were a deep red, with little pink spots shaped like hearts. They were a decent size, but not so big as to look bloated. Scrungle stooped down and picked one up. His nose snuffled around it to get a scent of how it might taste before he absorbed it into his skin by mushing it all over himself as if he were rubbing pastry in.

"Oi," said a voice.

"Hello,"

Scrungle threw out the reply telepathically and slowly turned his head to find the source of the 'Oi'. A fairy, no bigger than three inches, sparkling in yellows and greens, its little wings buzzing, floated into Scrungle's field of vision. The little face was red with annoyance.

"You've just ate my home, you big stupid twat."

The fairy waggled a tiny finger at Scrungle.

"Oh, I am sorry! Although I think it should have been 'eaten' rather than 'ate',"

Scrungle replied, brushing what was left of the little fairy's home out of his spindly hands. They stood staring at each other. The fairy flew closer to Scrungle, who went a bit cross-eyed trying to keep her in focus.

"What are you, the grammar police? What're you gonna do then?"

Her voice had a high-pitched sharpness to it that hurt the ears.

"Digest, I would imagine,"

Scrungle said after taking a moment to think about what the fairy had said. The little fairy, getting herself rather vexed, deliberately flew in and out of focus.

"If I had known, I wouldn't have eaten your home."
Said Scrungle, pleased with himself that he had accidentally made a rhyme.

"I had all my things in there."
There was an indignant tone to the fairies' voice. The happiness that Scrungle experienced with his rhyming prowess was short-lived after the fairy accusation of home wrecker. Scrungle did feel a little bad that he had eaten someone's dwelling, but the more they stood looking at each other, the more Scrungle thought that it didn't seem big enough to accommodate the fairy.

"Did it have a living room?"
He inquired, trying to get his head around how the fairy could have lived in such a small space.

"Yes, of course!"

"Where was the living room?"

"What are you, an interior designer?"
Said the fairy getting annoyed.

"I'm just trying to get a feel for the space."
The fairy hesitated for just a moment.

"It was in the stem."

"It looked a bit small to have a living room there; the stem was as thick as your body. Did you just stand all the time?"
Scrungle's tone was inquiring, but the question could easily be misinterpreted. He hadn't had many dealings with the wider world, so his social skills were a bit rusty.

"I'm flexible; I do pilates," countered the fairy. She had flown back a little and wasn't making eye contact anymore.

"Did it have a lot of rooms?"
Scrungle asked, trying to imagine the living conditions.

"I'm not going to describe my home to you. I'm minding my own business, and the next thing I know, a big, lumbering simpleton comes along and eats it!"

The fairy's face flushed red as she flew closer. Her fists were up and ready for a fight.

"Well, my father always said, Do unto others as you would have done unto yourself. I will help you find a new home."

Not expecting the reply to be as accommodating some of the fight melted away.

"Err, no, umm, I'm not happy with that. I want to be recompensed."

"Recompensed?"

Scrungle questioned, not sure what the little fairy meant. The fairy then crossed her arms while hanging perfectly still in mid-air, which Scrungle found rather impressive.

"Gold"

"I don't have any." Said Scrungle.

"Rubies, emeralds, sapphires, or diamonds, then?" Rattled off the fairy.

"I haven't any of them either."

"Precious metals: silver, platinum, ruthenium, osmium, rhodium, palladium, bitcoin?"

The fairy was becoming more and more desperate. Scrungle shook his head, then visualised his pockets. As they materialised, he started to rummage around in them for something that might help the situation.

"I have a hat stand."

He then started pulling out, hand over hand, a long, ornate wooden hat stand made out of cedar.

"My father made it from a single tree branch that fell and hit my mother on the head after a really bad storm. When she regained consciousness, she had no memory of who we were, who she was, or why we were all standing on a fridge. The next day she ran away, leaving a note saying she was going to seek her fortune as a french polisher."

Scrungle stopped for a moment and patted the hat stand as one would a jar full of methamphetamine.

"As a reminder of their love, my father whittled the tree branch into the hat stand using a salad fork and a spoon. He left not long after its completion to search for her. I now carry it with me to remember them both. When I have it, I don't feel so alone. You can have it to help pay for a new home or as a house-warming gift."

Scrungle ended the story, and then the fairy sighed and buzzed over to the hat stand to sit on it. She mumbled something that Scrungle couldn't understand. He moved over so he could hear her better. Then remembered he was telepathic, but moved closer, all the same as mumbling is mumbling.

"It wasn't my home." The fairy said it in a quiet voice.

"Oh." Said Scrungle.

"I was just sitting on it. I heard you coming and hid. I just thought I could make some cash out of the situation."

The fairy was still not looking at Scrungle, who then tilted his head.

"Why do you need the gold?"

"Bloody taxes! A stupid little man on a donkey came around, taxing everyone on behalf of bloody King Fromp. They're building some stupid new bypass that no one needs. I've had to downsize."

Scrungle heard this and thought of the day, which seemed a long time ago to him now, when an emissary to the King of Plomb had turned up sitting astride a small donkey.

The rotund representative of the king had started shouting up at Scrungle about paying taxes and his civic duty as a homeowner. Scrungles' engagement in the conversation came across as rather odd, as being telepathic. Scrungle was in a three-way conversation with the little man, and the donkey who he found out was named Kevin. He did try to include the little man, but he just kept shouting about taxes and who the hell was Kevin.

Scrungle found this terribly rude, so eventually he tuned out the little man and talked directly to the donkey. Scrungle had chatted away with Kevin about shoes, how tricky it is to get a good haircut, and what it would sound like to freeze to death while falling down a well. This one-sided conversation increasingly disturbed the little man, who started shouting even louder. It had a marked effect on the man's complexion as he proceeded to turn a nice shade of blue the more agitated he became. Eventually screaming himself into a very attractive shade of azure, giving up the demand for taxes and leaving on Kevin.

"Did you know that the donkey's name is Kevin? He's working on his portfolio of watercolours so he can put on an exhibition. I didn't like the man he was carrying either; he turned blue with shouting so much. All a bit odd, thinking about it."

The fairy looked up with surprise. Then surprise thought better of itself, realised it wasn't where it should be, and settled on the face of the fairy.

"You've met him, then? The fat blue bloke on the donkey?" She asked.

"Yes, obsessed with taxes, just seemed to go on and on about them. Then he got angry and went away."

The fairy paused, then sighed again.

"I'm sorry I lied to you. I'm just finding it hard to make ends meet at the moment. Thank you for the offer of the hat stand; it was really kind of you."

Then she smiled a sad little smile. Scrungle extended his thin hand for the little fairy to shake.

"Well, my name is Scrungle Bungus. You are?"

"Chicken Beak," said the fairy, brightening up a little. "Most people call me Chick, or Ken."

"Nice to meet you, Ken."

Then the fairy flew into Scrungle's outstretched hand and did a little dance to a salsa come boss nova rhythm that came out of nowhere. As she did this, Scrungle used his free hand to put the hat stand back in his pocket. He had to shake it a little to get it in.

"I've not seen you around here before," said Ken as the music did a nice even fade.

"No, I don't go out much, you see. I'm off to find some magic fungus that can help me get back into my house." Scrungle offered in the way of explanation.

"I understand. Rent arrears. Find them, sell them, and pay the landlord off."

"Well, not exactly. When I throw a piece of the mushroom up into the air, it breaks into tiny pieces, covering me like confetti and making me float. My house is high up in a tree, you see." Scrungle, mildly amused, that the end of the sentence rhymed.

"You own your own home? Well done, you. Why don't you put stairs in, though, or a ladder?" Ken said, trying to be helpful.

"Good point," Scrungle replied stroking his long white nose, it did occur to Scrungle that he had thought about installing a staircase, but being high up in a tree meant that no one bothered him. Most creatures just ignored his home, and he liked it that way. Admittedly, he did feel a little lonely at times; sometimes the winters felt too long, and having a good friend would certainly help pass the time. Maybe someone to talk to about mushrooms or play a game of 'Guess where I stuck my finger last.' Having stairs would mean that if he did make some friends, they could come and go whenever they pleased. On the other side of this reasoning was that he was never bothered by uninvited guests, and he didn't want any friends. Putting something in that could be used by strangers without permission or, fungus forbid, a tax inspector. That would never do.

"I think I'll stick with the fungus."

After a little deliberation, it occurred to him.

"You wouldn't happen to know where I could find some fungus like that, do you?"

"I never heard of anything like that," Said Ken, then continued.

"But in Plombree there is the Sorcerers Collective Society, or SCS for short. I did hear they had merged with Amazing Shine. Might be able to help there. It was a place to learn magic, but now it's just a place to buy a lot of stuff you don't need with guaranteed one-week speed delivery. Just keep following the road. Well, until you come to the roadworks and the detour,"

The little fairy took flight from Scrungles hand and flew up to his eyeline. Producing a wand from the folds of her dress she sprinkled a little fairy dust over Scrungle.

"A blessing, and a safe journey. Sorry, I tried to scam some cash out of you." Then she disappeared in the blink of an eye and a light popping sound. Scrungle pondered what Ken had said. He had never been to the capital or even a large town.

In his mind, Plombree City was a distant rumour, like the idea of garlic bread or statutory workers' rights, but it settled Scrungle's mind some, knowing that if he didn't find the magic mushroom by random chance, he could seek help from the SCS and Amazing Shine.

As he walked on he hoped that he would meet more people along the King's Road who were just as stimulating. The sun, low on the horizon, colored the sky in reds and purples of twilight as it began to set. He was very deep in the forest now. The road went straight on through the trees, lost in the distance without a turn or bend, its form blurring in the approaching darkness. The stone flags had become uneven, and the flags that had been put down instead of stones were filthy. Some of the paving at the edge of the road, lifted by the tree roots, had become a tripping hazard. Scrungle took all this in and still managed to take a tumble. Someone needs to put a warning up, he thought as he regained his feet. Further on, after dusting himself down, he passed a fox that was writing a sonnet. Its back was propped up against a tree. A lantern hung on a low branch.

A quill lashed to one paw with heavy twine and a piece of parchment glued to the other. The fox paid little mind to Scrungle only to ask if he knew of any word that rhymed with orange. Scrungle admitted he didn't.

Scrungle yawned and realised he had not walked this much for a long time. Where to sleep, he thought. Fishing in his pocket, he pulled out a loyalty card for the Inn of the Horseshoe and Bucket. It had been a gift on his eighteenth birthday, in case he ever went travelling. The franchise, he had been told, spanned the length and breadth of the land, with easy parking and a children's play area at every inn. He had used it once, while he was trying to find his father, who was looking for his mother, who was trying to find herself. He stayed at the first inn he came across, and since he didn't have any gold, he found it steeply overpriced. The trolls at the bar, seasonal workers under a nearby bridge, kept pointing and laughing at his nose. He decided after that day he would only use it in an absolute emergency. Now, standing on the King's Road at dusk, Scrungle wasn't sure if this counted as an emergency or not.

After a glance up and down the road, he realised he had no chance of finding one of the franchised inns tonight anyway. He had no option but to keep on walking. The forest, which had been welcoming under the bright day's sunshine, now started to take on a mildly spooky feel with the lengthening shadows. Scrungle was by no means the bravest of creatures; he now just wanted to find somewhere to set up camp. As luck would have it, within a few moments, he came across a signpost with rather nice writing. In the fading light, he could still read the sign.

**Recreational area, 10 yards.**

On the sign were little bumps, which Scrungle found to be braille for the visually impaired. Although Scrungle couldn't read braille, he stretched up and let his spindly fingers run across the little bumps, enjoying the feel of the little dots on the skin of his fingertips. Soon enough, he came to a small recess off the road. To some, it would be a recreational area, others a picnic point, and to others a passing place, but the vast majority of travellers, if polled by an impartial agency, would have said they couldn't give a shit what it was called.

It had two long stone benches, an ornately carved stone table, and an overflowing stone recycling bin with a wanted poster on the side and full of crumpled-up bits of parchment with the word orange written on them and then scribbled out.

"As good as anywhere, I suppose,"

Scrungle said out loud to no one but himself and he began pulling things from his magic pockets that could help make his makeshift campsite a bit more cosy. Presently, he had a hammock suspended between two trees next to the picnic table. Hanging on sticks speared into the ground were yellow bioluminescent fungi in jars. It gave the area a nice, homely glow. Scrungle then pulled out from his unfeasibly deep pockets the hat stand, plus a small set of bookshelves, a pajama set with little anchor motifs, a towel, a washcloth, a toothbrush (for no apparent reason, but it is the social norm for bathroom necessities), and a portable shower unit complete with curtain and drip tray.

The last thing he brought out was a small, ornate fireplace and mantelpiece. He put some logs into the fireplace with a healthy dose of lighter fluid. Taking a step back, he struck a match. After it caught a good flame, he threw it into the fire. There was a quick 'woosh' sound, and the fire was well ablaze.

"It'll have to do,"
Scrungle lay in the hammock, covered by an attractive strawberry-patterned duvet, thinking about what might lie ahead and the capital city Plombree. Not committing to any answer, he settled further into the hammock, enjoying the gentle breeze that swayed him from side to side.

Deep in the forest, a barbershop badger quartet sang songs about hunting for grubs at night, the latest fashion trends, and how long relatives should stay after a family gathering before it could be classed as outstaying your welcome. The four-part harmonies drifted through the woods, soothing and settling all that lived within, except for the larks, as they had been up early. The larks kept sending one of the flock to where the badgers were singing to ask them to be quiet. The badgers would quieten down for a while, but like all performers, they got into the groove, and the volume would go up, starting the whole debacle again. This didn't bother Scrungle, as he was very sleepy now. He could see some of the night sky through the treetop canopy and started naming the twinkling stars and the positions of the constellations. Their names he had learned from his time spent in his observatory and his vast book collection. Before he knew it, he had drifted off into a sound sleep.

# Two

## *Knights of Colour*

Scrungle was woken by the sound of horses. It was still early, and the sunlight wasn't doing much to penetrate the canopy of leaves as he lowered the duvet from his face to look at the scene before him. A group of knights in armour were hanging around the picnic area. The metal of the horseshoes clattered on the flagstones of the little recess.

A yell of annoyance came from the horse-riders whenever they trod on a flag pretending to be a stone. It would jerk the horse forward, nearly unseating their rider.

The riders had either not seen the seven-foot Scrungle suspended in a hammock between two oak trees or they had all just elected to ignore him. The first thing that Scrungle noticed was the individual armour they were wearing. It wasn't brightly coloured or garish; the hue was subtle but noticeable. A blue, red, black, white, and grey knight were in the picnic space. Scrungle had a vague idea that the grey colour was called cheeky camper, and the red was known as angry father. Like the capital city of Plombree, Scrungle had heard of the Knights of Colour, but this was the first time he had seen one, let alone five.

Sitting on a much smaller horse was a single squire. The horse was heavily laden with saddlebags and equipment, pulling a cart full of lances. Both horse and rider looked immeasurably tired, with the squire squinting periodically and yawning.

As Scrungle watched, the squire gave herself a hard slap across her face when her body started to slide out of the saddle.

"Well done, Sir Red. Your tracking skills have, as usual, proven to be the best among us,"

"You having a go at me again, Sir Grey?" The Red Knight turned his horse, so he was parallel to the Grey Knight. The Red Knight's hand was gripping the top of his sword's pommel, but not in a fun time way. His visor was up, staring intently at the Grey Knight who took off his helmet and shook out his long blond hair. He was gorgeous.

"Of course not, darling! What gave you that impression?" Said Sir Grey, adding a wink. The Red Knight bristled with irritation. The White Knight trotted over, understanding that the mood needed to be lightened.

"Gentlemen! Let us dismount and have something to eat. We can discuss tactics while the morning is young." This said, he got off his horse. After a moment, the rest of the knights did the same.

The yawning squire hurried over and took the horse's reins from the knights, tying them off to a nearby tree. Unfastening saddlebags from her horse, struggling with the weight, she dragged them over to the stone table. Quickly laying out provisions, plates, a griddle, a spit, a toasting rack, pots, pans, a fondue set, and a barbecue stand, then set about tenderising some chicken.

The oblivious knights sat chatting, seating themselves around the stone picnic table. Their armour clattered loudly on the stone of the bench. Each knight took their ornate helmets off, placing them next to the plates, goblets, forks, and napkins the squire was laying out.

All the knights were handsome, with strong jawlines and healthy complexions, which tend to come from being in the top percentile of the class structure. Maybe they have better access to a healthy diet and medical care, thought Scrungle in an absent-minded way. The Black Knight sported a short black beard, while the Blue Knight looked the youngest, with a well-kept face covering. The Red Knight had what could be called a 'Wild West' moustache. It suited his intense stare. The White and Grey Knights were similar in appearance, except for the Grey Knight's perfectly manicured nails and styled hair, which didn't look any worse for wear after being encased in the knight's helmet and gloves.

Now the hard-working squire had a little fire going and was toasting some bread while frying sausages. She stood on one leg, and the outstretched foot gripped a whisk, beating eggs into a creamy sauce. Looking down along the stone table, she shook her head, teeth gritted tight together.

Scrungle had been watching all this over the top of the duvet. None of the knights had said anything about the hammock and makeshift home beside them. He now felt things were getting a little awkward, and they were all subconsciously aware of the cusp of going over the appropriate time to say hello or for Scrungle to pull the duvet back over himself and pretend he hadn't heard all the racket.

"Hello," adding a little wave of his three-fingered hand above the duvet. The knights stopped eating their breakfasts and looked at Scrungle.

"I hope we didn't wake you," said the Blue Knight.

"It's the metal horseshoes you see. Very noisy," added the White Knight.

"Ah no, thank you. I was awake and thinking I should get up now anyway."

Scrungle, not wanting the knights to feel bad about disturbing his slumber, pulled the duvet back and swung his spindly white legs over the side of the hammock. Having never slept in a hammock before, his body weight shifted too quickly. He fell head-forward towards the ground. Not thinking, he instinctively tucked his large, round white head into his chest, did a forward roll, and then stood up in a kind of gymnastic pose that looked like he had been practicing. If it had been in competition, he would have scored a very respectable 8.9.

Standing there with his nose swinging back and forward like a pendulum, the heads of the watching squire and knights started to move in time with it. Grabbing the wayward appendage Scrungle stopped what could have turned into group hypnosis, the seated knights then gave him a spontaneous round of applause.

"Do you do that every morning?" Asked the Grey Knight.

"Ah no, truthfully, it was more of an accident." Said Scrungle. The Knights gave another smattering of applause.

"What's your name?" asked the Red Knight, not looking up while chewing on a chicken leg.

"Scrungle Bungus."

"Come and join us, sir. Have some breakfast," said the Blue Knight.

The squire rolled her eyes and looked on in annoyance at how she must seem invisible to the knights. Another seat at the table, and another mouth to feed.

"Thank you very much,"

Scrungle, still in his pajamas, sat down next to the Black Knight and stuck out a spindly hand. The Black Knight looked at the hand, then at Scrungle, then shook his head.

"No."

He took his hand back, looking around at the other Knights, wondering if he had made a massive blunder. Scrungle had very little experience with the wider world and social etiquette.

"Don't take offence. He doesn't shake hands with anyone. Terrified of getting dropsy or scurvy." Said the Blue Knight.

"Or limp leg, the scrumblies, or dead man's tang, wedge knee, the curlies," added the White Knight.

"Also, cholic, cold, Fang-dans-ear, or-" began the Grey knight, but was cut off by the Black Knight.

"I think our new acquaintance gets the point that I am watchful of communicable diseases." He said it rather testily, making the other knights smile and look the other way.

"Here," said the Blue Knight, passing over a plate of food to Scrungle. Hesitant, as he had only ever eaten fungus. But, not wanting to be impolite, he took the food.

"Thank you." Not wanting to upset the squire who was working so hard at making the food for everyone, Scrungle took bits of food off his plate and, when no one was looking, hid them in his pockets. Every time his plate was beginning to look empty, the Blue Knight would motion for the squire to put more food on it. Scrungle would try and protest at the generosity, but the Blue Knight wasn't having any of it.

"You are our guest. Please eat up."

Scrungle would then hide more food, hoping he could give the vittles away to a good home or mouth as soon as possible. Especially the Oyster Rockefeller, as it didn't look like it had much of a shelf life.

The squire scowled at the Blue Knight, feverishly cooking; she stabbed repeatedly at the burger in the frying pan. If there were any vestiges of sentient life left in the meat, the merciless attack certainly put an end to it.

"Tell me, sir, do you live in the woods? And I hope this is not too forward of a question: are you good or evil?" asked the White Knight. "We have to ask. It's the vows we take, you see. Vanquish evil and uphold the good,".

He was looking off towards the hammock and assorted items around where Scrungle had camped during the night. Scrungle had never been asked about his proclivity towards good or bad before. He was home-schooled by his father, and the question had never been raised. His father was much more concerned with conspiracy theories, eccentric drivel, and great teaching publications such as **Trust me, Mate, I Know What I'm Talking About';** a bi-monthly parchment scribbled out by Dave, the local vagrant.

His father's favourite conspiracy was that the world was a huge shoe. That's why the vast majority of beings are so downtrodden. His father also tended to make up answers to a wide variety of topics. When Scrungle was a little older, he had asked about the curriculum laid down by the local education authority, but his father insisted that the curriculum was just a set of loose guidelines and that his son would gain more practical knowledge by just listening to him. So ultimately, Scrungle had grown to be a truly kind creature but utterly clueless about the world at large and the intricacies found in any society that dictate the nuances of everyday life.

"Ah," said Scrungle. "I don't really know what I am. Just me, I would say. I don't live here; I am searching for some magic fungi that gets me in and out of my house. I have run out, you see."

"Magic fungus? Gets you in and out of your house? Sounds daft." Said the Red Knight, who was having little success at sticking a two-pronged fork into some penne pasta. The Grey Knight looked at the Red Knight and shook his head at his tactless behaviour.

"What does the magic fungi look like?" asked the Blue Knight.

"They have purple heads with little white speckles on top and are cream-coloured underneath. Then a purple stem with a black line going all the way down to the base."

Scrungle had become excited about describing the mushroom. The knights shook their heads, exchanging a glance between themselves to see if any of their companions had come across the fungi Scrungle was talking about.

"Like a go-faster stripe?" the Blue Knight offered, trying to be helpful.

"What's a go-faster stripe?" Scrungle looked intrigued.

"There, on my horse." The Blue Knight pointed towards the trees where the horses had been tied up. Scrungle noticed the long white stripe down the horse, from shoulder to haunches. Looking more closely at the horses tied to the tree, he noticed they all had some sort of livery. The Black Knights horse had TDI custom edition shaved into the rump. Sir Red had double stripes of red on black. Sir White had.

**'Sponsored by Charlton and Heston and son and another on the way.'**

embossed into the saddle.

"Does it make the horse go faster with the stripe?" Asked Scrungle.

"Can't say it does. It's more for the sponsorship and endorsements," said the Black Knight.

"Have you had any luck in locating these magic mushrooms?" the Grey Knight asked, pulling the conversation back on topic.

"No, unfortunately. But I have only been looking for one day." Said Scrungle.

"A day, you say? It can take a while to complete a quest. We all know that one, lads, don't we?" Said the Black Knight.

It was a tone Scrungle couldn't describe but knew he wouldn't be adopting its cadence to negotiate with a suicide risk.

"Can I ask what brings such noble knights out so early on to the King's Road?" Scrungle trying hard now to sound posh and upper-class.

"You haven't heard." The look of surprise on the White Knight's countenance echoed across the other knights' faces seated around the table.

"Sorry, I don't get out much." Scrungle felt rather silly and mildly embarrassed at his lack of knowledge of current affairs.

"Go on, Sir Grey. I always think you like to talk the most," the Red Knight said, chiding his compatriot. The Grey Knight flashed a smile that had the visual impact of saying that someone had poo in their beard. The Red Knight snarled lightly.

"As you can see, we are King Fromp's personal guard. The Knights of Colour to the great city of Plombree. Our compatriots, Knights Green, Yellow, Gold, Orange, and Silver, have gone north. We have come south. We are searching for Princess Isobella, who has, yet again, done a runner."

"Done a runner'?" Scrungle asked.

"Sir Grey is trying to get down with the kids." the Red Knight said sarcastically.

"Ran away, absconded, buggered off." The Blue Knight offered.

"Oh, I see. Have other Knights gone east and west?" inquired Scrungle.

All the knights stopped what they were doing as one and looked at each other.

"Bugger," said the Black Knight. The Knights looked towards the White Knight, who mused for a while.

"We are following the King's orders; that is all that matters." He said putting an end to it.

"Why has the Princess run away?" Scrungle said wanting to move away from this awkward pause in the conversation.

"The King wants her back to marry Prince Whackerknacker, you know, the prince of Flan. He's a right knob, but what can you do?" The Blue Knight said in the way of explanation.

"Yeah, right, our king wants his one and only daughter to marry

Prince Whackerknacker. Funny how that only came about after the king fell ill. Snivelling turd, Gumptrude, and Baroness Bakeasy?" Said the Grey Knight in a knowing, critical tone.

Scrungle was at a complete loss regarding the machinations within the kingdom's current political affairs.

"Sir Grey, that talk is heresy. Please, I ask you not to be so reckless. Gumptrude has a job to do," the Red Knight said, adding, "not to mention spies."

Sir Red had an unexpected yet slight hint of concern in his voice. The Grey Knight looked straight into the Red Knight's eyes, just for a moment. A little smile played on the corner of his mouth. Then he nodded in acquiescence.

"You wouldn't happen to have come across the Princess by any chance." the White Knight asked. He wasn't looking at Scrungle but up at the trees. A keen bird watcher, something had caught his eye. Brushing his blond hair out of his field of vision, the White Knight pulled a piece of parchment from under his breastplate. He marked the parchment with a little stub of a charcoal pencil. Next to the mark were the name and drawing of a bird.

"What have you seen?" the Blue Knight interrupted Scrungle's reply.

"The lesser spotted booby." The White Knight pointed to the tree opposite him.

The Blue Knight started giggling.

"If you see two together, is that a pair of tits?"

There was a clang when the White Knight punched him in the arm, Followed by an

"Ow."

The Blue Knight rubbed his armour-clad arm, and his bottom lip drooped.

"Any sign of Malcolm?" The Grey Knight interjected.

"No, but it's only been a week. I'm sure if there's anything to report, he will be winging his way to us. Sorry, I got distracted, my dear fellow. Have you seen any Princesses on your journey?" Said the White Knight, who looked at Scrungle and then smiled.

"No, sorry. Just a fairy called Ken and a fox writing poems." Scrungle added. "What does the Princess look like?"

"Raven black hair." Said the Black Knight.

"Beautiful blue eyes, clear as day." Said the Blue Knight.

"Full, red lips. Ripe as the ripest apple." Said the Red Knight.

"Fair complexion, and a laugh that sounds so sweet, happiness lives there." Said the White Knight.

"Alright figure. If you like that sort of thing." Mumbled the Grey Knight rolling his eyes.

"Well, if I do meet the Princess, I will let her know that you are looking for her."

The knights thanked Scrungle, then offered him contradictory advice on where to look for magic fungi. The Blue Knight asked Scrungle if he had any idea where to start looking. It became a similar conversation as it had been with Ken, and it was agreed by all the knights that he should get to Plombree City first. Then visit the Sorcerers Collective Society, which had now merged with Amazing Shine. Before Scrungle could stand, the Blue Knight, in youthful exuberance, jumped up.

"Selfie, selfie. Got to take a selfie."

"Sorry?" Said a confused Scrungle.

The Blue Knight started to marshal the rest of the knights to Scrungle's end of the stone bench. He put Scrungle at the centre of the group.

"Just a moment." Said Scrungle.

Walking over to the portable shower cubicle, Scrungle undressed from his pyjamas and returned to the group. Some of the knights had confused looks, while the Blue and the Black Knights smiled. It was paradoxical for Scrungle to undress to feel dressed.

"Come on Torpid, get a move on." The Black Knight was shouting at the squire, who was hurrying across with charcoal, a small easel, and parchment. Torpid hadn't stopped since cooking and had been nailing missing posters of the princes to the trees surrounding the campsite.

"Everyone look sexy, and Sir Red, you can smile if you try really, really hard." Said the Grey Knight.

The remark made the Red Knight scowl and the rest of the knights laugh. Torpid the squire with lightning speed, quickly sketched out the knights and Scrungle.

"It's a selfie not a bloody commission for a wall tapestry." Shouted the Red Knight.

In the blink of an eye, the squire gave a thumbs up, then turned the easel so the knights could see the picture. Appraising the drawing, each commented on how bad they looked, and they never took a decent speed sketch. Scrungle, who had never had any kind of drawing done of himself before, was absolutely delighted. It was brilliant, and there was not a single charcoal stroke out of place. Scrungle told the squire that it was amazing work, as the likeness of the ensemble of knights and himself was exquisite.

Never hearing this kind of praise before, the squire looked shocked, bemused, and on the verge of tears.

The Blue Knight asked Scrungle if he would like a copy. Taking a moment to think about it, making a copy would mean extra work for the squire, who had been on the go constantly all morning. Not wanting Torpid to have more work piled on her young shoulders, Scrungle declined. A look of relief crossed Torpid's face. Scrungle stood and moved to the side of the stone table.

"Thank you for the company, food, and all the very good advice. I think I should start on my journey again now."

The assembled Knights nodded towards Scrungle. Some said good luck and that they hoped he would find his magic mushrooms. The Red Knight leaned over, took what was left of the plate of food that had been given to Scrungle, and started to tuck in.

It didn't take much time to pack up his campsite, hammock, and other assorted items. Putting everything he had used the night before back into his pockets. Most of his time was wasted on the fireplace, as he had to clear the soot and embers away. He could hear the knights talking about which way to go next. Now and then, raised voices could be heard. Scrungle did notice that it was mainly between the Red Knight and the Grey Knight.

By the time he had his makeshift campsite put away, the knights were climbing back onto their horses. The squire looked ready to pass out after doing all the hard work but managed to get onto her horse without falling. Since Scrungle hadn't actually eaten during the knight's breakfast, he was starting to feel a bit hungry. As he was just about to walk off into the forest to do a bit of foraging for fungi, the Red Knight trotted over astride his horse.

"Sir." Said the Red Knight.

Scrungle turned to see the outstretched hand of the knight, holding a little figurine.

He motioned for Scrungle to take it.

"I take it you are heading to the city and the castle? This is a token of my house. If you get into any trouble from those trolls at the bypass, just show the foreman this. They're a bloody nuisance. They know me well, and they know I will give their leader a good thumping, should it be necessary." Said the Red Knight.

Scrungle took the figure from the knight with his spindly hand and looked at it. A silver skull with a sword through one open eye socket set against a kite shield. In very small writing on the back of the figure was a statement in ancient Plom. The Red Knight offered the translation.

"It says, 'Take That You Git.', or words along those lines." Said the knight with an air of superiority about the statement.

"Ah, thank you. I will keep it close." Scrungle was touched by the knight's generosity.

"Sorry, I don't have anything I can give you in return. Unless you have use for a hat stand?"

"No, no. It is a gift. I ask for nothing in return. Except to give a troll a good kicking in my name should the chance arise."

With that, he turned to catch the others; they were already heading down the King's Road in the direction Scrungle had walked up the night before.

"When you get to the city, watch out for the hobgoblins. Right little shits."

Shouted the Red Knight over his shoulder as he departed.

# Three

## *Up a Tree*

Scrungle stood, watching the knights slowly shrink in the distance as they travelled north along the King's Road. He then turned and made his way into the forest.

The sun was hidden almost immediately by a thick canopy of leaves. Moving slowly at first, letting his eyes adjust to the dim light, it didn't take long to move with confidence once they had adapted. For such a tall creature, he made very little sound.

Scrungle's tapering, wedge-like legs barely crunched the leaves on the forest floor.

Being as malleable as he was, he could traverse the forest and its interior rather quickly. Other creatures went about their business in the underbrush, but it was still relatively early, and no one was really up for conversation.

After some time had passed, he came upon a small clearing. A spring bubbled up from the ground, water trickling away to join a larger river down the slope. The soggy ground was ideal for a patch of brown and beige fungi to grow. Their long stems and wide caps shaded the ground beneath them. Stooping low Scrungle let his nose snuffle around the fungi. It didn't smell of anything. Learning from his earlier mistake, he stood straight.

"Hello? Is this anyone's home?" His hesitant voice telepathically shouted into the clearing. No reply. He bent again, grabbed one of the fungi, and started to absorb it. Mushing the fungi around his body, the taste was delicious. Within a very short period, Scrungle had eaten the lot.

"Ah, good breakfast." He said to no one in particular.

After he had finished the patch of mushrooms, Scrungle caught a murmur of barking and growling drifting through the trees. He wasn't sure where the sound was coming from and didn't want to find the origin, so he set off to try and find the Kings Road again.

Scrungle wasn't much of a forward planner. Some would say he lived in the moment.

He just did the things that made him happy, believing everything would turn out fine. And for Scrungle, this was often, if not always, the case. So, he simply turned and walked back in the direction he thought he had come.

However, he was heading in the completely wrong direction. The more he tried to steer clear of the sounds of growling and yapping, the louder the snarls and barks became. As if an unseen hand was guiding his path, nudging him gently towards the sound.

Now he could hear a mixture of commands being shouted. Before he registered what happened, Scrungle walked out of the trees into a little clearing.

A small pack of wolves was circling a lone oak, barking up at the branches.

Scrungle stood still, and then one of the wolves noticed the new arrival and stopped barking orders.

"Fellas, we've got a visitor. Fellas! Fellas, will ya shut up?" Said a

grey-white wolf.
He was the biggest, and Scrungle got the distinct impression he was the leader.
The barking and snarls tapered off, one by one the wolves looked at Scrungle, and Scrungle looked at them. They were all the same colouring, some fur darker than others, but all from the same pack.

Scrungle did a quick head count and came back with the number four. He then did another count using his fingers and came back with four again. He was pleased that the count stayed the same and that the number of wolves was under seven, as he only had six fingers.

"Hello," he said, adding a customary tentative wave.
The wolf that had seen Scrungle first ears pricked up, then walked over. He moved with a lithe grace that Scrungle thought wouldn't look out of place on a catwalk.

"I understood that. Not often do we come across someone we can talk to, but we saw the egg first, and seeing is nine-tenths of the law."

The wolf didn't sound threatening; he was just tired. Scrungle didn't say anything in reply, just slowly dropped his stick-like hand.

"Mate. We are starving, and it's a good size egg for an omelette." Saying this, the wolf then sat down and started to scratch his left ear with his back paw.

"Go away, I'm not an egg!" Said a squeaky, high-pitched voice from somewhere up in the tree. One of the branches quivered, shaking the leaves.

"That's what an egg hiding up a tree would say." Growled a demure-looking she-wolf.

"Can we have capers with the omelette?" Said one of the wolves. His eyes were independent of each other. One pointing left the other right. Like marbles in a sock.

"Where the bloody hell are we going to get capers from, you nugget?" Said the she-wolf.

"The grocer." Replied the wonky-eyed wolf.

"A grocer? Who's going to put a grocer's shop in the middle of the woods? What's the footfall going to be? A lost traveller, Hansel and Gretel, The cast of the Blair Witch?"

"I like capers." Said the wonky-eyed wolf.

"I like thrillers with lots of plot twists, but that doesn't help anyone does it." The she-wolf's tone was exasperated. Scrungle had the distinct impression that the wonky-eyed wolf was a bit on the dim side. While this exchange about the need for a remote woodland grocer was going on, the last wolf had come over to Scrungle and started sniffing him up and down. Scrungle felt a little self-conscious but had showered the night before, so he was sure he didn't smell too pungent. The wolf sniffed some more, then licked one of Scrungle's stick-thin hands.

"Have you just eaten chicken thermidor?" asked the wolf.

"I was sitting next to a knight who was eating it." Said Scrungle.

"My, my. Lucky for some." Snarled the now-annoyed wolf. "Haven't eaten in three days. Got a banging headache." Added the wolf.

"Go away, Leave me alone." Said the small voice from up the tree again.

"Come down. Don't make us come up there." Said the leader.
He had taken his place back up at the base of the tree and gave no indication he had any inclination to try to climb it.

"Olives, then?" Said the wonky-eyed wolf. Who then tripped over a gnarly root. The she-wolf rolled her eyes.

"The same thing you tit. Where are we going to get olives?"

"Grocers." Said the wonky-eyed wolf.

"Go away!" Said the squeaky little voice.
The she-wolf looked up at the tree.

"I'm so hungry…" She groaned.
Scrungle thought about the little voice and then looked around at

the wolves. He didn't want the little creature to be eaten by a pack of wolves if it didn't want to be eaten. Regardless of whether it was an egg or not, the wolves started barking again and telling the creature in the tree to come down.

"I'm so hungry." Said the she-wolf once again, pacing around the tree's trunk and whining. Scrungle suddenly remembered all the food he had saved from sitting with the knights at the picnic table.

"Oh, I have food!" Said Scrungle.

The wolves stopped at once and came straight over to Scrungle.

"You have food? I did hear you say you had food?" said the desperate pack leader.

"Yes, Yes! I forgot, you see. It's in my pockets."

Scrungle started pulling out the food that he had saved from his plate earlier while sitting with the knights, Scrungle tried to put it out in a nice picnic display with plates, napkins, and a chequered cloth.

The wolves, on the other hand, had a different idea and quickly dove in and ate everything Scrungle could produce. He even found a forgotten chocolate cake. It had gone a bit hard, and he could not, for the life of him, remember when he had put it in his pocket, but the wolves didn't mind at all. Scrungle did attempt to put a nice ribbon around it and present it on a cake stand, but had no chance as the wolves just got stuck in and demolished it in minutes.

Although the wolves did not wait for the niceties of presentation, they made sure that each of them had an equal and fair share, even the wonky-eyed wolf. He would stop eating and then stare off into the middle distance for no apparent reason, a gormless, almost frightened look on his face. As if he'd been accosted by the intrusive thought of his grandmother, whisking cake mix naked. But then, one of the wolves would shout out his name, and he would start happily munching away again, without a care in the world.

When every crumb and every morsel of food had been devoured, the wolves rolled onto their backs one by one. The day was beginning to warm up, and the little glade they were in seemed like a wonderful place to relax for a moment.

"Oh, thank you; that was amazing." Said the wolf with the cat's grace and the air of an alpha leader.

"Can you tell me your names?" Asked Scrungle.

"Of course." Said the wolf, "I'm Snickers; top dog, obviously. That's Melody."

He flipped an ear in the direction of the she-wolf. She was on her back letting the sun warm her belly.

"The one with a keen nose for chicken thermidor is Al, and the one with the need for capers is Wonky." Both the wolves barked their names and then went back to relaxing.

"Is there really an egg up that tree?" asked Scrungle, looking up into the branches.

"Oh, hey, I had totally forgotten about that." Said Snickers.

He sat up once again to investigate the tree. Scrungle followed, and he could make out a little, orange, egg-shaped figure hiding in the foliage. It did look egg-shaped, but strangely jagged as well.

"Hello, are you an egg?" Said Scrungle.

"I'm not an egg!" Squeaked the voice.

"I'm Scrungle Bungus. What is your name?" He said to the quivering shape up the tree in what he hoped was a gentle tone.

"Are you going to eat me?" Asked the voice. The foliage shook to give the statement emphasis.

"I am not. I only eat fungus. I can ask the wolves if they are still wanting to eat you, however," replied Scrungle. He turned to the wolves.

"What do you reckon, pack?" Said Snickers.

"I like eggs, but to be honest, I'm good for now." Said Melody. Her voice was kind of sleepy sounding. Wonky the wolf was snoring gently and didn't answer.

"I'm easy." Said Al. Snickers looked at Scrungle. "You can tell it that we aren't going to eat it."

Snickers then stretched out, turned around in a few circles, and curled himself up to sleep. Scrungle walked a little way around the tree to see if he could get a better look at the egg-like creature.

"Have they gone?" Said the anxious voice.

"No, but they did say that they weren't going to eat you anymore." Scrungle looked around at the wolves.

"And I think they have all fallen asleep."

A few moments passed, then the tree branch shook a little. Amongst the green leaves not too far from the ground, a little, round, orange egg shape scuttled slowly along its length. The creature's stance was very wide, so it kind of hopped from one foot to the other. Scrungle guessed its height was between a foot and a foot and a half. It had a sharp nose pointing off at an angle and soft, round black eyes. There was a nervous tension about it. Like a youth theatre play about wasps.

"Are you with them?" said a squeaky voice nervous. It pointed downward to the ground below with a stumpy limb.

"No, I was looking for the King's Road. I came into the forest for breakfast. I am on a quest, or so some knights I met seem to think I am. I was going to the city of Plombree to talk to a group of sorcerers about magic mushrooms. I, um, got a bit lost, you see."

With Scrungle talking and the wolves no longer barking and growling, the little creature had begun to relax, their shape becoming less jagged and more orbular.

"I'm Peetles."

"Nice to meet you. I am Scrungle Bungus."

"I want to come down now, please." Said Peetles.

Scrungle looked around. The sun was higher, dancing beams through the leaves. Golden pockets of light played over the forest floor. And as far as he could tell, the pack of wolves had all fallen asleep.

"I think it's safe to come down."

"Promise you aren't going to eat me." Said Peetles, their shape becoming ever so wobbly again.

"Promise." He replied.

Peetles relaxed and tottered back towards the trunk of the tree. Like Scrungle, Peetles wasn't designed for climbing, and almost immediately lost their footing and fell. Scrungle just stood and watched as they tumbled with little grace toward his face.

Then hit Scrungle squarely between the eyes. Scrungle, being the consistency of marshmallow, softened the impact for Peetles. For a brief moment, the impression of Peetles' body was imprinted on Scrungle's face. Peetles tried valiantly to grab the long white nose of Scrungle to slow their descent, eventually slipping off the end and onto the ground.

To Scrungle, it looked like Peetles had gone a bit spiky again. Shaking with anxiety, their body dancing about. Looking around to see if any of the slumbering wolves had woken up.

"Which way are you going?" Peetles whispered, their eyes large in their orange head.

"That way." Said Scrungle.

Sticking out a thin arm in the direction he thought the King's Road was. Peetles, with surprising speed, headed off with a sort of waddling bounce in the direction Scrungle had pointed.

# Four

## *Klepto and Steve'O*

After an excruciatingly long time and many misleading turns by sheer accident, Scrungle and his new companion Peetles found their way out of the woods and back onto the King's Road. Looking down the flagstone way, it didn't take long for Scrungle to realise they had come out only a few hundred yards further along from the picnic area where he had first ventured into the forest that morning. It left him wondering how anyone ever got anywhere in an adventure.

At the outset, Peetles hesitated to engage in conversation, fearing that the mere sound of their voices might rouse the nearby wolves from their morning slumber. Such a disturbance would undoubtedly result in a hasty retreat up a tree, seeking refuge from the canis lupus once more. Scrungle thought this prudent and opted for silence as well.

Putting some distance between themselves and the wolves, Peetles gradually began to ease into a less agitated state. The prickly tension that had gripped their little body began to subside, partly due to

Scrungle's reassuring presence. With this newfound confidence, Peetles enthusiastically started chattering about anything and everything that popped into their curious little mind.

"So, you have magic pockets that can carry anything you like in them?" Peetles asked.

"Yes, well, at least I think so." Said Scrungle.

"What about a tree? Could you put a big tree in your pocket? Like a really, really big one. Like an oak tree that's hundreds of miles high." Said Peetles, who was getting more and more excited by the idea of a tree in Scrungle's pocket.

"Yes, I suppose. But why would I want to?" Scrungle asked.

"Well, if it was an apple tree, you could just put your hand in your pocket and have fresh apples any time!" Peetle's was now hopping with speed from one foot to the other, like a pensioner heading to the bingo after a hip replacement.

"What a fascinating idea," Scrungle said not wanting to deflate the little creature's excitement by pointing out that he only ate fungus.

Peetle's little legs had to work twice as hard to keep up with Scrungle. So, moving to one side of the road, the pair stopped for a breather and sat on a rock that was suspiciously shaped like a camelback Ikea sofa. Scrungle inquired why the wolves had been chasing Peetles in the first place. Peetles was, in some ways, a lot like Scrungle, both of them living reclusive lives away from crowds and the hustle of large towns. The day was warm with a light breeze, so Peetles sat and told Scrungle his tale as best as a Peetles could.

There lives a strange and dodgy wizard called Klepto the Maniac, Peetles began.

Klepto had a home on the edge of the forest next to a small lake called **'Buffering Please Wait.'**

The wizard didn't live on his own, but within a little commune of displaced conjurers, limb-missing jugglers, disgraced city traders, fishermen terrified of open water, wheelwrights who could only work at right angles, and influencers.

Scrungle asked what an influencer did. Peetles said nobody knew.

The commune classed themselves as self-governing anarchists, not necessarily rebels, just wanting the choice to elect their leaders using the rule of democratic law. Rather than the archaic rights of divine luck, or as the commune members would say, 'led by inbred idiots through blind chance'.

As far as Peetles could remember, it had been a rainy Tuesday, just after lunch. Not that sort of heavy rain, or that rain that gets blown by the wind and comes in sideways; it was more that kind of rain that seems sort of misty but really soaks you through, and then you wish you'd listened to your mother and brought a jacket like she had told you too.

Klepto had been working on a new spell to levitate small items. Since he was an Amazing Shine premiere member, the spell had been delivered within the week. Scrungle wasn't sure this mattered within the context of the story, but the little creature seemed to be enjoying themselves recounting their tale, so he didn't interrupt.

The incantation consisted mainly of levitating wallets from pockets, gold coins and pouches of silver. Klepto, who wasn't the best of wizards, lost concentration halfway through the conjuration, distracted by two cows fighting over a tree branch shaped like a question mark. The spell casting went skew-whiff, rebounded off a polished silver dish, and twanged off the G string on a battered lute nailed to the breast wall. To Klepto's ears, it sounded more like an F as it hadn't been tuned in a while. It then struck a boiled egg sitting on a dark orange earthenware plate in the kitchen. The flash was blinding, and the loud bang that followed could only be described as a sad-faced clown's head smashing into the dashboard of a Ford Cortina. Eventually, when Klepto had regained his vision, the blurry image of the newly created Peetles greeted him, sitting on the drainer, blinking.

As far as Peetle's understood, it was how they had come into existence. The wizard, fascinated by what happened and, just as quickly, the potential exploitation of free labour, had kept Peetles around, washing his clothes, cleaning up, and having them run errands under the guise of wizarding research for the good of his fellow citizens.

It hadn't been a bad life, and Klepto had taught Peetles how to speak and read, as well as a few card tricks, which Peetles became uncommonly adept, if not alarmingly good at. This all changed when a fat man astride a donkey came into the commune. He stood in the middle of the town square, shouting that everyone had to be means-tested for the new tax rise. Scrungle inquired if they had gotten the donkey's name. Peetles said they had not.

The fat, blue-faced man with pompadour of urine yellow hair had been chased away from the commune; he had returned, unfortunately, even bluer, with a bunch of hobgoblins who went around behaving like a gang of England supporters at an away match.

After that, the wizard had told Peetles that he would have to let them go, as the new tax was on the number of sentient entities living at the residence, not the number of bedrooms. Klepto oddly had fifteen, most with an en-suite.

Peetles had then been hastily pushed out the door and given a knapsack. Klepto shouted after Peetles that they could find their fortune in the Capitol Plombree as a doorstop or a card shark. Or if things really didn't pan out, take their chance in the kingdom of Flan. Peetles had wandered aimlessly, losing the knapsack while being chased up a tree by a pack of hungry wolves who thought Peetles was an egg.

Scrungle felt sorry for the little creature as they started along the

King's Road once more. He told Peetles that they could travel with him for as long as they wanted or until Peetles found a vocation that suited them best. Peetles asked Scrungle where he was from and where he was going. Scrungle recounted his journey so far to find the magic mushrooms, his books, and the fact that he hadn't secured any content insurance before he left.

Scrungle took his time describing his lovely home in the Chana tree, saying that its real name was the Chanananananana tree. Peetles said it sounded like it had been named after falling down a well while freezing to death.

* * *

White clouds drifted lazily over the day's blue sky as they moved onward to the opening in the mountain range. They had walked a fair distance after the interlude with the wolves. The forest was tapering out as they climbed a gentle slope. The ground had become rocky on the approach to the pass. Scrungle and Peetles could see the end of the tree line and a bridge in the distance. As they drew closer, it became apparent that the forest and the mountains were separated by a deep ravine.

A wooden signpost stood with several fingers pointing out directions. One fingerboard pointed towards the bridge, informing travellers that Plombree City was eighty-seven miles away. The other fingerboard pointed the way they had come: Splandoolie, four hundred and one miles. The other two boards read Forest two yards left and Forest one yard right respectively. Scrungle felt that they could have been left out, and although he appreciated that the fingers all had braille accompaniments, there was a suspicion in him that the sign writer was getting paid by the letter.

After this, a roughly cut board was propped up against a large stone in the middle of the road leading onto the bridge. The sign read ~~**De tower**~~ with a line through it, then **'that way.'** The painted yellow arrow underneath had dripped onto the flagstones of the road and pointed to a dirt track running along the ravine to the left of the pair. It looked overgrown and dangerously close to the edge. Now they were out of the canopy of the forest, a quiet stole across the day.

Peetles looked up at Scrungle. "Should we follow the sign?"

Scrungle surveyed the bridge, which looked immaculate and in excellent condition.

"Let us try the bridge. If it feels unsafe, we can turn around and come back."

With that, Scrungle moved forward, and Peetles walked fast to catch up.

The impressive iron and stone suspension bridge spanned the cavernous depths to connect the forest side to the mountain pass. It was wide enough for two carriages to pass with ease. The decking was paved with flagstone, the same as the King's Road; however, the builders had used two different coloured stones to create a chequered pattern along the bridge's length.

The balustrade was decorated with statues of knees, ears, and the odd buttock.

Scrungle and Peetles didn't recognise any of the limbs and appendages but surmised they must be from illustrious people, creatures, or patrons who had paid for the bridge's construction.

Although it wasn't said, they both felt exposed, a little bit intimidated, as if being watched. The wind blew stronger now that they were in the open. Alien sounds, eerily haunting, funnelled upwards from the dark depths, playing across the verticals holding the bridge together. To keep their spirits up as they crossed the bridge, the pair fell into a discussion about what wine to serve when entertaining a unicorn, fishing for lost shoes or bricks in a pond, and what word would rhyme with orange. Just as they approached the other side, a loud, booming voice yelled out:

"Who's that trip trapping over my bridge?"

Peetles became instantly spiky and clung to Scrungle's leg. A huge green misshapen head appeared over the left side of the bridge, near the end. The shape was like an anvil had been dropped on a mouldy doughnut. Not a jam-filled one; more like a ring doughnut. On its massively lumpy head sat half a large coconut painted yellow. A string tied into a bow under its chin held the safety coconut in place. It was by law that all municipal employees of the crown had to wear a safety coconut when on duty. The small eyes, buried deep in the flesh of the head, stared intently at the two travellers.

"Hello." Said Scrungle.

"What?" Said the head incredulously. "You aren't goats! Are you wasting my time?" He seemed a bit vexed at the pair. Scrungle, working on the evidence before him, the large green head, shouting about goats, and definitely a bit thick, surmised it was a troll.

"We just want to get to the other side; we're going to the city." Said Scrungle.

"Do I look like I'm stopping you?" Said the troll, raising his eyebrows. He hadn't moved, and all they could see was his disembodied head above the stone railing. The nostril hairs seemed to dominate the vista of the troll's face. All Scrungle could think of was two hermit crabs trying to escape a house fire.

"Not really." Said Scrungle.

"Go on then."

The troll motioned his head towards the end of the bridge. Then it, and its imitation seaside crustaceans, disappeared back under the railings. With Peetles clamped onto his leg like an unwanted council tax demand, Scrungle limped forward. Just as they thought they were clear of the bridge, the gigantic, ten-foot-tall, green troll jumped out and barred the way. He was wearing a high-visibility tunic, brown shorts, and a badly embroidered badge stitched to his tunic, which said: Municipal employee Steve-O.

"Bridge's closed." Said the troll.

He wasn't looking at either of them, just picking dirt out from under his talon-like nails.

"Sorry, I don't understand." Said Scrungle.

At the same time bending down, trying to gently remove Peetles from his leg.

"The bridge is closed." Said the troll again, slower this time.

"We've just walked across it. How can it be closed?" Said Peetles, still clinging onto Scrungle.

"Well, it is." Said the troll. He had stopped with his nails and was now deliberately looking past them, just over their heads at the haze in the distance.

"Why is it closed?" Inquired Scrungle perplexed at the troll's statement. It had been a long time since he looked up to talk to someone. It felt odd.

"It hasn't been issued a safety inspection certificate, laid out in the King's statement, for the treatment and safety of travellers on the King's Road. Pending full and due notification under the Judiciary Act, Section 3 of the Sheriff and Knights Governance, circa the last coronation. All bridges spanning ravines, rivers, chasms, ditches, gabs, or any other hole deemed to be a hazard to the movement of goods and chattel will by law hold a BS101 parchment relevant to the year of issue. Failure to produce such a document at the bridge or construction for the traversing of the latter definition will then be classified as condemned and closed. As ordered by Chancellor Gumptrude," The troll rattled off at some speed.

He had this bit of information totally memorised, but it had brought him out in a sweat. Scrungle stood perplexed. Several thoughts ran through his head. Well, his thoughts never really ran; they ambled, occasionally stopping to have a look around at the scenery and then starting again at an easy-going pace.

His first thought was: A barrier stopping travellers would have been very useful rather than a badly designed sign saying, '**That way**'.

If the troll had allowed them to cross to this point, then the bridge was safe to cross the rest of the way, surely?

The most prominent question, which had taken some time to come to the forefront of Scrungle's mind, as it had taken a nice little wander with another thought before it bubbled to the surface, was:

Why was the troll under the bridge and not guarding it on top?

"Why were you hiding under the bridge?" Scrungle asked.

"Wasn't hiding." The troll's gaze had dropped and he was now looking at his feet.

"It looked like you were." Squeaked Peetles.

The troll shifted on his feet, then looked around as if scared of being overheard. In doing so its nasal hairs were caught by the wind, and Scrungle thought of the seaside again. He moved in a little closer to the pair as if to give up a great secret.

"I know it's not really part of the job but, you know, the whole 'pop-up thing' and then the 'trip trapping over my bridge' stuff? It's kinda expected, and well, goats get a bit disappointed if I don't do it. I used to have a whole tribe of goats travel from far far away to do the old troll on the bridge routine. A full day out for the family. 'Who's that trip trapping over my bridge', such fun. The number of times I was knocked off this bridge, banged up at the bottom of the ravine well, I couldn't guess. I was renowned for it. Goats came from miles away to knock me senseless. But then they cut the health insurance; unless you went private and had bridge cover, you couldn't do it. I miss the old days."

His eyes had teared up a little, his voice wistful while he recounted this to Scrungle and Peetles.

"I always thought it was a herd of goats." Peetles offered, now standing next to Scrungle with one stumpy appendage holding onto a leg.

"It can be that or even a flock. Usually, it's a herd for a larger number of goats. Smaller numbers it's more concise to say tribe." Said the troll.

While they talked, Scrungle had an idea. It wasn't a great idea, but an idea all the same. He slowly started to edge around the troll. Peetles followed, holding his leg for comfort. Not obviously looking like he was edging around, just a slight sort of shimmy. Shifting from one foot to the other or in Scrungles case, stump, gaining ground ever so slightly.

Scrungle figured that the troll enjoyed the sound of his own voice so much that, if he inquired as to the troll's well-being and situation, the troll would likely be so caught up in his woes that he wouldn't notice them moving at all.

"Why don't the goats come anymore?" Asked Scrungle shifting a little as he said this. He was now at an eighteen-degree arc from his first position of zero degrees at initial contact with the troll. Not that Scrungle had any idea about trigonometry, as he had never been taught it. Either with or without the help of trigonometry, Scrungle was ever so slowly moving around the troll, at a similar speed to that moment when you drop a piece of toast, and it falls ever-so-gradually to give you the false belief that it won't land butter side down but invariably does.

The troll followed the pair, shuffling around, with Scrungle and Peetles, oblivious to the position change, as if he were part of a shit dry-land synchronised swimming team.

"It's this blooming by-pass. I mean, it has employed a lot of my people. When I say 'my people' I mean trolls, not ogres. Often, we are confused as the same. All the delays and road closures—you see, they've caused all sorts of problems. Delivery carts from Amazing Shine. Well, you should hear some of the language. I mean, take yesterday, for example; the Knights of Many Colours came charging along the road. Now, would you stand in their way? 'Course not, but 'the bridge is closed!' I shout to them. Then the red one clips me right around the ear!"

The troll rubbed his left ear, a hurt look on his misshapen features, remembering the lump there, which was odd after his monologue about being battered by goats regularly.

Scrungle and Peetles had now arced to a sixty-four or sixty-five-degree position from the zero degrees of initial contact. Scrungle was confident that if the troll should argue, they had to return the way they had come; the pair had surpassed the threshold for positional superiority. Fortunately, the troll seemed not to have noticed the change or the new dynamics of the situation. More content to continue rambling on about how no one ever took any notice of him.

"It's been nice to meet you." Said the pair as they started to edge away up the hillside road towards the mountain pass.

"Of course, I am sorry; I can't let you pass. Orders are orders. I mean, you are very polite travellers. Just trying to get to where you need to be. But if I let one through, then word gets around, then everyone wants to be let through, and if I don't, everyone thinks you're mean. Probably why we trolls get such a bad reputation. It's not like we set out to be disliked. Oh, they've gone..." Said the troll, with a sad note in his voice.

Peetles tapped Scrungles leg and said that the troll seemed lonely. So pausing on the winding road towards Plombree City and castle, they did turn and waved one last time to the troll who vigorously waved back. Shouting all the time he was sorry he couldn't let them pass. Then the pair walked over the ridge of the hill, disappearing from view into the mountain pass.

# Five

## *Mountain Pass*

As the road through the mountain opened up before them, they were greeted by a cool breeze; a welcome relief after the climb. Ahead, stretching out like a memory, they could see the King's Road. Their eyes followed the flagstone path as it wound its way through the mountains, broken in places, weather-worn by water and frost turning to a dull grey blur in the distance.

Spellbound they stood looking up at the snow-covered mountain peaks on the skyline. Clouds clung to the top, swirling as if dancing to a silent tune. Running alongside the King's Road was a river fed by waterfalls that cascaded down the sides of the mountain range, deep, clean, and clear. The falling water thrummed with energy. The deep, rolling sound of raw power added to the breathtaking scenery. Each little tributary filled the river, which rolled and meandered, making its way at an unhurried tempo.

The sloping sides of the mountains were covered in heather and bushes, the colours deep purples, greens, and browns. Evergreen trees clung to the steep sides, becoming little copses of woodland closer to the mountain base, lining themselves along the river as if in vigil, creating homes for the birds and shade for the travellers. Now that it was summer, budding wildflowers added much-needed hues to the landscape. Blues, reds, purples, and yellows spread dots of colour as far as the eye could see. The heads of the larger flowers were nodding in the wind funnelled by the geography of the pass and mountain slopes. Brightly coloured fish jumped up from the flowing river to have a quick look at the two travellers. They hung in the air for a few moments, wide-eyed, then decided they weren't that interesting and splashed back into the water. Every facet of the pass was vibrant, bursting with new life.

Scrungle and Peetles noticed the flags that had been in place of the stones were all but gone and deep grooves were cut into the stone of the road, where the constant roll of carriages had marked their passage. The pair took their time as they walked on, as in some places the stone paving was slippery with moss.

"Good walking weather don't you think." Commented Scrungle.

"There's so much colour; it's lovely. Can we stop? I'm very thirsty." Peetles added, pointing towards the river. Scrungle came to a halt as a thought bubbled up in his mind.

"Just a moment Peetles."

Taking his time to rummage through his unfathomable pockets, he soon had a wide variety of objects strewn by the side of the road, including a hair dryer, snow shoes size 11, a surfboard, and a cage for a hamster. Eventually, he found what he was looking for and presented a large, round lemon-coloured water bottle with a carry strap to Peetles.

"A gift." Said Scrungle.

"Ehh, this is the best; I've never been given a gift before." Peetles hopped and danced from side to side, hugging the water bottle that was only a little smaller than themselves. Scrungle started to put the other things back in his pocket.

"I love it. What is it?" Said Peetles, looking up and smiling at his travelling companion.

"It's a bottle you can fill with liquid, like milk, strawberry cordial, or cement. Normally, it's just water." Scrungle explained.

"Why do you only eat mushrooms?" Peetles asked, still investigating the water bottle, plugging and then unplugging the stopper.

"I don't know. They're all I've ever eaten. All my parents ate. It makes me so happy to discover all the strange and wonderful tastes. Like my mother used to say, life is like a mushroom salad; you never know what you're going to get."

"Life is a mushroom salad?" Peetles sounded confused.

"It's a metaphor."

"What's a metaphor?"

"I would imagine it is like a meta-three but with one more," Scrungle said. He was running a hand up and down his long nose, which he did when he was thinking.

"What's a meta then?"

"Nothing. Is there anything-a-meta with you?"

"No, I love my gift," said a very happy but slightly confused Peetles. Before continuing the journey, it was decided that they should gather and store as much food and water as possible. While Peetles carefully filled his new gift with water from the river bank. Scrungle found fungi in numerous places along the side of the road, next to the river, and in the shade of rock formations or stunted trees where mushrooms flourish. There were quite a few mushrooms of different varieties, sizes, and tastes. With Peetle's help, they safely stored everything they had foraged in the magical pockets.

Scrungle ate as many as he gathered while Peetles was content to just drink water, but when they both felt they had enough provisions, the two companions began their journey once more through the mountain pass.

Scrungles lolloping gate could cover quite a bit of ground. The movement was the essence of a balloon filled with water being pushed down a flight of stairs. It wasn't long before Peetles started lagging. The little creature's hopping bounce combined with a full water bottle made their progress slower and slower, eventually coming to a stop.

"Can I have a sit-down, please?" Said an out-of-breath Peetles. There wasn't anywhere nice to sit and take a break. The left side of the road was covered in brambles, and the riverside was lined with trees. Having a thought, Scrungle bent down to Peetles.

"Do you want to ride on my head?"

Peetle's eyes lit up at the thought.

"Oh, yes, please!"

Scrungle stayed bent, Peetles reached up and Scrungle gently picked up the little creature around the middle and plopped his travelling companion onto his head. It took a moment for Peetles to balance, eventually deciding to just splay their legs out across Scrungle's round head like a two-pronged arcade claw machine. Peetles wouldn't let go of the water bottle, which tried to dislodge him with its shifting centre of gravity. Eventually, with Peetles' butt firmly pressed into Scrungle's soft cranium, they agreed that it worked and started along the mountain road again. A few moments passed, and then Peetles spoke.

"You're the bestest friend I've ever had, Scrungle."

Scrungle tried to look up and make eye contact, but in doing so, wandered off the side of the road. Tripped on a small divot of grass, then corrected himself.

"I mean, I think you're my only friend too, but it still counts." Peetles continued. "Thank you for not eating me, and offering your pocket space to me, and letting me ride on your head, and, and, and for everything."

Peetles had become jagged from the emotions bubbling up and was digging into Scrungles head a little.

"You're welcome, Peetles. I think you're the best friend I've ever had too."

He raised a spindly hand towards his head and gently patted Peetles on the leg. A warm yet unfamiliar, tingly feeling filled Scrungle's stomach. Not dissimilar to the feeling of peeing in the ocean, but more heart-warming and with much less pee involved.

"I'll help you as much as I can to find your floaty fungi, I promise," Peetles said. "What does it look like?"

"They're that classic mushroom shape; they have a purple top with little flecks, a cream underbelly, and a darker purple stem with one black line going down to its base. Like a go-faster stripe on a knight's horse or on horse livery where the owner has little in the way of personality." Scrungle explained.

Peetles listened intently, nodding away.

"They sound very unusual. I've never seen that kind of mushroom anywhere before. But if I do, I'll let you know straight away!"

As nice as the sentiment was, within half an hour, Peetles had forgotten what they looked like and asked Scrungle to describe them all over again. Scrungle soon discovered that Peetle's ability to retain information was oddly selective, with utterly no recognisable pattern.

For the next ten days, Peetles and Scrungle walked without much incident along the mountain road. They came across wooden signposts stating how many miles to Plombree and which side the mountains were on to where they stood, which was a bit daft as they were huge and you couldn't miss them. It rained at times. Fortunately, Scrungle had packed a large, rainbow-coloured umbrella in his unfathomable pockets. It was more than big enough to keep the pair dry.

They weren't alone on the road, passing other travellers, mainly on carts pulled by donkeys, horses, or the occasional moose. Most of the travellers heading to Plombree were on the road to find work if they could. The taxes on homes and businesses had become too much, forcing people and mythical creatures to sell up and find work elsewhere. Others were bringing goods to market; quite a few were laden with cake ingredients of every kind.

The ones travelling away from Plombree City were invariably dressed in blue and yellow. The front of their tunics had a large letter A sewn onto it and an S on the back. They never stopped just galloped past, pulling carts full of brown cardboard boxes of different sizes. They gave no heed to fellow travellers or any kind of road etiquette, just barging through as if they owned the road. Sometimes fellow travellers would stop and chat with Scrungle and Peetles. To chat would be the wrong term; it was more of a complaining monologue about having to take an extra week out of the journey to go round since the bridge was closed and how barmy Steve-O was. Others who had been to the city before would rant about the delays on the bypass, the customs charges entering the city, and the number of cones that had been laid out for no apparent reason.

Scrungle would listen politely, still getting used to being around people and creatures he would normally try to avoid. At some point, either Scrungle or Peetles would remember to ask about the magic mushrooms. No one had ever heard of this kind of fungus and just turned the conversation back to lamenting to the pair about how the 'whole blooming kingdom was falling apart' and that 'the Princess is missing.'

The statement Scrungle and Peetles heard the most was 'bloody broken, from top to bottom.'

"Why do you think there's so many problems with the new bypass? And what's a bypass?" Peetles added.

Scrungle thought for a moment.

"I'm not sure. I think it might be something that you pass by, or a pass you buy, or the pass has gone bye or perhaps the trolls they've hired keep getting distracted by herds of goats."

"Tribes" Peetles corrected.

"Yes, tribes, quite right." Scrungle nodded.

"It's a little sad that they don't get to do the bridge thing anymore," Peetles said quietly. "The troll scared me, but I'm sure the goats must have loved it. It must be hard not being able to follow your passion in life."

"Health and safety gone mad." Said Scrungle.

The road had plateaued as it coiled its way through the mountains. Walking was pleasant, and the small inclines or little stone bridges over the feeder rivers were easy to traverse. The pair would stop now and then just to admire the view or watch the birds of prey fly to their homes in the lofty peaks. Abandoned, crumbling watch towers and attached courtyards would poke out through the trees. The pair would investigate, and Scrungle would find a fungus or two that he had never seen before and many new exotic tastes. Beef and custard, leather, and a taste that he could only describe as licking a house brick on a lunar eclipse. To his disappointment, it was never the magic floating fungi he needed.

Here, or maybe by the side of the road, if it was pleasant, Scrungle would snack, and Peetles would then take a few small sips from the ridiculously large, Scrungle-sized water bottle. The first few attempts to drink from it had toppled Peetles backwards, spilling the water all over themselves. Luckily, Scrungle had put Peetles down, and they both saw the funny side and laughed together. It was in the mountain pass that Scrungle, with the help of Peetles, fashioned a makeshift harness for the water bottle. Peetles could now shoulder it across their back and carry it like a rucksack. The little creature learned quickly that it was not the best idea to overfill it.

At night, Scrungle, with the help of Peetles, would set up his makeshift campsite.

This was usually in the alcove of a passing point, which were dotted along the road. Neither wanted to stay in the old watch towers; in the darkness, they became eerie and a little daunting. In the hammock they would top-and-tail, looking at the stars. Relaxing Scrungle would tell Peetles all about the different constellations. What were planets, what were comets, and how the celestial bodies move through the heavens.

Peetles in turn would tell Scrungle how many times they had blinked that day, if rubbing essential oils into your thighs warded off ghosts, the history of group chanting and how to card count to win at blackjack. Their talk would often go on into the wee hours before drifting off to sleep together. It was in these days that Scrungle and Peetles became friends. Their likes and dislikes, favourite colours, hobbies, and bonding over many, many games of 'Is it Heavy,' and 'Where did I put my finger last?'

When there weren't any trees to hang the hammock from, the pair improvised, turning the hammock into a little tent held up between the hat stand and the fireplace.

Scrungle had an inflatable yellow dinghy that they would sleep in, and it felt doubly safe just in case of rain. It was never deflated, Peetles would stand transfixed whenever they witnessed Scrungle put it back into his pocket.

"Is it not easier to put away when it's down?" Peetles said one day after watching the magic pockets at work.

"Yes, I believe it would be. But how would I blow it up again?" Said Scrungle.

This left Peetles pondering how it was blown up in the first place, as Scrungle didn't have a mouth and the dinghy was a decent size. Then the thought turned to smoke as the little creature became distracted by a stone that looked like a ferret.

Finally, the mountain road began to descend as the pair started another day of walking. For the moment Peetles was content to walk next to Scrungle, taking in the morning on their own two feet. For breakfast, Scrungle had found mushrooms that tasted of egg mayonnaise, and Peetles, as usual, had water.

* * *

The morning was young, bright, and fresh as they turned a sharp bend between two sides of a worked rock archway, and the panorama changed completely. Before them, they could see the land below laid out in all its wonder. The first thing to grab their attention hazy in the far distance, was a castle set on the top of a natural hill. They could just make out the tall white spires, high defensive walls, and glinting silver-topped turrets.

From there, Central Plombree expanded haphazardly, sprawling with little symmetry outward down the hill. The buildings after the castle walls looked to be made of stone, but it was hard to tell from where they were. The whole of Plombree was protected by an outer wall, outside of which were the farmsteads and farmlands that covered the vast plains around the capital city. Crops of different kinds covered the fields, creating a beautiful chequered pattern filling the world with colour. It reminded Peetles of a patchwork quilt that they used to sleep on when they lived with the wizard.

In some of the fields, they could see specks of cattle grazing. A vast woodland off to their left covered the rolling hills. To the right a great lake. Fed in some part by the huge waterfall that now fell thunderously down the side of the mountain to their right.

The King's Road zigzagged down, left, then right, along the

mountainsides to the land below. When it reached the bottom, it headed straight to the castle, cutting a long, grey line through everything in its path. Not far from where the road met the bottom of the mountain, they could see little figures moving around a construction site.

"Is that the bus pass?" Said Peetles.

"I imagine it is." Said Scrungle.

They could just make out a long queue waiting to get through the contraflow system and figured, contrary to what they had heard from other travellers, that the works must have only just started, as not a lot of progress seemed to have been made.

On one side of the construction was a huge pile of something. Being unsure of what the pile was, they both became very curious about it.

"It all looks very big." Peetles had a little bit of the spikey lumpiness going on.

"Indeed," was all Scrungle could say.

They both looked at each other and took comfort in the fact that trepidation was etched in their companion's face. It was all a little bit frightening.

Scrungle smiled at Peetles. Not a real smile, as he didn't have a mouth, but more of an imaginative one. Maybe Peetles sensed this and smiled up at Scrungle.

"Come on, Peetles."

Then, placing the little creature firmly on his head, they began their descent towards the City of Plombree. The road leading down the mountain wound back and forth many times to keep the incline as gentle as possible, this was to accommodate for heavy goods and coaches. The distance of the winding road had been deceiving, and it took most of the day to get to the bottom. Here, the pair had a better idea of what was happening at the roadworks. Which, admittedly, didn't seem to be a lot.

To get around the roadwork obstruction, they talked about walking through the farmland to the city. Scrungle didn't think the farm owners would be very happy with Scrungle and Peetles trampling their crops. There might be pathways through the myriad of fields, but they came to the joint conclusion that it would probably put many extra days on the journey.

"Let us find more food and water first. Then we can decide." Suggested Scrungle.

"That's a good idea. Good ideas are like a hot pie." Replied Peetles.

"I think you need to illuminate, elucidate, and illustrate that statement, as I am unclear as to its meaning," Scrungle said, getting carried away by the words sounding similar to each other.

"Well, ideas fill your head up, just like a pie needs a filling."

"Yes, that is very true if you put it that way. Pie and ideas are, indeed, very much the same."

Putting the little creature onto the ground. Scrungle then walked off the flagstone road and into the waist-high grass, hoping he would be able to sniff out some fungi at the base of a tree or on the bark of a fallen branch. Red and golden butterflies took flight, displeased at being disturbed. To show their annoyance, they flew into the shape of a rude word and then scattered.

"Sorry." Said Scrungle after reading it. Peetles followed behind, trying to keep up with Scrungle as he cut a path through the long yellow grass. It didn't take long, however, before Peetles lost sight of Scrungle and started heading off in the wrong direction.

"Scrungle!" Shouted Peetles in a squeaky voice.

Being lost in the tall grass and out of Scrungle's sight panicked the little creature's sensibilities and they began to get a little bumpy and spiky. Before Peetles knew it, Scrungle was there, stooping down to pick them up. He held Peetles in his stick-like arms.

"Thank you. I got lost." Said Peetles, a note of relief in their voice.

"Sorry, it's my fault. I forget that I am very tall and that you are very small." Scrungle said with another smile on his face, but in reality just in his head.

# Six

# *At the By-Pass*

Once fed and watered with Peetles safely perched back on his head, Scrungle walked towards the bypass. Approaching the tailback, they could now see a multitude of temporary signs along the King's Road. The first of these read.

**'Work is scheduled to begin on the first day after grouse touching just before lunch'.**

Scrungle didn't know when that was but assumed it must have already passed.

The next sign was triangular and depicted two parallel lines, but halfway down, one of the lines bent outwards away from the other. The pair decided it was either to show that the road going forward was narrowing or that someone up ahead had just bought a new pair of drain pipe trousers and wanted to show the world. The next read.

**'SPEED LIMIT 1mph.'**

The sign after that showed a rudimentary stick figure holding a quill. A speed sketch artist had been employed to capture a portrait of anyone contravening the speed limit. Large, orange witches' hats with white sashes tied around them had been laid out in the middle of the highway. Stopping for a better look, the witch's hats went on as far as the eye could see. Neither Scrungle nor Peetles could work out for what purpose, as the closed lane seemed perfectly fine. With a little shrug, they started walking again, passing wagons, carts, drays, and other wheeled carriages laden with cake mix, paper, cardboard, and a few angry-looking A-to-S workers who were pulling empty trolleys.

A large wagon full of day-trippers who had been at the roadblock for nearly a week had turned their transport into a holiday let, with favourable reviews on Trip Advisor.

Some of the waiting travellers, watching a group of actors nodded and said hello, recognising Scrungle and Peetles from the mountain pass. The acting troupe had set up a makeshift theatre in what looked to be a naturally formed stone amphitheatre, just off from the front of the roadblock. An impromptu song and dance show was in mid-performance; most of its content deriding the road traffic management of the kingdom.

Next to them a group of cyclists in different coloured jerseys had put their bikes on the kickstands and were sitting in a circle playing cards. Scrungle and Peetles were fascinated by this, not so much the card game but the bicycles, as it was the first time they had seen one. A few mythical creatures were also at the roadblock. A well-dressed unicorn nodded to Peetles and Scrungle, a look of weary sadness settled on its features as some young children were using its horn as a ring toss.

Close to the front two griffins were getting rather uptight about the charabanc full of day-trippers. The rowdy bunch was making a loud racket and singing a folk song about a lumberjack following in his father's footsteps by chopping down trees wearing high heels and a bra. The griffins were insisting that the group should quieten down and there were others in the queue trying to read or sleep. A large woman in a paisley dress taking up two seats on the charabanc turned to the griffins pointing out they could fly and wondering why they were in the queue to begin with. The griffins tried to keep the argument going but soon piped down. After a moment or two, they shuffled slowly to one side, trying hard to go unnoticed. When they thought no one was looking, they took flight up and away towards the castle.

As Scrungle and Peetles approached the front, there were a few disapproving looks and a few shouts.

"There's a queue, you know!"

"Sorry." Said an apologetic Scrungle as they walked alongside the waiting wagons.

"Just going to have a look at the big pile," said Peetles. Although he had no real idea what was really going on. At the front of the waiting wagons, a troll, dressed in similar attire to the bridge guardian Steve-O, held up a sign. Black letters on a red background, it read

**'Stop'.**

The penmanship was atrocious. On the other side, white writing with a green background said.

**'Go'.**

The cart owner at the front sat tensed, poised in avid concentration, not taking his eyes from the sign the blank-eyed troll was holding; the reins of his wagon held between clenched fists in anticipation of giving the horses a 'Giddy Up.'

Another vacant-looking troll in a high-visibility tunic with a yellow coconut safety hat stood beside the first troll. This second troll would wait for a carrier pigeon to land on a plinth. When one did, the troll would unwrap the message attached to the pigeon's leg.

The little scrolls had the words 'Go' or 'Stop' written on them. Once the troll had deciphered the word, he would signal the troll with the sign. At this moment as Scrungle and Peetles ambled up it had just turned to,

**'Go.'**

The cart owner shouted and slowly started to move forward. However, being laden with goods, the wooden wheels and tired horses took a few moments to gain momentum. Invariably, by then, a second pigeon had landed, the message deciphered, and the sign had flipped around to,

**'Stop.'**

The owner of the lead wagon had barely moved. Scrungle and Peetles, now close enough, heard the cry of despair, then watched the man put his head in his hands and start to sob.

Scrungle and Peetles looked down the King's Road to its vanishing point in the distance. It was now a single lane on the left-hand side. Some of the orange witches hats had been blown by the wind and had ended up in a ditch at the side of the road. Nothing moved along the flagstone road except wishful thinking. Although they couldn't articulate it, it all felt a bit depressing.

The rest of the trolls were either walking, talking, sitting, or standing in little groups. The only work being carried out was a large wagon with brand-new flagstones being unloaded. The flagstones were put into neat stacks, slowly counted, and checked off. After this was done, they were moved to a new location near the huge pile of broken flagstones. A single troll with a sledgehammer would then take one of the new flagstones, carefully lay it down between two tree stumps, and violently smash it to pieces. Another troll would load the brand new, smashed-to-piece's of flagstone onto a wooden wheelbarrow, then trundle them over to the huge pile that had been steadily building since the work had started and dump them off. Scrungle and Peetles looked at each other.

"Is it some form of road building?" Peetles asked looking to Scrungle for an answer.

"None that I've ever read about," Scrungle replied.

"Hello," Said Scrungle turning to the troll with the 'Stop' sign. The troll at the front had the same look of imbecility as his colleague Steve-O at the bridge. His nasal hair was just as prolific. Scrungle took a moment to put Peetles down, as he felt he would exude a little more authority over what might happen next if he didn't have an orange egg-shaped entity with a huge water bottle on its back sitting on his head. The troll said nothing.

"Hello." Said Scrungle again.

The name badge on the troll said 'Municipal employee: ave'. The first letters stitching had unravelled, so Scrungle guessed that it would be Dave. It could have been 'Save, Cave, or Rave'; however, he thought it highly unlikely. Dave, his eyes blank, demeanour similar to a pencil drawing of a cat, just stood looking at Scrungle. Eventually, he blinked.

"Look mate, just wait in the queue. Nothing I can do here." Said the troll.

A wild idea had rushed headlong into Scrungles mind that if he rhymed, it might come across as rather jovial and lighten the mood of Dave with a silent D.

"Nothing to bother, nothing ado. I just wondered how long we would be waiting in the queue."

After another long pause.

"Fred, get Billy, we got a couple of troublemakers here." Said Dave, his voice as flat as his expression.

Scrungle looked down at Peetles who was beginning to get a bit spiky and moved closer to the little creature. A moment or two passed, then off to one side, close to the huge pile of broken flagstones the biggest troll Scrungle had ever seen came out of a rather ratty-looking hut. He was wearing a fez, which signalled he was important. In his hand, he held a flagon of something hot; they could see the steam rising into the air. Walking over to Scrungle and Peetles with an air akin to that of a racing pigeon enthusiast who had just won. His tag read 'Billy, foreman.' The troll stopped close to Scrungle and looked down at the pair.

"Hello." Said Scrungle a third time.

"Right lads, what's the problem here?" Said Billy the troll.

"Problem? What problem?" Squeaked Peetles and looked around to see if he could spot one. Billy the foreman took in a breath.

"That's the way we're doing this then, is it?" Nodding his head as if he had just discovered a clue. Scrungle unable to identify a problem turned his attention back to Billy the foreman.

"I was curious as to how long it would take to get to Plombree?" Said Scrungle.

"Look, mate, just get back in the queue. It'll take as long as it takes." The expression on his large green face implied that this was the end of the conversation.

"Can we walk along that bit?" Said the small voice of Peetles, motioning to the cordoned-off section of the road.

"What?" Said Billy, trying a little harder to intimidate the pair. Peetles shrank behind the thin wedge-shaped legs of Scrungle. With his long stick-like arms, Scrungle pointed to the coned-off side of the road that Peetles had already motioned to, where nothing was happening.

"The road looks perfectly fine to me, as far as I can see," added Scrungle, feeling he was on a bit of a roll still finding time to try and rhyme.

"Woah, woah lad, what you trying to say, eh? We're working on that bit. That's why it's coned off. Proper pair of worky tickets." Said Billy, exasperated.

He was now shaking his head as if the pair had overcharged him for a pint. Scrungle had moved his thin hand across his brow to cover the sun. The only work he could see was the slow decay of the witches' cones into the cosmic dust to which all things inevitably return. Billy shook his head in even larger exaggerated movements, then leaned in a little to frighten the pair; now they could count the individual hairs around the outside of his ears.

"I can't see any work happening." Replied Scrungle.

"Look, mate, this is by orders of the king, passed by Chancellor Gumptrude. Now, there's a queue. Go wait in it. That over there is blocked off for a reason."

The troll then, without thinking, took a drink from his steaming flagon, burning his lips and mouth. Besides the flash of agony crossing his face and his eyes watering heavily, no one would ever have noticed.

"Why is it cordoned off?" Asked Scrungle in an honest attempt to understand the situation.

"Right, that's it. If you don't go back into the queue I will forcibly remove you." Billy stood, flexing his biceps. They stood looking at each other, then Scrungle bent down and lifted Peetles up, turned, and started to walk away from the troll.

"He was mean." Said Peetles, who looked rather sullen now.

Scrungle thought the same, then remembered the token the Red Knight had given him. He stopped and put Peetles back down. The waiting roadside queue, having not much else to do, watched the confrontation intently. Billy the foreman troll was still standing there, looking at them depart. Ordinarily, Scrungle would have just walked away, avoiding conflict, and waited in the queue with everyone else, but something was different today. Maybe having Peetles with him, or just being out in the world for once, or just having the need to find the mushrooms that made him float so he could go home, he decided to turn back. The troll rolled his eyes as Scrungle walked up to confront him.

"Hello." Said Scrungle for the fourth time.

"What now?" Billy said, his tone angry.

Scrungle put his hand in his pocket and pulled out the Red Knight's sigil.

"A friend of mine gave me this. Said it might help." holding out the token for the troll to see. Billy's hand shook, wincing as he slopped some of the hot drink on his high-visibility tunic. Then his eyes darted around, looking everywhere at once.

"Is he here?" Said an unsettled Billy.

"Who?" Replied Scrungle.

Billy the foreman paused.

"Alright, alright, I get ya." Rubbing the back of his head, remembering the lump he had been given there. Billy walked off quicker than he had approached, towards a couple of trolls playing hopscotch by the side of the road. Scrungle and Peetles watched as Billy the troll did a lot of talking, head shaking, and pointing towards Scrungle and Peetles. At one point, the trolls listening rubbed the backs of their head in unison. Eventually, one of the trolls walked off to the hut to retrieve a couple of high-visibility tunics and approached Scrungle and Peetles, who tried to decline the work wear, but Billy the foreman came over and insisted they wear them. He then walked to the closed lane and started to move the cones to one side. The onlookers in the queue were getting restless. Then, a shout could be heard.

"Hey!"

"We've been waiting bloody days!"

"Hey, that's not right!"

Billy, the foreman, walked over to the front set of wagons.

"Priority travellers. By order of the king." Nodding towards Scrungle and Peetles.

Peetles tugged at Scrungle's leg.

"It doesn't feel right, just jumping ahead of everyone." Getting a bit agitated and spiky-looking.

Scrungle looked at the queued coaches, drays, wagons, and assorted travellers. A sea of faces looked back, awash with annoyance, frustration, and hopelessness.

"Peetles, I think you are right. We should invite our friends in the queue to come along as well." They walked over to the start of the queue, where the lead wagon waited. The driver's eyes were still puffy from crying. He looked up.

"Hello, I would like everyone here to come along with myself and Peetles as our guests while we travel to the city to find the Sorcerer's Collective Society." Said Scrungle in a loud, telepathic voice.

A cheer went up from the long queue, as well as a few shouts and calls of "they're having a sale."

Billy the troll looked distraught.

"You can't do that!." He shouted, waving his arms, and walked over to block the lead wagon. Scrungle, who thought the troll had been rather brusque and rude, didn't bother waiting for him to say anything more. He would be the first to admit that it wasn't in him to create conflict. His instinct was to actively avoid a quarrel. A tactical move that had rendered perfect results every time he employed it. However, manners and a kind word never hurt anyone. Well, as far as he knew, he wasn't sure about the phrase,

'Please put the crossbow down; someone could get hurt.'

While it was both polite and kind, he imagined that a lot of people who may have said it got hurt regardless.

"Come along!" Shouted Scrungle in everyone's mind. Then he moved more witches' hats aside so that the lane was now wide enough for the larger wagons and carts to pass. Billy moved to confront Scrungle, but Scrungle held up the Red Knight's sigil, and Billy stopped immediately. Another cheer went up from behind them as the waiting assortment of people and mythical creatures started to move. Billy the foreman moved to stop the lead wagon but was forced to one side when it showed no signs of slowing. The trailing people and creatures in the queue quickly gathered their belongings and jumped onto their respective wagons, carts, and drays.

The charabanc of singing travellers pulled up alongside Scrungle and Peetles.

The large woman in the paisley dress got down from the open seating at the back to the relief of the horses and suspension. She insisted that Scrungle and Peetles hop on and travel to the city with them. As soon as Scrungle and Peetles were sitting comfortably after removing the silly-looking high-visibility tunics, a rousing 'For they are both jolly good fellows,' was sung by everyone who had been waiting. The heroes of the road congestion queue looked back at Billy the foreman. Billy was still shouting but when no one showed the slightest sign of stopping, he threw down his fez, jumping up and down on it. The flagon of hot liquid splashed everywhere. After one last shake of his fist, he walked off to his little hut in a huff.

Scrungle and Peetles were the toast of the wagon train.

## Seven

# *The Horse Shoe and Bucket*

As the wagon train slowly passed the watching fields, Scrungle and Peetles listened to the passengers on the charabanc educating them both on the Plombree City, the castle, and all the latest gossip. A passenger with a delightful green afro, wearing pointed-toed shoes with little bells on the ends, turned and introduced themselves.

"Hello, most wonderful creatures, My name is Sando Sando Sando. My friends call me Doris. Thank you once again for getting us all moving. Did I hear you say you are headed to Plombree? Have you seen the new promotional art for the castle?"

Before Scrungle or Peetles could reply, his travelling companion sitting opposite jumped into the conversation, not in the literal sense, as he was sitting down. He was wearing a thick yellow rain slicker, stained from years of being out at sea. A striped blue and white high-neck jumper underneath. His pants matched his rain slicker and were tucked into his heavy-duty black rubber wellies. The smell of crab sticks and fish was pungent. On his head was an origami hat made of folded cardboard recycled from a popular breakfast cereal; it resembled a sea-faring hat known as a sou'wester. It had seen better days after becoming soggy in a rainstorm and then drying out again. It was odd that a paper hat, which would lose its material integrity within minutes of being introduced to copious amounts of water, would be of any use against the elements when taken out to sea. Neither Scrungle nor Peetles pursued the matter, although Peetles did ask.

"Where is your boat?"

The bemused friend of Doris looked at Peetles as if the little creature was mad.

"Hate the water; I'm an apprentice baker."

Doris pressed his fellow traveller, the apprentice baker dressed as a sailor, to continue the conversation so they could all get past the awkward moment.

"Oh, yeah! It looks so good! That Baroness, Bakeasy, really knows what she's doing. I love the cardboard aesthetic; it's so in season right now." Said the apprentice baker dressed as a sailor, excited by the new paper fashion. The paisley-dressed woman bristled in her seat. Then leaned forward.

"It seems silly to me that people are going gaga over this Baroness when everyone is struggling with all the taxes and this silly bypass nonsense. I'm Gladis, by the way." She thrust her hand out at Scrungle, then Peetles, who both took a turn to shake it.

"Who's idea was the pass by?" Said Peetles.

"Bypass." Said the apprentice baker, dressed as a sailor.

Gladis looked to Doris, who then looked at the apprentice baker dressed as a sailor. Who then took off his cardboard hat, scratched his head, looked at Gladis, and shrugged.

"It was Chancellor Gumptrude that wanted it." Said Doris.

"I thought it was the King, but then it was put to a vote." Said the apprentice baker dressed as a sailor.

"Well, there was a referendum." Said Gladis.

"Referendum?" Scrungle asked, not sure how a referendum worked.

"Everyone gets a vote." Doris chipped in.

"In the kingdom?" Said Peetles.

"No just Plombree." Said Gladis.

"No one asked me if I wanted to vote?" Said the apprentice baker dressed as a sailor.

"I thought you said you didn't live in Plombree." Said Doris

"I used to." Said the apprentice baker dressed as a sailor in a tone that was edging on the defensive. A falcon landed on the side of the wooden planking of the charabanc. The little group stared at it. Scrungle was just about to say hello when the wheels hit a bump in the road, and the falcon took flight, deciding it was safer in the air.

"All I'm getting at is there was a vote for the bypass.' Gladis picked up the conversation again. "All the proclamations and town criers were saying that the King wanted the bypass; it would help with trade, and we would save money on health care fees and ointments, also stop outsiders coming to Plombree and taking all the jobs."

"Were all the outsiders taking all the jobs?" Said Peetles.
There was a pause then Doris said.

"Not really."

"I am very sorry, but I am not sure what the connection is between the road works and the new interior designer who specialises in cardboard." Said Scrungle stroking his long white nose.

"I'm getting to it." Said Gladis, raising an eyebrow and pulling a face akin to finding a hair on a custard cream.

"You see, everything was better before the Baroness Bakeasy turned up. I don't blame the Baroness, you see; I blame Gumptrude for not keeping an eye on the finances. I don't think the King cared at all about the bypass, and then he went and got himself ill." This in

Gladis's mind explained everything.

"I see." Said Scrungle, completely lost as to what direction or point the conversation was heading. Gladis hadn't finished, however.

"With the King being ill, Gumptrude does his best to convince everyone the bypass is going to be good for the city. Then you look, and it doesn't seem to have any work done on it. Costing a bloody fortune. And now money's being spent on those hobgoblins and sheriffs." She nodded and crossed her arms, a stern look in her eyes. If she had been a judge at that moment, someone would have been sentenced to death.

"So everyone voted to have a new road built that no one wanted." Said Scrungle trying to get his head around all the different aspects and what the point was.

"Well, it was more like forty-eight percent against and fifty-two percent for. It was a narrow margin." Said Doris.

Gladis felt she had another point to make.

"Well, some wanted it, some didn't, and don't get me wrong. I'm not a mytholophobe, but the bypass was also meant to stop the trolls coming into the city. I think trolls should stay where they belong. But now they're taking all the stone mason jobs on the road. A friend of a friend of a friend's neighbour told me that their uncle's cousin just can't get any work as a stone cutter because all the trolls have taken the work. Undercutting prices if you can forgive the pun and everything."

"I see." Said Peetles, who didn't, but wanted to stay included in the conversation.

"So the people of Plombree used to do all the stonework." Said Scrungle.

"Not really, it was mainly trolls." Said the apprentice baker, dressed as a sailor.

Scrungle sat stroking his long white nose.

"So the trolls are doing a job that they have always done that no one else wants to do, but no one is happy that they are doing it for a bypass that people voted to have that they don't want. This was to keep the prices down for goods and health care, which have now gone up." Scrungle summed it up, trying to understand.

"Well, when you say it like that, it sounds daft. It's more the trolls you see; they are beginning to settle here and not go back up the mountains where they belong." Said Gladis.

"Or back under the bridges." Said Doris.

Everyone nodded at the comment.

"Taxes are just getting out of hand. Everything is just getting more and more expensive. There's already plenty of marches and unrest. Broken from top to bottom." Said the apprentice baker, dressed as a sailor.

The wagon train trundled on as the travellers sat in contemplative silence. Scrungle and Peetles had no real clarification of what was transpiring within the kingdom. They both felt even more confused after the conversation. Deciding that it was far too complicated a subject to get any more involved with.

Scrungle sat back, and he and Peetles watched the farms and homesteads slowly pass them by. A wheat crop in the field opposite looked a bit wilted. It had grown tall and seemed in desperate need of harvesting. Next was a field of corn, the heavy husks sagged in the heat of the sun. Another field of plants that neither Scrungle or Peetles could identify. Deep purple leaves, and the fruit a sapphire blue, overripe ready to burst.

The pair waved at an elderly man at the side of the road wearing nothing but bib overalls and a straw hat. He didn't wave back, just made a rude gesture. Scrungle wondered if he was related to the farmer back where the Chana tree grew.

Peetles asked Doris why the crops weren't being harvested. Doris said the bypass had caused problems for seasonal workers who would travel in and help, but the kingdom had been assured by Chancellor Gumptrude that things would improve once the election was over. He asked the citizens of Plombree to have a little patience and promised that everything would be fine very soon.

Scrungle had a distinct impression that their travelling companion thought the chancellor was a complete and utter half-wit.

The good spirits in the charabanc, that they had started in, were now evaporating. There were problems in the city that Scrungle and Peetles were witnessing first-hand. Some of the travellers in the convoy turned off the King's Road and headed down dirt tracks and cobbled lanes towards farms and homesteads.

As the dwindling convoy trundled onwards, talk between the passengers turned to the fact that the journey to the city was going to take longer than a day thanks to the wait at the roadworks.

To the right of the King's Road, behind a copse of oak trees, a large building poked out. Seeing the approaching convoy, it tried to hide but couldn't as it was a building, so it just had to sit there looking pensive. The structure boasted a white-washed stone façade adorned with black wooden beams, standing tall at three stories high. An array of sash windows informed the convoy of the numerous rooms within. The inn was comprised of two wings flanking a central section, with a charming courtyard nestled in the heart of the arrangement. At the rear were stables, along with an adjoining play area.

It was one of the franchised inns that Scrungle held a loyalty card for.

'The Horseshoe and Bucket' read the branded swing board. The hand-painted sign hung from an L-shaped bracket on iron chains. It depicted a confused-looking horse with one hoof in a bucket. What was chilling about the sign was the smiling elderly father figure smoking a pipe, looking down at the animal through the cross hairs of a loaded crossbow.

The driver manoeuvred the charabanc into the crowded stables, trying their best to find a place for the passengers to disembark. The stable hands were busy; it was difficult to assign places at such short notice for the assorted animals that had been pulling the wagons and carts. Since the roadworks had started, their jobs had all but stopped. Turning up for a working day and lounging about had become the normal way of doing things. Hardly anybody stopped at the inn, as they were either all stuck back at the roadworks or simply couldn't stomach staying at the inn for any longer than an evening. Now it felt like the whole world had descended onto the inn in the blink of an eye.

Their idyllic, do-nothing attitude was a thing of the past.

Scrungle and Peetles dismounted the charabanc and stood under an overhanging pergola next to a poster of the missing Princess, to watch. One young stable hand kept shouting to the driver of a cart chock full of baking soda, being pulled by a moose, to back up slowly. The moose did everything at a random speed: fast, slow, moderate, and just kept getting jammed.

Gladis hurried over to the pair and assured Scrungle and Peetles that their room and lodgings would be paid for by their new friends on the charabanc.

"That's uncommonly kind of you." Said Scrungle.

He then pulled out his top hat, putting it on his head, tilting it to Gladis, letting it sit on his head for a moment, then putting it back in his pocket.

"We don't know how to pay you back." Said Peetles.

"No need, my dears; it's our pleasure. Stuck at that roadblock for bloody days." Said a smiling Gladis. Scrungle pulled out his loyalty card and held it out to Gladis.

"Is this of any help?" Said Scrungle.

Gladis took the card.

"Brilliant. This will get a good fifteen percent off the whole bill." Gladis then hugged Scrungle, stretching on her tiptoes to kiss the side of his cheek. Beaming a smile, she headed inside the inn.

"Your cheeks have changed colour." Peetles pointed out.

"Oh, they have? What colour are they now?"

"A kind of a pinky-reddish."

"I think, Peetles, this is what they call 'being embarrassed'. I read it in a book, but never actually experienced it." Scrungle held a stick-thin hand to his cheek to feel the warmth.

"What's embarrassed mean?" Asked Peetles.

Their conversation was interrupted by a loud crash, as one of the wagons had caught a central beam holding up the roof of the stables. A small section of the roof sagged, creaking, shedding a few reddish slates for good measure. The roof now looked like a mad grin that could give way at any moment into a gasp of surprise. Two of the stable hands began pushing each other, shouting about who was at fault.

The landlord burst through the onlookers with a bucket of cold water. He looked between the two stable hands for a moment, then threw it over the smaller of the two.

"Peetles, I think we should find our rooms. Too much excitement can make you overweight or so I have read." Said Scrungle.

Peetles nodded sagely at this, and they turned to check in and find their rooms. The foyer was in chaos, crowded with many of the people and creatures from the convoy. Gladis had taken it upon herself to try and coordinate the sleeping arrangements for the little party of the charabanc. Everyone was shouting contradictory things to each other, and an assortment of mythical creatures were asking pointed questions about the accessibility of the four-legged kind. A centaur had knocked over a centrepiece in the main foyer and was refusing to take the blame for it, saying it was a stupid place to put a full-size statue of the King. Above the racket, Scrungle heard:

"I am not a horse. Look at the bloody horn! I'm here on official business." The unicorn was there, refusing categorically to go into the stables.

"It seems as mad in here as it was outside," said Peetles.

Scrungle lifted Peetles onto his head, and the little creature settled into their normal sitting position. He then walked over to the unicorn's side of the foyer, which looked a little less crowded.

"Look, you have to go in the stables. All creatures that pull or push carts or wagons are housed outside. It's company policy." Said an elf who was trying to appease the unicorn. For a working unicorn, it was rather fashionably dressed.

"I bloody will not. I'm on my way to court by appointment, you little tit." Shouted the unicorn, dropping its head and pointing its horn at the chest of the elf.

"Excuse me. Sorry to interrupt, but the unicorn did walk here on its own hooves, neither pushing nor pulling a cart of any kind." Scrungle said trying to help.

"Yes, we saw him entertaining the children." Added Peetles.

The elf let out a long breath.

"Alright, alright, I will see what I can do."

"Ground floor." Said the unicorn, who then turned to Scrungle. Before the unicorn could say anything in the way of an introduction or thank you, Gladis shouted,

"Scrungle, Peetles, come here, please!"

The crowd parted to let the champions of the roadblock through to the check-in counter. A harassed-looking elf with a feather quill looked up at them.

"Hello," said Scrungle.

"Dietary requirements?" Asked the tired elf.
Scrungle stood and thought about the question, then realised he only ate mushrooms when the elf cut in with a pointed

"no." Then proceeded to check off a box on the registration parchment. "Have you, in the last six months, been convicted of any offence against the crown?"

The elf looked up at Scrungle. It became apparent that there was a very limited time for a reply. Scrungle, who liked to consider what he was about to say, had no chance of being victorious in this little encounter. The elf then checked the next box. This went on at speed for the rest of the questions: a quick look up as the elf filled in the last box, a key was thrust into Scrungle's hand.

"Room three. Top of the stairs, turn left, right, then a left, left again, down, then a right. If you come to a fish tank full of house bricks you've gone too far. Breakfast, in here, the minute the cock crows. Enjoy your stay. Next!" Shouted the elf.

Gladis smiled at the elf; it sent a shiver through most of the people who saw it. She then started to list a long list of inquiries, low-grade demands, and a request to get more than fifteen percent off the bill for everyone, thrusting Scrungle's loyalty card into the face of the elf. Scrungle and Peetles turned and made their way to the stairs. Accompanied by many shouts from the crowd,

'Sleep well!"

"See you both in the morning for breakfast!"

"SCS are having a sale."

## Eight

# Homicidal Cockerel

Scrungle was already awake when he heard the cock crow, not so much as a cock-a-doodle, more a scream of pure aggression. He had watched the dawn brighten the room for a while now, so he thought the cockerel must have overslept or been on a homicidal rampage by the sound of its wake-up call, and lost track of the time. Peetles, lay on the bed next to him, fast asleep still clutching the lemon-coloured water bottle. The little creature murmured something about griffins then rolled over onto their side.

Lying there on the straw mattress, looking up at the dark wooden beams in the low-ceilinged bedroom. His thoughts returned to the recurring dream he'd had the night before. In the dream, he was living under a tatty, dirty bridge, and every morning he had to pick up a large flagstone only to find that there weren't any mushrooms under it. Just a tiny blue man with yellow dead hair shouting 'Taxes'.

He now felt an immense longing to be home, making a mushroom salad, reading a book, or just looking out from the Chana tree at the peaceful valley below.

Scrungle's review was broken by a long, gentle fart from Peetles, then a dreamy giggle, and then a fart again. Peetles dream-mumbled something about the king of diamonds having too many shoes, and the correct pronunciation of the word donkey was with a silent 'k'. Feeling a familiar twinge in his stomach, Scrungle decided to wake his companion and go down to breakfast.

The day was clear, so they dined outside on wooden tables. Scrungle had a full continental breakfast, which ended up being just a plate full of mushrooms. Peetles asked what a continental breakfast was, but the elf serving broke down crying, running away to hide in the kitchen.

Peetles felt bad about this, but the neighbouring table's occupants said that the elf had been doing it all morning and not to worry about it. Scrungle just helped himself to the serving dish that held the grey, overcooked mushrooms. They tasted like something he had never tasted before. He then realised that this new flavour could be the actual taste of mushrooms.

Doris appeared just as Scrungle finished the last fungi and joined them. The serving elf had reappeared, her eyes puffy and red from the tears asked what he would like. Doris inquired about the continental breakfast, the elf burst into fresh tears. Scrungle consoled Doris by telling him it seemed to be something she did to anyone who asked. In the end, Doris helped himself to apples and cheese from the buffet. Peetles commented that his new hair colour, a bright blue, suited him.

"Well, my friends, a little further, and we will be back in the city. Will you be heading straight to the Sorcerer's Collective Society?"

"Yes, we are. Although I do not know how to get there." Scrungle stroked his long nose.

"Are you going all the way to the city?" Said Peetles.

"Yes, I am going to see my sister and her husband. He is a farrier and has a small stable not far from the museum. I am a builder by trade, and I'll be helping them rebuild their house, which has a very bad lean and will fall if not corrected and time is of the essence so thank you for getting us moving. As for finding the sorcerer's building, if I remember correctly, it should still be there. There is a carved wooden map of the city at the plaza where the charabanc stops. Very big; you can't miss it." Explained Doris cutting an apple into segments.

They talked more, and Peetles asked what a farrier was and Doris explained. Then he warned them not to trust some of the people and creatures who may approach them.

The city could be a dangerous place at the best of times, and these were definitely not the best of times. He especially disliked the hobgoblins who had been contracted to help the sheriffs. If Doris had his way, every one of them would be thrown off the high walls of the castle. Scrungle was just about to ask more about the King's illness when Gladis appeared.

"Come along, everyone. Come along. Onto the coach, the drivers waiting." Gladis, who seemed to be a natural at people-marshaling, barked out the command.

She handed the loyalty card back to Scrungle and said she had gained a lot of points on it. Scrungle thanked her and then watched her get everyone, including a sleepy-looking apprentice baker dressed as a sailor, onto the charabanc and away in a relatively short period of time.

Scrungle and Peetles just sat and listened to the conversations from the passengers while the city approached. Ambling along, the convoy of wagons headed towards the outskirts of Plombree City, the road still split by orange witch's hats. The farm fields to either side started to dwindle, winding cobbled stone roads and houses with small terraces taking their place. The passengers began opening bags and cases. Pulling out parchments. Checking over the handwritten documents as they approached the twenty-foot-high outer wall of the city. Chiselled into the stonework of the archway spanning the opening to the road beyond was the message.

**'Welcome to Plombree. Please don't stay any longer than you have to.'**

A barrier barred the way, manned by castle guards dressed in full chain mail with the emblem of the city on the outer tunic. Some carried pikes, while the guards checking the wagons and documentation going in and out of Plombree had long swords at their sides. Gladis, sitting next to Scrungle, was holding her documents.

"What are those?" Scrungle pointed to the documents.

"Identification. They won't let you in without them." Said Gladis.

"We don't have any." Scrungle was looking at Peetles, who had fallen asleep next to him.

"What. Oh, my Scrungle they will turn you away. It's all the new things they have done to stop immigration. You have to apply at least 6 months in advance if you're not a resident unless you have immediate family in the city." Said Gladis, who for the first time since Scrungle had met her seemed at a loss. Gladis looked around the charabanc assessing the options. After a moment, she stood up, holding onto the back of her seat for support.

"Listen up, everyone. Scrungle and Peetles have lost their papers. I know we all owe them a lot for getting us this far. I have a little plan to get them through customs. Is everyone with me?"

The tone of Gladis's voice was such, that if anyone had voiced anything other than yes, they would have made an enemy for life. Doris stood up.

"How can we help."

Gladis looked around at the charabanc passengers.

"Right, this is the plan."

* * *

It wasn't long before the driver of the charabanc slowed the horses to a full stop.

The guard approached and talked for a moment with the driver. Happy, the guard, walked to the back of the charabanc and climbed on board. Gladis sat with Scrungle at the endmost seat of the charabanc, with Peetles asleep on Scrungle's head.

A ribbon had been tied around Scrungle and a decorative bow to look like a wrapped present. Gladis had told Scrungle to look floppy and kind of mushy as it might help with the deception.

"And whatever you do, don't blink," Gladis whispered.

"Papers please." Said the guard, inspecting documents. He was efficient without being pedantic. Now and then, he would ask if the person was here for business or pleasure. Also asking if they had any exotic diseases on their person, as it was an offence to bring a plague into the city. The guard reached Gladis, who felt the eyes of the other passengers on her, even though the whole company on the charabanc had found something other than Gladis, Scrungle, and Peetles to look at. Smiling her best smile, she handed her documents over. The guard nodded to Scrungle and Peetles.

"What's that."

"Oh, it's a present for my nephew. Took me ages to stitch it all together. Stuffing it took even longer." Gladis informed the guard; she was very convincing.

"Looks real." Said the guard, who then poked Scrungle in the stomach with his finger. Peetles, who was still asleep let out a wheezy fart as if on cue which set the guard off laughing. He poked Scrungle again, who made no sign of movement, but as if by divine intervention, Peetles farted again. The guard was now in gales of laughter and was about to poke Scrungle a third time when Gladis slapped the guard's hand.

"Stop with the grubby hands; by the time you've finished, it'll be broken, dirty, or both."

"Sorry to be a pain, but is this going to take much longer?" Said Doris.

Then everyone on the charabanc started to ask questions. The guard, not realising this intervention by Doris was a deliberate distraction, turned and addressed the passengers.

"All right, ladies, gentlemen, and creatures. All done here." Turning he handed Gladis her documents back.

"If you decide you want to go into business and make those, I'd be interested as a partner. That is absolutely hilarious." He tapped the side of his nose with his finger in confidence. Then jumped down from the back of the charabanc and waved it on through the barrier.

Scrungle and Peetles entered Plombree City for the first time. When they were at a safe distance from customs, everyone on the charabanc laughed, whooped, and clapped.

Once again they had beaten the officials. Scrungle scratched where the guard had poked him. He had never felt so itchy and nearly lost his composure, wanting to scratch where he had been touched. Peetles shifted on his head.

"Where are we, Scrungle?" Said a sleepy-sounding Peetles.

"We are now in the city of Plombree."

Reaching up so he could put Peetles on the vacant seat next to him. They stared at the world around them. To Scrungle and Peetles, the fringes of Plombree looked run-down. In many places, grass and weeds had gained a foothold, popping through the stone verges along the roadside. A missing fence panel here and a half-broken wall there. Detritus of discarded and damaged possessions lay abandoned in boarded-up doorways and side streets.

Half of the buildings were still occupied, although bearing numerous 'for sale' and 'to let signs', just to keep the tenants on their toes. Businesses and homes that were empty had 'Repossessed' painted on a piece of wood that was either hammered into the ground or nailed to the front door. Underneath the same contact information.

**'Gum & Trude estate agents 1 Rich B'stard Lane, Central Plombree.'**

The buildings themselves were mainly made of timber: one-story dwellings, then two. Then grander designs made of sandstone or brick, the closer they got to the castle. Mixed in with the residential houses were assorted trades.

The outskirts had most of the heavy industry, with stone masons, wood yards, rope manufacturers, leech farms, and gravediggers. Then the more elite trades, baubles for every occasion, the latest in paper fashion stores, cake suppliers, butchers, bakers, and candlestick makers were all closer to the castle. There was no order to the crisscross of streets that wound everywhere, up and down, here and there, through and far between.

One thing that Scrungle or Peetles had not contemplated was the noise which grew louder the closer they got to the city centre. From every corner, top and bottom came the sounds of some form of activity. Shouts, laughter, hooves on cobblestone paths, and sellers shouting for attention. There was music of harp, lute, and brass as buskers sang songs to entertain or ballads to lament the state of the country.

On every other street corner, a beggar stood asking for pennies, who would then scurry away if they saw an approaching sheriff or hobgoblin. A few shouts came from the residents of Plombree up to the charabanc, asking if the bypass was complete.

The curiosity was sparked by the fact that the travellers were riding on the wrong side of the right side of the road. Peetles tugged at Scrungles arm and pointed at a badly angled sign saying 'BEND.' The 'B' had a line through it, then there was a slow realisation that it was meant to say 'END,' and the city was just trying to save money.

At the sign stood several trolls; one of them was engrossed in writing on a small piece of parchment. His lips moved spelling out the word 'STOP.'

Next to the troll was a wicker basket full of pigeons cooing, itching to take flight and escape the confined space. All the trolls were dressed the same as their fellow workers at the other end of the road works. His slack-jawed associate held up a sign saying

**'Stop'**.

He stood very still as if made out of stone. Behind the sign were many drays, coaches, wagons, and A to S delivery riders waiting to use the contraflow system to exit the city and start their long journeys. The trolls stared at the convoy coming down the coned-off lane. Some scratched their heads, trying to understand what they were seeing. Nothing the trolls did indicated that the travelling wagons were contravening any kind of by-law. Thus settling any idea of repercussions, as everyone in the convoy understood that by the time the trolls had processed what was happening, they would all be long gone.

Not long after coming out of the cones, the coach driver maneuvered the charabanc off the King's Road and entered a huge plaza adjacent to a large fountain. The plaza was filled with coaches and wagons of different shapes and sizes, with dismounting passengers and others boarding to be taken around the city or to other long-distance destinations. The charabanc pulled to a stop, and the driver shouted:

"Plombree Main Plaza! Please check your belongings as you depart. No refunds given, and remember to tip the driver. Thank you for travelling with Mad Bongo Tours."

"Why do we have to push the driver over Scrungle?" asked Peetles as they dismounted the carriage.

"I think it's a different kind of tip," Scrungle replied, moving forward.

As they passed the coach driver, who stood with his hand out and held a smile that was closer to a junior mortician practicing technique than the genuine article Scrungle said.

"Death is a lot like living, just without the breathing,".
Nodding sagely, he picked Peetles up, putting the little creature in their accustomed place on the top of his head. The pair walked off in what they felt was the right direction for the SCS building, which of course it wasn't.

The coachman looked at the departing Scrungle and Peetles in disbelief, then began shouting something that started with the letter 'B', but was drowned out as Gladis called after them.

"I hope you find what you're looking for! Take care, Peetles, Scrungle." Gladis waved vigorously, beaming a smile then she turned and was lost from view.

The pair came to a stop, standing next to a vendor selling yellow coconut safety helmet halves. They stared at the world around them. Central Plombree and the Plaza were utterly enormous. Numerous building styles were crammed together and loomed over the pair. White stone town-houses with three floors stood next to thatched roof wattle and daub. Greystone architecture of municipal buildings focused on symmetry and proportions. Columns with intricate detailing made out of marble were contrasted against red brick and concrete. Some buildings had medium-pitched roofs, while others were flat, hip, or pyramid all mixed in together, which made the skyline patterns an interesting panorama.

The duo did a slow turn, taking the vista in. Decorative door surrounds mixed with the plain and functional. Signature half-timber detailing, long vertically placed decorative wood beams created a two-toned exterior. Steeply pitched roofs; plain or colourfully painted brick; ornate gables; rooftop verandas; octagonal or round towers; and generous wraparound porches. The floors of the buildings had wide planks or red slate tiles, others grey. Archways of different designs seemed popular everywhere they looked. Sprawling homes with enormous courtyards sat next to tiny houses for the smaller residents of Plombree. The look was of many different styles, materials, and constructions, depending on the occupant and the time in which it was built.

The city had tried hard to keep as much foliage as possible. Trees lined streets and wall-climbing plants with blooming flowers covered many walls and courtyards.

Then, above it all, on the hilltop stood the castle. A high white stone wall enclosed its white towers, casting long shadows over Plombree-like dials on a clock.

It was Peetles who noticed there were a few vacant buildings even here with a '**To Let**' sign on them; these empty abodes had a mass of posters plastered on the walls and doors. Some said:

**'Vote for Gumptrude on Article 16.'**

Others stated a reward for information leading to the whereabouts and safe return of the Princess and her travelling companion.

On top of the visual spectacle of Plombree City was the constant movement. Now and then a cyclist would speed past, giving them a start as the contraption was still a revelation. It was quite an experience for the pair, as they had never had such an assault on their senses. The residents that thronged the plaza and surrounding streets all had some form of paper adornment. It looked to Scrungle that the more affluent the creature or person, the more ostentatious the dress and colour.

Bright green neck ties of cardboard, yellow scarves of connecting paper, and handbags made from parchment. To Scrungle, it felt like he was being swallowed up and drowning simultaneously. He had never imagined that there were this many people or creatures in the world.

During his little journey so far, Scrungle had felt pangs of being homesick, which would just as quickly disappear, but today, for the first time since leaving the Chana tree Scrungle would have given anything in his possession to be back there, curled up in his reading chair.

"Are you alright, Scrungle?" Said Peetles, who was getting a bit spikey. The huge bustling city made them anxious.

"Yes, Peetles, thank you. I just miss my home, and it is very noisy here." Said Scrungle.

Peetles gently patted Scrungle's head, trying his best to console his very tall friend in his own little way.

"Well, let's get away from the noisy things and find the thingy place where they might have the mushrooms," said Peetles.

"That is an excellent idea," Scrungle said. "Can you see the wooden map that Doris talked about?"

Peetles had a very good vantage point to see the myriad of streets and alleyways leading out of the plaza. A cluster of people and mythical creatures stood in a circle near a shopfront selling multicoloured fish.

"I can see something over there."

Scrungle looked up to see where Peetles was pointing then followed Peetles directions. Moving through the circle of people and creatures, they could now see an impressive three-dimensional model of the city. Carved out of dark wood with a dense grain, heavily varnished. Little plaques of brass had the names of notable buildings engraved on them.

**'Museum of Contemporary Carts,'**

**'Royal Observatory,'**

**'Slaughters Quarters of Dragon Hall,'**

**'House of Cake.'**

**'The Temple of Crushed Nuts.'**

The brass nameplates went on and on. Slowly circling the miniature layout of Plombree, Peetles shouted that they could see it. The plaque said,

**'Sorcerers Collective Society and Amazing Shine.'**

The carving showed a building with a gable roof and many windows and turrets.

In comparison to its neighbours, it looked very big. Scrungle noticed a little flag close to the edge, and underneath the flag was **'You Are Here.'** Scrungle studied the map while Peetles looked around at the Plaza and Plombree.

"That's the fountain." Said Peetles pointing to a large water display to the left. Made of black and red marble and depicting a huge dragon eating a strawberry while water sprayed from its ears.

"Which is that there," Scrungle said, identifying it on the map.

"So that way must be to the sorcerers building." Peetles was now pointing to his right. "I think, Scrungle, I can just see the roof from here."

"Excellent job; well, then Peetles lead on."

Peetles beamed a grin at the world and navigated them through the winding streets toward their goal. They passed a myriad of shops and businesses, getting distracted, watching an old lady in a confectioner's boil hardened sweets in the shape of little ducks, which, when cooled, quacked noisily as if alive until she smashed them to pieces with a toffee hammer. Despite being in a city full of magical creatures, the pair kept getting a lot of confused looks. They were stopped at one point by an elderly lady dressed all in lilac cardboard, who asked where Scrungle had purchased his hat.

After explaining that Peetles wasn't headwear in the traditional sense, she shuffled off, a little disappointed that she couldn't get a sentient hat of her own. Now and then, they would pass a lamp post or wall, and plastered on it would be the same wanted poster.

**'Have you seen this woman or this penguin?'**
On it was a very good black and white wood-cut print of an attractive woman wearing regal clothing, and on her head an expensive-looking tiara. Then a smaller drawing of a penguin called Sergio.

It read: **'Princess Isobella and her retainer Sergio cash for information without reservation as to her location, no negotiation for this fee.'**

Scrungle and Peetles read the sign over a few times. Discussing why the Princess had a penguin as a retainer and what did a retainer do. Then they started to make up a tune to the lines of the poster, as it had the rhythm of a song, entertaining themselves as they walked along.

At a covered square at an intersection next to the civic hall of Plombree, a crowd had gathered. It was made up of magical creatures and residents of the city.
Wooden placards and woven wool banners stated 'Cut the tax rise,' 'Gumptrude must go,' 'Stop the road works,' and 'Three for one at SCS.' On a raised step under the canopy of sycamore trees, next to a statue of a famous foot, stood an activist minotaur promoting himself as the opposition to Gumptrude for the interim high chancellor of Plombree while the King was ill.

As Scrungle and Peetles watched this several hobgoblins dressed in blue and red braces, blue pants rolled up to the calf, revealing white socks, and black hob-nailed boots barged their way into the crowd. Pinned on their black shirts was a silver star. Most were wearing caps that said, 'Make Plom Great Again.'

The sheriffs in more regular uniforms of brown and green began telling the crowd to disperse by order of the King. The hobgoblins, with no provocation, started to aggravate the crowd. Next, a punch was thrown, and one of the hobgoblins ran away, holding his nose and crying. The other hobgoblins hid behind the regular sheriffs and shouted names at the crowd from a safe distance. Scrungle and Peetles beat a tactical retreat and headed onwards up a cobblestone road toward the Sorcerer's Collective Society.

# Nine

## *At the SCS*

It didn't take long to spot the huge, walled courtyard coming directly off the street.

The entrance was through an extravagant and decorative portcullis. Above this was an enormous draping banner that said 'SCS & Amazing Shine.' The hand-stitched logo was an attractive red colour. Standing at the gate was a griffin in a red and blue blazer, in keeping with the banner.

As Scrungle and Peetles walked past, the griffin took a step forward and stopped them. Peetles went a bit spikey but relaxed when the griffin said.

"Enjoy your visit today; there's a sale on." Thrusting a parchment into Scrungle's hand.

"Would your hat like one too?" added the griffin after watching Peetles blink.

"Yes please." Said Peetles.

The pair stood to one side, opening the parchment. Peetles read the opening paragraph out to Scrungle.

***'The use of magic always requires a form of sacrifice. Whether it takes the shape of a light nap after a spell or something far greater, balance will always be restored; if something is given, then something of equal measure will be taken.'***

This statement made by a long-gone king resonated with Scrungle; its honesty held ominous overtones. Reading on, it explained the history of the SCS. It was set up more than four hundred years ago by King Flipchart the Fifth for a better understanding of magic. In its golden years, scholars travelled from far and wide to the well-respected seat of learning to pursue a better understanding of magic in all its varied forms.

Publicly funded, with academics in residence, a vast library had been built for anyone with an up-to-date library card to use, study, and explore magic. This all changed when the financial crash happened. Brought on when the city financiers speculated on property prices in the neighbouring kingdom of Flan. Not taking into account that the place was a bit of a shithole and everyone defaulted.

To make up the deficit, the SCS was swiftly sold off by the state to Amazing Shine and became a hub for the sale of all things magical and even more things non-magical, with one-week delivery on most items. It pushily promoted the idea of signing up for the Shine deal, which included an extended warranty on most purchases and access to numerous discounts as well as money-off vouchers.

Despite being the reason the SCS had been set up in the first place the learning bit had become a small section with the library and resources now relegated to the basement of the huge sandstone building.

Peetles handed their parchment back to Scrungle, who put it away for safekeeping. Then they walked on through the huge open archway and into the halls of the Sorcerers Collective Society's building.

Buzzing with activity, the sound echoed off the vaulted ceilings.

Everywhere they looked were stands with signs announcing half-price sales. Customers laden with goods, milling around as if in some form of trance. It was a struggle to decipher who was a customer and who worked there. The pair had never seen so many stalls, all stocked with strange knick-knacks and paraphernalia, and quite a few with a wide assortment of cheeses and paper apparel.

Walking through the rows, Scrungle, in idle curiosity, picked up a mug in the shape of a small cauldron.

"What a bargain! This has just gone on sale!" Shouted an overly excited harpy who had appeared from just outside of their peripheral vision. Peetles screamed and nearly fell off Scrungle's head.

"Sorry, I didn't mean to scare your hat." The sales assistant said at a more reasonable volume. The beautiful harpy had long jet-black hair, dark purple eye shadow, and the wings of a bird sprouting from her back. The blazer she was wearing was the same as the griffin who stood at the entrance. Scrungle lifted Peetles off his head, putting the little creature down. Peetles held one hand against Scrungles leg for reassurance. Scrungle looked at the tag on the cauldron-shaped mug.

"It says winter sale here."

"We like to get the bargains out to the customers as early as possible."

"It's summer." Said Peetles.

"I rest my case." Said the harpy holding an inane smile. They stood in an awkward silence no one said anything.

Can I help you with anything?" The harpy asked eventually and a little too loudly making them jump once more.

"Yes, please. I was told to come here, you see. I'm looking for a particular mushroom—a magic one." Scrungle said, a little hesitant. He was still trying to understand the winter sale's pitch. The harpy winked.

"Having a party, eh?"

"No, I just want to get back into my house. It makes me float." Said

Scrungle not getting the hint.

"Of course it does." The harpy added another wink and a sly smile, just for the hell of it.

"What? Eh? Well, I'd throw it into the air, and it would explode like confetti, making me float," Scrungle explained.

The harpy looked at Scrungle, then Peetles. She wasn't sure if the pair were making fun of her or if they had just escaped from a high-security wing of a mental hospital.

Before she could make up her mind, A loud crash was heard. Then three hobgoblins dressed similarly to the halfwits Scrungle and Peetles had witnessed at the rally earlier, came running out of an aisle two lanes down, laughing.

"Little gits." Said the harpy and rushed off to see what they had done.

"There is someone who might know," Peetles screamed again at the sudden appearance of the new sales agent. They both turned to stare at the harpy, who looked exactly like the one that had left and was just as loud.

"Where can we find them?" asked a tentative Peetles.

"In the basement with the other academics. Can't miss her hacking cough. I can hold that at the till for you."

Scrungle looked down and realised he was still holding the mug in the shape of a cauldron. Now that he had handled the mug was it expected that he should buy it? Since he didn't have a mouth or the need for a mug in any scenario, he began to panic a little. Would his deficit of an orifice be mentioned, Would questions be asked? Why did he pick it up in the first place if he couldn't use it? Was it now shop-soiled and couldn't be sold? Would security be called, and then he and Peetles taken away? He panicked more as the harpy was staring straight at him with a wide, unflinching smile. He handed the mug over.

"Thank you," Scrungle mumbled.

The harpy smiled her customer satisfaction smile, but before Scrungle could follow up on his inquiry about how to get down to the basement, the harpy had moved on to a young man holding the same mini cauldron mug.

"What a bargain! This has just gone on sale!" Said the loud harpy, just out of sight of the man's peripheral vision. He jumped at the sound of her voice, spinning on his heels with a balled-up fist, ready to punch. The harpy didn't flinch as if used to this reaction and just smiled a fake smile. He relaxed immediately and apologized.

Peetles said that it would be best if they refrained from touching anything but the floor to walk on until they were out of the building. Scrungle agreed, picking Peetles up and placing the little creature on his head. They moved further into the huge interior.

It was Peetles from his vantage point that saw the sign hanging over the archway and the stairs that descended into the bowels of the building. It was lit with torches that didn't smoke and gave off a blueish light.

At the bottom of the first flight of stairs, they stood on a balcony, the spindle railings intricately carved with spells and glyphs. The illumination was subtle and came from globe lights hanging from long chains. From here, they looked down into the vast room. Thick pillars held the ceiling up, and just like the railings they were covered in detailed carvings.

Row upon row of very high bookcases extended the length of the basement. The symmetry broken by study areas at regular intervals. On the shelves were assorted scrolls, leather-bound volumes, books of different sizes, and parchments of all kinds. Scrungle felt a rush of excitement run through him, dizzy with the scent of ancient knowledge. The idea that so many books were in one place touched him deeply.

It was also a blessing to leave the noise behind. Here in the basement, there was an air of calm. The whisper of a page being turned or the sound of a hacking cough were the only things to disturb the gentle repose.

The stairs from the balcony were split left and right, leading down to the floor of the basement. Scrungle elected to go down the left-hand side as he felt the sound of coughing to be stronger on this side. At the bottom, Peetles wanted to examine the library themselves, so Scrungle put them down. The little creature ambled off down a passage of brown-bound leather books about glyphs, all the while keeping half an eye on where Scrungle was.

Under the balcony was the librarian, writing entries into a ledger on the counter-top. The sphynx didn't look up, so Scrungle just decided to follow the sound of what could be described as someone trying to bring a lung up. The coughing grew louder as they walked to the back of the library, passing rows of books on every subject of magic.

The white magic section on the right held alchemy, conjuration, divination, thaumaturgy, hydroponics for the indoor gardener, easy spells for beginners, and many more. The left-hand side of the rows was dark magic: taxes, politics, banking, accounting, and the restricted area. How to be a bastard and work for Universal Credit.

Passing through the different aisles, they could see a pot-pourri of different scholars sitting at the tables. Trendy sorcerers, mainly dressed in black to match their eyeliner sat together. Wizards with stars and moon symbols on their cloaks were far more flamboyant with the hues and tended to sit alone. Witches dressed in various colourful garments usually had a cauldron on the go.

Nearly all of the scholars had magnifying glasses in some shape or form. Mainly because the light was so soft down here and most of the scholarly texts were handwritten. A gnome sat engrossed in a huge volume of a book entitled 'Why do gnomes fish?' A mermaid in a wheelchair was writing in a textbook. As they passed her, she poured a small bottle of water over her fishy bottom half. It was only later that it crossed Scrungles mind to wonder how had she managed the stairs.

Although Scrungle enjoyed fiction most, the idea of reading through the rows and rows of books, stacked from top to bottom with the wisdom of the ages was intoxicating. If it wasn't for the cough echoing around the library, a reminder of why he was there in the first place, he would have explored and read every inch. Scrungle tarried awhile in the 'Magic for beginners' section of the library; however, a tap on the leg by Peetles kept him focused.

Under an archway at the back of the basement, behind a table hidden by all manner of foliage and dying indoor plants, they found the source of the cough. The light here was at its most subdued; candles had melted onto every available flat surface. Only a handful were lit. The soft yellow glow added to the tomb-like feel. Within the tangled mess of plants, something moved. Now and again, it would heave, and the hacking cough would start up again. The whole back end of the basement smelled heavily of cigarette smoke, pipe tobacco, and pot noodles.

Scrungle and Peetles edged closer, not sure whether to disturb whatever creature was living there. After a long pause a light tap once again on Scrungle's leg by Peetles, who was looking decidedly spikey and bobbly, galvanised Scrungle into summoning up enough courage to speak.

"Hello," Scrungle said to the mass.

The mass shifted slightly, and a wrinkled face peaked out from beneath the brim of a densely woven brown and green hat. Eyes filled with a sharp keen intelligence that seemed to radiate light inspected the pair.

"Oh, aren't you both something?" The mouth on the wrinkled

features croaked.

Then the face came out of the shadows, moving forward to get a better look.

On closer inspection, Scrungle could see that the mass was an old lady, wrapped in layers and layers of coarse, sullen wool. Her pointed witch's hat was crooked. The roadwork's flashed briefly through Scrungles mind.

"Hello." Said Scrungle once again.

"Are you a witch?" Peetles asked in a timid voice.

The old woman cackled a laugh, which then sent her off into a coughing fit.

She repeatedly banged her hand on the table. It didn't do anything to help get her in control. It just made the young scholar in a red and gold wizard outfit, sitting a few tables away look over and roll his eyes. Eventually, the coughing subsided.

"Yes, my little one, I am a witch. I am the witch Waynex, and I have been waiting for you to come and find me."

"Ohhh, has it been foretold? Are we in a prophecy?" Peetles voice was hushed, respectful.

The bumpy, spikey lumpiness subsided a little. Getting excited at the prospect of being in a prediction.

"Yes, it was foretold by the floor manager, telling me that you two were coming downstairs." Said the witch Waynex. Then she chuckled but managed not to fall into another fit of coughing.

"What can I do for you, child of the forest, and you, my little innocent?" Said the mass of wool that had an old woman wrapped up in it.

"Am I the innocent?" Said Peetles, looking up at Scrungle.

"Well, I do live in a tree," Scrungle said, stroking his long nose.

"But you did find me in a forest." Peetles countered.

"Yes, that is true. I have lived a very innocent life, I think." Scrungle said to clarify the statement.

"But I am little, and you are tall."

"Ahh, good point, but it might have been an antiphrasis." Said Scrungle, his head slightly cocked, thinking the greeting over.

"Shit a cucumber sideways! It was a greeting, not a question for debate." The witch Waynex shouted, which brought on a coughing fit. She pulled on a smoking cigarette resting in an ashtray below the table and took a long drag from it to calm herself. To Scrungle's surprise, it strangely suppressed the cough. The witch Waynex blew out a large volume of smoke. Filling the little alcove. The wizard, who had rolled his eyes, looked over, tutted loudly, and pointed to a sign that said,

**'No smoking.'**

"Blow it out your neck, beard face." Said the witch Waynex. Which was an odd thing to say to the wizard, as he was clean-shaven. She looked back at Scrungle, her eyes fixed on his, mesmerising. The strangest of sensations began to fill his consciousness as if she were sitting next to him in his mind. Hunting his memories, picking through them like tulips, searching his soul for meaning.

"Go on, my dear, ask what you're here to ask." Her voice was the sound of infinity.

"I'm looking for some fungus to help me get back into my home." Said Scrungle, besides Peetles it felt like this was all he ever talked about with other people.

"I see." Said the witch. "Do these mushrooms make you float, by chance?"

"They do! They do." Said Scrungle excitedly.

For the first time since leaving the Chana tree, he was excited. In this forgotten corner of the library, he had found someone other than himself who knew what he was talking about. Someone who might be able to help in his search, and have the answer to Scrungle reclaiming his home. A sense of joy and relief washed over him.

The witch smiled a knowing, wise smile. Her gaze was intense, aimed directly at Scrungle. It made him feel like he was being appraised while getting a shower.

"Do they have a black go-faster stripe down the stem?" Said the witch.

"They do." Said a very happy Scrungle

"You're looking for the Hu-" She spluttered into another hacking cough. Scrungle and Peetles stood patiently.

"The Hu-" The word caught in her throat again, and another fit of coughing began. Scrungle and Peetles stood powerless. An anxious impotence gripped them, unable to help the phlegmatic witch. Was she going to keel over before she gave the name of the fungus he had been searching for? Scrungle moved in closer, not knowing what to do to stop the coughing other than a swift kick to the stomach.

"The Hu-" The witch wheezed, holding onto her desk for balance. She coughed and coughed and coughed, spraying spittle in every direction. The red-and-gold-clad wizard closed his book with a slam and walked off. At this point, the pair didn't know if they should stay, call for help, or get a towel. Finally, after long, uncomfortable minutes, the witch seemed to regain a little of her composure. Giving up on trying to speak and scribbling something onto a piece of parchment, the witch chucked it over to Scrungle while she finished off the last of the coughing. Scrungle turned it around and read.

"The Huba mushroom." Said Scrungle.

Then bent down so Peetles could read it. His companion blinked, then nodded. Straightening up he addressed the witch.

"The Huba mushroom, if you don't mind, where can we find it?"

The witch nodded at the question and then leaned in across the table. In the two bony fingers of her left hand, she held a newly lit cigarette. She beckoned them closer with the index finger of her right. Peetles clambered onto a chair next to Scrungle and the pair stared into the witch's eyes, the witch managing to stare into both their eyes simultaneously. The smell of smokey tobacco, crab sticks, and stale curry was overpowering. Expectancy hung in the air—the same feeling you get—not knowing if it's wind or a parking ticket.

"The path to the fungus you seek is hidden. I will tell you where to go, but you both must promise me that when you find where they grow, you will tell no one else how to get there. The Huba mushroom has many magical properties; it is only for the pure in heart." The tension had climbed up a notch. Now it was the feeling of unwrapping a Christmas clothing present, an Armani shirt, or a home-made knitted jumper.

"I promise," Said Scrungle and Peetles in voices that were barely above a whisper.

"Well, that's what I've been told; it could all be bollocks." Said the witch, then shrugged and sat back, destroying any tension that was in the room like a cold shower.

"We still need to know?" Said Peetles in a small voice. The mass of wool with eyes nodded.

"Alright then. First, you must answer three riddles. I can only accept your first answer." Adding a cough at the end.

"Why?" said Peetles.

"Standard etiquette," replied the witch Waynex.

"Who started that up?" asked Peetles.

"No idea. Just the way it's done," Her tone flat.

"Well, do we have to stick with convention? Can't you just tell us?" Said Scrungle after a moment's thought.

"Look, I'm just sticking to format. How many times have you heard, you can have as many goes as you want to get the answers correct at a pivotal story point? Or just cough up the answer, love, and we'll be on our way," The witch's patience was beginning to wear thin.

"Why do you think this is a pivotal moment?" Scrungle asked.

"I just assumed it was." There was a pause, then the witch Waynex added. "Don't get a lot of visitors."

"Oh, I am sorry to hear that. Just the three questions seem a bit arbitrary." Said Scrungle.

"We could mess with the format." Peetles chipped in.

"No, that's just wrong. Do you want to know the way to the island of the Huba mushroom or not?" The witch paused for dramatic effect.

"Sounds like we don't have much of a choice," said Peetles a little aggrieved.

"An island?" Scrungle said, a little taken aback by the island bit. It felt like the witch Waynex was thinking about just getting it over with and telling the pair. Eventually, she shook her head and thought better of it.

"Can't. You're both very likeable, but I think you should put a bit of work into it. Plus, if word gets out and stuff, well, that's my reputation gone. Alright then. My first is." Then the witch coughed.

"A cough, that was a cough; the answer's a cough." Said Peetles.

"That wasn't a riddle, but I will give you that one for trying."

Peetles beamed a smile, and Scrungle gave his friend a nervous pat on the head.

"My second is, who am I?"

Before the witch could carry on with the rest of the riddle Peetles, excited at doing so well with the first riddle and not thinking about what was at stake, blurted out.

"Lord Sebastian Bigglesworth the third."

"What? Who is Lord Sebastian Bigglesworth the third?"

Scrungle was incredulous at the answer. The witch, exasperated that there had been so much debate carried on.

"My third is, at night I shine, by day I die, you can find me in the sky. What am I?" The witch's eyes flashed brightly.

"Are you a cricket bat that was set on fire, then thrown into the sky to herald the coming of the dark lord?" Said Peetles, hopping slightly from one leg to the other. Believing wholeheartedly that what they had just said was the correct answer.

"Not even close." Said the witch Waynex.

"Noooo!" Exclaimed Scrungle in a long, heartfelt wail. The thought spread out in every direction. Library readers turned around at the noise. A few shushes could be heard. Scrungle just stared at the witch, then at Peetles, then at the witch again. He gave out a long sigh and sat down in a chair next to Peetles. Putting his head in his stick-like hands, Scrungle started to rock back and forth. If he could have cried, he would have. Peetles jumped down from their chair and waddled over holding Scrungles leg to comfort his friend.

"I'm so sorry, Scrungle. I didn't think; I got excited." Peetles was spikey and bumpy. The little creature was on the verge of tears.

"Can we have another go?" Peetles pleaded with the witch.

"No." Came a swift reply.

Peetles was about to break down and cry when the old witch coughed and said.

"To get to the Isle of the Huba Fungi, you will need the moon-dial made by the mighty sorcerer Flurdenburgengerdun. It is in the Land of Badly Designed Signs, and the cheese man guards it. You will ask him three questions; the answers you are given will tell you how to read the moon-dial."

Scrungle dropped his hands from his face and looked up. Peetles took a breath.

"I don't understand any of that and I thought we got the riddles wrong." Said Scrungle.

"You did, bloody terrible answers, but all I said was that you had to answer them. I didn't say they had to be right." The witch replied with a smile on her face.

Scrungle jumped up, grabbing Peetles as he did so, and danced around the little alcove. Both companions laughed together. There were a few more shushes and 'Will you be quiet?' but for that moment, they didn't care. Scrungle just kept saying 'Well done, Peetles' over and over. Peetles giggled in delight. Eventually, after the gnome walked over and said he would curse the pair if they didn't calm down. Scrungle put Peetles on the chair, and they both turned to the old witch.

"I will mark on this map the place you need to go and the questions you need to ask." Peetles let out a small, captivated ooooh, and the witch began to write with the occasional look upwards for inspiration. She stopped entirely at one point to duck under the table for another phlegmatic coughing spree, then sat up and continued. Finally, she held out the handwritten map but pulled it back as Scrungle reached out.

"There will be trials ahead for you both. Others need your help. Are you prepared to give up what you want for what you truly need?" She asked.

Scrungle didn't fully understand but thought about his home and how much he missed his simple life. Then, looking at Peetles, who was smiling with an unadorned trust back at him decided the matter. Scrungle was sure that whatever was to come, they would work it out together.

"We're ready,"

The witch nodded, then handed over her rolled-up scroll of directions into Scrungle's spindly hands.

"I wish you a safe journey, and be careful who to trust. It is your duty to make sure the Huba mushroom and the island of fungus stay safe, and if you don't mind, I've popped a couple of things down. Be a love and just pick them up for me."

With this said the witch took a long drag from her cigarette, blowing smoke out like a train whistle. Scrungle began coughing, and soon Peetles joined him. There were still several other questions that Scrungle wanted to ask, but the alcove was filling with smoke so dense that neither of the pair could see a thing, just the waxy glow of the candles.

A cry to Scrungles left informed him Peetles had tumbled off the chair and onto the floor. Disoriented now, he moved forward to try and help his friend, then tripped over an overflowing ashtray and half-eaten curry. They kept shouting at each other, finding it difficult to orient themselves. The only thing coming back to their ears was 'Hush, Please be quiet,' and 'For the love of the king, shut up.'

When the smoke eventually began to subside and the pair could open their eyes without them stinging they were back on the ground level of the SCS and Amazing Shine, looking up at the huge banners saying there was a sale on, while a harpy just out of the pair's field of vision was exclaiming two for one-on-eye baths.

## Ten

# *Hob-Goblins are Bell Ends*

Dusk settled over the city. The last golden rays of sunshine danced off the windows of the SCS building. The coloured glass bathed the interior with beautiful spectral hues. Scrungle and Peetles their eyes clear of smoke, watched the sparkling beauty, overcome with a corporeal feeling of oneness.

The sudden, scream of a banshee, made everyone in the building jump in unison—the equivalent of group electrotherapeutic shock treatment. The scream announced that would all shoppers please make their way to the tills and conclude their final purchases.

Scrungle, with Peetles on his head, walked out of the huge arched entrance. It felt like an age had passed since they entered. All the companions wanted now, was to find a quiet place to investigate the map, absorb what the witch had said, and rest up a little.

"Hello, you've forgotten your cauldron mug." said a far too loud voice at the side of the pair. A startled Scrungle nearly dislodged Peetles from his head at the sudden appearance of the persistent harpy assistant.

"If you just come back inside, we can complete your purchase."

"I'm sorry, I don't carry any gold." Said Scrungle, not wanting the mug but not wanting to upset the sales harpy.

"We take silver, precious gems, bitcoin." Her eyes sparkled, her smile wide.

"Sorry, none of that either. I don't really have a need for a new mug. I don't have a mouth, you see." Scrungle didn't want to admit this but needed to extricate himself from the conversation. He lifted his long nose so the sales harpy could see what he meant.

"We can set up credit terms with easy monthly repayments."
Being on a percentage, she ignored Scrungle's lack of an orifice for imbuing any form of liquid or food and pushed on. Talking continuously about finance, and what an ideal purchase the mug would be for any kitchen. This went on until the pair stepped over the threshold, and the harpy skulked away, annoyed that they hadn't closed the deal and secured the commission.

* * *

Having no real plan of action but elated at the information on the elusive mushroom, they decided to head back to the fountain and the wooden model of the city. Retracing their steps, the pair eventually found the plaza, its fountain, and its map.

Scrungle slowly walked around the wooden carving to see if he could find a horseshoe and bucket for the pair to spend the night. He was sure that, with the points Gladis had acquired on his loyalty card, they wouldn't need any money for a room.
Growing at the base of the fountain, Peetles spotted a very small, fluorescent patch of fungi that had sprouted up along a weathered crack in the stonework. Pointing it out to Scrungle.

"It will do as a snack," Scrungle said almost to himself. Giving up on the map for a moment, he ambled over. Absorbing it all up, then told Peetles it tasted like horseradish and pancetta. The little creature had jumped off Scrungle's head and onto the edge of the fountain. The dragon was no longer sprouting water from its ears leaving the water still and clear.

"Is that a fish?"

Peetles pointed to a stationary house brick at the bottom of the water.

"I believe it is known as an orange oblong," Scrungle explained. "It lives in clear water and feeds on the bottom. They don't move much and are hunted to make houses and buildings; you don't see many in captivity. Well except when they are dried and stacked up on top of each other."

They sat on the edge of the fountain and watched the street lights being lit. Flaming torches of yellow and white housed in ornate glass and iron cradles took over from the retreating sun. Round balloon-like hanging lanterns stretched a zigzag along the street at tree height. It was a beautiful sight, the illuminations in the city of Plombree.

It was a combination of centaurs and men in heavy leather long coats doing the job of lighting the way.

The men would get down on all fours, and then the centaurs would clamber up and stand precariously on their backs to reach up to light the wick in the gas- or oil-filled lantern. The hooves dug deep into their arched backs. Muffled cries of pain as the weight of the half man, half horse would bear down on them. Watching the centaurs inflict long-term disabilities on the men for no apparent reason, was rather disturbing and a completely upside-down way of doing things, as the men could barely stand after each lantern was lit. Just sit for a good five minutes before the pain subsided enough for them to move onto the next street light. Scrungle reasoned that he shouldn't judge, he wasn't a council member or city planner and had no idea about the job description or risk assessment involved.

Most of the shops and street sellers were closed, along with the cafes and eateries. There weren't many people or creatures around, either. Anyone they did see hurried along with their heads down, intent on their destinations. Scrungle and Peetles watched the city become brightly lit but deserted.

"It seems odd that everyone has gone home. I thought there would be more people out eating and relaxing. Just look at all the lanterns; they are lovely," said Scrungle, admiring the surroundings.

"Should we find somewhere quiet and put up the hammock?" Peetles said looking around the now-empty plaza.

"Well, I can't see a horseshoe and bucket inn on the map. We might have to," Scrungle replied, thoughtfully stroking his long nose.

"Arrr, what ya deein here like? Gan on, get lost." Said a snotty-sounding voice from behind the fountain.

Looking to find the source of the voice, they watched as two hobgoblins appeared from either side of the round base of the fountain. The hobgoblins or bell ends had mean little black eyes, not black eyes that come from being punched in the face, although they could have done with a good smack to the head. Just the pupils were black. Sneaky little mouths and sour expressions. It was only by accident and not design that the pair made a textbook-enveloping pincer move, as neither had enough brain cells to read a bus timetable, let alone make a coordinated tactical maneuver that Hitler would have been proud of. Dressed similarly to the hobgoblins the pair had seen at the gathering in the square. Peetles and Scrungle watched in fascination as they pulled at their braces in unison.

"Who ya starin at like!" Said the slightly taller of the two-shaven-headed bell ends.

"Nee rough sleeping in Plombree here, like." Said the slightly shorter of the two-shaven-headed bell ends.

"I'm not asleep. Are you Peetles?" Said Scrungle.

"I don't think I am, as I usually dream about ham sandwiches, which is odd, as I don't like bread, ham, or sandwiches." Said Peetles.

"Ye been funny, like, eh?" Said the slightly taller of the hobgoblins. Then tried to intimidate Scrungle by extending his braces in what he assumed was a threatening manner but being two and a half feet shorter, it wasn't going well.

Peetles little body started to become spikey and bobbly. Scrungle picked Peetles up and put him on his head.

"Arr, is that a threat like, puttin ya mate on ya heed?" Said the smaller hobgoblin, while taking a step back.

Plombree suddenly felt menacing. The plaza was empty, with no other creatures except for Scrungle, Peetles, and the two little shits poncing in front of them. Adding to the tension was that the pair found it hard to understand what the two pants-brace-wielding idiots were saying. The dialect was strange, a cross between strangling a goose and being hit by a runaway cart in thick fog.

Scrungle and Peetles were also bewildered by the aggression from the two little bastards. Not for the first time, Scrungle wished he was home in the safety of the Chana tree, looking up at the stars from his observatory.

"Reet where's ya papers, like." Said the taller hobgoblin.

"Papers." Said Scrungle, knowing that they didn't have any.

"Whey, it looks like there's a bunch of vagrants here. Reet you're gannin with us," said the smaller of the hobgoblins, who pulled out a billy club. Scrungle lifted his hand to hold Peetle's leg as he was about to turn and run away. Hurried steps could be heard out of the shadows, accompanied by the sound of little bells. A cloaked figure ran up to the group.

"Hello, my friends, so sorry I kept you waiting." The cloaked figure took off the hood, and Doris stood before them, still jingling.

"Come, come; my sister's house awaits your arrival."

Doris smiled and nodded at the hobgoblins then produced his identity papers, all the while ushering Scrungle away from the little gits. The hobgoblin glanced at the papers and then handed them back to Doris.

"Divent, let us catch ya oot again after curfew reet," said the slightly bigger hobgoblin after the retreating trio. He then flexed his braces at full extension. The button popped off and the brace's metal clasp hit him hard in the face. A satisfying squeal could be heard as they left the plaza.

Scrungle started to question the curfew, but Doris said they should talk when they were safe indoors at his brother-in-law's house. Hurrying on through the streets, they came across other hobgoblins patrolling and flexing their braces.

Doris just smiled and waved, telling them he had an ear infection, and that Scrungle and Peetles were caterers. Then, up a winding, cobbled stone bank to the south-east of King's Road, Doris pointed to a very thin, three-story house with a thatched roof and a pronounced lean.

"My sister's house, missus Morris, and her husband, Mr. Morris of the clan Sando."

The whole dwelling looked ready to fall. As if a harsh criticism of the cement pointing would collapse it into a heap onto the street with a light sigh of 'I did try to warn you.' Numerous wall plants covered the exterior; next to each was a lantern spilling amber light, inviting the trio onward. The weight of the hanging baskets inviting the wall outward. It was, in all aspects, a potential death trap, the equivalent of catching your genitals in a blender and asking Genghis Khan to turn the electricity off. Scrungle remembered that Doris was a builder and that this was the reason why he was at his sister's house. The dwelling had a small courtyard at the rear, a stable, anvil, and a furnace, with horseshoes of every size and shape hanging from the walls.

Doris led them through a horseshoe-motif front door. Inside, he introduced them to his brother-in-law, Morris, a strong-looking man in his late thirties; his wife, Missus Morris, wearing a horseshoe print dress, her hair tied back in a kind of horseshoe shape; and their three children. The eldest girl was thirteen, called Morris; the other daughter was eleven, called Morris; and their six-year-old son, called Morris Minor.

Peetles whispered to Scrungle that it made it easy to remember everyone's name.

(Later that night, as Peetles dropped off to sleep, the little creature asked Scrungle what they were all called again.)

Before long, they were all sitting around a wooden table. A black-bodied kettle hung across the grate boiling water for tea. With the curtains drawn and a fire in the hearth, the duo felt safe.

The house had a unique charm, with everything leaning to one side. Scrungle was given a small plate of dried-out mushrooms. Missus Morris apologised that they weren't fresh. Scrungle thanked her and said they tasted nice enough, but he did feel that he could do with a fresh batch. Peetles drank berry-infused water. After they had relaxed and eaten, Doris's brother-in-law, Morris, took his leave and went out to prepare the workshop for a client in the morning. A very picky unicorn, a good payer but a pain in the arse to work for.

Doris's sister, Missus Morris, took the children up to their beds. The children wanted to stay and hear all about Scrungle and Peetles, their journey so far, the Chana tree, and Knights of Colour. missus Morris assured the children that they could talk to the guests in the morning, but what they needed now was a bedtime story and sleep. None of the children wanted a story; still coming to terms emotionally with the last one their mother had told them. missus Morris insisted that it developed character, so she read them the story of a miner digging for rubies.

*Once upon a time, A divorced miner had a beautiful, gentle, and sweet daughter. However, she caught a fungal infection while messing around with the communal weights at the local gym. All because no one bothered to clean them down after they did a session. The infection on the palms of her hands became so bad, that it stopped her from playing the banjo. Since the government of the land had decimated the healthcare budget the miner had to find the money for treatment and go private. The miner teamed up with seven other miners all of whom, were short in stature, minor miners as they were called.*

*The work was dangerous and hard as they dug deep but eventually, they found the biggest ruby that had ever been. It would not only pay for his daughter's remedy but also a good few nights at Fanny Bucket's Fun Time House and pie shop. Just as they are celebrating this good fortune, the mine collapses, killing them all, and a puppy the major miner had just found, which he was going to give his daughter as a present because it was so cute.*

Missus Morris told the children that the whimpering cries of the trapped, terrified puppy could still be heard. The daughter never follows her dream of becoming a world-class banjo player in a Cajun band; taking the safe option as a financial advisor and ends up an alcoholic by the age of twenty-three. The moral of the story was to join a union. Utterly depressed the children cried themselves to sleep.

"Thank you so much for coming to help us." Said Scrungle after the sobs began to fade and Missus Morris had said her good nights.

"My pleasure, my pleasure. You are the heroes of the road works. Lucky it was that I was out late sorting the supplies and things needed for fixing the house." Said Doris, waving his hands in the general direction of everywhere to illustrate his point.

"It is strange; don't you think that I am there at the right time?" Added Doris.

"Why were the Hobgoblins so mean?" Said Peetles

"They're just made that way. You see, the hobgoblins were introduced by Chancellor Gumptrude to help the sheriffs. Helpers, they call them. The bypass and rising taxes have caused a lot of unrest. I don't agree with a lot of things that Gladis said, but she is right that things have been getting worse since Baroness Bakeasy turned up and the King became ill. Now the Princess has run away, and the Knights of Colour aren't around to keep things in check. Well, things are bad," explained Doris

"They did seem very honourable and like to start the day with a hearty breakfast." Said Scrungle.

"Yes, they bring a sense of safety when they are in the streets. But now, with them away, trade is low as no one goes out at night. The curfew was introduced to stop the meetings and rallies." Doris sighed. The sound was sad. He looked away, not wanting to show his guests his melancholy mood. He then got up taking the empty plates to the small kitchen, putting them in the sink to soak.

"Did you find what you were looking for at the Sorcerers Collective Society?"

"Yes, well sort of." Said Scrungle.

"We met a really nice witch who gave us a map and smelled of curry," said Peetles, sitting on several cushions, so they were at table height.

"The map smelled like curry?" asked Doris.

"No, the witch."

Doris nodded understanding.

"You seem to be doing a lot of travelling to find these mushrooms, but I have to ask. Why don't you put a staircase into your home? Then you won't have to float up or down."

Scrungle didn't say anything for a moment as he was thinking about what the witch had said about keeping the way secret, who to trust, and how long his eyes had stung after their meeting. Scrungle believed that Doris was trustworthy; he just felt it, and as for abandoning the search for the magic fungus, he came to the same conclusion as before.

"If I put a staircase in, then anyone could come and disturb me. It feels safer if that makes sense,"

"Well, you could put in a door, and you'd have a key," said Doris with a smile.

"Then it would feel like a house, not a tree. If people knock, I would be obliged to open it and say hello. Shouting up at a tree puts people off from disturbing me," said Scrungle, smiling inwardly at the rhyme between 'tree' and 'me.'

"A tree-house," said Peetles. The little creature was trying hard to join the conversation but was a beat behind. Scrungle sat, lost in thought.

"It wasn't my intention to upset you, my dear Scrungle," said Doris, who had stopped tidying up and just stood looking at him.

"No, of course you didn't. I was just thinking that I feel that I have to find the fungus. I don't know why, but I have started now. I have to finish," He reassured Doris that everything was fine.

"I still want to help," said Peetles, smiling.

Doris nodded, although it didn't make much practical sense. He knew what Scrungle meant.

"I believe that you have a quest, and it is your choice to follow it. I admire your conviction. So, my friends, the house of Sando will help as best we can." Doris said this, taking his place back at the table.

"The witch said that I shouldn't tell anyone, but I feel you have a good heart."

Doris clasped his hands together and bowed his head towards Scrungle, then Peetles. Scrungle pulled the hand-drawn map out of his unfeasibly deep pockets. Laying it out across the table.

At the centre of the map was Plombree, drawn out with fine detail. The pair could see their journey so far along the King's Road and the mountain pass. Scrungle's eyes followed the road from the bypass to the western gates where they had entered the city. Opposite was the eastern gate leading to the harbour many miles away. A small island of Slightly Broken Stuff was just off the coast. Further over on the map was the kingdom of Flan, separated from Plomb by a narrow sea. Following the coastline, the road forked and went through other villages and small towns. A river leading to the sea cut the road in half. It was marked with a ferry crossing, then into more woodland, and after that the Hills of Badly Designed Signs.

The hills had a red X through them. The witch had made sure they knew where they had to go. A lot of the map was blank and just inscribed with.

**'Here be dragons.'**

**'The wilderness.'**

**'Toner ink running low.'**

This last remark no one at the table understood. Doris's chair creaked lightly as he sat back and contemplated the map. Next to the Hills of Badly Designed Signs, the witch had written instructions in very tiny script.

"Can you read that?" Said Doris, pointing to it.

"No. But the witch said that we have to ask questions to the cheese man when we find the moon-dial and also if we could pick up a few things for her." Said Scrungle, Peetles nodded in agreement.

"We can buy a magnifying glass in town tomorrow. Did the witch say how you use the moon-dial?" Said Doris.

"No, just where to go," Peetles said trying to be helpful.

"I assume the information we need is in the tiny writing," Scrungle said rubbing his long nose. There was a note of concern in Doris's voice, and when Doris looked up at Scrungle, he shook his head.

"I have heard only dark tales and uncanny rumours of this place." Tapping his finger on the map next to the Hills of Badly Designed Signs.

"I'm sure that it will work out for the best, and when I am home with my books and my telescope, I will appreciate them all the more."

Said Scrungle nodding a little. After a moment of silence, Doris took a breath.

"I believe, my friends, that it has been a long day for us all. I will show you to your room, sleep, and make a plan, as tomorrow is another day."

* * *

Doris took the pair up a tight, winding staircase to the attic room. Holding a brass candle holder made out of an old horseshoe to light the way. The room up here was more askew than the rest of the house, listing as if drunk. It was small, with a skylight shaped like a horseshoe. There seemed to be a theme running through the house's décor, but for the life of him, Scrungle couldn't put his finger on it.

Leaning to stay straight, Doris moved through the room and lit more candles. Dominating the space was a double bed with a straw mattress. In the candlelight, they could see the blankets were adorned with horseshoe motifs. In the corner was a washbasin made of blue porcelain and a small chest of drawers.

"Thank you and your sister and your brother-in-law for the room and everything." Said Peetles looking a bit nervous and spikey at the generosity being shown them. Doris smiled at the pair.

"Sleep well, my friends. You are safe in the company of missus Morris of the house of Sando tonight."

With that, he gently closed the door and descended back down the stairs, the bells on his shoes jingling.

## Eleven

# *A Unicorn*

Scrungle and Peetles came down the next day to find breakfast waiting for them.

Missus Morris had been out early with the children to collect fresh mushrooms from some of the parks and green places dotted around Plombree. It had been a bit of a frugal search. Then they went to the mushroom seller. In hindsight, she realised that she should have gone there first and saved herself a lot of time, before whisking the now-late children off to school.

The dining table was crammed with bowls full of different fungi: White Button, Crimini Portabella, King Trumpet, and many other varieties. For Peetles, Missus Morris had infused water with apples and berries. After drinking, Peetles exclaimed how delicious it was, then asked Scrungle for the lemon-coloured water bottle so it could be filled.

Morris, with Doris assisting, was in the stables, shoeing a rather snooty-looking unicorn. Scrungle and Peetles wandered through to watch. The unicorn was a magnificent white; over the front haunches, it wore a black and grey satin jacket embroidered in gold. The four-legged equine looked at them directly. A moment passed, and then the unicorn nodded at the pair, its demeanour instantly changing as it recognised them as the ones who had come to its assistance at the Inn of the Horse Shoe and Bucket.

"Hello," said Scrungle.

"My dear fellow, how are you, thank you for getting us through that terrible roadblock." Said the unicorn.

Morris, sweat dripping from his brow, wearing a heavy black leather apron, was filing down the stump of one of the hooves of the unicorn, ready for shoeing. Doris, his hair bright red now, holding a bucket, stood next to him. Both Doris and Morris looked up, surprised at the change in the unicorn, who had been testy and rather pedantic about the whole shoeing process. Now that Scrungle and Peetles were present, the unicorn seemed downright courteous.

"You know I never introduced myself properly. I am Lord Sebastian Bigglesworth, the third. Call me Biggles; everybody does. I didn't know you were friends with the farrier."

Biggles then lifted a hoof for Scrungle to shake, at the same time taking a heavy dump right next to Mr Morris. The unicorn shit looked like ordinary horse shit, except that it was multicoloured and sparkled with flecks of glitter. Mr Morris looked at Biggles, then the shit, then back to Biggles.

Something snapped behind Mr. Morris's eyes. Incensed, hot, stressed, and sick of the unicorn's derogatory comments he started towards Biggles, muttering curses under his breath. He raised the shoeing hammer intending to smash it repeatedly into the unicorn's head. Doris grabbed Mr Morris, and there was a silent but desperate life-and-death struggle between the two until Doris eventually wrestled the hammer out of Mr Morris's hands, gesturing emphatically for him to calm down.

Scrungle kept shaking the hoof while this went on. He could feel Biggles trying to pull away, but he wanted the unicorn to keep his concentration in front of him unaware that he had been close to becoming glue.

"I need that back." Biggles eventually pulled the hoof away from Scrungle.

"Can you remember what you said to the witch, Waynex Peetles?"

"Was I wearing a raincoat?" Peetles was investigating a small horseshoe.

"No." Scrungle knew at that moment that Peetles had forgotten most of what had happened the day before.

"Is it important?" Peetles said getting ever so slightly bumpy.

"It's alright, Peetles. It doesn't matter and is certainly not important." Scrungle said in an easy manner.

"Is this your first visit to Plombree?" Inquired Biggles.

"It is, and it is very noisy, but Doris and family Morris of the house of Sando have made us very welcome." Said Scrungle. Then he bent down to pick Peetles up and put him on the lid of a barrel that was full of horseshoe nails.

"They are good people," Biggles said, managing to make it sound patronising.

Scrungle watched Morris roll his eyes and then make a very specific hand gesture. Doris had to stifle a laugh as he shovelled the unicorn manure into the bucket he had been holding.

"We went to see a witch; she was a bit scary. She did give us a map." Said Peetles. Picking up a small tack hammer and investigating it.

"A map sounds interesting. Where are you going?" Inquired Biggles.

Scrungle remembered what the witch Waynex had said about not telling anyone. He was sure that Peetles would get mixed up anyway, but grabbing at the first thing that popped into his mind, he said,

"I'm going to see my aunty; she lives on the island of Slightly Broken Stuff." Scrungle and Doris exchanged a knowing look.

"Oh dear, that is a terrible place. Why anyone would live there is beyond me." Biggles said this-looking Scrungle up and down.

"She sent me a letter. She needs the grass cutting." Scrungle added for no reason.

"Well, it's your aunty; do what you like." Biggles dismissed the matter, no longer interested.

"Do you like your new shoes?" Said Peetles as Mr Morris started hammering on the new horseshoe. They were gold-tipped.

"I have to keep up with appearances. The crown wants to borrow more money from my investors." Said Biggles. "How are you getting there?"

Morris dropped the shod hoof and picked up a polished steel plate so the unicorn could admire himself.

"I think we are happy just to walk." Said Scrungle, looking at Peetles, who smiled back.

"Sounds very demotic. Why not hire a carriage or, at the very least, a bicycle? They are becoming all the rage in Plombree. It will be so much faster than walking. It'll knock days off the travel time," said the unicorn.

Scrungle didn't want to admit to the snooty upper-class prat that they didn't have any gold or silver. It was unlike Scrungle, but the fabled creature made him feel humiliated by their lack of funds.

"Is that that thing that has two wheels and a seat?" Asked Peetles.

"That could describe a lot of things," Biggles replied, managing to sound condescending and aloof at the same time. Mr Morris made another gesture to Doris, who picked up a tack and stuck it in his hand so he didn't draw attention to himself by laughing.

"They had handles to the bar to turn the front wheel. Then other bits that you pushed down on." Peetles explained, trying hard to be more helpful in the description, not registering the fact that the tone of the unicorn was that of a proper twat.

"Yes, Peetles that is a bike. They look a bit dangerous, and where would Peetles sit?" Said Scrungle getting annoyed for Peetles. Biggles shrugged, which looked daft for a horse with a horn in the middle of its head thought Scrungle.

"You can get a basket on the front for Peetles." Said Doris.

"Or I have seen them with a sidecar attached." Mr Morris chipped in. He had moved over to the small forge and was heating a new shoe to beat into shape for the unicorn's hoof. Pumping the bellows to heat the coals was Doris. Sparks flew up from the furnace, like mini stars as he pulled it out to inspect. To Morris's practiced eye, it didn't look right. He then plunged it back into the heat.

"Some of the carriage shops have them. We could ask there. There is a good one not far from the eastern gate. Then we can buy a magnifying glass; once I have finished helping here, I will take you there." Said Doris.

"What do you think Peetles?" Said Scrungle.

Peetles looked at Scrungle and smiled; that was all that was needed for the decision to be made. Picking Peetles up, they said goodbye to Biggles, who immediately asked how long the shoeing was going to take and if Mr Morris's workshop always smelled the way it did.

Outside, they found a little wall to sit on across from the garden of the leaning home of Mr. Morris of the house of Sando. Side by side the pair watched the city.

To their great delight and a favourable portent of things to come, a bicycle came past with a basket on the front full of parcels and letters. The rider was an elderly gentleman in a red uniform with the words 'Post by Royal Command.' embroidered on the back. They both surmised that he was a postman, then they remembered the apprentice baker dressed as a sailor and thought the man on the bike could have been a harpoon salesman for all they knew.

It didn't take long for Doris to finish helping Morris with the shoeing of the unicorn. He also saw to the start of the scaffolding work on the house. Showing the workers, two women and one dim-witted troll with a rather jovial disposition, where to brace first.

Doris then took Scrungle and Peetles on a little tour of Plombree. Scrungle asked about the road leading out of Plombree. Doris informed them it was just like the King's Road. Better in places, before it forked one way to the harbour town of Harbour and the other towards the Hills of Badly Designed Signs.

Doris explained the harbour was called Harbour, as the founding fathers thought that it wouldn't confuse people as to where it was. Not many towns and cities that weren't on the coast were called Harbour. Also, they just couldn't be bothered to·come up with a decent name.

The other road wound its way through towns and villages for many miles before entering the Hills of Badly Designed Signs.

"How did the hills become the place of Badly Designed Signs?" The question had been on Scrungle's mind since hearing it from the witch, unlike Peetles, wide-eyed in wonder, without a coherent thought entering their head, just sitting in their usual place as they walked through the streets of Plombree, heading to the carriage works.

"A long time ago, a wealthy family of cheese-makers lived in a huge estate on the tallest of the hills. One day, a sign designer who had been appointed by the king, who would have been our king's great-grandfather, was sent out to make professional-looking signs throughout the land. He stopped at the wealthy family of cheese-makers and asked if they needed any signs made.

I did hear it was a very tempting offer, as he was giving discounted rates because the state was footing the bill. Well, before anyone knew it, the sign designer and the daughter of the wealthy cheese farmer fell in love. Sadly, the father didn't want his daughter to be with the sign designer, as he thought the sign designer had a bit of a funny walk, talked in a high-pitched voice, and pointed at things using three fingers."

Doris gulped in a breath. "So to get rid of him, The wealthy cheese farmer went and replaced the fancy signs with badly spelled ones. Signs that pointed in the wrong direction or others that just didn't make any sense. The king called the sign designer back to the city and imprisoned him for being shit at the job. The daughter of the wealthy cheese farmer was heartbroken and decided to run away to the city and petition the king to get her true love back. The tragedy was that one of the signs giving her direction was written by the father, and she fell down a well and died."

Doris had only taken a single breath since starting the monologue and promptly passed out on the busy street next to a man selling watermelons. The man selling watermelons noticed the unconscious man on the pavement with bright red hair and thought this was the perfect moment, to ask Scrungle if he would like to try a segment. Scrungle politely declined, putting Peetles down so he could help Doris. Peetles, on the other hand, gave it a try and were delighted with the taste and the fact that this was something they could ingest. While the interaction was happening, Doris regained consciousness and sat up.

"Are you alright?" Said Scrungle. Doris nodded, still sitting on the ground. Scrungle held out his hand. Taking it, Doris helped himself up.

"Sorry about that, I forget to breathe sometimes."

"That'll be four taploons." Said the watermelon man, bending down to stare at Peetles.

"I don't have any money." Peetles edged away, getting a bit spikey and lumpy.

"You better pay, or I'll call a sheriff or a hobgoblin."

"Here," Doris said. Giving the watermelon man some silver coins with shaky hands, his brain still fuzzy from passing out. The watermelon man scowled at Peetles, then walked off. Scrungle picked his little ally up and put him on his head.

"You get nothing in this city for free." Said Doris as they walked on.

"Sorry that we are eating your sister's food and using her home. The only thing I can offer you is a hat stand. My father.." Scrungle was interrupted by Doris.

"No, no, not at all. You are my guest, and you saved the day. If it wasn't for you and Peetles, my sister and Morris would have lost their home; it was ready to fall."

Just as Doris finished talking, they turned a corner, and in front of them was a coach and livery hire shop. The name above the entrance of the large double gate read.

**'Charlton and Heston and son and another on the way.'**

Doris pushed through a smaller door in one of the double gates. Scrungle remembered Peetles and set them down as they followed. Inside the courtyard, several carriages were lined up in tidy rows. Different colours, signage, and design. Basic models, from black and affordable to the more luxuriant, trimmed velvet with gold leaf piping silk curtains hung on the inside for privacy. Three-quarters of the interior of the building was filled with stalls for horses. Scrungle and Peetles said hello as they passed. None of the horses responded; they just munched away at the feed tray hay.

At the back, in an alcove, stood several bicycles and a single tricycle. The tricycle was painted a banana yellow, chipped and rusted in places. Attached to the front was a tatty basket; on the right handlebar was a little silver bell. The wheels were large, but the tyres looked worn without much tread.

"Hello, how can we help today?" Shouted the sales harpy, appearing as if from thin air and standing far too close to the trio. Peetles screamed, and both Doris and Scrungle jumped. The harpy exuded far too much enthusiasm for carriage rental. Her long, jet-black hair flowed around her shoulders, with dark purple eye shadow, and the wings of a bird sprouting from her back. The sales harpy was just as beautiful as the ones the pair had encountered at the SCS and Amazing Shine.

"Have we met?" Said Peetles.

The sales harpy brushed a lock of hair from her face. Smiled and nodded in a way that conveyed she heard that statement frequently.

"Bicycle hire." Said Doris.

"Brilliant, we have several fine transportation devices for hire, two and three-wheeled for the most discerning of taste."

"I like the yellow one there," Peetles said then did a bouncing walk to the tricycle and tried to get on it.

"How much is the rental?" Asked Doris.

Scrungle picked Peetles up, placing them in the basket on the front. Peetles tried the little silver bell; it 'tinged', setting the pair giggling. They took turns flicking the little catch 'ting, ting' and it started the pair laughing harder. The harpy steered Doris away from the alcove to discuss business. After a moment, Doris walked back to Scrungle and Peetles, looking rather forlorn.

"I believe we have to go." Said Doris, who didn't wait and walked back to the gates. Outside on the street, Doris told the pair that the rental for just a week was far too expensive.

"You have said you don't have any gold or silver, but it is far too much for me to give you. In all honesty, it would be cheaper to buy a bicycle than hire one. I am sorry." Doris looked at his feet.

"Oh, I feel we have become a burden to you. I have never needed to buy things." Scrungle was fiddling with his nose as he admitted this.

"Come. Let us go to the entertainers green take our minds off things. I find that when you don't think about it, the answer will present itself, and we still need to purchase a magnifying glass," Doris said, looking up and smiling.

Scrungle felt deflated. His journey so far had taught him many things. For one, there are a lot of silly regulations in the world that do nothing to help anyone. Another was that people and creatures did many stupid things because someone in charge had told them to do it. Common sense wasn't that common, and anyone in a position of power was usually an idiot. However, above all else, it was apparent that the world and most of its problems were routed in the want of money, and Scrungle just didn't care for wealth. He just wanted to get some Huba mushrooms so he could get back into his home.

## Twelve

# *Never Bet*

They walked through Plombree, up towards the castle. Doris explained that the entertainer's green was an open area just outside of the drawbridge and main gates. Musicians busked, wizards wizened, and jugglers usually maimed themselves.

Lounging around on street corners, they would come across hobgoblins in two's or three's flexing their braces. It wasn't unusual for them to shout out.

'Get ya dog on a lead, 'cal that a haircut mate.' Or 'look at the ginger'. Ignoring the hobgoblins was the best tactic, as they would get bored and pick on someone else.

Once they were on the King's Road, which led directly up to the castle gates, it didn't take long to get to the green.

The castle guards at the drawbridge policed the area, so there were no hobgoblins or sheriffs to spoil the day. Stone tables were scattered around the green, with people and mythical creatures watching different performers.

At one of the tables, a snappily dressed wizard in yellow and black was doing a card trick known as Find the Lady. The wizard kept saying to the group betting, 'find the princes' and then laugh at his joke.

The cluster of gamblers or suckers included two burly-looking men, their faces tattooed with spider webs stretching out from the nose. Peetles thought they must really like the taste of flies. Opposite them was a middle-aged woman dressed in paper and boxed cardboard, making her look like she needed to be posted, and three smartly dressed young women in court uniforms of green, purple, and red, wearing hats made with paper in the shape of a candelabra.

The people at the table were engrossed in watching the wizard move the three cards that were face-down on the stone table. Doris, Scrungle, and Peetles sat at the table next to them, staring at the impressive amount of gold and silver that had built up in the pot. Peetles climbed onto the table to get a closer look at the card game.

A young man approached them dressed in a long knee-length jumper. He held a wooden bucket filled with water and a bag full of goblets. He asked if anyone would like some water for one taploon. Doris bought one for each of them.

The young man thought this was the ideal moment to tell everyone he was an aspiring bard and start to sing one of his compositions in the new street style. It had a repetitive quality that was rhythmic and rhyming. Just saying the words rather than singing.
Scrungle could only make out that he was angry at digging and dogs, as he kept admonishing bitches and hoes. Rubbing his temples after the third hoe, Doris, abruptly shouted that he would beat the young man to death with the bag of goblets if he didn't move on. He scurried off grumbling that they knew nothing about art or what it was like in the hood.

Sitting in silence the three companions thought about how they could make some money. Now and then, Doris would sit forward, hold for a second, look like he was about to say something, debate it in his head, and then sit back, convinced that it was a bad idea.

"It's in the middle." Said Peetles to no one.

"Sorry," Scrungle said pulling his mind back to the moment, as he had been thinking about farm tools and livestock.

"The queen's in the middle." Peetles pointed to the wizard and the pot of money on the other table.

The group pointed to the card on the farthest right. The woman in cardboard stretched over and turned the card. It was a jack. Amazed, they watched the wizard turn the middle card, and the queen of hearts was revealed. Doris, who had been watching this in a kind of half-hearted way, sat up straight. Cajoling the group, the wizard said they would get it right on the next go. There was a lot of discussion, and then one by one, they put in another round of bets.

"Keep your eye on the Princess," called out the wizard laughing. He then picked up the three cards. Shuffling them around the table his hands quick and fast. The gamblers watched intently until he stopped, and then the wizard invited the group to guess again.

"Where is it, Peetles?" Said Doris.

"In the middle again." Peetles sat swinging their little legs back and forward, not concentrating on the game of chance.

"I am convinced it's on the left." Said Doris.

"Definitely in the middle." Peetles was now looking up at the castle, admiring the flags flying from the ramparts. The wizard kept up the performance, asking them to pick. The group, as one, decided on the left-most card. With a flourish, he revealed it was still in the middle. A groan of dismay came from them as they looked at the pile of coins sitting heaped on the stone table. Double or nothing, said the wizard. But shaking their heads one by one, they concluded that they would just lose even more money and declined the invitation.

"How did you know it was in the middle?" Asked Doris, looking to

Peetles, then the wizard.

"Klepto taught me; I used to do the game at the market." Peetles smiled at Doris.

A fevered look had crept onto Doris's face, looking from Peetles to the wizard, then Scrungle. He jumped up and shouted across to the group.

"Double or nothing."

"Private game, mate." Said one of the men who self-identified as a spider. He didn't want two chancers to come in and win the pot. The wizard looked at the tattooed man.

"Does that mean you want to have another bet?" He smiled a slippery smile at the congregation at the table. There was a bit of conversation amongst the group, then the ladies of the court said no. The burly, tattooed men shrugged and said no.

"Then this is mine, and I can take on any challengers." Said the wizard in a conciliatory tone, all the while thinking this was his lucky day. He beckoned them over. Doris looked at the gold and silver on the table while pulling out his purse. The burly men gave the trio an embittered look.

"I don't think this is a good idea. You can't risk your money on a game of chance. Not for us; your kindness has been enough." Scrungle wasn't just thinking about the game being one of luck but also Peetles short attention span as well as the little creature's ability to get over-excited. Scrungle was also feeling unbelievably indebted to Doris, and this was playing on his conscience. Doris, on the other hand, wasn't listening to Scrungle anymore. The frenzied look of the degenerate gambler had taken over. Peetles had opened a full can of worms.

"Can you match what's on the table?" Said the wizard.

Doris looked into his purse, counted, and then nodded. Scrungle had a terrible thought that the money was family Morris's savings to fix the house.

"Bollocks," said one of the tattooed men, and then they both put money in. Eventually, everyone at the table did.

"Please don't." Begged Scrungle.

Doris shook his head and looked at Peetles, who was standing on the table next to Scrungle, watching some butterflies. Doris motioned to Scrungle.

"Peetles can't see from there." The urgency in Doris's voice made Scrungle ask Doris once again not to bet.

"Pick Peetles up and put them on your head before I pull that nose of yours off and beat you to death with it."

Doris, eyes as big as saucers, clenching and unclenching his fists, enunciated every word. Scrungle, now mildly terrified, picked Peetles up and wore them as a hat once again. The wizard and Doris locked eyes, but the wizard didn't move until Doris dropped the bag onto the pile of coins on the table.

"Watch the lady."

Flashing a smile of perfect teeth, at the same time as showing where the queen of hearts was in the three-card shuffle. His hands were a blur as he moved the cards around the table. Doris's sole focus was watching the wizard's hands.

"Pick a card." Said the wizard, looking at Doris.

Doris, realising this was the moment, looked at Peetles.

"Where is it, then?" Doris said it with the tension of fifty thousand volts in his voice.

"Sorry." Peetles turned around to look down at Doris.

"Weren't you watching?" screamed Doris.

Peetles started to get spikey and lumpy.

"I saw a cloud shaped like a cloud." Peetles was happy that they were on Scrungle's head and away from the angry face of Doris.

"My dear Doris, what has come over you? Please calm yourself." Said Scrungle.

"I'll dear fucking Doris you, you useless white seagull shit. Where's the queen of hearts, ya little tit?"

Doris was screaming, making heads turn. He suddenly lunged towards Peetles. Scrungle put out a spindly arm to keep Doris at bay.

"Stop that," said Scrungle as Doris tried to pull Peetles from Scrungle's head.

"Middle. It's in the middle." Squeaked Peetles.

"What? Are you sure? You better be sure." Shouted Doris. Not caring anymore about the attention that was now being directed at them. Everything was now wrapped up on the bet.

"Yes, please don't be angry at me." Said Peetles, who was now quite lumpy on Scrungle's head. Doris rubbed a hand across his eyes and shuddered. The assembled people stared at the unfolding scene, not knowing what to do. The guards at the gates were looking over, trying to decide if they should investigate or keep lounging against the wall of the castle. It didn't take long for lounging against the wall to win.

"Are you sure you want to say the middle? I do believe your little friend was looking the other way." Said the wizard.

The inflection in his voice was conciliatory, but his eyes had a sharpness that wouldn't have been amiss on an investment banker. Doris, on the other hand, looked demented. He took a moment to scan the faces of the people at the table, then Scrungle and Peetles.

"I don't know. I don't know. I've been so good." Then broke down, crying.

The wizard pulled a sad face.

"Let's just forget the bet. Eh, thank you everyone; it has been fun entertaining you today." Said the wizard, throwing Doris's bag of coins back to him. Just as he was about to pick up the cards and the cash.

"Wait a moment, please. Are you sure it is the middle one?" Said

Scrungle, putting his trust in Peetles.

"Yes. But." Peetle's voice was small and hesitant.

"But?" Scrungle wanted to know more.

"When I did it, if anyone got it right, I would palm the card."

"Palm the card; what's that?" Said Scrungle.

The two tattooed burly men on hearing this stood up immediately, turning to look at the wizard, who opened his palms outward and shrugged.

"Swap it when you pick them up to show the idiots. Well, that's what the wizard Klepto told me to do." Explained Peetles.

The table erupted with shouts at the wizard. Doris was still crying into his sleeve. Moving to pick up the cards, the wizard was stopped by the tattooed men, grabbing an arm each. The woman dressed as a cardboard box stretched over and uncovered the middle card. It was the ace of spades. There was a collective gasp. The wizard pulled his arms free from the tattooed men.

"As you can see, the guess was wrong. I have never been so rudely treated in my life. Now if you'll excuse me, I'll be on my way," said the wizard, who then sniffed.

"Turn the other cards over." Squeaked Peetles.

"No, no, no, I have had quite enough of this. I'm going," said the wizard, who then moved forward to pick up the cards and money. Before he could the cardboard box woman turned the two remaining cards over. The king of clubs and the jack of diamonds. The queen was nowhere to be seen. The moment was filled with deadly silence.

"Oh my, how could that have happened?" Said the wizard, his voice at its most innocent in the deceptive quiet.

"You cheating little git!" shouted one of the tattooed men. Both men nodded to each other and started stripping the wizard of his cloak and jacket, searching for hidden cards. Several items started falling out: jewellery, necklaces, pocket chains, rings, bracelets, a chicken leg, half an apple, a full deck of cards, and then the queen of hearts. Protesting and struggling, but with little effect against the men, the wizard was soon down to his shorts and vest. One of the king's court women looked at the necklace lying on the ground. She put a hand to her neck and realised that her locket and chain had gone.

Throwing a tirade of abuse at the wizard which made the guards give up on the lounging and walk over to see what the fuss was about. After a discussion with the men and ladies of the court, the wizard was dragged away to the cells in the castle, all the while protesting his innocence.

The guards gave Peetles two free entry tickets to the castle, grounds, and gardens, off-peak times only, for catching a thief and a cheat. Everyone congratulated Peetles and Scrungle. The little group divided up the money on the table, giving the bigger share to Peetles for saving them from being robbed. One by one, they left, going back to their jobs or businesses.

Doris, however, during the whole episode, just sat crying at the table with his head buried in his crossed arms. Now and then, hitching with a sob. Peetles jumped down off Scrungles head and onto the table. Scrungle sat next to Doris and put an arm around him.

After a moment, Doris put his head into Scrungle for comfort. Rocking gently they sat until Doris had composed himself enough to speak.

"I am so sorry; I have a problem. I gambled my house away, all our savings, I gambled my wife away to a pirate on a game of 'what made it wet'. I thought coming to see my sister was a good idea. Start over. I had it under control, but when Peetles got it right over and over, I just couldn't help myself. How can you ever forgive me?" Doris's confession came in a choked and halting voice. Peetles eyes had filled up, and a tear made a straight line down their round face.

"It's alright." Said Peetles.

"No harm done, and look, we have more than enough to get a bicycle." Added Scrungle

All three sat watching the rest of the entertainers and the city play on until Doris was capable of looking at Peetles without bursting into fresh tears. The shadow of the castle towers cut across the city, marking time.

"I think that we all deserve ice cream."

With this, Scrungle stood up from the table, picked Peetles up, and put them on his head. Then held a hand out to an embarrassed and red-faced Doris.

Scrungle sent Doris an imaginary smile. Doris must have picked up on it as he smiled back. Taking the offered hand, they headed away from the green to buy a bicycle.

On the way, they stopped at a stall selling ice cream. Neither Peetles nor Scrungle could eat them, so it was for appearances only, as it was fun to hold them as they ambled around Plombree. Doris ended up eating all three and getting sphenopalatine ganglion neuralgia. A passing doctor told them this, then said it was more commonly known as brain freeze or Brian freeze, depending on whether they were or weren't paying attention to the spelling.

Deciding not to go back to Charlton and Heston's, they walked around the city looking at thrift shops to see if there were any bicycles for sale. Outside a second-hand shop of oddities and out-of-tune pianos, not far from an Amazing Shine depot, was a battered and broken tricycle. They had more than enough money to buy it twice over. Doris told them that, between himself and his brother-in-law Morris, who was good with metalwork it would be in tip-top condition in a matter of days.

Peetles was a little sad that it wasn't yellow. Doris, still atoning for his behaviour at the green, assured Peetles that it would be the brightest, best yellow he would ever see and so much finer than the one at the coach hire.

Peetles and Scrungle kept a little walking-around money but gave the lion's share of what was left of the gold and silver to Doris to give to Missus Morris for the expense of looking after them. It was only later that they remembered they needed a magnifying glass. Doris said fixing the bike would take a while, so they had plenty of time to get one in the days to come.

# Thirteen

# *Sugartits Lane*

The next day, a lilac-haired Doris, still apologetic, suggested that Scrungle and Peetles should go out and take a stroll around Plombree without him; this way, they could see the city and buy a magnifying glass. He had written an extensive set of directions for the pair to follow to get to the Magniphorim, along with a detailed drawing.

Scrungle and Peetles gave an inward sigh of relief that it wasn't SCS they had to go to for the magnifying glass. Neither wanted to face the sales harpies again or the unremitting, relentless, persistent pressure to buy something, anything!

On the back of the written directions were light blue dotted lines and folding instructions. Doris said that if you folded it along the marks, it would make a paper airplane.

"What's an airplane?" Asked Peetles.

"It's what the witch said when I bought the paper from her," Doris added a shrug of his shoulders as manned flight hadn't been invented yet, and at the time of purchase, he didn't want to appear dim by asking in case it was a new type of hat.

"Was it the witch Waynex by any chance?" Scrungle asked out of curiosity.

"No, she was called Wayup."

"It might be a relative, an aunt, or an uncle, or maybe someone holding a grudge." Said Peetles.

Doris looked confused and, with backward glances at Peetles, took his leave of the pair. Missus Morris, delighted with the money she had been given, ensured there would be a lavish meal fit for a king later that evening. Telling them before they set off, to be back well before curfew and that if they were lost, to ask for directions to Sugartits Lane.

Some believed that it had been named after the common blue tits that nested in the cherry trees lining the street, and also in part because of the nearby warehouse that refined raw sugar cane. Mr. Morris insisted it had nothing to do with the prostitutes who plied their trade on the street corner in the evening. Mr and Mrs Morris exchanged a look that neither Scrungle nor Peetles could quantify. Then Mr Morris swiftly disappeared into the stable to repair the second-hand bike.

With Peetles perched on Scrungle's head, the pair strolled casually through the streets. Heading in a slow, leisurely way towards the Magniphorim and Doctor Optics Crazy Lenses.

Outside the entrance of '**Charlton and Heston and sons and another on the way**' Scrungle and Peetles met the life-size painted wooden figure of the White Knight.

A speech bubble was written above the promotional wooden cut-out.

**'The only place I buy a saddle.'**

Children standing next to it were having speed sketches made.

Following the smell of ginger and cinnamon, the duo came upon an open square surrounded by bakeries and patisseries. While Scrungle and Peetles were looking around at all the wonderful cakes, it started to fill up with residents of Plombree, magical creatures, and people alike.

A lone sheriff and several hobgoblins marshalled the gathering. It was another rally supporting the opposition to Gumptrude. It started peacefully with a band, jugglers, and an alternative comedian. Once the crowd was warmed up, an old man dressed smartly in a paper waistcoat came forward to talk to the crowd about his vision for Plombree and the kingdom.

The hobgoblins, however, had a different idea and started pushing and taunting the people and creatures who were in support of the old man calling them 'radgies.'

The sheriff, dressed in what appeared to be a purple one-piece jumpsuit covered in anti-climbing paint, was doing her best to maintain control over both sides of the engagement. Spent most of her time telling the hobgoblins they were there to help, not add to the problem or behave like a pack of idiots. It didn't take long for the confrontation to escalate and the crowd to retaliate, tossing rotten vegetables and then hard pieces of cake at the hobgoblins.

Taunts of 'Gumptrude is a turd' and 'Bakeasy is kinda sleazy.' enraged the hobgoblins, who supported the chancellor. At her wits end, the sheriff called in the fire department. A hand-pulled fire wagon was deployed. The elves vigorously operated the fire engine's pumps and sprayed water into the crowd on both sides of the commotion.

It effectively took the fight out of the crowd and hobgoblins alike. Damp and miserable the majority left leaving soggy cardboard everywhere. Scrungle and Peetles watched all this from a safe distance, not wanting to be caught up in any altercation, moving on when the fire engine ran out of water.

As the pair wandered the city, they sensed an increasing undercurrent of unrest.

On the surface, the citizens of Plombree went about their daily lives. Hugging their children, eating fruit, having affairs, and staring aimlessly into space waiting for death. Contrasting this was the growing number of protest marches and rallies calling for the interim chancellor, Gumptrude, to step down.

Overheard conversations and grumblings of the residents of Plombree at the ever-increasing taxes and curfew, put Scrungle and Peetles on edge. No matter where they looked, people and creatures were being harassed by the deputised hobgoblins. Outsiders as they were, in a foreign world, Scrungle just wanted to resume his journey and find the Huba mushroom so he could float back into his home. He had never thought the world outside the Chana tree was such a complicated, contradictory place.

"Who's Chancellor Gumptrude?" Asked Peetles.

"I'm not really sure, Peetles. I do feel though that I would not trust this Gumptrude."

Peetles suggested that they take a small detour from the directions that Doris had given them and look around Painters Point. It was located on the flat thrust of the hill, the city had grown around. A triangular courtyard had been built, with two triangular-shaped entrances. Inside were painters of many different styles and abilities. Crowded with tourists admiring the work, Scrungle and Peetles , enjoyed the art and calm atmosphere, after witnessing the threat and noise of the rally. Some people and creatures were sitting to have caricatures done. Other artists painted landscapes from memory. Completed paintings filled all available spaces, covering the walls and tiled floor.

As the pair walked through, Scrungle saw Kevin the donkey. His watercolour paintings had been framed and displayed across a section of the courtyard. A decent number of admirers were looking at them.

Kevin clip-clopped over.

"Scrungle Bungus, it is you." Brayed the donkey. It sounded like Kevin made a loud 'eey orr' sound to everyone else.

"Hello Kevin, how are you? Are these all your work?" Scrungle said this while looking at the framed watercolours around him, splattered hues everywhere, disturbed brush strokes that screamed out from the paper. To Scrungle, it was the work of a distressed mind that had been left too long in a dark room.

"Yes, do you like them? That one there is Plombree main plaza. I really think I got the light perfect on that one." Brayed Kevin.

Kevin tilted his large head at the painting closest to Scrungle. From the angle he was viewing it, Scrungle had the impression Kevin had thrown up a heavy volume of sick, then decided to swirl it around with his hoof, while inebriated.

"What's happening, Scrungle?" Said Peetles, who was a bit spikey because all they could hear was a donkey making loud donkey sounds.

"Ah well, this is the Kevin that I mentioned. He came with the blue man who screamed at me. These are his watercolours. That one is the plaza where we first arrived." Scrungle pointed to the desperately bad painting.

"It doesn't look like the plaza; it looks more like the insides of a small animal." Said Peetles in a voice loud enough, only for Scrungle to hear.

"Can your friend understand like you do Scrungle?"

"Eh, sorry no."

Kevin realising he was disturbing people and only Scrungle could understand him, stopped 'eey orring as loudly as he had been.

"Pity. It's so much easier when I don't have to tap a full sentence out on the boards. Does your friend like it?"

"He does." Said Scrungle. He told a little white lie, not wanting to upset the donkey, who was as utterly charming as he had been the first time they had met.

They were interrupted by two well-dressed elderly-looking women who asked for the price of a small watercolour. To Scrungle and Peetles, it looked like Kevin had tripped over the paint and landed badly on the paper. Kevin moved over to a wooden board on the ground painted with the letters of the alphabet. With surprising speed, Kevin tapped out with his hoof the price of the piece and its title. Scrungle worked out that the price Kevin tapped out was three times more than the money they had won at the card table. What dumbfounded Scrungle was that the women were impressed with the painting and the price. Kevin tried to pick the watercolour up and wrap it while they counted out the gold.

After five awkward minutes, the women politely said it was fine the way it was, and they had to go, as they were up on charges again for GBH, goblin-bashing-halfwits, and due in court. Passing Scrungle, he heard them say Kevin's work was becoming rather collectible.

Peetles asked to be put down so they could explore on their own and waddled off to look at the other artists' work.

Kevin inquired about Scrungle's presence in Plombree, prompting him to explain his quest for Huba mushrooms and, amongst other things, his encounters with Knights of Colour. Curious, Scrungle asked if Kevin was still in the service of the rotund blue man. The donkey said that he no longer worked for the court. Having found success with a pitch at the Painters Point he was happy to leave the blue man's employment.

"You could stay and work for me. Be an interpreter. It can take so long to tap out the price, especially when people want to haggle." Said Kevin, knocking on the wooden board of painted letters with his hoof to illustrate the point. Scrungle politely declined the offer, and then Kevin said he could have a painting, free to choose anyone he liked. It was a kind offer but Scrungle said he didn't have anywhere to hang it. All the while thinking the art was the visual equivalent of watching someone being crushed by falling masonry.

"It has been lovely to see you again and I am glad you are a success, but I have to go and buy a magnifying glass." Said Scrungle.

Wishing each other success in their separate endeavours, they said farewell. Catching up with Peetles looking at a set of paintings portraying a lake and mountains, Scrungle called to them, but the little creature didn't acknowledge. Crouching down, he called to Peetles once more. Turning to Scrungle there were tears in his little friend's round eyes.

"Oh my Peetles, what's the matter?"

Peetles pointed to one of the paintings. It was titled

**'Buffering Please Wait.'**

"That's where I used to live."

Scrungle knelt as best he could to get a better look at the painting and, in the closeness, comfort his friend. The landscape was beautiful—greens and browns, tall trees, a crystal-clear blue lake. He could understand why Peetles was upset; it was a good place to live.

"Well, at least we are together."

With that, he picked Peetles up, held him as best he could in his stick-thin arms, and they left Painters Point.

Talking as they walked, it didn't take long for Peetles to regain their happy temperament. Holding the directions while sitting on Scrungle's head, the little creature directed them towards Doctor Optics but somehow managed to send them in the wrong direction, and they found themselves in a gravel courtyard of a large grand building. White roses in tended borders flanked the driveway to an open section under a first-floor balcony. Here a decent-sized crowd had gathered

Scrungle and Peetles watched from a distance. The security was a mixture of private guards, hobgoblins, and a couple of sheriffs.

Standing on the balcony was a group of similar-looking men. Their hair was yellow like a sick man's urine and backcombed into a pompadour, all were overweight, and had puffed-out lips like a duck. It was hard to tell from where Scrungle and Peetles stood, but it looked like they had a blue tinge to their skin. Dressed in purples and blacks, gold chains hung around their necks,

An air of arrogance, similar to a sewage works, exuded from them. One of these sad, overweight men was shouting inane platitudes, willing the crowd into a mild hysteria. Soon the shouts of, 'Gumptrude. Gumptrude.' could be heard.

A woman, in dark travelling clothes, her face hidden by her hood shouted, 'Is a tit.' between the 'Gumptrude.' chant. The morons closest to her turned hostile, telling her to leave. They lost interest when Gumptrude walked out and addressed the thick mud of imbeciles below him. Many in the crowd started shouting

'Make Plom great again' and 'levelling up'.

Gumptrude raised his hand in a calming motion. His appearance was similar to the other men on the balcony, although the hair was more pretentious, his duck-like lips thicker, and his gold chain the biggest. Behind Gumptrude was a tall blonde woman, elegant, dressed in the latest paper fashion. To Scrungle, even from this distance, he had never seen a woman so top-heavy.

"I'm sure that is the fat man who was shouting up at me while sitting on Kevin," Scrungle said.

"It's the same man that came to the village and had me leave." Said Peetles.

"So that is Gumptrude," the pair said together.

Gumptrude smiled a rubbery smile and addressed the crowd.

"It is so good to see so many loyal supporters out today. I think the only difference between me and other candidates is that I'm more honest, and my women are more beautiful. Just like our own Baroness

Bakeasy." Gumptrude turned and acknowledged the woman behind him. She stood, impassive as if waiting for a kettle to boil.

"I mean, think about it. The beauty of me is that I'm very rich. I think I am actually humble. I think I'm much more humble than you would understand. I'm intelligent. Some people would say I'm very, very, very intelligent. People love me. And you know what? I've been very successful. Everybody loves me. My fingers are long and beautiful, as, it has been well documented, are various other parts of my body."

There was a round of applause from the crowd.

"What is he talking about, Scrungle? What he's saying doesn't make any sense. Why is he talking about his fingers?"

"Maybe he has had a blow to the head." Scrungle offered. The crowd, however, seemed spellbound and called out.

'Gumptrude for high chancellor.'

The fat loony pointed at the crowd and clapped them. Someone threw a hat up to the balcony. MPGA had been stitched into the front. Gumptrude picked it up and put it on his empty head. The crowd went wild with applause.

"I will tell you something else. A person who is very flat-chested is very hard to be a ten. You know, it really doesn't matter what the opposition says as long as you've got a young and beautiful piece of ass. Number one, I have great respect for women. I was the one that really broke the glass ceiling on behalf of women, more than anybody in the city. My relationship, I think, is going to end up being very good with women."

"I hate that man." Said the hooded woman.

She had heard enough and turned to leave. Her face was obscured but her eyes caught Scrungle's as she brushed past. Just for a moment, he felt he should know who she was, then the next moment she was gone. A lingering scent of an exotic perfume was left in her wake.

"The worst thing a man can do is go bald. Never let yourself go bald." Said Gumptrude, the crowd applauded even more.

"I think Peetles, we should leave and buy the magnifying glass, as this Gumptrude seems to be a complete and utter pillock."

# Fourteen

## *It's Yellow*

They both rose late on the fourth day of their stay in Plombree. Scrungle felt a certain relief now they had everything they needed to get on with the next part of the journey. He kept catching himself thinking about how far he had travelled, underestimating what would be involved in replenishing the amphora jar and the adventure so far. He was glad that Peetles was with him. At times, a complete and utter twit, but a good companion and a loyal, trustworthy friend. Not having had an ally before, Scrungle was at a loss to know if he was a good friend in return.

Now the building work was underway; all Doris had to do was keep an eye on its progress, so Doris, Scrungle, and Peetles spent the morning studying the map, that was laid out across the table. Doris moved the magnifying glass over the tiny writing the witch had scribbled.

"I don't know why we have to ask questions. I mean, should it not be the other way around." Said Scrungle.

"Who is the cheese man?" Asked Peetles.

"I have no idea, but I know everyone avoids the hills of Badly Designed Signs. It is said that once you go in you can never find your way back out again." Doris didn't look up while he said this. Concentrating on copying the tiny writing to a readable size.

"I do think, you may want to return to the sorcerer's collective society and get some magical help." Said Doris.

"I don't know what else they could help us with, and the witch sort of disappeared at the end of it all," Scrungle said while stroking his nose.

"I was thinking of a protection charm or a health potion. You know something that might come in handy in a pinch." Doris said.

"What do the tiny writings say." Asked Peetles as Doris finished the copying.

"Well, the first little bit is a list of ingredients. Cheese, tomato, chlorinated chicken, seasoning, and a nip of mango rum. Then these questions. I don't understand them, but the first is: I have an apple and three pears. How long will it take to bake a cherry pie to a golden brown at gas mark six? The answer must be to the exact second."

"That's what we have to ask the cheese man," Said an incredulous Scrungle. If he had eyebrows, they would have furrowed. Doris shrugged and nodded, as he had no idea either.

"The second one is what is the boiling point of cheese and the last one is pick a number from one to twenty-four. No primes and must be divisible by nine and it's not eighteen."

Doris scratched his thick hair, which was the colour of saffron. He had the look of a man who was negotiating a tricky bowel movement.

"Why she didn't just write nine is beyond me. Then there's this thing." Doris showed his writing, so both Scrungle and Peetles could see it.

**In the kitchen put a pan on your head.**

**Turn to the corridor stand on what's red.**

**You will need the love that was left behind.**
**To chase the coats and hats you find.**
**The clock will strike one. Up the stairs you must run.**
**Catch the moon and then you'll be done.**

Doris put his handwritten note down.

"Daft. This is another reason to go back to the SCS and see if the witch can shed some light on all this. I can come with you and ask. I mean, how long will you have to sail to get to the island? Are there things on the island that you need to stay clear of? Does the moon-dial come with a user manual, warranty, free returns?"

After a little bit of debate, it was agreed, and soon the three companions headed out to SCS and Amazing Shine. Doris was on a mission and walked straight past the sales harpies that tried in earnest to thrust a two-for-one voucher on specific items into his hand.

Heading downstairs, they stood on the balcony, looking out across the rows of tall bookshelves. Scholars in sorcerer's robes and the occasional wizard were all they could see. It was eerily quiet, with no sound of coughing.

Following Scrungle's lead they headed toward the back of the library, where the pair had first encountered the witch. The desk she had been sitting at, as well as the paraphernalia that surrounded her, was no longer there. Smelling of pine disinfectant it had been scrubbed clean. Now in its place was a stack of unsorted books and a life-size cut-out of the Black Knight looking depressed. Above his head was the legend. Barry's the Butcher, the only pork sausage I will eat.

"This is where she was." Said Scrungle keeping his thoughts low.

Doris nodded, then turned and they walked to the reception under the balcony stairs. Scrungle put Peetles on the counter-top. A Sphinx librarian, her hair hidden underneath a top hat, wearing heavy red eye shadow and half-rimmed spectacles, was looking up the meaning of bastard in a leather-bound dictionary. She underlined the entry:

**Person or persons who work for Universal Credit.**

"Excuse me." Said Doris, keeping his voice low. The Sphinx stopped what she was doing.

"Yeessssss." The Sphinx's voice started in a low register up to a high'sss.' It made them all think of escaping gas.

"We are looking for the witch Waynex." Said Doris. The Sphinx assessed the trio over the top of her half-rimmed glasses.

"Oh, she's gone. Taken away by the sheriffs and hobgoblins. Plotting against the crown and chancellor Gumptrude. She made such a racket; biting, kicking, and cursing a few of the hobgoblinsss, well until they shoved a gag in her mouth. Are you friends of hersss?"

Doris, Scrungle, and Peetles stood dumbstruck under the probing stare of the librarian.

"No, she owed us money; well, a refund, really." Said Doris, thinking on his bell-wearing toes. This seemed to reassure the Sphinx, who stopped staring as intently as she had been.

"What had she done?" Asked a bumpy Peetles.

"No idea. She did have a visitor before she was taken away. The sheriff seemed very interested in them as well."

Scrungle and Peetles tensed, both thinking maybe they were the reason the mad old bugger was in custody.

"What did they look like?" Asked Doris.

"Like a witch, coughed a lot, pointy hat made out of wool and." Doris cut the sphynx off.

"No, the witch's visitor."

"A woman, I think. Lovely perfume, wrapped up, couldn't see her face. You are asking a lot of questions."

The sphinx's hand had started to move towards a large viking horn sitting on the counter-top with the words 'Blow for Assistance' carved into its side, .

"Never get that bloody refund now. Come on." Said Doris, looking annoyed. He turned and walked off. To keep the pretence up, Scrungle plonked Peetles onto his head with a "Good day to you, sir."
And followed Doris out of the library, in what Scrungle thought was a self-important strut.

* * *

Back at the Morris's, they debated what might have happened. Should they be worried, were Scrungle and Peetles under surveillance? Who was the woman who had seen the witch last? Did this have anything to do with the map, and if the witch had been taken to the dungeon, did it have visiting hours like a hospital? Maybe take some grapes in and a word search.

The discussion was interrupted by Missus Morris.

"We have something to show you." An excited Missus Morris, then made the trio get up and follow her into the stable.

Before they entered, she told Peetles and Scrungle to close their eyes and promise not to open them until she said they should. Positioning the pair side by side she stood to one side.

"Alright, now you can look."
Standing in pride of place was the tricycle. It had been freshly painted yellow and couldn't have looked any better coming out of the showroom. The handlebars, known as ape hangers with a cross member, were brightly polished chrome and now had leather grips. Brand new rubber tread on the chunky wheels looked like it would grip no matter what the terrain. Each spoke of the wheels was finished to a high shine. On the mudguards over the back wheels were long sticks with triangular flags at the top. Written on the left was Scrungle, the right Peetles.

It didn't have a seat when they brought it back from the second-hand shop. Now it had a cushioned leather arrangement with a high back and a little overhang to help with shade and rain. Scrungle had a pang of longing for his reading chair, and the wardrobe where he kept his smoking jacket.

A wicker basket on the front now had two holes for Peetle's little legs to stick through. Attached to one side of the handlebar was a beautiful ahooga horn.

A smaller one was attached to the basket for Peetles. Peetles squealed in delight, and Scrungle forgot all about the map, the witch, and the wardrobe.

"Go on, give it a try, but be careful of the paint; it's still drying. I'm going to give it one more coat of lacquer once it's dry," said Mr Morris.

Scrungle gingerly put a leg over the tricycle and settled himself in. Mr Morris had modified the pedals for Scrungle's non-existent feet.

"How do the pedals feel?" Said Mr Morris.

"They fit like a glove or cone, maybe it fits like a glone ." Said Scrungle.

Peetles, using a little metal peg that Morris had attached to the front wheel, clambered up and into the basket. They both squeezed their horns together. It made a great two-tone sound that set everyone laughing.

"Oh my word, it is magnificent." Scrungle was quite overcome with emotion.

"I got this today at the market."

Missus Morris handed over two pairs of goggles and sheep-skin hats with ear flaps. Peetles hat fell over his face, and Scrungles sat on his head like a crown. Mrs Morris pointed out that they had each other's, so they swapped. Urged on by Mr Morris, Doris, and Missus Morris, the stable was just big enough for Scrungle to do a tight circle. The tricycle moved with smooth speed.

"You have three gears." Explained, Mr Morris, after Scrungle brought the tricycle to a stop. "This here." He put Scrungle's hand on a T-shaped lever in the centre of the frame.

"That's uphill, that's flat, and downhill. The last one there, 'P', is to park it."

Scrungle clicked through the gears, then put it into 'P' and dismounted the tricycle. Peetles got out and shimmied down the tricycle's front wheel. Scrungle picked Peetles up, walked to the family Morris of the house Sando, and tried his best to give a long group hug to them all. Missus Morris, with tears in her eyes, said she would make a little food. Mr Morris said that after watching Scrungle on the tricycle, he would make some minor adjustments to the seating height and peddles.

Behind the seat, he showed Scrungle a carriage lantern that could be attached to the front under Peetles basket. Doris demonstrated to Peetles the canopy, which would cover the basket if it started to rain.

"Oh my, that is so clever," Peetles said.

"Come let us eat." Said Doris.

Just as they started to leave the stables, Mr Morris slapped his forehead.

"Nearly forgot."

He motioned for Scrungle and Peetles to watch closely. Moving the tricycle into the centre of the room, he pulled on a lever under the seat. A clanking ratchet sound could be heard as the seat rose, flattening out at the same time until it was nearly touching the stable roof. Out from the sides came a wire frame and canopy.

Mr Morris, Scrungle, and Peetles stood underneath as it covered them like a huge umbrella. Both Peetles and Scrungle clapped and whooped in delight. Doris said it was probably the best work his brother-in-law had ever done and Mr Morris took a bow.

The children were now home from school, so everyone ate and

talked about how Mr. Morris might go into the bicycle trade, as he'd had so much fun modifying the tricycle for the pair. The children wanted to play with Peetles but Missus Morris said they had to finish their homework about applied control engineering and fluid mechanics.

Peetles offered to help but he didn't have a clue, so they ended up colouring-in the diagrams instead. Scrungle wanted to take the tricycle out for a test drive, but Mr. Morris said it would be best if they waited until it had the last coat of lacquer applied.

The rest of the evening was spent with the trio studying the map, formalising plans, and wondering about the witch, then joining the family to play a game of 'Is it heavy?'

# Fifteen

## Castle Tours

On the fifth day, which would come to be the last day at the home of Doris's sister, Mr Morris said the tricycle was ready, but to give it the day to dry completely and set off the next morning. Missus Morris mentioned the free passes to the castle tour Scrungle and Peetles had been given and said it would be a great thing to do to pass the time. While Mr Morris dismissed it as a ploy to make commoners foot the bill for its upkeep, Doris took the pair to one side, saying it might be an idea to see if they could get to the dungeon, and talk to the witch Waynex. It was a long shot, but what did they have to lose?

The pair now had a working idea of the layout of Plombree. So it didn't take long to navigate back to the castle entrance. Upon arriving at the green, they were greeted by a bustling scene filled with performers and onlookers, just as busy as the day they had won the money and exposed the cheating wizard.

With Peetles comfortably perched on Scrungle's head, they walked up to the majestic castle walls, white towers, and defensive turrets.

Flags fluttered gracefully in the breeze, bearing the emblem of Plombree, a clenched fist with a thumbs-up set against a yellow background. Soldiers in royal colours and chain mail moved about on the ramparts.

Approaching the outer guard towers to the drawbridge, they saw the two soldiers who had intervened on the day of the cheating wizard, in their customary position, leaning against the wall, having a deep conversation with two young women. As Scrungle and Peetles ambled over, one of the guards looked up.

"Go ahead, mate. I remember you from the other day. Got a merit from the captain and a day off for the collar."

"I am pleased," Scrungle replied.

Although he was at a loss as to why wearing a collar had earned him a day off, they crossed the wide drawbridge.

The archway of the keep now towered above them. The imposing black iron portcullis hung high, locked in place. Once inside and surrounded by fellow visitors, Scrungle consulted a poster of the castle's layout.

A red dot with **'you are here'** informed the pair that they were in what was called the bailey.

A young elf dressed in red cotton pants and a brown woollen jacket held a placard stating the next tour would commence in five minutes. The tour insignia was the logo of Gumptrude Enterprises.

"This way, everyone! Over here, over here!"

They recognised the assertive voice of Gladis in her role as an unofficial people marshal and headed through the bustling crowd towards it. Gladis let out a delighted scream when she saw them, startling those nearby and setting a child off crying. A guard went into a defensive stance, causing a guide dog to snap at its owner's hand.

Scrungle overheard the dog explaining that it had panicked. The owner didn't understand the barking and shouted at it until it stopped.

"Scrungle! Peetles! So lovely to see you again. How are you enjoying the capital? Are you joining the tour as well? I've heard it's fantastic," said Gladis, dressed in a colourful cardboard and paper ensemble adorned with numerous folds, She now resembled a combination of a cone-shaped mountain range and a broken accordion.

"Yes, we wanted to see what the castle looked like from the inside. It's easier than trying to see what it looks like on the inside from the outside," Peetles replied.

Gladis raised an eyebrow at Peetles but then half-smiled, trying to comprehend if the little creature was being facetious or just a bit daft.

"I thought you didn't like the castle or the Baroness." Said Scrungle.

"Oh, that was then. I was grumpy from all the waiting around. I mean, when in the city, you have to see the sights, don't you? And we were given free tickets by the hotel manager. That was after the incident with the ferret and step ladders. I said they were getting a one-star review from the town crier trip advisor. Anyway, Gumptrude's the idiot; the Baroness is just an interior designer who likes paper and a throw cushion or two." Said Gladis.

"Hello, everyone," The tour guides timid voice was just slightly louder than the crowd. The elf waggled the placard and spoke again. Lacking authority in his voice, most people paid little attention.

"Shut up." Said Gladis. Her voice, not much louder than the tour guides, carried an unmistakable controlled rage and practiced menace, that silenced all chatter instantly.

A few in the crowd absent-mindedly rubbed their arms and the backs of their necks, unaware that the fine hairs were stood on end. Her smile intended to reassure, seemed to add to the intimidation factor. The tour guide gave Gladis a nervous little smile.

"Thank you, thank you. It's great to see so many people today. My name is Chockoblocko, and I'll be your guide. Please remember, this is a fully operational castle, and the king's health isn't at its best, so kindly keep the noise to a minimum once we enter the grand gallery. Lovely, thank you."

He now led the group along a stone path adjacent to the gatehouse. Everywhere they looked, on just about every other surface, was some form of paper addition. The castle guards had fancy paper scarves, doilies lay on every flat surface, crocheted mats and throw cushions littered the granite floors and the flagstone walkways. As the tour progressed the elf provided some background and history, explaining that the castle had been meticulously crafted from quarried limestone and quartzite. Over the years, it had undergone expansion because Queen Shoesling the Thirteenth enjoyed swimming in the moat. So another wall was constructed around the moat to keep her safe, which had over time become the primary defence wall.

To the tour guides knowledge, it was the only castle with a defensive moat on the inside, with absolutely no defensive quality whatsoever. Peetles looked over and could see punts moored at a small jetty and ducks in the water.

The buildings within the primary bailey encompassed the armoury, sleeping quarters, kitchen, and stores. The most luxurious building in the bailey was the tower of the knights of colour. A chivalric order formed over five hundred years ago to marshal the different armies in the nipple-ripple ring wars and to protect the royal house.

The tour pressed on, crossing the moat's single wooden arch bridge towards the inner wall, magnificent grand gallery, and regal throne room. Everyone marvelled at the main trio of towers that served as the royal residence for the king and his family. It housed the living quarters, main throne room, store rooms for essential ingredients for baking cakes, and, of course, the dungeons.

Outside the entrance to the grand gallery, a row of tacky stalls offered an array of souvenirs, plush toys resembling the king and

Princess, every paper combination that the mind could devise, cushions with the royal crest, doilies, and crochet kits, intricate wooden toys depicting the castle, tin knights that you could paint your favourite colour, DIY construction sets with 'Make your own roadblock,' stamped on the side, and refreshments that came with a price tag the king would have choked at.

The tour guide suggested taking some time to explore the stalls, as the grand gallery was occupied with official proceedings, and an hour needed to pass before they could gain access.

Amidst the stalls, Peetles noticed a young woman deftly demonstrating the workings of a cup and ball toy. Curiosity piqued, Peetles asked Scrungle if he could have a go.

"We don't have any gold or silver now. We spent the last on the magnifying glass." Said Scrungle, delighted at the rhyme of last and glass.

"I don't want to buy one; I just want to give it a try, see if I can get the ball into the cup."

Scrungle acquiesced and gently placed Peetles on the ground. The young woman bent down and handed the toy over. Peetles gave the ball a few flips, missing the cup completely. Determined, he gave it one last shot, which was a bit too vigorous, causing the ball to snap off the string and bounce away. Careening across the flagstones it rolled into the grand gallery's entrance. Peetles at once, followed after it.

"You better find that; otherwise, you'll have to buy it." The young girl looked at Scrungle, then at the tower guards practicing with spears. Driving them into straw-shaped men on the grass field inside the bailey. Scrungle, not wanting to be made into a pin cushion, or disturb an ill king, chased after Peetles and watched the little creature disappear through the grand entrance.

Following moments behind Scrungle walked into a long vaulted corridor. Alcoves recessed into the walls held busts of marble figures, adorned with hats or scarves made of paper or card. Paintings and tapestries hung on the walls, depicting the history of Plombree, its kings and queens, and one painting of a large turnip that had been coronated nearly two hundred and fifty years ago. By all accounts, it was the most peaceful and affluent time the land had ever seen.

At the centre of this corridor, were closed black iron double doors; so big a horse and rider could have passed through without dismounting. White marble stairs on either side of the corridor led down on the left and up on the right. Two guards stood at attention blocking entry into the chamber beyond. Their gaze fixed on nothing, just looking straight ahead. Peetles stood in front of one of them and was asking if he had seen a ball.

"They don't talk or move." Said Peetles mildly agitated and looking a bit lumpy.

"I think they are statues." Said Scrungle

He then raised a finger to touch the nose of one of the motionless guards. Just as he was about to make contact, the guard moved with lightning speed, putting his sword to Scrungle's non-existent neck. The other was also in attack position, with his sword at Peetles. No one moved. Scrungle was about to say hello and offer a hat stand when they heard a click-clack of hooves on the stone floor.

"Stand at ease." Said a voice Scrungle and Peetles recognised.

The guards moved back to attention without a moment's hesitation. Scrungle and Peetles turned to look at who had rescued them. It was Biggles, resplendent in his new horseshoes and trimmed jacket.

"Hello." Said Scrungle.

"Hmm, we meet again. Are you here on court business?"

"We lost our ball." Said Peetles.

"That sounds lovely, now move along. I have my place in court. The guards are instructed not to talk or let anyone in they don't know. Don't get too close to them as they will start cutting at things."

The unicorn moved forward, approaching the guards. Scrungle and Peetles scurried to one side.

"Lord Sebastian Bigglesworth the third of Unicorn Investors. Here by command of the King." Said Biggles.

The guards drew to one side, then moved to open the doors to the throne room. Biggles trotted in and the doors were closed swiftly behind them. Scrungle put Peetles on his head and moved away from the entrance. Lumpy and bumpy from the guard's behaviour, Peetles said.

"We can't go back. We haven't found the ball yet."

"Well, I don't think we are going to get much help from the guards. Maybe it went down the stairs there." Scrungle pointed to the leftmost stairs.

"It could have went up." Peetles pointed to the other set of stairs. After a moment of hesitation, Scrungle descended the stairs that were wide enough for three abreast. Torchlights were recessed into the walls, and along with high slit windows, lit the way down. The light reflected off the white stone of the walls and stairs of the lower levels.

The pair followed the steps as they spiralled downwards until they came upon another long corridor leading west. Several doors could be seen along its length, and another set of stairs just as wide as the ones they had descended, led further down into the bowels of the castle.

"I don't think we should be here." Said Peetles who was looking decidedly lumpy.

"Well, Peetles, the guide said the dungeons were downstairs so we might see the witch and find the ball at the same time."

They walked along the corridor heading towards the stairs leading down. Stopping in their tracks when they heard voices coming up. Peetles went as spikey as a blowfish, hopping from one leg to the other.

"We're caught. We're caught." Cried Peetles.
Scrungle tried the door next to them. It swung open and revealed a storage space, filled with cleaning materials, a stack of cake display cases, a mop, and a bucket.
Bent nearly double, Scrungle slid into the space with Peetles at his feet, just as the bodies belonging to the voices entered the corridor. Squashed as they were against the inside, Scrungle could see out of the little ventilation holes drilled into the door. A rotund squat man with a bluish complexion and yellow hair the colour of dying wheat fields was in the corridor. Scrungle recognised Gumptrude immediately. Unmistakable as the the incoherent rambler, who addressed the crowd from the balcony.

He was walking quickly, to keep up with a woman who rustled loudly as she strode along the corridor. On the very top of her grey-white hair was a sparkling silver tiara.
Her hourglass figure was complemented by her considerable cleavage, intentionally weaponized and amplified by a combination of cardboard, paper, and felt. Jewels sewn into the gown glistened in the torchlight.

Scrungle realised it was the woman who had been on the balcony with Gumptrude, and it must be Baroness Bakeeasy.

"What I won't do is take in two hundred thousand trolls who could be well terrorists.
I have been watching this migration. And I see the trolls. I mean, they're all male. They're mostly men trolls, and they're strong trolls. These are physically young, strong trolls. They look like prime-time soldiers. Now it's probably not true, but where are the women trolls?... So, you ask two things. Number one, why aren't they working for their own lands? And number two, I don't want these trolls coming over here."

Gumptrude had blocked the way, and Bakeasy had no choice but to stop and listen. He wasn't holding eye contact, but addressing the mountain peaks before him. His lips puckered out when he talked. Watching him, Scrungle thought of a sucker fish eating a lemon while trying to hold a conversation.

"Where did you get the number two hundred thousand." A note of disbelief in Bakeasy's reply.

"They are here to build your bypass. A bypass you promised the people who voted for it. I have done everything to elevate your status. You are on the way to being head chancellor now, I had the king introduce those hobgoblins that you like so much. What more do you want? You really are a moron, aren't you." Bakeasy sneered.

"I'm intelligent. Some people would say I'm very, very, very intelligent." Came Gumptrude's retort.

Bakeasy looked up and down the corridor, then at Gumptrude. Her brows furrowed.

"Who are you trying to convince? Just keep the peace until the vote is over and you are elected. Things will happen fast after that." Said Bakeasy.

"Are you not happy with your share. A lot of people would be happy with your share. I mean we need to make it last, money doesn't just happen. It comes from things." Said Gumptrude, licking his rubbery lips, while staring at Bakeasy's chest. Bakeasy was getting irritated with Gumptrude. Her eye was twitching sporadically.

"We can't keep pushing taxes up and nothing happening."

Gumptrude looked peevish.

"It wasn't me who lost the Princess. Marry Wackerknacker. That was your plan. A plan is an idea, and ideas are plans. I have a really big brain, people say I have, a lot of people. Ask anyone."

Bakeasy grabbed Gumptrude by the collar and pushed him against the door Scrungle and Peetles were hiding behind. Peetles clamped a hand over his mouth to stop a squeak from escaping. Bakeasy looked around to make sure that no one could hear.

"Listen to me, you little tit. My plan with the King of Flan and his soppy son is none of your business, and if plan A doesn't work, we go to plan B. Do not forget. It was me who put you where you are. I can take it away; you just remember that. Keep the riff-raff under control. Otherwise, you might find yourself head first down a well."

Gumptrude looked like a child who was being potty trained at gunpoint turned blue and sniffed.

"You don't have to get so like that, I have a big brain." He turned to take a step towards the stairs leading up. Next thing, Gumptrude was propelled by an unknown force across the stone floor towards the wall, which he expertly blocked, using his face to spare his body any damage. Knocking himself unconscious, he lay on the floor.

"What the fu…" Began Bakeasy.

She had started to walk over to see what had happened. The next thing, she was pin-wheeling her arms, trying hard to keep her balance. Watching this, Scrungle was sure she would have succeeded in staying on her feet if it hadn't been for two combining factors. The first was her two combining factors, gripped by gravity, moving with independent elegant grace, pulling her towards the centre of the earth. Then Gumptrude's unconscious form, tricked her in a cunning move, by not getting out of the way.

She kick-tripped over Gumptrude's head, then fell forward. Bakeasy smashed into the wall as Gumptrude had, using her face to break her forward momentum. Sliding slowly down, she came to rest on top of the prone chancellor. The little wooden ball that had caused the mayhem bounced a few times across the stone floor, coming to rest at the tight vertex of the splayed legs of Bakeasy.

Scrungle and Peetles fell out of the closet. Mop buckets and cake display's scattered everywhere.

"Brilliant, they found the ball." An excited Peetles hop wobbled over to retrieve it.

"Spies." Said a drowsy Baroness Bakeasy, trying to point a finger at them. Scrungle looked at the glazed eyes of the woman, and without another word, he picked Peetles up and ran for the exit.

# Sixteen

## *Windmills*

When they returned, and after explaining everything that had happened on the castle tour to a blond-haired Doris, he declared a family meeting. Missus Morris, who had spent the day setting out a lavish farewell meal for Scrungle and Peetles, insisted they leave immediately. The children Morris started to cry, worried for the pair's health, their parents' safety, and their health and safety. Doris was not so convinced.

"It was a silly accident; it wasn't anyone's fault but the manufacturers." Picking up a vol-au-vent and starting to chew.

"Didn't you hear what Scrungle said? They heard plotting. Bakeasy and Gumptrude are up to something." Countered Mr Morris.

Scrungle rubbed his long nose. Deep down, he was already thinking about the family's safety.

"I'm so sorry." Said Scrungle.

"Enough; Bakeasy is paranoid, and Gumptrude is a fascist. If they remember anything, they will come looking for them. It's time to go." Missus Morris looked stern, the men nodded knowing she was right.

Peetles collected what little belongings they had, while Scrungle filled his pockets with food Mrs Morris was now wrapping up for him. Outside the day was beginning to shorten as they mounted the tricycle. Doris had drawn a map with the quickest route to the east gate.

"If they come looking, they will come here. What will happen to you?" Said Scrungle.

"We will tell the truth and say you rented a room and left." Said Doris.

"But they might be mean," Peetles said, getting spikey and lumpy. He didn't want anything to happen to the house of Sando.

"It will be fine. By what you've said, I think they'll not remember or just dismiss it as a dream." Said Mr Morris.

It was far from the departure Scrungle wanted. One by one, Mr Morris, Missus Morris, Doris and the children Morris, hugged Scrungle and Peetles. The pair donned their goggles and riding hats, settling them on their round heads. With one last wave and a sad heart, Scrungle pushed down and pedalled towards the east gate. Turning constantly to look at family Morris, who had been nothing but kind to them. The family waved their goodbyes until they were lost from sight.

Although the pair were now afraid the guards, hobgoblins, and sheriffs of Plombree might be hot on their heels, it didn't stop their unabashed beaming smiles as they sped through the streets of the city.

It was magical; the tricycle glided along as if it had a mind of its own. Whatever Mr. Morris had done with the bearings and gears was nothing short of miraculous.

Scrungle, concerned about attracting attention, told Peetles not to use the little horn.

No matter how they tried to look inconspicuous, people and creatures stared in fascination as the pair sped past. They were, after all, still one of a kind, even among the magical creatures in the land of Plom, and there weren't that many tricycles around either.

Following the map Doris had drawn, they were at the east gate in no time at all. A long queue waited to exit the city. Across the sandstone arch chiselled into the stonework was,

**'You are now leaving Plombree; please take your crap with you.'**

On the opposite side of the city gate was a longer line of people and a few magical creatures trying to gain access to the city. Most were bringing goods from the harbour and the outlying lands. Hobgoblins lounged around, not doing anything.

A single customs guard was checking over the wagons, making sure anyone entering had the correct papers. As they approached, Scrungle could see the exit barrier being raised so that a wagon full of empty beer barrels could pass through.

Pedalling fast, using the wagon as a shield, the pair glided through the raised barrier.

A shout went up from one of the hobgoblins for the pair to stop.

"Sorry, I'm a doctor. I'm chasing a badger with trench foot."

Not knowing why he shouted what he did, Scrungle, just grabbed the words that filled his mind. The flag-stoned highway leading out was flat as far as they could see, with very few flags made to look like stones. Soon Scrungle built up a respectable head of speed.

Along the road on either side were small farms and little huts. In the fading light, the pair could see it was even more run-down here than around the western gate, where they had entered.

Scrungle felt at home on the tricycle. His legs pumping the pedals easily, feeling the road through the springs, the tricycle responded as if alive. The habitats dwindled, and soon they were surrounded by a forest of yew trees. Peetles beamed in delight and shouted to

Scrungle that it was amazing.

Scrungle shouted back that he thought it was as good as burning a tramp. Peetles asked if Scrungle had something to confess, but Scrungle said he had overheard the phrase while they walked around Plombree, and was sure it just meant 'to have great fun'. Not stopping, as with every mile behind them they felt safer, they managed to fit the carriage lantern to the front of the tricycle. It lit up, shining a clear, wide beam on the darkening road.

Speeding onwards, they passed others travelling towards Plombree, but most heading away, towards the windmills and the harbour to pick up goods. As the duo sped past their fellow travellers, the little flaps of their riding hats fluttered like wings in the wind.

Their progress was remarkable, but Scrungle was beginning to pall; it had been a busy, scary day. Peetles saw a passing point or picnic area with its customary table, stone seats, and overflowing bin. Pointing it out to Scrungle, who applied the brakes a little too enthusiastically, they slid to a stop, while pulling a respectable skid at the same time.

"This is so much fun. Sorry, you have to do all the peddling, Scrungle."

"I am enjoying it, and we have made such good progress. It makes me wonder why we didn't get a tricycle right at the start."

"Is it because we didn't know they existed until we got to Plombree?" Said Peetles, trying to be helpful.

"Ah yes, that will probably explain it."

They got off the tricycle and sat on the stone bench. Fear of being chased and imprisoned had pushed all other thoughts from their minds. But now that they had stopped, sitting in the light of the tricycle lantern, they both felt ravenous. Scrungle pulled out Peetle's lemon-coloured water bottle and handed it over. Then a wicker basket full of mushrooms for himself and some melon slices wrapped up in grease-proof paper for Peetles.

"Should we make camp tonight, and where are we going again?" Peetles asked.

"I think making camp is a good idea. I do think we should go a little way into the forest. If we are being followed, it will be harder for people to see us. We are headed to the hills of Badly Designed Signs."

"Oh yes, I remember now." Peetles paused while nibbling on a slice of melon. "Is that a good idea? Last time, it took us ages to get out. You know, the forest, I mean." Peetles had gone a bit spikey, thinking of the wolves.

"I will tie a string around a tree close to the road. We can make our way back using that."

This reassured Peetles and they sat eating the late supper. The night set in quickly, so using the carriage lantern, they found a little hollow where the trees were sparse. Scrungle didn't have string, but he found some ribbon in his pocket. This was for wrapping presents he would send himself on his birthday and at Christmas. Peetles asked when Scrungles birthday was. Scrungle said he had two, as he came in two pieces. His first birthday was on July the fourth for his head, and his second was on the third of February for the rest of him. Peetles said he would get him lots of presents, for being such a good friend, on all of his birthdays and Christmas. The little creature had no idea what Christmas was and soon forgot while they got the campsite ready.

The tricycle canopy worked a treat, and then Scrungle, with the help of Peetles, set about putting the other things out. Soon it was cosy, with a roaring fire, a mantle piece, and other amenities for the pair. It didn't occur to either of them that the fire and stick lanterns illuminated the space with a soft glow of amber light, that could be seen from miles away.

Top and tailing in the hammock the pair woke at dawn and then spent a little while foraging for mushrooms. Because they had gone undisturbed the night before, both Scrungle and Peetles believed that the incident with the Baroness had most likely been dismissed as a mere fantasy caused by mild concussion.

Packing up the campsite didn't take any time at all and the pair were back on the open road, Scrungle pedalling at an easy pace. The forest thinned out, becoming high grassland stretching out as far as they could see.

Unlike the King's Road leading into the city from the west, which, once out of the mountain pass, ran in a straight line to the castle gates, the east road followed the land's natural contours. As Scrungle pedalled away the morning, the landscape began to change again. The instinctive arrangement of the world, a state of random organic growth, slowly matured into an ordered design.

The road wound its way around small hills and along long stretches of constructed dams. Everywhere they looked, they saw small lakes and canals, with embankments that separated the water from the fertile soil of the rolling flower fields.

The scene was a patchwork of long rows of flowers in every imaginable colour. Tulips, pansies, carnations, and many other varieties flourished in between the low-level waterways.

On the horizon, windmill sails lazily turned in the breeze. Beautifully painted in primary colours and immaculately constructed, they created majestic arcs across the sky.

Neither Scrungle nor Peetles had ever seen a windmill before, and to Peetles, they appeared almost alive in their graceful movements.

Captivated by curiosity, they couldn't help but wonder about their purpose.

A tall black signpost in very tidy garland script stated they were now entering **'Ileccelfechen-Havyamate.'**

The road was now bordered by flower arrangements and neatly trimmed hedgerows, and a notice board with forth-coming events pinned to it, including a poster of the missing Princess and the penguin.

Pedalling up the brow of a small hill to get closer to one of the windmills, they were confronted by a cluster of protestors. Milling around were about thirty people, a few griffins and a vacant-eyed troll. Some of the gathering were holding signs.

'Vote Gumptrude,'

'Make Plomb great again.'

'SCS sale now on.'

Most were wearing the hats with 'MPGA.' on the front that they had seen in Plombree.

A single sheriff was standing to the side, looking pensive. A spokesman for Gumptrude stood on a cart full of hay bails, using it as a platform. Behind the cart was a large banner that read, **'Windmills give you cancer. Burn coal; that's our goal.'**

The man was dressed similarly to Gumptrude; his purple and black cloak fluttered around him in the breeze. Unlike Gumptrude, his urine-yellow hair was unkempt, as if he had just woken up from a heavy drinking session.

He was overweight and talked with a posh accent. A couple of hobgoblins stood near, flexing their braces and nodding their heads, as he addressed the crowd before him. Scrungle and Peetles shared a look, wondering if the idiot was from Plombree Court.

"I am supporting Interim Chancellor Gumptrude purely out of cynical self-interest. I know myself that it is easy to make promises; it's hard work to keep them. So I will tell you this, my friends: as I have discovered myself, there are no disasters, only opportunities. And, indeed, opportunities for fresh disasters."

Scrungle pedalled closer to the lunatic on the cart. The sad yellow-haired fellow had stopped for a moment to wave at the crowd, nodding his head as if agreeing to himself that he was nodding.

"I know, and I can say in all honesty, that the chancellor Gumptrude wanted to be here today. He apologises for this, but I have a speech that the chancellor penned himself for this very occasion."

The group watching cheered and applauded. The idiot nodded his head like a spring-loaded chicken. Then broke the seal on a rolled-up scroll. The crowd calmed a little, waiting for the words of their beloved chancellor to be read out.

"Now I never understood wind. You know, I know windmills very much. They're noisy. They kill the birds. You want to see a bird graveyard? Go under a windmill someday. You'll see more birds than you've ever seen in your life." The idiot gestured to the windmills behind him, which moved with harmless charm.

"But they're made tremendous if you're into this, tremendous fumes. Gases are spewing into the atmosphere. You know we have a world, right? So the world is tiny compared to the universe. So tremendous, tremendous amount of fumes and everything fumes are spewing into the air, right? Spewing. It's our air, their air, everything, right? And they say the noise causes cancer."

The idiot on the cart rolled the scroll up and looked at the crowd. His posture was that of a man who had explained the meaning of life to the assembled group. The protestors applauded the idiot and booed the windmill. Then, from out of the crowd came the chant.

'Burn them down, burn them down.'

Although not explicitly exciting the crowd, the idiot did nothing to keep them in check.

A torch was lit, and the crowd moved towards the nearest windmill. The sheriff, who had become more and more unsettled as the loony on the cart talked, moved forward and tried to stop the protestors. Pushed to the ground almost immediately, she regained her feet and ordered the hobgoblins to stop the crowd. Adding to the confusion, the hobgoblins just started chanting 'burn it down.' and joined the protestors.

The idiot, seeing that he had antagonised the mob into a killing frenzy, jumped down off the cart ready to make a hasty exit. The nearest windmill was painted a lovely orange with black piping. A low hedge surrounding it was perfectly trimmed. In the garden, rows of neatly planted vegetables grew, ready to be picked. The white sails, pristine and bright in the morning sun, looked new or recently cleaned.

Scrungle and Peetles watched as the protestors marched towards the idyllic setting with murderous rage.

"Oh dear, they are going to hurt the big turny thing." Said Peetles, who was very anxious and spikey now. Scrungle pedalled over to the tousled sheriff, who now had a bloody lip. Disoriented, she was looking around for help.

"Hello, I'm Scrungle Bungus, and this is Peetles. I think you need to stop them."

Scrungle pointed to the group who were at the gate of the windmill's front garden.

The miller had come out and stood in front of the crowd, trying hard to calm the situation. Behind him was his wife, holding their children close as she stood watching from the doorway.

"I joined the sheriff's department to help, not this. Where did that cretin go? He's the only one who can calm this lot down now."

She set off in the direction of the hay cart to try and find the Gumptrude look-alike who seemed to have vanished. Peetles had become even more spikey and lumpy.

"Scrungle, we must do something. It can't get hurt; it's not right."

The pair watched as the miller shouted to the mob.

"Please. Please calm down. What's all this about? It's a windmill for pumping the water to the field."

"You should be using coal. You're poisoning the air. We don't want to hurt you; just come out, and we will burn it down. Make Plom great again." Shouted the closest of the cretins, in the mob, at the miller.

"I live in the windmill you tit. How's burning coal going to help the irrigation system?" Ordinarily, Scrungle Bungus would have turned and made a tactical retreat. But with Peetles alarm and his time away from what was familiar, he felt different in some subtle way. Scrungle had an innate sense of fairness, but now he had found something else. Maybe this was courage; he didn't know for sure; he just knew he had to help. Watching the miller and the windmill, he clung to hope that if it was the Chana tree and he stood where the miller was now, someone would offer assistance.

"Do unto others as you would have done unto yourself," Peetles turned and looked up to Scrungle from the basket.

"I'm with you, Scrungle." Then pulled the flaps down on their hat and settled the goggles onto their face, giving Peetles what they thought was a determined goggle-face look. Scrungle, summoning up the courage he never knew he possessed and understanding it was alright to be afraid, pedalled forward.

The leader at the front of the protestors, not waiting for any further discussion, borrowed bravado, and with a mob of creatures behind him, pushed through the gate.

Some others in the mob started hacking through the hedge and depending on your socioeconomic perspective, were making a terrible mess, or a contemporary art installation, depicting the cost of living crisis.

Scrungle had pedalled around the mob, finding a side gate. It crossed Scrungles mind to look for dead birds, but on neither side, front nor back, was there a single victim. He did see bird boxes in the garden and the trees next to the windmill.

At the front garden, Scrungle managed to put the tricycle between the miller, who was brandishing a small hand trowel, and the leader of the mob.

"Hello. I'm Scrungle Bungus." He announced as loudly as his trembling telepathy would allow. Peetles managed a squeak.

"You one of those windmill lovers." Shouted a voice from the crowd.

"Burn it, burn it." Started the mob again.

"Make Plomb great again." Shouted the crowd.

"Two for one at SCS." Shouted a lone voice.

"I have a hat stand," Scrungle said as loud as he could.

It was the only thought that bubbled up in his mind. The mob took a collective moment to contemplate what Scrungle had said, then shouted at him to get out of the way.

Peetles sat terrified and spikey in his little basket. Scrungle wondered if his luck had finally run its course. Attempting to appease the enraged mob with his much-loved hat stand, now looked like an ill-advised move.

The mob, as deranged as they were, was determined to wreak havoc on the cancer-bearing windmill and anyone who obstructed their path. The leader, a student on a gap year from studying the Dunning Kruger effect on mob mentality at Plombree Academy, was handed a flaming torch. He swung it at Scrungles face, who was momentarily blinded by the heat and light.

# Seventeen

## *Picnic in the Garden*

Had the two Knights of Colour not come upon the scene, calamity might have befallen Scrungle, Peetles, the miller and his kin. However, fortune smiled that day, tripping over fate, falling on circumstance, and landing arse first on what was just and right.

In doing so, it would entwine their lives together. The torch-wielding bag of shite at the front, clad in a sheep's fleece and a horned hat, was struck on the side of his head by the flat of a sword. One of the horns spun free as he staggered to the side.

The horn did two more spins until it came to rest, pointing at the ground. So fixated on reducing the unfortunate windmill to ashes, he had failed to hear the approaching hooves of a horse, the gradual hush of the crowd, or the lone cry from the mob:

"Behind you, dude."

Holding the side of his head, he turned to see who had hit him. A knight in green armour, sitting on a magnificent stallion towered over him. The knight's visor was down; only the eyes could be seen.

Pointing at the young man was the business end of the knight's blade. The knight motioned with the tip, for the young man to get out of the garden.

The miller retreated into the windmill and shut the door. The young halfwit stumbled out and into the safety of the mob. The Green Knight made a tight turn, trying their hardest not to trample the flower beds, then walked the horse through the gate towards the mob. The crowd backed off, keeping a safe distance, stopping as one when they realised that another knight in yellow armour, sitting on another horse, was behind them.

Perched on the forearm of the Yellow Knight was a large falcon. A murmur rippled through the crowd, but no one was shouting now.

"Put the torch out." Said the Green Knight.

The oddly pointing-horned halfwit complied immediately. Scrungle thought this was the end of the silliness, but a voice in the crowd shouted.

"We're taking back control. Make Plom great again."

The Green Knight stared at the mob, then dismounted, in no hurry, walked with absolute authority to the slovenly-looking fellow who was stupid enough to shout.

The crowd parted as one would if an iguana entered a lift. When the knight drew close the man gulped.

"I have rights." His voice trembling.

To all onlookers, the next few minutes happened in slow motion. The knight grabbed the man's ear and knelt, bringing the man with them, so they were now over the knight's knee. With one deft movement, the knight pulled the man's dirty breaches down and started to smack the dirty-pants man's arse resoundingly. Trying hard not to cry, dirty-pants man made an effort to rise, but the knight twisted his ear until he complied.

After each word, a hearty smack could be heard. "Are." Smack "you." Smack "going." Smack "to." Smack "burn." Smack "the." Smack "wind." Smack "mill." Smack "down." Smack.

After the second hit to the bottom from the metal gauntlet dirty-pants man was denying any possibility that he would be looking at a fire, let alone lighting one ever again. The knight, however, carried on. Most of the crowd watching this unfold, were now looking at their feet, shuffling, embarrassed by the whole scene. In no uncertain terms, the drive to incinerate a windmill for no apparent reason had now left the mob.

The knight pushed dirty-pants man off, then stood. Dirty-pants man, in a panic, with his breeches around his ankles, tried to run away and tripped over. Stumbling back to his feet, only to trip again after a couple of steps. This happened a few more times until he had reclaimed the lower garment to the level of his large belly. Crying, he faded into the throng. Surveying what was left of the mob, the knight's voice was low but audible.

"Now bugger off home. Catch anyone trying to burn anything or acting like a mob or, king forbid, shouting vote for Gumptrude, I swear by all the knights before, now, and yet to come. You'll be heading with me to the castle and spending the rest of your days in the dungeon."

The Green Knight's voice had taken on such authority that Scrungle felt a sudden urge to comply. The mob started dropping their placards bearing the inane statements onto the street. The heart had gone out of the protest, and Scrungle felt relieved as they started to slither away.

"Take your crap with you, or you'll get a hot bot as well."

The protestors, who had dropped the placards and signs, swiftly picked them back up, looking back over their shoulders at the Green Knight to make sure they weren't being singled out for a smack. The Yellow Knight urged the falcon to take flight, then dismounted and walked over to the Green Knight.

Trailing the horses behind them the knights approached the windmill.

Scrungle pedalled the tricycle out of the garden. The miller, who had been watching from the door, now came out and joined them. Unclasping the leather straps and buckles, the knights took their helmets off. The plumage on each matched the knight's colour. The Green Knight's hair was a lush brown, which tumbled out, over the plate armour covering their shoulders; the Yellow Knight's hair was short, blond, and kind of punky-looking. They were both female, or at least Scrungle thought so, but didn't want to enslave anyone to a gender they weren't comfortable with.

"Hello. I'm Scrungle Bungus, and this is my friend Peetles."

He took off the sheepskin hat and goggles, pulled out his top hat, put it on his head, tilted it at the knights, and put it back in his magic pocket. Peetles, who was still a bit spikey, did a cautious wave from the front basket, then took their hat and goggles off.

"Where did that little toe-rag go?" The Green Knight was looking over to where the cart had been. The idiot was nowhere to be seen.

"When we rode up, he was away down the road, heading for Plombree." The Yellow Knight said this in the way of explanation.

"Word will get back; I wonder if I'll be in stocks by the end of the week."

"I don't think any of us would let that happen." A stern look crossed the Yellow Knight's delicate features, and then a smile.

As they talked, Scrungle looked around and saw that there was a sign just off to one side of the mill's front garden. Like so many others he had seen when travelling, it was a tall black post with pointed wooden fingerboards. The segments on the post read, **Harbour 85 miles, Plombree 43, Windmill 2 feet to your left.**

The writing was in elegant bright white garland script and underneath braille for the visually impaired. Why did the board single the miller's home out? The question hung in his mind for a moment until it was interrupted by the miller.

"Thank you for saving me and my family. Please come in; I can provide tea and a light lunch."

Not waiting, the miller ushered them all through to the back garden. Another sign fixed to the side of the windmill in the same graceful garland script said: **Back garden, 3 yards**, with an arrow leading the way and braille accompaniment. Further along, was another arrow pointing up. The writing said: **Windmill sails 4 feet up,** with its braille accompaniment. Scrungle read these and mused again that it was just a tad odd as to who needed this information, but how elegant and legible the writing was.

A high green hedge separated the front and side of the garden from the back. Providing privacy for the family to relax in. On entering, the knights, Scrungle, and Peetles, who were now on their own little feet rather than Scrungle's head, were greeted by a camomile lawn enclosed by a rock border. A high old stone wall took over from the hedge, which also ran the length of the garden at the back.

At the far end was a well, with a winch, bucket, and circular tiled roof. Years of weathering covered its grey-green slates in moss. The miller's wife had put out deck chairs for the company. The knights managed to sit; it was more like a controlled fall into the deck chairs, which creaked alarmingly as they lounged nearly horizontally in full armour. Scrungle and Peetles sat on a long bench. A blanket was laid out on the lawn for the miller's family. The miller's wife and children were busy setting out food and drink on a round table.

"My name is Minimal Decimal Miscellaneous, but most people call me Milly. This is my wife Windy, my son Indy, and daughter Mindy." The family gave shy little waves and nods as they were introduced.

"What was that all about?" Said Windy.

"Hmm, it is the election. It has the whole kingdom riled up. Article sixteen has been triggered. Since the king's illness and the Princess has gone into hiding the court is to elect a high chancellor to rule the land in her absence." Said the Yellow Knight, her voice sweet and soothing.

"Why doesn't she want to be found," Windy asked, handing out drinks to the knights.

"Because she won't marry Prince WhackerKnacker." Said the Yellow Knight.

"High chancellor my breastplate." The Green Knight said stretching to get some food. The Yellow Knight gave her companion a swift sideways look.

"What happens if there isn't an heir." Said Milly.

"Well if we can't find the Princess and the king you know doesn't get any better then the court scholars search the records for the next in line."

The Yellow Knight answered, then became thoughtful, working through the idea of not having a King or Queen.

"Has this ever happened before?" Scrungle asked wanting to understand.

"About two hundred and fifty years ago, the whole royal family was killed in a complicated game of where did I put my finger last. A high chancellor was elected until archives revealed that a third cousin to the late queen was the next in line. A duchess, or countess of some sort." The Yellow Knight explained to Scrungle.

"What's a duchess and a countess?" Peetles asked.

"A duchess is the wife of a duke, countess the wife of an earl." Said the Green Knight, between mouthfuls of food.

"Is a Baroness the wife of a baron?" Asked Windy.

The Yellow Knight nodded in an absent-minded way, deep in thought.

"Glad you're versed in this legal stuff. Does my head in." Said the Green Knight. She then took a bite of some cheese and crackers.

"Wow, where did you get the cheese."

"The wife made it," Milly said, a look of pride on his face.

"Nice job." Nodding at Windy who smiled at her feet.

"I learned how to make it from my mother." Still not looking up and not used to such praise

"You need to go into business; that is amazing." The Green Knight then ate what was left, paused a moment, and then cut off another large slice from the block of cheese on the table.

"Did you make the signs?" Said Scrungle.

"Alas no they were made a long time ago by my father, he was very good at writing. He and my mother settled here and built the windmill together."

Windy looked at her hands, either self-conscious or afraid she had said too much.

Scrungle sat thinking, he could feel something tugging away inside his mind but couldn't for all the mushrooms in Plombree, put a spindle-like finger on it. His thoughts scattered as the miller thanked them once more.

"Can't thank you all enough, coming to help. How's the hand." Said Milly.

"A bit sore but not as sore as his arse." The Green Knight laughed and the rest of the company joined in. Whatever tension there had been in the air, was now completely dispelled. Mindy and Windy set about pouring more drinks, while little Indy sat sucking his thumb.

"You two were very brave, coming between the mob and the windmill." said the Yellow Knight. Both knights saluted Scrungle and Peetles with their mead. Peetles became a bit spikey, being made a hero; and Scrungle for the second time in his life, blushed.

"I met some of your companions on the road. Over the mountains."

The Yellow Knight sat forward interested in hearing about her fellow champions.

"Oh, which colours."

"Blue, Black, White, Grey and Red. Uncommonly decent fellows. Very hearty breakfast." Said Scrungle, thinking to himself how it now felt like such a long time ago. The two Knights exchanged a laugh and a look.

"Yeah, that sounds like the lads. Were they having any luck finding the Princess?" The Green Knight searching Scrungles eyes.

"Unfortunately not, I did say If I came across the Princess, I would get word to them, but so far I have no news to share." Scrungle was a little sad he could not be more of assistance. The knight sat back as the canvas deck chair, creaked under the weight of the armour.

"Never met one of your kind before. Or your kind." The Yellow Knight nodded to Scrungle and Peetles.

"If I may be so bold, tell me. Why are you on the King's Road?" Scrungle told the knights about the other knights, the wolves, and everything else in a condensed version, from setting off to find what they now knew was called the Huba mushroom to the fracas at the windmills. Peetle's attention had wandered, and halfway through the conversation, they had jumped down from the bench and gone to play with the daughter and son of the miller. All three ran in circles around the old well, trying to catch each other.

Scrungle thought it would be best not to mention what they had overheard on the castle tour, or anything about the moon-dial. Would the knights be obliged to take them back to face the Baroness and Gumptrude? Also, he and Peetles promised to keep the location of the Huba mushrooms safe. Travelling in the wider world had taught him that prudence was a good bedfellow. Both knights listened saying little.

"And you have been told the best place to find these mushrooms is in the land of Badly Designed Signs." The Green Knight asked still lounging in the deck chair.

"Yes." Scrungle felt bad that he wasn't telling the whole truth to the knights as they seemed honourable.

"What you think Lady Yellow." The Green Knight looked at her companion. The Yellow Knight was looking to the sky to see where the sun was. How far the shadow of the windmill had stretched since they had been here. Taking a moment to struggle out of the canvas deck chair the knight stood.

"I think Lady Green we should be going. The day is beginning to get away from us. We must bid you adieu. We have to meet with our compatriots at the harbour"

The Green Knight rolled her eyes at this, she was getting comfortable in the deck chair, enjoying what looked to be a vegan waldorf salad with a side of chips.

The Yellow Knight held out a hand to the Green Knight and after a little bit of heaving, managed to get her out of the deck chair and standing. The Yellow Knight turned to Scrungle.

"It would seem our road is the same, how would it sound if we travelled together for the time being."

"That would be splendid." Scrungle sounded happy but a little apprehensive, thinking about what had happened on the castle tour. Scrungle called Peetles but he couldn't see his friend. He walked over to the wishing well. Peetles sat with the children, they were touching the braille engraving on the opposite side.

"Peetles it's time to go."

Peetles did their hopping bounce, coming around to Scrungle.

"I was touching the bumps on the well, it was a copy made by their grandad for their grandma. They made it up so only they knew how to read the bumps, but Grandma told Windy, who told Mindy who told me."

"Yes, it is for the people and creatures who can't see as well as everyone else," Scrungle said nodding to his companion.

Leaving the hats and goggles off for the time being, Scrungle and Peetles settled themselves back on the tricycle. The yellow Knight told Milly if they had any more problems raise a red flag, high up on the top of the windmill. Malcolm the falcon would see it and let the knights know.

The Green Knight then gave the family their sigil. Reassuring the family, should anyone at all cause problems, just show them the emblem of the Green Knight's house and say they were under their protection. Mounting their horses the company then said farewell to the miller and his family.

# Eighteen

# *Travelling with Malcolm the Falcon*

They set off at a steady pace. Scrungle and Peetles felt safe with the two knights at their side. Scrungle lightly tapped Peetles to get the little creature's attention, telling them quietly, to say nothing about the castle and what they had overheard.

Having seen others in Plombree, but none so elegant, the knights complimented the pair on the tricycle. Marvelling at the build quality and how smoothly it moved. Peetles told them about Mr Morris and how good he was at shaping metal and had made it bright yellow just for Peetles.

The knights said when they eventually returned to the capital, they would go and see Mr Morris of the house of Sando. This delighted Scrungle and Peetles, knowing an endorsement from the knights would elevate Mr Morris's business.

Scrungle tried conversing with the knight's two horses, but the horses were hesitant to engage in conversation. They felt that, without the knights understanding what was being said it was a betrayal of their loyalty.

The company passed the ruins of an old keep with a walled enclave. The sandstone wall, crumbling and weather-worn, had been breached and fallen in several places. Only the weathered posts of the entry gates were left. It had been a decent size at one time, with two high towers squared with slate roofs. The coat of arms chiselled into the stonework was now illegible after years of wind, sun, and rain.

Scrungle looked at the knights, wondering if he should talk about the general unrest they had witnessed in Plombree. His attention drifted when he noticed that the Green and Yellow Knights had nothing in the way of go-faster stripes or promotions on their horses.

"The other knights had go faster stripes." Said Scrungle. The Yellow Knight laughed and the Green Knight grimaced.

"Yeah, that's the lads for you." Said the Green Knight eventually, after calming down a little.

"Why don't you have any?" Said Peetles, directing the question to the Green Knight.

The Yellow Knight interceded, as there was a look of thunder on the Green Knight's face.

"Well, the endorsement and personal appearances are all a bit pretentious. Gets a bit tacky. We aren't concerned with that as much as the lads are. Just don't need the hassle with the agents and all the promotional stuff they have to do." The Yellow Knight looked off into the hills as if searching for something.

"When you are all together, who is the leader." Asked Peetles.

"I don't think that's very polite somehow Peetles." Said Scrungle.

"No not at all." Said the Yellow Knight. "Every four years we have a tournament. Anyone can enter, It's a five-day event and brings the whole of Plom together. Jousting, swordplay, archery amongst others. The best is then crowned leader. That knight then wears the gold."

The Yellow Knight manoeuvred the horse around a flag that was in place of a stone and then added. "I am a little surprised you've never heard of it before."

"I don't get out much." Said Scrungle, then had a shock, realising this was the longest he had ever been away from his home in the Chana tree.

"And for the last eight years, it's been the same lass." Said the Green Knight her voice proud that it was a woman who was the alpha leader.

"Does the Gold Knight get lots of sponsorship?" Asked Scrungle. This was the trigger, and the Green Knight launched into a rant about how the female knights do the same job, but for some reason, it's the lads that always get the sponsorship and endorsements. It was a quick education for Scrungle and Peetles that there was a large pay gap between the two sexes, and female knights not only knew this but were deeply annoyed by it to differing degrees.

"And then Gumptrude comes along and ups the beard-trimming allowance. Do I look like I have a beard?"

The Green Knight thrust her silky smooth jaw forward and pointed at it.

* * *

The landscape was changing to marsh as the reclaimed floodplains were now behind them. Tall grasses and dark brown pools of water dotted the landscape. Swifts flew low across the marshland, catching insects. Far off, a bird of prey could be seen, flying in a straight line towards the company. When it was overhead, it circled and circled.

The company stopped, and the Yellow Knight extended her left arm. With practised ease, the bird of prey swooped down and landed perfectly on the gloved hand. The Yellow Knight had strings of raw meat and fed them to the falcon. One of the horses muttered something about the falcon being a show-off and the knight's favourite.

Turning her horse, the Green Knight brought herself close to her compatriot and produced a small cup from her saddle bag, holding the cup in one hand and metal pellets in the other. The falcon picked a pellet out of the hand of the Green Knight and dropped it into the cup. It rattled for a moment until it settled. Both Knights looked at the falcon but it didn't do anything more, just preened itself.

"Anything else Malcolm. Eh, anything else? Who's a good bird of prey eh? Who's a good bird?"

The Yellow Knight cooed at the bird, which sat impassive, staring at the knight. The look could have been easily misinterpreted as 'Keep up the baby talk, and I'll peck your eyes out.'

"Roads clear as far as a league." Said the Green Knight turning to Scrungle and Peetles in way of explanation.

The Yellow Knight raised her arm, and the falcon slid down onto the shoulder and perched on the pauldrons of the armour plating. It had been adapted so the talons of Malcolm the falcon could grip.

The company set off again, with the knights talking about the Princess and what strategy to use to find her. Scrungle concentrated on the falcon. He wasn't sure if he should tell the knights that he could talk to their scout. In a way, he felt he was being a little dishonest, but it would be polite to say hello. Peetles seemed happy sipping from the lemon-coloured water bottle and counting the flags on the flagstone road.

"Hello." Said Scrungle.

The falcon turned around on the shoulder of the Yellow Knight so it was now looking at Scrungle.

"Alreet, you Scrungle Bungus mate?" Asked Malcolm.

"Yes thank you and my travelling companion is Peetles." Scrungle nodded to the basket. "If I may inquire, How do you know my name?"

"It's the lads fella. The White Knight talked about you. Mind you, we did meet briefly when you were on your way into Plombree. I landed on your coach for a quick breather. The Blue Knight says you can narf put it away."

"Oh, so are they here." Scrungle inquired, not understanding what a narf was.

"Na mate, they're far north now. Looking for signs of the Princess. I'm given messages to take to them. You see." Malcolm lifted one of his legs to show Scrungle where a message would be attached. The knights, oblivious to the conversation between Scrungle and Malcolm, had moved on to tell each other jokes about Gumptrude and Prince Whackerknacker.

Malcolm talked more about how he scouted for the knights, also carrying messages to and from the two search parties. Scrungle asked about the pellets and the cup. Malcolm explained the system: he would drop a pellet if the road was clear. Two pellets for bandits or if there may be trouble, and three if there were other knights on the road. A fourth pellet would indicate that there was news about the Princess.

Scrungle asked if the falcon had ever been to the Hills of Badly Designed Signs. Malcolm said that it was always covered in mist, so they had stayed away from it. The pair talked more. Each asked questions about where they grew up and why they were on the road. It didn't take long for them to realise they would become good friends.

"Why aren't there more scouts? It seems you have a lot to do." Asked Scrungle.

"Budget cuts, mate. I mean, back in the day, when they cared about stuff, there were a few of us. Plus, nearly half of the team had squires. Like everything now, supposedly can't afford it, which is never the case for chancellor's expenses, claiming for a second home or yearly ministry banquets, which get more and more lavish. Not to mention the cake budget for Bakeasy. I blame Gumptrude; he was a jumped-up arse when he went around collecting taxes. Now he'll probably be voted premier, now that's a real problem. But what can you do? The idiots love him."

Malcolm flexed his wings a few times.

"If you don't mind mate." He then turned back towards the front and took flight.

"Need to stretch the wings plus I'm a bit peckish." He screeched this over his shoulder as he ascended into the sky.

At midday, the little company found a nice area beside the King's Road to stop for lunch.

It wasn't a stopping area with a stone table and bin, but the trees around had been felled, so there were plenty of tree stumps to sit on. As they ate, Peetles asked the knights when they were last in Plombree and if they had missed it.

"We've been looking for Princess Isobella for at least four weeks now. I really miss a good cheese and onion pastie from Greggory's." The Yellow Knight looked a little sad at the thought.

"Do all the knights have to look for her?" Asked Peetles.

"Well now you mention it, I've been thinking the same thing. I mean it only takes a couple of us to go searching. We were given express orders five south five north, no one east or west. Why?" Said the Green Knight.

"It is not our job to question the king. We all saw the order, king's seal and signed" Replied the Yellow Knight.

"Yeah brought to us by Baroness Bakeasy. I mean the king on his sick bed gets enough energy to sign a decree. Doesn't feel right."

"Just stop there Lady Green." The Yellow Knight who had put her food down turned to look straight at the Green Knight. "we are in company."

She nodded in the direction of Scrungle and Peetles. Her blue eyes fixed on the hazel eyes of her friend and fellow knight. Struggling with an internal debate, eventually, the Green Knight dropped her gaze.

"You're right, you're right. Sorry, Scrungle, Peetles I shouldn't be talking like this and it isn't safe or fair for you two to hear it either." She then turned back to the Yellow Knight. "I'm calling a conclave when we meet up with Gold at the harbour."

"I'm right there with you sister." The Yellow Knight agreed, with a light tap on her friend's arm.

To lighten the mood, Scrungle asked Peetles if they could show the knights a card trick or two. Spending the rest of the lunch watching Peetles demonstrate sleight of hand with a battered deck of cards. Then Peetles urged the knights to shuffle the pack and pick a card. After several goes where Peetles named the card correctly every time, the knights sat back, amazed.

"How do you do that? You must be using some magic." Said the Yellow Knight.

"I don't know any spells, but somehow I just know; how I know, I don't know." Peetles, feeling self-conscious at being the focus of such attention, took a drink from the water bottle a little too quickly, dousing themselves as it toppled them over. The knights tried hard to stifle their laughter, but Peetles started to giggle, which set them all away.

As they travelled, it became apparent to the knights that Scrungle and Peetles had little knowledge of the kingdom. Soon both the knights were educating the pair on some of the history and traditions of Plombree, the kings and queens, and some notable battles.

The rhythmic clip-clop of the hooves and good company made the journey slide by.

It felt surprising when the light began to wane and night started to descend. Scrungle could barely see, the road that ran straight, to the horizon then split between two hills.

"Just around the next hill is the Dangles Inn. It sits between the fork in the road. I suggest we take rooms for the night." Said the Yellow Knight.

"We don't have any money left." Said Peetles.

"You are our honoured guests. Anyway, we can claim this on expenses, so pick the best room you fancy." Said the Green Knight with a laugh.

She stopped her horse, and the rest followed, coming to a halt in a line. The Green Knight unclasped her helmet, which had been hanging on the pommel of the saddle since the windmill incident. There was a glint of mad mischief in her eye as she pushed it down over her head, then she flashed a smile at them.

"Oh no I've seen that look before." Said the Yellow Knight reaching for her helmet.

"Bugger." Said both the horses that only Scrungle could hear or understand.

"Fancy a race to the Inn." Said the Green Knight looking at Scrungle.

"I don't know." Said Scrungle in surprise.

"Put your hats on lads. Last one there's a Gumptrude supporter." Said the Yellow Knight.

Scrungle and Peetles swiftly donned their bike hats and goggles. The moment they were set, both knights shouted a loud 'giddy yap,' digging their spurs into their mounts and galloping away at a blistering speed.

"Come on, Scrungle, go." Said an excited Peetles getting into the idea of a race.

Scrungle plunged onto the peddles, and away they went. The knights were neck and neck as they raced away. Scrungle put the gears on low, peddling furiously to build up speed. Flying along, he pushed the T-bar gear handle into normal, then downhill. Scrungle's legs pistoned up and down. The torque was higher, but the speed increase was amazing. All the while Peetles shouted words of encouragement to Scrungle.

"We cannot solve problems with the kind of thinking we employed when we came up with them." Peetles had seen that one on a wall in Plombree.

"Hammock." Shouted Peetles, because it made them think of Scrungle.

"Always keep a potato peeler handy." It had popped into Peetle's head, and it sounded inspiring.

Scrungle was gaining, skimming across the stone flags, and delighting in the idea of the banana-yellow tricycle sprouting wings and taking flight. He could see the horses had started to slow down after their opening sprint.

Both knights' heads were down, bodies hunched, driving their horses forward. Scrungle deftly steered the tricycle to the side, forcing the pedals to turn even faster as they rounded the hill. Down a little slope was the inn, and bright lights shone from the many windows. Scrungle and Peetles honked the horns together, laughing all the way. The Green and Yellow Knights were behind the yellow tricycle as they came speeding into the open courtyard. Scrungle braked hard and started a skid. The tricycle hit an empty barrel and threw the pair off, landing in an empty stall full of hay. The knights, seconds behind, clattered into the courtyard, pulling hard at the leather reins. Skidding on the cobblestones, the horses worked hard not to lose footing.

Dismounting, the knights took their helmets off, all the while laughing. Coming over to pull Scrungle and Peetles out of the hay. Immediately, the pair went over to the tricycle. After a quick inspection, it was a relief to know the tricycle was fine and hadn't suffered any damage from the little collision. With all the commotion, a couple of the inn's staff, holding lanterns aloft in the gathering dark, had come out into the courtyard to see what all the fuss was. On seeing the knights, they ran back into the inn to tell the owner the Green and Yellow Knights were there.

"Well, that contraption is fast." The Green Knight was now looking at the tricycle with a new sense of interest.

"That was a good race. We might have to trade the horses in for one of those." Said the Yellow Knight between breaths. Her cheeks, flushed with excitement.

"Usurper." Said one of the horses.

"See what you've done. Bloody knackers yard and glue for us, you burke." Said the other horse, who was panting loudly. Before Scrungle could say anything in his defence, a small fawn came out of the back door of the inn.

"Lady Green and Lady Yellow." Shouted the faun.

The Knights grabbed the fawn and hugged him tight. Then introduced Scrungle and Peetles. The faun stuck out a hand crushing Scrungle's stick-like appendage, in a hearty shake. Then knelt to shake hands with Peetles, grabbing their flipper-like appendage.

"Some call me Dingle, some call me Dangle."

"Hi, Dingle Dangle." Said Scrungle and Peetles together.

This set the knights off laughing. Scrungle nor Peetles got the joke. Before they could ask why it was funny, the fawn started to push them towards the door he had just come out of.

"So good to see you both. Bloody hobgoblins are causing all sorts of problems. Stupid Gumptrude followers getting everyone riled up. Bloody taxes skyrocketing. Can't you bang some heads together and get things back the way they were? Whole country's went daft."

Talking all the while, Dangle took the company through a series of corridors lit with hanging lanterns, towards the main room.

"Not tonight, Dangle. Me and the Lady Green are off the clock. So no politics, Gumptrude, or any other idiot to deal with." The Yellow Knight said this while unclasping some of her armour.

"Yep, it's mead, food, and a game of darts." Said the Green Knight.

"As you wish. My house is your house." Said Dangle, as he opened the door to the common room. A cheer went up from the assembled patrons, as the two knights entered. Scrungle and Peetles felt a certain pride in being the guests of the knights. Word would spread that the knights were at the inn, and all would be safe for many leagues.

"What about the tricycle?" A concerned Peetle asked, looking up at Dangle.

"Don't worry my little friend. The contraption will be well looked after, just like the horses."

Dangle moved to his customary place behind the bar. Reaching up, the faun rang a chunky brass bell hanging from one of the roof beams. The loud clang silenced everyone.

"Lady Green and Lady Yellow, what are you drinking?" Dangle paused for effect. "Anything you like as the first ones on the house." He shouted.

Another louder cheer went up from all assembled, and then everyone surrounded the knights, asking questions about the Princess, Plombree, Gumptrude, and if the SCS still had a sale on.

## Nineteen

# *Fork in the Road*

After waking from a deep sleep, the pair ventured down to the common room to see if they could get breakfast. The evening before had become a bit of a blur.

The knights were well-known and liked to party hard. It wouldn't be a stretch to say that more than one flagon of mead had been drunk. The Green Knight had kept the locals and the inn's guests entertained with lots of funny stories as well as a great impression of Gumptrude that had everyone in fits of laughter.

The Yellow Knight took on all comers, beating everyone at darts, ring toss, and what made it wet.

Peetles had tried a bit of mead, and not long after, was standing on a table reciting a dirty limerick about a goat, a milkmaid, and a bucket. Unable to imbue liquid, Scrungle sat and watched, laughing along in his way, like everyone else.

When Peetles had started to slur his words and then fallen off the table, he had taken his friend up to the room to sleep.

Now in the common room, they saw Dangle kneeling at the

open hearth, stoking the coals back into life. An elf they had been introduced to the night before, called Skid, came over and ushered them to a table by the window, then asked what they would like for breakfast.

Scrungle asked for mushrooms, and Peetles asked for anything that would help with a bad head. Since Peetles was nearly all head, Skid said he would make it a large remedy. Then went away to find some mushrooms.

Before long, they were joined by the knights. It took a moment for Scrungle and Peetles to recognise the pair. No longer in armour, just long cotton under-shirts, boots, and leather trousers. Their eyes were red-rimmed, hair designed by gas explosion as they moved in a sunken shuffle finding a corner table and hiding from the sunlight streaming through the windows.

The Green Knight asked Dangle if he could poke the fire, a little bit more quietly.

Dangle laughed, then went into the kitchen to make his famous morning-after tonic.

It wasn't long before he pushed a plate of shelled boiled eggs in front of the hung-over pair, a salt shaker, two small glasses of spiced ginger, and a leaf of parsley

"You know the drill." Said Dangle.

Neither knight looked up. Just sat with their heads in their hands as if they would fall apart if they didn't. Dangle left the pair to recover and joined Scrungle and Peetles who were looking out onto the grey-green fields surrounding the inn.

"Did you sleep well Scrungle, Peetles?"

"Very well thank you. Peetles head is a little sore today." Peetles looked up at Dangle blinking.

"How long has the inn been here?" Asked Scrungle

"Over a hundred years as far as I know. I've owned it, Oh about."

The faun did a count using his fingers. Searching through his memories for dates.

"Twelve years I think. I was given it by the old fellow who owned it. He went to live with his grandson by the sea."

"That was very kind of him." Said Peetles.

"I think he felt I'd earned it. In my former life, I was an assassin, killed a few of his enemies and his wife."

A shadow fell across the room, a cloud covered the morning sun. Scrungle looked at Dangle, whose happy smile now held a sinister twist. Peetles had gone a bit spikey.

"Oh." Was all Scrungle could say.

"Only joking." Dangle started to laugh. "Won it off him in a game of what made it wet."

Scrungle gave an inward sigh, Peetles a nervous chuckle. Dangle's comedy routine might work for Dangle and his friends, but Scrungle thought it decidedly off-putting. Skid had come back and was placing the mushrooms down for Scrungle. Handing Peetles a glass of cloudy water he told Peetles it would help with the bad head.

"Have you been to the hills of Badly Designed Signs," Peetles asked after sipping the drink.

"Oh, you don't want to be going there." Dangle's manner abruptly changed.

"We have to." Said Scrungle.

"Those hills are cursed. Strange tales that make your head spin and your pee turn orange." Said Dangle, trying hard to put the pair off.

"I don't pee." Said Scrungle.

"I'm orange." Peetles offered.

Scrungle told Dangle what he knew about the cheese farmer and what he did with the signs. Dangle nodded but then said that was only half the story.

"After losing his daughter, the cheese farmer became a recluse.

Broken hearted, he cursed himself and his land after sending off to the SCS for a DIY cursing kit. Being an Amazing Shine member, it was guaranteed delivery within the week. By all accounts, the curse was on the expensive side and was guaranteed to work, well until it was broken.

Legend has it that on the first full moon after the delivery, a fog rolled down the hill from the manor house and has covered the land ever since."

Dangle bent forward a little, his voice quiet. "To keep people from disturbing his grief, he summoned a race of terrifying creatures. No one was sure about their origin, only that these egg-like beasts called Farnys surrounded the land of the manor.

It is said that when the Farnys catch you, and they always do, they devour you whole on the spot. The cheese farmer was able to afford the Farnys because the cursing kit came with a promotional half-price voucher."

Dangle finished his story by saying that he had never known anyone who went into the hills of Badly Designed Signs to come out again. Well, except for an old woman called Waynex.

"Witch Waynex," said Scrungle. The common room was eerily quiet, the sun no longer as bright as it had been.

"That is your choice, but I caution you not to go to the land of Badly Designed Signs." Dangle admonished.

"No, we mean witch Waynex." Peetles chipped in to try and clarify the statement.

"You've just asked me that."

"Yes, but I mean witch Waynex."

"Sorry, which way what? Have you just said the same thing twice? Either way, it's your choice." Said Dangle, totally confused now, and gave the pair an odd look. Skid called his name as he couldn't find the hammer and chisel to open the till. Dangle excused himself to help the elf.

Outside, the pair went to check on the tricycle. The frame had been cleaned down, and the wheels had been washed clean of mud. Scrungle and Peetles thought the employees of the inn must not have had that much interaction with tricycles as it had its own stable, hay feed, and a pail of water.

Putting Peetles in the accustomed place on his head, Scrungle pushed the tricycle out into the courtyard. Then went to look in on the knight's horses.

Scrungle said hello a few times, but the horses just ignored him. Both the horses, after a long night of discussion, were now certain they would feel a swift, sharp blow to the back of the skull when the knights returned to the city. Trading the pair in for nice new bicycles.

"Huffy pair, aren't they?" Said a familiar voice. Looking up, Scrungle saw Malcolm, the falcon, perched on the overhang of the stable roof.

"I really am sorry I raced the knights. Should have lost."

"It was a fair race Scrungle." Said Peetles.

"Look, that thing will never take over from the horses. I mean, look at it; you have to do all the hard work. Whereas these daft lads will do all that for you."

Malcolm said this, then glided to a wagon that was used to take feed to the animals in the fields. He perched on the drop gate at the back, so when Scrungle walked over they were at eye level with each other.

"Good point."

"Thank you." Said Peetles, thinking Scrungle was talking to them.

"You two still heading to the hills?"

"Yes, I suppose I have to go. I have no other way."

"Sorry Scrungle I don't understand." Said Peetles.

"I was talking to Malcolm." Said Scrungle.

"Who's Malcolm?" Said Peetles, looking around, thinking he had missed someone's approach.

"The falcon." Scrungle pointed to Malcolm sitting on the wagon.

"Hello." Said Peetles.

"Can Peetles understand us?" Said Malcolm.

"No. Sorry." Said Scrungle.

"Sorry for what?" Said Peetles

"I was talking to Malcolm."

"Who's Malcolm?" Said Peetles.

The confusing conversation was interrupted by the sound of metal on stone. The Green and Yellow Knights dressed in their armour walked over, clanking on the cobbles of the yard. By the looks of them, the morning after pick me up provided by Dangle seemed to be working as their eyes weren't as bloodshot.

The Yellow Knight held out her left hand, and Malcolm flew over. The Green Knight produced the cup and pellets, but Malcolm just preened his left wing.

Saddling the horses, the knights set about getting ready for another day's travel. Dangle came out and handed over provisions, preserves, and water to the knights and Scrungle. Dangle knew the inn would be full for the next week or two. This was good news for the inn and his bank balance. Just having them turn up chased the riff-raff and troublemakers away. Locals would flock to the inn wanting to hear the latest gossip, who the knight's travelling companions were, and if the knights had left any Amazing Shine vouchers.

Dangle walked with them to the crossroads, which was more of a mincing canter to keep up with the horses and tricycle. Like the knights, the faun commented on the tricycle and how well it looked and moved. Low grey clouds now obscured the sun, the overcast morning reflected the company's mood. Where the intersection of the roads split, a badly designed sign read:

**'Harbour town 300 miles,'** which it wasn't, and the fingerboard it was written on pointed straight down. What was even more annoying was that the lettering was in different fonts. Another fingerboard on the black post read:

**'Piss off the way you came 300 miles.'** pointing back in the direction they had travelled.

The last arrow pointed in the direction of the hills. It was a mixture of fonts, capitals, and lowercase letters; for some reason, this annoyed Peetles the most. It read:

**'Clem Fandangos Knee 300 miles'** which, in all honesty, didn't help anyone. The little group that had saved the miller and family from the baying mob now stood, facing each other, the mounted knights on the road to Harbour. The tricyclists Scrungle and Peetles on the road to the hills.

"Are you sure about going to the hills? What if the mushrooms you seek aren't there?" Said the Green Knight " I fear for you both."

"I think it's my quest. Well, that's what the other knights thought, and I don't know what else to do but try." Said Scrungle.

"It's our quest, Scrungle." Peetles was smiling, not sensing the danger everyone was trying hard, to persuade the pair, to avoid. The knights nodded, and a breeze blew the Green Knight's hair across her face.

"A quest is a quest so I wish you every success." Said the Yellow Knight. She then set Malcolm away to scout the next leg of their journey. Malcolm flew over Scrungle, calling out that he would keep a falcon's eye on the road for them. Circling once the knights scout headed off towards the sea. With one last salute to Dangle, Scrungle and Peetles, the knights set off down the King's Road in the same direction as the falcon. The two companions settled their goggles in place and pulled down their hats.

"Thank you, Dingle Dangle." Said Scrungle and Peetles together. Turning the tricycle in a tight arc, they set off towards the Hills of Badly Designed Signs. Dangle stood watching them depart, returning to the inn a little sadder.

* * *

No longer in the presence of the knights, the pair felt a little subdued. As if on cue, a light rain started to add to the gloomy mood. Scrungle took a moment to extend the overhang on the top of the tricycle seat, while Peetles pulled the rain cover over themselves and the basket. As the road climbed, Scrungle dropped the gears to make the peddling easier. The tricycle's grip was impressive even with the flagstone road becoming wet.

At the top of the incline, the land before them rippled out like a throw rug that caught your feet when you least expected it, scalding your fingers while holding a cup of tea.

The King's Road wound through the hills and rock formations that poked through the uneven ground. Far-off smoke rose in a spiral from what they assumed was a chimney. Cattle and sheep roamed the grasslands, penned in by dry stone walls.

With one last wistful look, they scanned the road behind them. Knowing in their hearts that the knights would be long gone, but searching for them anyway. Dangle's inn was just a dark speck now, and the fork in the road could just be made out.

Then, just for a moment, Scrungle thought he could see movement. A dot of a figure moved along the King's Road, moving at speed as if running. There was a flash of silver, then the light changed, and the moment was lost.

Scrungle pushed the gears to the downhill position and pedalled on into the countryside. The road soon levelled out, and the pair came across another black signpost with arrows pointing in all the wrong directions. The topmost fingerboard said:

**'Plombree, 3 half miles.'** It pointed straight at a thorn bush.

Then another wooden arrow read, **'U smel shitphace 1 mile.'** Written in Comic Sans, the handwriting was so poor it was nearly unintelligible, which aggravated Peetles, who became spikey and a bit lumpy reading it. The little creature shuddered, then pulled the sheep-skin riding hat lower. Scrungle slowed the tricycle a little and looked down at his friend.

"You don't have to come with me, Peetles. I can take you back to the inn and wait for my return. I am sure Dingle Dangle will look after you."

Peetles turned to look directly at Scrungle.

"We are bestiest friends. We go together like rainbows and cress. I will help you to get the fungi I'm sure, I promised."

Glad of the company and that neither was on their own. Scrungle consulted the map. At some point, as long as they stayed on the King's Road, they would come to a river crossing. Since it was not to scale, there was no way of telling how long they would have to pedal to reach it. Putting the map back into his unfeasible pockets, he released the brake, and they continued.

The light rain turned heavy, continuing for the rest of the day. Now and then, they would happen across a badly designed sign. Covered in vines so severely in need of trimming that they were nearly impossible to read, not that any of them made any sense. Dirt roads and gravel tracks led off to homesteads and little villages. They understood that any travellers searching for an unfamiliar place were well out of luck. When they did see anyone else, they would walk by head down, or turn off the road. No one greeted them or said hello.

After two more days of travelling the pair came to the ferry crossing.

* * *

The river was wide and slow-moving. The water sparkled, catching the mid-day sun. Consulting the map, Scrungle saw it flowed to the sea from the great lake next to Plombree. If the river or lake had a name, neither he nor Peetles had thought to ask when they had the chance.

A wooden one-story house stood next to the jetty. It was run down and long abandoned. Slates were missing from the roof, and the overrun garden was full of grass and weeds. A weathered sign at the front gate said:

**'Ring for, attendant.'** Under the sign, hanging by a rusted chain was a bell with a handle. Scrungle stretched across and gave it a ring. The bell snapped off from the handle and rolled away with a clang. After a moment of just staring at the bell, Scrungle pedalled the tricycle onto the wooden jetty. The boards protested at the weight but held. Tethered to a post was a rope that spanned the river to the opposite bank. Dismounting they stood looking across the river and could see the flat wooden ferry on the other side.

"How do we get across?" Peetles asked.

Scrungle rubbed his long nose thinking.

"I believe the ferry should be on this side."

"Oh." Said Peetles then after thinking for a little while, "Can we pull it back across from here?"

"I believe it works that you stand on it and pull across using the rope. So if we can't stand on it we can't pull it."

"Oh," said Peetles.

Scrungle was unsure what to do next. Peetles walked to the edge of the wooden planking. Looking down into the river.

"I know it's only for sleeping in, but can we use the dinghy?" Said Peetles watching the rippling water. Scrungle picked Peetles up, laughing.

"Peetles you really are a marvel."Scrungle swapped the tricycle for the dinghy in his magical pockets, and soon the pair were using the rope to pull themselves across the river. Scrungle wasn't the strongest of magical creatures and Peetles was just too small to help. It was slow work and took far longer than expected. On the other bank, they camped for the night a little way in from where they crossed.

They spent the next day cycling slowly beneath the canopy of a rather tatty forest. The King's Road was becoming more cracked and broken, falling further and further into disrepair. It had not gone unnoticed to the pair that the closer they came to the Hills of Badly Designed Signs, the gloomier the world around them became. Like that relative who's a bit too serious about life comes to stay, and everyone starts to feel oppressed by their presence and you start counting the days down for when they leave.

All around were abandoned farms, crofts, and cottages. No one moved along the King's Road, and they hadn't seen a fellow traveller for days. Signs of life had all but deserted the land.

At noon the next day, they came out of the forest after spending a restless night in the strangely quiet woods. The road was now a mixture of dirt, gravel and the occasional flagstone. The wheels of the tricycle still worked miracles and gripped the varying terrain.

All around them, once-tended fields of staple crops had been left to fallow. The tracks leading to small holdings and farms were overgrown with tall grass and wildflowers.

A wooden fence that followed the track had fallen into disrepair, with most of the main posts rotten and snapped. Scrungle thought about the past, imagining when the land had been well-tended and full of life.

Grey clouds hung low, as oppressive as their feelings. The impression of abandonment grew ever heavier as they approached their destination; not a soul lived here or anywhere near the Hills of Badly Designed Signs. Scrungle felt a sad longing to be in the Chana tree, sitting on the veranda, absorbing a mushroom salad, and enjoying the view.

Peetles, sensing his tall friend's sadness, chatted away about whatever Mr Morris of the house of Sando had done to the suspension, which was an expression of perfection because neither of the pair ever felt a bump or hole in the road.

Up ahead was a ravine covered with trees, beyond which they couldn't see anything. Scrungle pedalled the tricycle up, and then, as if passing through a curtain, they were in the Hills of Badly Designed Signs.

It was a sudden change; one moment they could see the world around them, and the next they were plunged into a thick grey fog.

Scrungle stopped the tricycle and lit the carriage lantern. It was a powerful light, but it did little to illuminate the world before them. Down they pedalled. The road no longer had the occasional flagstone, just hard, compacted dirt and gravel. Scrungle slowed the tricycle as neither of the pair could see more than a couple of yards in front. The only sound was the crunch of the all-terrain tyres on the rough track.

The path began to rise again. Scrungle, pushing down harder on the pedals. With no point of reference other than a bush or a tree looming out of the mist, the duo became discombobulated quickly.

Following the rough track, the pair had no clear idea how long they had been travelling, only agreeing that it had the same feel as a run-down council estate.

An uneasy lumpy Peetles sat in the front basket squealed when out of the mist loomed a dark, unnatural, menacing shape. Scrungle stopped the tricycle. There was a sigh of relief between them when they could make out that it was a badly designed sign. All the finger arrows on it were pointing the same way.

**'Swimming pool 1 mile.'**

However, the road split off in three different directions.

"How do we find the Cheeseman?" Said Peetles in a tentative voice,

"I really don't know. we can't use the signs as they are all so badly designed." Said Scrungle who just sat looking at the daft signpost.

"Should we shout? You know, like. Hello Mr Cheeseman are you there?" Asked Peetles.

"We could but for the moment let us not." Said Scrungle.

Whilst they were sitting there enveloped in the mist, wondering what to do next, a low rumbling started. Like the chatter of a large group of people discussing knitting patterns behind closed doors in a conference hall. As the moments passed, it became louder, with many voices saying the same thing over and over but with no clear rhythm, just a deep grumble.

The mist obscured the sound's source, making it all the more terrifying. Neither Scrungle nor Peetles could decide which way to go. The sound grew in intensity—a light shake of the stones on the path. Joining the deep, rolling rumble was the sound of clacking. All Scrungle could think of was teeth biting together. Peetles tried to climb out of the basket, but Scrungle pushed them back.

"Stay there Peetles if I have to pedal I want you as secure and safe as possible."

The sound bounced around the pair, threatening to swallow them whole. The clacking of what could only be described as numerous teeth was the thing of nightmares. The tricycle and the ground it stood on began to shake. Rattling the lantern and bouncing the flags attached to the back of the tricycle that had Peetles and Scrungle's names on.

"I'm scared Scrungle." Said a lumpy, bumpy, spikey Peetles.

It was too much, just as Scrungle was going to turn the tricycle and head the way they had come. Bursting out of the mist came the source of the sound, and both companions screamed.

# Twenty

## *Oh Bugger*

The mist gave way to egg-shaped creatures that Dingle Dangle had said were either myth or monsters. Scrungle didn't know what the collective noun would be for the Farnys, but his mind tossed up the word 'Bugger,' and he didn't question it.

They were about two feet high, although this varied in many cases, as with their colouring, which ranged from light beige to white. The only limbs the Farnys had were a double set of thick, muscular legs with a backward knee joint. On each of their four feet were wooden clogs, Scrungle understood immediately that it was the source of the clattering, cacophonous biting sound. A single eye in the middle of the egg-shaped torso blinked rapidly through thick black eyelashes, and the mouth, a small round, beak-shaped orifice, was saying.

"Farny."

The single word out of so many mouths at the same time was an incomprehensible, deranged mush. Sweeping the tricycle up, screeching, and shouting 'Farny', they ran into the mist. Then, from some silent command, they turned as one and headed down another of the rough dirt tracks hidden by the mist. The tricycle and its occupants bounced along as if being attacked by a late-night drunk in a garage forecourt.

"What's happening Scrungle." Squealed Peetles, their eyes squeezed shut.

Scrungle after the initial shock, saw that the Farnys were transporting the tricycle as if they were flotsam bobbing along in a sea of eggheads. The creatures would abruptly turn like a flock of unhinged starlings and head into another part of the mist.

Scrungle's initial fear when the Farnys came charging out of the mist was subsiding. Due primarily to the fact that the pair had not been instantly torn apart or scrambled. It was also, in part, because the jostling tricycle was making his nose swing from side to side so aggressively that it was slapping him in the face in a rather annoying manner.

A reminder, if ever he had needed one, that this wasn't a dream, unless he had passed out on a stag do.

As Scrungle got a more focused handle on the bouncing and the generally deranged atmosphere of the situation, he was beginning to think the Farnys were unaware of what they were doing. The mist hid how many there were; the sound, however, made Scrungle believe that there was a large herd or bugger of Farnys. Listening more intently, the chattering of 'Farny, Farny, Farny.' had a hint of desperation to its timbre, even mild panic. He had the distinct feeling that the Farnys were being chased.

"I have an idea Peetles." Shouted Scrungle to his terrified friend.

"Does it have anything to do with using your fingers to eat tinned pilchards?" Peetles his voice, a rickety, wobbly epitome of fear.

"No, it has more to do with what's happening at this moment in time. Although I can't see why you can't eat pilchards with your fingers."

Scrungle was doing his best to shout as loud as his telepathy would allow above the constant noise of the Farny's.

"However I do believe it would be beneficial to us both if we addressed the matter in hand. I will count to three. When I say three we will both blow our horns as loudly as possible." Peetles gave no indication that he had heard Scrungle, so he just went ahead and started to count.

"One, two, three." Scrungle squeezed the ahooga horn with as much pressure as he could. Peetles did the same. The horns cut through the clamour, startling the little creatures. For good measure, Scrungle shouted,

"Stop you silly buggers!" At the same time.

The tricycle came to an abrupt halt, bouncing on its springs three or four times, jolting the pair against the frame as the Farnys scattered in every direction. Scrungle got control of his random slapping nose, then looked around, seeing where they had ended up. The mist, still as dense as before, hid everything after a couple of feet.

"Have they gone?" Said Peetles

"I think so, you can open your eyes again now," Scrungle said in a gentle manner.

Peetles did, then tried to move around in the basket but were wedged solidly with lumpy bumps sticking out everywhere on their little body. Scrungle could still hear the word 'Farny.'

"Can you hear that Scrungle?" Peetles said even more fearful, thinking the mad jostling ride was going to start again. Scrungle, turning his head from side to side, tried to identify where the sound was coming from. Putting the tricycle into park, with slow, deliberate moves, he dismounted. Peetles, seeing Scrungle get off, managed, after a struggle, to extricate themselves from the basket. Peetles took off their hat and goggles, Scrungle did the same and stored them in his magic pockets. Peetles quickly scrambled down the wheel to stand next to him. Slowly, they approached the source of the sound. Trapped under the seat and the back two wheels was an egg-shaped Farny. The one eye of the Farny encircled by thick, lush lashes was huge, wide, and staring at Scrungle; its whole body was shaking the frame of the tricycle in fear.

"Hello." Said Scrungle.

Scrungle bent down so he could make eye contact with the little creature. Hoping it would help calm the Farny to see his face.

"Farny, Farny, Farny." chattered the Farny.

"Well, it's like my brother once told me; don't cry because you're useless, smile because you're an egg"

"Sorry, Peetles what does that mean." Said Scrungle.

"It's written on the back of the egg head." Peetles pointed to the Farny.

From where Peetles was standing, they could read the writing. It looked like it was embossed into the shell. Scrungle had knelt onto all fours and was extending one of his stick-thin arms to pull the Farny out from between the wheels.

It may have looked to the creature that it was about to be skewered by a three-pronged fork. So it began pushing itself as far away from Scrungle as physics would allow. Its agitation passed from shaking to vibrating in fear, Peetles seeing that the creature was more scared of them than they were of it, started to talk and reassure the Farny that nothing untoward was going to happen.

Bending further, Scrungle managed to grab the little creature, pulling it free by one of its legs. It felt surprisingly light as he stood holding it upside down while it vibrated like a tuning fork, its little legs trying to gain purchase in mid-air.

Just as Scrungle was going to put it down. A wolf came out of the mist and bit a decent-sized chunk out of its side. Scrungle panicked and dropped the wriggling four-legged egg, which landed on its feet, dashing off, screaming.

"Farny, Farny Farny."

The wolf went to chase the Farny then stopped. It sniffed the air, turning, it barked.

"Scrungle."

The next moment, the wolf was rushing at Scrungle, jumping up and knocking him over, licking his face with a long red tongue, and wagging a tail so fast it looked like the back end of the wolf would snap in two.

Peetles screamed, then rushed at the wolf, ready to defend his friend by sacrificing themselves as a starter. The wolf's tongue lashed away at Scrungle, who realised it was Snickers. Rolling over, Scrungle managed to shuffle the excited wolf to one side and pluck the charging Peetles up at the same time.

"Scrungle, how you doing? So good to see you. Didn't have you pegged as a creature that would like the taste of Farny?" Said Snickers, still excited that they had met their friend.

"Snickers, my dear wolf. How are you? Em, I don't think I do, although that was the first Farny we have come close to. You look well."

Scrungle had settled Peetles onto their accustomed place on his head, raising his arm, he patted the leg of his friend in reassurance.

"This is Peetles, whom you thought was an egg. Peetles isn't an egg, just Peetles."

"Oh yeah, I remember. That's interesting. Gives a second, and I'll call the rest of the pack. I can't see a thing in this fog. It's so good to see you."

Snickers started barking, with a few howls thrown in for good measure. In return, other barks came out of the mist. The mist had an odd quality, as it would bounce the sound around, making it hard to pinpoint the source. Bit by bit, the disconnected barks found their way to Snickers.

Melody and Al came first and when they saw Scrungle, bounded towards him, jumping up and yapping that it was good to see him.

Wonky turned up last and sat down, his glazed expression as thick as the mist. The wolves all started to talk at once. Scrungle found out that the pack had come over the mountains in search of food. It hadn't been planned to come this far; they had just wandered into the mists and found the Farnys.

Scrungle was given conflicting reports of what the Farnys tasted like. Snickers said they tasted of white chocolate and were delicious. While Al said beef, Melody cottage pie, and Wonky capers, To Scrungles eye, it looked like the wolves had gained a few pounds.

"I feel a bit sorry for the Farny's but we all need to eat something." Said Scrungle. Not liking the thought of the little egg-shaped creatures being someone's dinner. Snickers assured Scrungle that they never ate a whole one.

"You just take a bite, and they just grow back. I mean, within minutes, they're whole again." Melody said in the way of explanation.

"That's unusual." Said Scrungle.

"We're not complaining, although you never get the feeling you're full, and thirty minutes later you want another one." Said Al.

"Maybe that's what happens with fast food." Said Wonky.

"Yes, Wonky," Melody said, then sat down next to the dozy wolf. Throughout the exchange, Peetles had been sitting terrified on Scrungle's head.

To Peetles, it sounded like growling and barks.

"What's happening, Scrungle?" Said an all-clumpy, bumpy Peetles.

"Ah yes. Sorry about that Peetles. We were talking about Farny's, but introductions first. Now that is Snickers."

Scrungle pointed to the lead wolf, who gave a solid bark, which translated to Peetles meant, 'Alright, mate.' Scrungle introduced the rest of the wolves in this way. Since they had found a decent food source they had no interest in eating Peetles. Scrungle assured his friend that there was absolutely nothing to worry about.

"Are you lost, Scrungle?" Asked Snickers. His ears were up and Scrungle assumed that he was listening for Farny activity.

"I'm not sure. We're trying to find someone. Not really sure where to start." Said Scrungle, then added. "Are you?"

"To be honest we can't seem to find a way out of the mist. It's OK though we have plenty to eat. Gets a bit boring with the grey all the time. Who you looking for anyway?" Said Snickers

Al was sniffing one of the rear tires of the tricycle in suspicion. The group had formed a tight circle to see each other in the mist.

"The Cheeseman." Said Scrungle.

The pack looked at each other one by one and shrugged.

"Never heard of him. Sorry mate." Said Snickers then took a moment before adding. "This'll sound a bit odd but there's a definite smell of gorgonzola over that way."

He nodded his snout in the direction behind him. The rest of the pack agreed with Snickers although there was some debate about what kind of cheese the aroma was.

"Come on I'll take you." Said Snickers. Sniffing the air, the wolf eventually caught the scent his nose was searching for.

Peetles stayed spikey and lumpy, only settling a little when Scrungle placed him in the relative safety of the basket. Having never seen the like before the wolves gave the tricycle a wide berth. Wonky would have a lunge at the back wheels. Melody or Al would be there to pull him back or get in the way.

As they walked and pedalled, the wolves began sharing more stories of their travels. Scrungle in turn, recounted his and Peetle's adventures so far. Taking the time to keep Peetles abreast of what was being discussed. When the Princess was mentioned, to his surprise, the wolves had seen her.

"Well, I think it was the Princess. She was hiding in the woods. She looked like she had been there awhile. Still managed to smell good, her nails done to perfection." Said Melody.

"Had this waddling black and white bird with her." Added Al.

Scrungle thought about Malcolm and if he could get a message to him.

* * *

The mist never let up, but they could all sense the sun climbing in the sky, a dull light dissipated in a grey world.

Snickers led the way, stopping now and then if the scent became elusive. Then the pack would join in and work as a team to pick up the aroma of cheese. Time wore on, lost in the grey haze. Sometimes the group would get stuck, having to backtrack if they came to a boggy stretch of ground, stunted trees in a decaying forest, or the occasional wall. At times, Snickers would stop and say they didn't want to go a certain way. Telling Scrungle that he could smell the bodies of lost travellers that way.

This panicked Scrungle, Asking the wolves how long they had been in the Hills of Badly Designed Signs.

"Not sure, can't remember the last time we saw a full moon." Said Al.

"Seems like forever, really," said Melody.

"Oh dear." Said a very worried Scrungle. It was dark now, the only light was the tricycle lantern.

"What's that Scrungle?" Peetles said pointing to the edge of the track they were on.

On closer inspection, Scrungle could see a border of white stone running along a rudimentary path. It was hard to see now that it was dark and overgrown with grass. Snickers sniffed and said the scent of cheese was in the same direction. As they followed the nose attached to Snicker's body, they neither heard nor saw a Farny. The road began to climb, becoming a paved road of sorts.

Out of the mist in the darkness loomed a signpost. The lettering was a mixture of capitals and lowercase; it simply said:

**'Back Go.'**

"Go Back. Can't anyone write a sign around here? Back Go, how can you get that wrong?" Peetles was losing his lumpiness while shouting at the sign.

At the top of the climb, once-ornate wrought iron gates barred the way. Grey, wilting vines had woven themselves into the swirling patterns of the metal, then wrapped around the stone pillars on either side. The entrance was wide enough for the largest of wagons to pass through. Shining the lantern around, they could all see it was the entrance to a walled estate. Everyone in the little group could now smell cheese as they cautiously moved forward.

"Have you been here before?" Scrungle asked Al who was next to him.

"Na the smell interferes with Farny hunting and in all honesty it's a bit spooky." Replied Al.

Scrungle got off the tricycle and pushed at the gates. The dead stems protested at the intrusion, not wanting to give up their iron captive. Snapping only when the wolves added their combined weight. Waking up the silence with a squeal that felt to Scrungle as if they were being announced, the old hinges fought against them but eventually swung back wide enough for the tricycle to fit through.

The mist was thicker here; creeping forward the little group stayed close together.

The pack as a whole had their ears on high alert, listening intently for anything that could be a threat. Snickers sniffed the air, expecting trouble.

"There's something up ahead." Melody's eyes were the keenest of the wolves.

A dilapidated old mansion could be made out. Its outline darker against the grey. Scrungle shone the carriage lantern around, trying to pick out the indistinct features. It was hard to tell, but the mist seemed to be coming off the very building as though it had been out for a run in the cold weather.

Snickers padded up a short flight of stone steps that appeared out of the darkness and disappeared into the mist.

"Snickers." Shouted Scrungle fearing for the wolf. It was only moments, but felt like a lifetime before he reappeared in the glow of the lantern.

"Come on this way." Said Snickers.

Scrungle put the tricycle into park, picked Peetles out of the basket, settled the little creature on his head, and got off. A patient Snickers waited at the bottom of the steps. Staying together, they approached the open doors of the mansion. Nothing could be seen on the inside.

"Wow, now that's one heavy-smelling cheese." Melody choked a little.

"Yes," Scrungle and Peetles said together.

The scent was overpowering, wafting through the black mouth of the doorway, assaulting the noses of all those present. Snickers moved closer and then slipped into the hallway.

"Wait," Scrungle said, alarmed at the wolf's show of bravery.

With no reply from Snickers, Scrungle, upset that the wolf was on his own, crossed the foreboding threshold, and then the rest of the pack followed.

Once inside, the carriage lantern shone brightly, illuminating the hallway. Dank with mildew, black fungus corrupted the walls. Heavy crimson curtains torn and moth-eaten hung on either side of the long row of sash windows. Old cobweb grey with a layer of dust added a slightly over-the-top creepy aesthetic. Above them, the biggest chandelier any of the company had ever seen hung, dirty with age. At the far end of the hallway was a grand staircase, one flight arching left and the other arching right. Under the balcony, closed black doors, led to what Scrungle assumed was the back of the mansion.

Looking around, he thought the place needed a once-over with a mop and bucket or a flame thrower. No one could see Snickers, just the impression of the wolf's pad prints on the dusty floor. Standing together in a tight little knot, Scrungle took a step forward.

"Hello." Speaking into the oppressive surroundings. Nothing came back, not even the creak of a floorboard.

"Hello," Scrungle said again, moving a little further into the mansion. They all did a little jump at the sudden appearance of Snickers from a doorway at the end of the corridor under the grand stairs. Lantern light reflected from the wolf's eyes. They hurried towards him, glad that he was fine.

"No one home but the smell of cheese is stronger in there though." Snickers turned his head to a set of double doors to the right of them all. Above the door was a plaque. On it were expertly crafted bumps like brail.

"You didn't have to come in. I just needed your help to get here." Scrungle felt he was putting everyone in danger and should be here on his own.

"Don't be silly, you're part of the pack now and Peetles, obviously." Said Snickers.

"What's happening Scrungle." Peetles voice was small in the hall. Scrungle told Peetles what Snickers had just said. This calmed the little creature down, confirming him as one of the pack. Moving over to the doors with the strange plaque above the lintel. Scrungle tried the handle. It didn't budge, then, as if the mansion had been waiting for this moment, a low moan was heard by the little company. It echoed around the corridor, bouncing off the walls and rattling the chandelier.

The wolves ears flicked around, searching for the source. Then it came again, and the hackles of the wolves stood on end.

"Oh my, Oh my." Peetles once again lumpy and spikey.

The moan surrounded them, then a voice ominous and menacing.

"Who disturbs the door that can never be opened."

Then the front door slammed shut with a loud bang, blowing dust and leaves into the air. The floorboards in the corridor creaked and then rippled as if made of water. An oil painting of an elderly man dressed as a monk moved as if alive, reaching out of its frame to grab Scrungle. The scents of Camembert, Livarot Munster, and Stinking Bishop like a festival portaloo wafted through the corridor ruffling the fur of the wolves, who had started to sneeze and gag at the stench.

"Oh my, Oh my," said Peetles once again.

Another loud moan, but this time Scrungle swung the lantern up revealing where the horrifying sound was coming from. Standing above them on the grand staircase balcony was a rippling mass of yellow cheese. It was at least seven feet tall and man-shaped. Mixed in with the cheese were lumps of tomatoes, gherkin, and lettuce. Its black mouth opened, and out came a low, rumbling moan.

"I see you." It said then laughed.

To Scrungles ears it wasn't a joining-in laugh but more the sadistic laugh of a member of parliament cutting child benefits.

## Twenty-One

# *The Mansion*

Trapped as they were, panicking as one. The wolves and Scrungle with Peetles on his head ran towards the door Snickers had come out of earlier. It was an unspoken group decision, just wanting to get away from their unwelcoming host.

On the other side of the door, they were confronted by a short corridor with multiple doors to choose from. Not waiting to investigate, they ran on, Scrungle would have fallen if he hadn't bumped into Wonky, who sat at the top of a short flight of stairs.

The moan of the Cheeseman receded a little, and Scrungle took the lead to light the way down the stairs and through a set of double, hinged doors at the bottom into a huge kitchen at the rear of the mansion.

Spiders skittered across the floor as they entered. Scrungle shone the light up to the high windows—too high for escape, he thought. The kitchen had been white-tiled, but most were cracked or missing. It made Scrungle wonder what it would be like to have teeth.

It was as dusty in here as everywhere else, with black and green mould on the ceiling. Fungi grew in the corners of the kitchen, but for once, Scrungle showed little interest in discovering their taste. At the far wall was a door that must have led out into the mansion's rear gardens. Scrungle put down the light, and they tried to open the door. Sealed tight, it didn't budge.

"We're stuck." Said Melody.

"I'm getting a bit worried mate. What happens if we can't get out." Snickers said scratching at the back door.

Scrungle looked around the kitchen, bench tops covered in dust, and sinks rotten with gunk. Unused utensils and pots hung from rusted hooks. Staring at the hanging pots and pans, something started to tug at his mind, like the image of a bear wearing a thong.

"Scrungle, does the witches' writing have anything on it that might help?" Said Peetles.

Scrungle's magic pockets manifested themselves, and he pulled the map and the notes that Doris had written out. With the lantern next to him, he looked at the rhyme the witch had given them.

"In the kitchen, put a pan on your head." He mumbled softly to himself.

"Did you say something?" An agitated. spikey Peetles was digging into Scrungles head. Scrungle lifted Peetles and put his friend down so they could stand on the counter-top.

He then laid the writing out for Peetles to read.

"Look." Scrungle pointed to the rhyme.

**In the kitchen put a pan on your head.**
**Turn to the corridor stand on what's red.**
**You will need the love that was left behind.**
**To chase the coats and hats you find.**
**The clock will strike one. Up the stairs you must run.**
**Catch the moon and then you'll be done.**

Scrungle and Peetles read it over a few times, exchanging glances.

The wolves were circling the kitchen growling when the sound of the Cheese man was heard.

"We have to try." Said a frantic Peetles.

Scrungle walked over to the large hob, where a selection of pans covered in years of dust hung from hooks. Picking up the largest copper pot, Scrungle put it on his big white head. The moment it was sitting snugly, the door they had been trying moments before, with a squeal of its hinges, cracked open a little.

"What are you doing, Scrungle?" Barked Snickers.

After a quick explanation, they tried the door again, but even with all of their combined weight, it wouldn't budge. Scrungle took the pan off his head, deflated that it hadn't worked, and the door closed tight once more.

Scrungle then put the pan on his head, and the door opened a little as before. Off and on, he put the pan on his head, and the door followed suit, opening and closing but not getting any wider. Peetles, watching all this from the bench-top, started an excited hopping bounce.

"Scrungle, I think I might have an idea,"

Scrungle was at a loss as Peetles wasn't that strong on ideas, thoughts, and original thinking as a whole.

"I need a pan."

Scrungle unhooked the smallest of pans and slid it over Peetle's head after a little bit of pushing, as the little creature was still spiky and bobbly in fear. Once again, the door opened a fraction, then Scrungle donned his pan, and it opened wider still. The moan of the Cheeseman drifted into the abandoned kitchen louder now.

Scrungle lifted the rest of the pans down and put them one by one on all the wolves' heads. The door opened wide enough so even Scrungle could get through.

" I think the witch Waynex left us some rather vague and cryptic instructions." Said a much-relieved Scrungle, picking up Peetles, the lantern, and Doris's notes..

A louder moan echoed down the corridor from behind the closed doors of the kitchen. They huddled around the door at the back of the kitchen. Metal clanged now and again as the pan handles clashed with one another when one of the wolves forgot they were wearing them. Al stuck his head into the corridor beyond.

"Dark in there," he said pulling his snout back out. "It's odd though; it should lead straight to the outside. Why is it so dark?"

"I'm coming to get you." The horrible gurgling sound of the Cheeseman filled the room. Snickers not waiting; took a step into the corridor, moving in one fluid motion, under the impression that if he moved fast enough, things would be fine. No more than two steps into the corridor, a flame whooshed down from the ceiling. Yelping, the wolf jumped back into the kitchen, the pan on his head clanging against the door. The fur on his back was singed and smoking.

"Who puts a flame thrower in the ceiling? That's a health and safety issue if ever there was one," Snickers snarled at the empty corridor.

"I like fireworks." Said Wonky, one eye on Snickers the other eye looking at a rack with dirty plates on it. Snickers just stared, yet again at a loss as to what was happening inside his friend's head. Scrungle held out the carriage lantern, illuminating the room beyond.

It was a long corridor with faded leopard-print wallpaper. How anyone thought leopard print looked good on anything other than the leopard was beyond him. There was no time to lose as the sound of banging doors outside the kitchen startled them all.

The Cheeseman was getting closer to his prey. The carpeted floor was patterned in squares, yellows, blues, blacks, and reds. Scrungle handed the instructions to Peetles.

"Stand on what's red. Do you think it means the carpet?" Said Peetles.

The first square that Scrungle could see that was red was a good step into the room.

"I do hope it means that." Scrungle then took the step into the corridor.

As his stilt-like legs touched the red-tiled carpet, a jet of fire came down from the ceiling. Scrungle was saved from being burned badly by the pan on his head. He stumbled nimbly back into the room. Smelling of toast, horse chestnuts, and charged ozone particles.

"Hmm, that didn't go as well as I hoped."

"Bloody stupid this." Said Melody.

There was a loud moan, the Cheeseman was getting closer.

"Stand on what's read." Said Wonky then yawned.

"Don't worry mate everything is going to be fine." Said Al thinking Wonky needed comforting. Scrungle looked at Wonky and something tickled round the edges of his thoughts.

"Stand on what's red," mumbled Scrungle to himself.

Repeating the phrase over and over, Scrungle laid the map out on the floor of the toasting corridor. The little group stood watching, wondering what the tall white creature was up to. He then stepped onto it. Nothing happened. Scrungle came back out and neatly split the map into two.

The Cheeseman was getting louder; he would be in the kitchen any time now. Using the map pieces as slippers, Scrungle put Peetles on his head and told the wolves to climb onto him as best they could. Snickers on his stick-thin arms, Melody and Al clamped to his legs, and Wonky clung to his rounded shoulders. It looked as though he had gone all out to accessorise in furs without the necessary culling and skinning first.

He slowly shuffled across the floor on the map pieces, the pans clanging together as the wolves slipped and clambered for purchase. It was a cumbersome balancing act as Scrungle was also holding the lantern, but they successfully made it to the opposite door. Turning the handle, it swung open, and the wolves immediately jumped down into the next room.

The doorway was too small for Scrungle and Peetles to get through together, so he put Peetles down, who picked up the two map pieces for Scrungle as he entered. The moment they were clear of the door, it slammed shut, cutting off the sound of the Cheeseman.

Bunched together in the corner, they surveyed the room. Furnished with a long settee, a writing table, three cushioned seats, and a Welsh dresser. It was full of clothes, strewn across every available surface. Shoes, socks, ties, pants, dresses, shirts, and a varied assortment of hats. At the far end of the room, there was another door. Snickers, yet again, took the lead, heading for the exit at the far end.

A woollen jacket the wolf stood on immediately wrapped itself around him, buttoning itself up. Snickers panicked and started attacking the jacket, trying to tear it off. In doing so, he stood on a pair of socks and then a pair of braces. Within moments, he was casually dressed for a lunch meeting with investors.

Melody and Al jumped into the fray, trying hard to rip the clothes off their pack leader. In doing so, every time they stood on a garment, it would wrap around them. In no time, the wolves were extremely overdressed for a possessed mansion. It didn't stop, and the cursed clothes kept adding themselves on top of each other, heavier and heavier until the legs of the wolves buckled under the weight of so many garments. All three were now on the floor, panting. Hats of different styles were jumping up and balancing on top of the pans.

"Help us Scrungle." Moaned Al, barely able to lift his head.

Scrungle and Peetles, stood shocked, watching the madness unfold, then Scrungle bent down closer to Peetles.

"What does the rhyme say Peetles."

"You will need the love that was left behind. To chase the coats and hats you find."

Scrungle swung the lantern light around, hoping for inspiration, as the verse made no sense. Although the wolves had stopped moving, other items of clothing were slowly making a rippling crawl towards them.

"We must do something. Scrungle they'll suffocate, be crushed... thrown in a landfill."

There was a frenetic sound to Peetle's voice making it sound even more squeaky.

The wolves started to howl and whimper. Wonky was off to one side near the door they had entered, sitting, chewing on his back foot. The wolf stopped for a moment.

"My mum used to say, coats on hooks and hats on stands, where's your dad, it's bin day tomorrow."

"That's as bad as what the witch wrote, doesn't rhyme or anything you silly doggy," Peetles said their little face scrunched up, annoyed at the stupid phrase. Scrungle, terrified for the wolves and not knowing what to do, latched onto what Wonky had just said. A daft rhyme at the wrong time.

A vision of his father came to him, whittling away at a hat stand. A hat stand that was a token of love for his wife and Scrungles mother. Suddenly he yelled,

"Fungi pie," as the answer came to him. Pulling the hatstand out of his magical pockets, he stood it on the floor. The minute he did this, the nearest items of clothing recoiled as if in fear.

"That worked, Scrungle. Use it like a wand; swing it around." Peetles shouted excited, bobbly, and scared. Scrungle with the lantern in one hand grabbed the base and waved it at Al, who was the closest. The clothes jumped off immediately. Al panting gained his feet snarling at a pair of brown trousers, Peetles stayed close, tugging at Wonky's ear so the batty wolf would follow. Scrungle waved the hat stand at Snickers and Melody. The items of clothing dispersed, crawling away from the hat stand as if it were a cup of lentil soup. The two wolves shook themselves down and moved close to Scrungle.

The door at the far end opened on its own, and they went through to find themselves back in the main hallway.

"Arr, shite." Barked Melody. Now back more or less where they started the little group looked at each other. A feeling of resignation that they would end up going around in circles forever went through everyone's mind.

The only comfort was they couldn't hear the moaning taunts of the Cheeseman. Then from nowhere came a chime of a clock.

"The clock will strike one. Up the stairs, you must run. Catch the moon and then you'll be done." Peetles said, looking at the instructions Doris had written out.

To everyone's bewilderment, two Farnys sprang out of a battered grandfather clock and ran up the right side of the stairs.

"Excellent I'm starving." Said Al, all thoughts of terror now gone as lunch had arrived. The wolves, including Wonky, chased the little Farnys, acting on their stomachs, completely forgetting the madness that had just happened. Up the left side of the stairs, they ran to cut them off at the top; the Farnys, seeing this, abruptly turned and ran back down. Snickers turned and ran to catch them at the bottom. Back and forth, they ran. The wolf pack followed Snickers at every turn of the Farny's, running up, then down.

"It makes me wonder, Peetles, how they ever caught one." Said Scrungle, watching.

"What does the writing mean by catch the moon, then you'll be done? What about the Cheeseman? It's still around." Said Peetles, hopping in fear.

"I am at a loss yet again, Peetles, as to what the witch meant by her instructions. Also, how dangerous this is? She didn't warn us, the unhinged old fart."

Peetles was shocked at what his tall friend had just said, but Scrungle's patience was wearing thin. He had naively thought he could just walk and find some of the Huba mushrooms under a tree, near a stream, or hidden in another jar. Why couldn't the Huba mushroom be stocked by the SCS? He would have even signed up for an Amazing Shine membership, for that matter. No, he had to travel the width and breadth of the country dealing with monsters, Farnys, and enchanted clothes.

Snickers was urging his pack to move faster, but for all intents and purposes, they were beginning to slow. The Farny's, on the other hand, showed no signs of tiring. It had also slipped everyone's mind that maybe now they could take the pans off their heads. As the two Farnys ran up the stairs side by side, Scrungle noticed something.

"Peetles what do the Farnys look like when they run together."

Peetles giggled.

"They look like a bum."

"And what's another name for a bum." Said Scrungle.

"An arse." Peetles giggled.

Scrungle took a moment.

"True but also a bum is sometimes called a moon."

"How do you know that?" Peetles was genuinely curious.

"It was in a book I read."

Peetles blinked a Peetles blink, and Scrungle left it at that.

"Follow me Peetles."

Putting the lantern down on a side table shaped like a half-moon, they walked to the bottom of the staircase, where the Farnys were running. The wolves had just run up the other side, although slowly, as the vigour with which they had started was now gone.

The Farnys had turned and were running down towards Scrungle. The moment they realised that Scrungle and Peetles were at the bottom, they turned and ran back the other way. Snickers was at the top of their stairs now. The Farnys panicked and turned to go back down. After a little way down, they realised that it was blocked, turned, and ran up. Snickers had taken a step down and growled, which would have been menacing if he wasn't wearing a pan on his head.

Now trapped, the Farnys became more and more frantic, spinning from one way to the other. Scrungle with Peetles took a step onto the staircase, while Snickers, Melody, and Al took another step down. Wonky had lost interest and was chewing on the baluster of the bannister. Now the Farnys started to fuse into the lovely arse shape of a well-toned cyclist or celebrity bum double.

"Look Scrungle they make a lovely bottom." Said Peetles.

The Farnys were no longer saying 'Farny, Farny' either. It had turned into a loud-pitched squeal, vibrating and spinning faster as they slowly began to rise off the stairs. Fusing as one, they were lifted above Scrungle. It would be later that Scrungle would think of a pale moon rising. The pitch of the squeal went higher and higher as the vibrating, spinning Farnys went faster and faster, becoming a perfect sphere. The wolves watched in fascination and then howled as the pitch went beyond normal hearing.

It didn't last long before the frequency jumped again and went above all hearing. The spinning moon of the Farny coupling hung in the air, glowing from within, radiating light. Then a loud bong of the gong as the clock struck one, and the Farny Moon infusion exploded.

The sound was more of a plop than a detonation, and the fused matter splattered everywhere. The wolves, not wasting any time, were moving around, licking the staircase, bannisters, and walls of what moments ago had been Farnys. It was later that they told Scrungle that it tasted like warm custard. Something still hovered above Scrungle's head, defying the laws of gravity, and then fell into his outstretched hands. It was either the moon-dial or an ornate paperweight.

The circular disc was approximately two inches deep. On closer inspection, it was made from several concentric rings layered one after the other. Each ring was made from grey and white marble, but the outermost one was jet black. Numbers and lines were engraved everywhere on the surface of the thing except for the black ring which was blank. A triangle-shaped dial known as the gnomon sat in the centre on its side. Scrungle had no idea how it worked.

"What the bloody hell's this? Have you just exploded two of my Farny's"

Scrungle, Peetles, and the wolves jumped at the loud, booming voice? The Cheeseman was in the corridor, slowly moving its yellow mass towards them. The strange embossed plaque above the locked door that they had seen when they first entered started to glow. The Cheeseman had grown in size, and the smell hadn't improved either. The wolves descended the stairs to line up with Scrungle and Peetles growling at the monster. Scrungle, frightened beyond anything he had ever known, felt a stronger sense of love for the wolves and Peetles standing with him, defiant against the cursed mansion and its host. It was the reason he found the courage to do what he did next. He took the pan off his head, hung it on the newel post of the staircase, and took a step forward.

"I was sent by the witch Waynex. I have the moon-dial." Scrungle held out his hands showing the Cheeseman the device.

"And." Said the Cheeseman.

"Aren't you the Cheeseman?" Peetles asked their voice small.

The yellow rippling monster rippled an irritated ripple. The voice that replied loud and menacing.

"No, I'm covered in cheese as a lifestyle choice. Next daft question."

Terrified, the little group huddled closer. No one said anything; it stretched out into an awkward pause. Unable to bear it any longer, Scrungle took an imaginary breath.

"Can you answer some questions so I can use the moon-dial." The Cheeseman took a rippling step forward.

"Only when you have answered my question first. If you do not my house or I will kill you."

The Cheeseman produced a cheese knife the size of a sword from the mass it was made from. The other hand pulled out a shield made from a huge sesame seed bun. Then the house itself pushed in on the little group, becoming darker as the walls closed in.

"The witch said nothing about answering a question." Scrungle had put down the moon-dial and was frantically searching the map and Doris's notes for help.

"Then you will die." laughed the Cheeseman and took another step.

"What's the question?" Peetles squeaked.

The yellow mass of cheese stopped and raised the cheese knife using it to point to the plaque.

"I need to know what does it say above the room you cannot enter?" The plaque pulsed with a pale light. Time stood still then Peetles said in a whisper.

"Wendy from Wendol meet me by the well where we first met at midnight." Said Peetles.

The plaque stopped pulsing, shone brightly once, and then went out. The doors below opened up to reveal a banqueting hall. Beyond them, they could see that the room was full of ornate and beautifully designed signposts. Scrungle was sure that they must have been the original directions that the daft signs replaced.

"What." The Cheeseman's voice had changed drastically to the point where it sounded almost human. Dropping the cheese knife and shield, it ripply ran at Peetles, lifting the little creature off the ground. The wolves snarled and then dived into the Cheeseman as Scrungle retrieved the pan and swung it at the yellow mass as best he could.

Peetles, spikey and bobbly, squealed in the Cheeseman's hands. Soft, yellow over processed cheese ran down the sides of the little creature. The Cheeseman was oblivious to the bites of the wolves or the assault from Scrungle.

"How do you know what it says? Are you making it up?" Shaking Peetles for answers.

"It's the same as the one at the windmill, It was on a well in the garden as a reminder. The little girl said her grandad put it there for the grandmother. She couldn't see very well so it was bumpy, Windy the miller's wife made lovely cheese. Said her mum had taught her. They built the windmill for her and the family to live at."

The Cheeseman dropped Peetles, who landed on the dusty floor with a thump, rolling over. Scrungle helped his friend up, making sure he wasn't hurt. The wolves backed away from the Cheeseman after it let Peetles go. Spitting and coughing trying to rid themselves of the lettuce and tomato they had swallowed from the attack. The whole house shuddered as if getting ready for a sneeze.

The yellow mass had stopped rippling, now shedding cheese in big lumps, revealing a figure underneath. A very old man stood in front of the group. His once-fine clothes were stained and torn, but so old they were back in fashion. He fell to his knees and looked up at Scrungle.

"I took the sign down; they were sending messages to each other; he had left it for her. I thought my little Wendy had killed herself."

"You thought, Wendy missed Wendol and fell down the well." Scrungle, unable to contain himself, enjoying the couplet. Tears ran down the old man's face.

"I couldn't find her; I just wanted her to be safe. He was going to take her away."

Scrungle suddenly felt sad for the old man, who had until recently been covered in ultra-processed dairy.

"She lived. They made a new life. You have grandchildren now." Scrungle took a step forward to help the old man up.

"I cursed myself as punishment. I've wasted my life." Said the ex-Cheese man, who then fell forward, dying of extreme old age and hardening of the arteries. Wonky walked forward, sniffed at a bit of the cheese that pooled next to the old man, and took a bite.

"Wonky man," said Snickers, moving forward to stop the inappropriate behaviour.

The house gave one more shudder, and the front door swung open.

## Twenty-Two

# *Lets Howl at the Moon*

They all stood, looking down at the old man, and then as if in respect, the pans dropped from the wolves and Peetle's heads to clatter loudly on the dusty wooden floor. Now that the front doors stood wide open, a refreshing blast of cool air flowed in, bringing with it the light of the new dawn.

"How are you, Peetles? Well done for saving the day." Scrungle, with Peetles in his stick-thin arms, was looking the little creature over. Peetles smiled and then blinked.

"I'm fine; just feel sorry for the Cheeseman."

Scrungle, wanting to get out of the mansion, put Peetles down, picked the moon-dial up, and put it safely in his magically appearing pocket. There was a moment when he thought of keeping the pan, but it felt like stealing, so he stopped himself. Peetles hopped over and picked up the map pieces and Doris's notes that had been dropped when the Cheeseman had attacked.

"Scrungle, is this the cheese the witch asked for?" Peetles pointed to the yellow globes surrounding the body.

"Oh dear, I had forgotten all about her list. It feels in such bad taste, but I think it would be the kind of thing the batty witch would want."

"It tasted rather nice, to be fair," said Al.

"I'd agree but not the lettuce and tomato," Said Melody.

There was a bit of a discussion between them about the niceties of scooping up discharged cheese from a dead body, but Scrungle eventually put some of it in a glass jar, sealing the lid tight and then into his pocket for safekeeping.

"What should we do with Windy's granddad?" Peetles asked, looking at the shrivelled old man on the floor. The body was shrinking as the cool air reached it.

"There's not much meat on him, but we could have a go at." Snickers said, sniffing around the body.

"No!" Scrungle said, cutting in to stop the wolf from finishing the sentence.

"What about chucking him down the well? You know to be with his daughter," said Al.

"She didn't fall down the well. That was why the curse was lifted." Replied Scrungle at a loss.

"Yeah, Oh, must have missed that bit. Where's she now?" Said Al.

"She died," Peetles answered.

"Down the well?" Melody Asked.

The talk concerning who or what was down the well, what to do with a dead body, and what everyone thought about eating pilchards directly from the tin went on for some time. Eventually, it was decided, and Scrungle, with the help of the wolves, dragged the old man by his feet up to the grand bedroom, where they laid him down on the old four-poster bed as if he were asleep with bite marks on his ankles.

* * *

Relieved to be outside and away from the claustrophobic madness of the mansion, Scrungle extinguished the carriage lantern, attaching it to the tricycle. The sun was climbing above the horizon as the wolves padded along next to Scrungle and Peetles. Nothing was said as everyone headed down the path in the thinning mist and through the rusted gates, wanting nothing more than to be off the grounds, putting as much distance between themselves and the insane building as possible.

They had lost any sense of time; it felt as though they had spent days in the possessed abode of the Cheeseman, A similar feeling to waiting for the local council to respond.

Little by little, the mist was evaporating, tracks and paved roads spreading out like veins. It was Snickers, scouting ahead, who found a little hollow. Scrungle was happy about this, as the most recent episode had tremendously strained his sensibilities. Incredibly tired, all he wanted to do now was sleep. With the Cheeseman gone, he had no idea how to use the moon-dial. So far, his experience in the Hills of Badly Designed Signs had been too much, and he wanted to go home more than ever.

With Peetle's help, they set up the tricycle canopy and a fire in the surround. Sitting together in the dinghy, next to the tricycle, the friends snuggled together under the strawberry-patterned duvet. The wolves settled themselves, lying next to the fire. Past events caught up with them all, and one by one, they dropped off to sleep as the new day began.

Scrungle woke to find the wolves had left and the day was almost done. Peetles was still asleep, so he got up, stretched, and watched the evening sky that all in the Hills of Badly Designed Signs could now see. It was as if the land was waking from a long sleep. Pockets of mist clung to low-lying areas; trees and grass withered, but there was potential there, under the surface, buried in the roots, waiting to start again. Taking out the moon-dial, Scrungle studied it, trying different combinations of turns to the rings on the mechanism. Nothing happened; it just lay inert. He wasn't surprised as the different combinations were astronomical. Scrungle's tinkering was interrupted by Peetles.

"I didn't mean for him to die."

Peetles had woken up with one thought and had gone bobbly and lumpy realising Scrungle had no way of using the moon-dial. The questions that the witch had given them would stay forever unanswered. Peetles started tearing up saying they were sorry over and over. Scrungle put the device back in his pocket and sat next to his little companion, putting a stick-like arm around them.

"My dear Peetles, without you, we would never have left the cursed mansion. Without you, we would all be in a very sticky situation. How could you have known, my dear Peetles? I would imagine people must shed cheese and collapse all the time around here." Scrungle said, trying to ease Peetles feelings.

"How will you get the answers to the questions now?"

"Well, as my father used to say at times like this, if it looks like an orange and smells like an orange, then it probably fell out of the fruit bowl, and if I would be a good bungus and pick it up and put it back," nodded Scrungle, deep in thought.

"I don't understand." Said Peetles blinking.

"Yes, I never understood it either."

Scrungle handed Peetles his lemon-coloured water bottle as he ate mushrooms, and they watched the evening fade to night. It was in the darkness that the wolves came wandering back into the camp, reporting that the surrounding area was safe. Although Snickers and Al were a bit unsettled as they had picked up a strange scent and followed it for a while before losing it at a row of stepping stones crossing a stream.

Scrungle asked what it smelt like, and they both agreed it was rather pleasant reminding them both of Midnight Fantasy by Brittony Spears.

"Whatever it was, it isn't around now." Said Melody.

Scrungle took out the bioluminescent lights, putting them on sticks; Peetles added logs to the fire; and they all settled down to watch the crescent moon low in the sky. The wolves were still hungry, only having a lick of exploded custard Farny to eat, but Snickers was confident it would be so much easier to catch a Farny now that the mist had gone. All they had to do was wait for the morning. Scrungle's suspicion that the Farnys might have evaporated like the mist was left unsaid.

In the relative comfort of the tricycle canopy and the warm glow of the fire, it was decided the best thing for Scrungle and Peetles to do was to go back to Dangle's Inn. As it was a well-known stopping point for travellers, if Dangle couldn't help, he would surely know of a creature wise enough who could decipher the moon-dial.

The wolves had been happy in the Hills of Badly Designed Signs before the mist dispersed and had no intention of moving on now that it was gone. Knowing within a season the land would be back to where it should be, and although they were still waiting for signs that the Farny's still roamed the land, they were confident they were out there as easy as a ready meal.

In the morning, the wolves were confident about which way to go to find the King's Road and set off along the same rough dirt track from the previous night. After a mile, it led down to a long valley of grey flat grass. At the bottom, a small arching stone bridge spanned a slow-moving stream. Now that the cursed mist had lifted from what it had been hiding, the landscape was becoming pleasantly surprising. A clear sun showed that at some point in the past, it had been beautiful and full of life. Approaching the bridge, Scrungle pedalled around a badly designed sign that had fallen, half on the road, blocking the track.

His attention had wandered, thinking about trolls. cones and safety certificates Peetles read the fallen sign.

"Scrungle look." Slowing to a stop Scrungle looked at what the excited Peetles was pointing at. The black-finger posts could still be read.

**Apple and three pears. 3 miles** on one finger.

**Cherry pie to a golden brown 6 miles.** The finger had snapped off completely and lay in the grass. The last finger, sitting at an odd angle read:

**Bake a pie 33.3 miles.**

Badly spelled, and the writer had used backward 3 as 'e', and the 's' was a '5'. It looked more like a ransom demand, but what it stated could not be doubted. Scrungle pulled the instructions out of his pocket along with the moon-dial. He handed the paper over to Peetles, who read it out.

"I have an apple and three pears. How long will it take to bake a cherry pie to a golden brown at gas mark six? The answer must be to the exact second."

Scrungle looked at the device and deduced that the two innermost rings could be aligned in increments of points. Shaking with nerves, he turned the first ring to 33 in line with the pointed end of the flattened gnomon. It was a wild guess, as he had no real idea what to do. Then turn the next ring to .3 in line with the end of the gnomon.

Scrungle nearly dropped the device when there was a low click as the tumblers fell into place. An unseen mechanism started inside the moon-dial, and the triangle gnomon raised itself from the surface, standing straight in the sun's light and casting a shadow across the marble top of the moon-dial.

"It works, Scrungle." Shouted an excited Peetles who wiggled in the basket, turning to his friend.

"Remember the stories about the hills. The Cheeseman was the owner of the mansion; he made the signs that got the sign writer arrested." Said Scrungle.

Chasing butterflies across the grass, the wolves came running back over the bridge. Barking what was the matter? Scrungle relayed what had happened, explaining that the signs dotted around the Hills of Badly Designed Signs may have the rest of the answers to how to use the moon-dial. Before Scrungle could say anything more, they sprinted off in four different directions, excited to help.

"Should we follow them?" Said Peetles.

Scrungle stroked his long nose.

"Let us wait a moment as I think they will be back." Putting the tricycle into park, the two friends dismounted and stood on the bridge, watching the water flow underneath them. Peetles heard a bird sing, then they watched a flock of swifts pass by, it was a good omen.

Wonky came back first with what looked to be the remnants of a garden chair. He dropped it at Scrungles feet and asked for capers. Al was next, then Snickers and Melody together.

"I was over the next hill, then I remembered I can't read." Said Al.

"I think we need a little plan." Said Scrungle.

He then tried to explain what they had to look for next. After a brief but illuminating tutorial on the basics of language, symbol imagery in letter formation, and its connection to sound, it was decided to abandon any idea of the wolves learning to read.

Melody suggested they search in two's, and Scrungle and Peetles would stay by the bridge. When a pair found a sign, one would stay next to it and howl, while the other would come and round everyone up, and then Scrungle or Peetles could read it. They would then start again from this new position. To everyone's astonishment, it worked extremely well.

The land had suffered under the curse that had covered it for so many years. Now that it was gone, they would come across empty farms, holdfasts, and small stone keeps. At one point, they passed through a whole village that had been abandoned. It wasn't the only thing they saw, but Snickers would take special care to avoid what was left of the lost travellers.

By the end of the day, Scrungle and Peetles had pedalled to four different signs. They were out of luck, but at the fifth, it read: **Hot Cheese: 42 miles.**

Excited Scrungle turned the next ring on the moon-dial to 42, in line with gnomon. It clicked, and they stood watching as the last ring, which had been blank, glowed with numbers from 1 to 24. Scrungle's fingers shook a little as he turned it to 9, in line with the other numbers and the point of the gnomon. The moon-dial glowed blue for a moment, then stopped doing anything at all.

"Oh." Said Scrungle.

The anti-climax had everyone looking around at each other, wondering if anything more would happen. Scrungle, holding the moon-dial, looked around at his companions.

"I think we will have to try this again tonight. It is after all a dial for the moonlight." Peetles was so much happier; the feeling of letting Scrungle down had lifted.

Snickers took them on a shortcut through the fields. The tricycle did remarkably well on the soggy terrain. The wide, chunky tires stopped them from sinking into the wet earth. The pack leader was leading them all towards the King's Road.

To the wolves' delight and their bellies, they saw a bugger of Farnys off in the distance. Giving chase, they left Scrungle and Peetles, who in turn decided that hunting for food was a great idea; spending the rest of the evening filling up on fungus for Scrungle and water for Peetles. Scrungle replenished the basket that Mrs Morris had given them with as many fungi as he could find.

Chasing the Farnys the wolves found an open circular folly with tall, thick posts of marble and a stone slab table in the centre. It had been built to memorialise Barry Gland, the only person who had ever died from being offended after he heard a woman express an opinion. Melody led the way and Scrungle and Peetles set up camp for one last night in the Hills of Badly Designed Signs.

Scrungle was a nervous wreck, waiting for the night to come and the moon to appear. Walking back and forth, constantly fidgeting with the moon-dial that he'd laid on the slab stone table. The anxiety started to rub off on Peetles and the wolves.

To his dismay, as the darkness came, so did the cloud cover. The wolves, already tense, felt the pull of the moon as a soft spot of haze behind the clouds.

After rearranging the moon-dial for the umpteenth time, Scrungle sat with Peetles and waited. In the darkness, the minutes moved intolerably slowly. Scrungle felt like he would burst with the wait, but just before he stood once more to go and rearrange the device, the clouds parted.

The moonlight, full and bright, shone down and illuminated the little folly. Washing its cool silver light over the moon-dial. Everyone held their collective breath.

The surface of the device glowed, and the gnomon slowly at first, but picking up momentum, began to spin manically in different directions, flipping one way then the next until it orientated itself and pointed to the northeast. A clear beam of blue light as thin as a pencil shone from the top of the gnomon, showing the way.

Then Peetles asked. "How will we know which way to go when the moon isn't around,"

Scrungle walked in reverence over to the moon-dial and lifted it to the sky. Using his knowledge of the vast constellations he knew which stars to navigate with.

"I will know Peetles. I will know."

If Scrungle could have smiled he would be beaming from cheek to cheek. He picked Peetles up. The wolves no longer able to contain themselves began to howl at the moon.

"I think we should join in with our friends." Said Scrungle.

"I don't know how to howl." Peetles looked a bit bobbly.

Scrungle placed Peetles in the tricycle basket and blew the ahooga horn. Peetles, now understood, joined in and they all made a hell of an annoying sound in the middle of the night.

A bright sun shone the next day as the company made their way to the start of the King's Road. Passing the sign that read **swimming pool 1 mile** ahead, they could see the start of the large, heavy flagstones of the real King's Road.

It was a sad farewell. Peetles and the wolves had become fast friends. Scrungle was fond of all the wolves in equal measure. They both promised to come back and say hello once they had been to the island of the Huba mushroom.

With tears in their eyes, they donned their sheepskin hats and riding goggles, then slowly pedalled away. Turning one last time to wave to the wolves, now small little specks on the landscape. Scrungle and Peetles heard a long, sad howl, and then the pack disappeared into the awakening woods and were gone.

## Twenty-Three

# *Wanted Criminals*

Heading downhill, Scrungle put the tricycle in low gear and let gravity do the work. The yellow tricycle cut a smooth path, moving at an easy pace along the flagstone road. It all looked so different now, unrecognisable from the terrain they had encountered on their approach. The malediction that had spread out of the Hills of Badly Designed Signs had been like a sloppy cheeseburger that wouldn't stay in the bun.

Scrungle was happy to have played his part in lifting the curse, taking comfort that the world around him was beginning to heal. Trees had colour in their leaves, butterflies buttered, bees buzzed, and birds flew in circles across the meadows and low hills, trying to eat them both. In no hurry, wanting to find the travelling rhythm they had when the friends first met, the pair would stop if Scrungle saw a particular fun-looking fungus or if Peetles wanted to look at a pretty flower or some old ruins.

It was next to a lone oak tree that the pair came across an old well, reminiscent of the one in the garden of the Millers. Both of them wondered if it was the one Wendol had told Wendy to meet him at. Searching his magic pockets for pennies, Scrungle came up empty. But he did have spoons, so they took one each, threw them in, and made a wish.

It was a simple journey now, with the moon-dial pointing with a certain promise towards their destination: the island of the Huba mushroom. They travelled this way for the better part of the day, talking about the mansion, Windy and her connection to the Cheeseman, and how the Farnys exploded when trapped.

Up ahead, the road went through a natural split in the hill made long ago by a now dried-up river. Trees and raspberry bushes covered either side, reaching down to the very edge of the road. Only days had passed, but now fragmented and half-remembered, neither could remember this point; it had all looked so different.

Scrungle consulted the moon-dial, its direction still in line with the King's Road. Acutely aware that it was the only one of its kind, he put it back in his unfeasibly deep pockets and away from any prying eyes.

Pedalling onwards, Peetles asked if the white bits on top of mountains weren't coloured in because they were too high. Scrungle tried once again to explain to his little companion that it was snow. In the middle of the now-dry ravine, they were brought to an abrupt halt.

"Stop in the name of the Chancellor, Gumptrude." Shouted a voice. Rushing out of the woods on either side, a handful of hobgoblins similarly dressed to the ones in the capitol, all wearing MPGA hats and brandishing billy clubs, surrounded the pair.

The sheriff and leader of the group held a short sword in his chubby hand, which was in harmony with his tubby belly, chunky legs, and fat head. His attire wasn't the green and brown they had seen in Plombree. These garments were more in keeping with how the Chancellor and the other council dipsticks had dressed. On the breast of his tabard was the logo **'Sheriff. Gumptrude Security.'**

His hair was lank and greasy, hanging over his monobrow. A podgy, round face, covered in the remnants of bolognese sauce, was a warning not to skip a regular wash.

To finish the look, he had that white foamy stuff at the edges of his mouth, and a breath mint wouldn't have gone amiss.

"Stop in the name of Chancellor Gumptrude." Shouted the sheriff once more, then belched. He stood now directly in front of the tricycle.

"Aye, do as he says, or we'll knack ya." Said one of the hobgoblins, swinging the billy club around and managing to hit himself on the side of the temple.

Peetles, suddenly lumpy and anxious, tried to climb out of the basket as Scrungle brought the tricycle to a stop.

"Off," said the sheriff.

Scrungle, shocked, not comprehending what was happening, just sat and stared. The only thought that crossed his mind was that he had left something perishable in the fridge.

"Off the bike." Said the sheriff, brandishing the sword at Scrungle's long nose. Slowly getting off the tricycle, Scrungle picked Peetles up and was about to put his little friend on his head.

"None of that. Put it down." Said the sheriff, brandishing the sword as if he were cutting lettuce. Scrungle put Peetles on the road next to him, who then clung to Scrungle's tapered legs, terrified of the sheriff and hobgoblins. Scrungle shaking and mildly terrified, thought it best to say something.

"Hello," said Scrungle.

The sheriff said nothing and used his free hand to pull out a crumpled poster, looking at it, then at the pair. The wanted poster had the likeness of Scrungle and Peetles on it.

"It's them, alright. Put your hands up." Showing the hobgoblin closest to him.

The hobgoblins crowded in, swinging the billy clubs to intimidate the pair, but unintentionally hitting themselves. There were little yelps of pain, and 'Watch what you're deein ya tit.'

"What's happening, Scrungle?" Peetles was knobbly and spikey, hopping from one foot to the other. They both stood there, hands in the air.

"What's happening? I don't understand. What have we done?" The fear was evident in Scrungle's thoughts.

"Don't do anything rash; otherwise, you'll get this." Said the sheriff, now brandishing the sword as if he were fending off a block of cheese. "Right, lads, get them secured."

Two of the hobgoblins came forward and, after a bit of pushing and biting, to see who was going to climb on the other's shoulders to reach Scrungles arms. The winner then tied them together behind his back. Scrungle would have just dropped his arms if they had asked, but they didn't. At the same time, the goggles and riding hoods were pulled off the pair and thrown onto the road.

Leg manacles appeared, and another hobgoblin tried to attach them to Scrungle.

It was evident they were going to be impractical since he didn't have feet; they just kept slipping off. The hobgoblin, oblivious to the obvious, kept trying.

"Just leave them off, you idiot." Shouted the sheriff after watching them try and fail for the umpteenth time.

Peetles, who had started to cry at the loss of his hat and goggles, was being taunted by the other hobgoblins, who took great delight in upsetting the little creature.

Scrungle pushed forward to stop the bullies, but a rough woollen hood was thrust over his head. Before it covered his eyes, he could see Peetles had a similar hood thrown over them. It was so large for

Peetles, who was effectively trapped in a sack. An iron collar was now being attached between his head and non-existent neck. Scrungle felt intensely scared and vulnerable.

"Just stop this; we haven't done anything wrong." Said Scrungle. A low, menacing voice to the side of him said.

"You are wanted for acts of terrorism against Chancellor Gumptrude and the Baroness Bakeasy. For being part of a terror cell advocating terrorist activities in the Kingdom of Plomb."

Suddenly transported back to the episode of the escaped ball in a cup and the acrobatics of the chancellor and the woman who had landed with easy access when she fell.

"It was an accident. It was just an accident. We are sorry." Said Scrungle.

No one was listening, and all Scrungle could hear were the taunts directed at Peetles and the little creature crying. He could sense his friend's absolute terror. Pity subdued his fear, and tuning everyone else out, he talked directly to Peetles. Telling his friend that everything would be fine and that it was all just a mistake and not to say anything if the little creature could.

"What we ganna dee with this like." Scrungle heard one of the dim-witted hobgoblins ask.

"I will ride it. It's evidence," said the fat sheriff. He then got on the tricycle and settled into the seat. Scrungle heard the springs protesting. Then a crunching sound and moronic laughter by the hobgoblins. It wasn't hard to guess that the goggles had been smashed. A rope was attached to his collar, and then Scrungle was jerked forward by their captures toward Plombree City.

The pair had no idea how long they walked, but it went on for a long time. Peetles hood stretched over them; anyone looking would think they were pretending to be a ghost.

The little creature tripped several times, falling over onto the stone flags. The hobgoblins would laugh while they kicked Peetles until they were back on their feet.

Scrungle would shout for them to stop, but no one took any notice. He would then tell Peetles that everything was going to be alright, that it was all a mistake, and that the knights would probably come along and sort the whole thing out.

Peetles didn't reply; all he heard was a little hitching sob. Scrungle had never felt true anger in his long life, but by the end of the day, he was incensed and would very happily set every one of the hobgoblins on fire if he had the chance.

Sometimes the hobgoblins would hit either Scrungle or Peetles with the billy clubs just for fun. It hurt Scrungle, and he would have bruises later, but his body was soft, malleable, and absorbed a lot of the impact. He could hear the thuds when they hit Peetles, who cried out in pain.

A brief halt was called when the hobgoblins and the sheriff stopped to eat. It was a warm day, and they both could have done with water and mushrooms. Nothing was forthcoming from their captors, and Scrungle didn't want to tempt fate and a billy club to the head by asking. Peetles was so frightened that they couldn't talk at all, retreating into themselves emotionally and shutting down.

"There has been a huge mistake." Said Scrungle, hoping that the sheriff could hear him.

"No, there hasn't. I mean, you're pretty hard to mistake. You and this little thing are terrorists and illegal immigrants. Any more chat, you and the sympathiser here will get a proper good hiding. Shut it."

The sheriff was close as Scrungle could smell his bad breath. He fell silent and hoped that maybe Malcolm might see them. Then he heard one of the hobgoblins kick Peetles and laugh when Peetles started to cry.

"Leave Peetles alone you horrible bully." Shouted Scrungle.

"Or what you ganna dee like," said the hobgoblin.

"Enough. They both need to be able to walk. I want to be over the river as soon as possible." Said the Sheriff.

A few moments later, Scrungle and Peetles were on the march. Between the Hills of Badly Designed Signs and the river crossing, two days passed. During the forced march the hobgoblins just kept up the constant bullying and kicking of Peetles. Scrungle tried on several occasions to stop the hobgoblins, and at one particular instance, he just wouldn't walk any further until they promised to stop.

The sheriff took Scrungle's hood off, producing a wicked-looking short knife and poking it into Peetles. Peetles screamed in pain. The sheriff assured Scrungle that if he didn't keep walking, his friend was going to get a lot more scars. Scrungle walked on.

He talked to Peetles, constantly worried about his small friend's emotional state. Telling his friend that he would show them how to play chess or recounting his favourite stories from all the books he had read, where he had found his reading chair, and how he had happened upon the mind projector. In doing so, Scrungle had never felt so homesick.

The hobgoblins kicked up a fuss at night when a watch was ordered on the pair, complaining to the sheriff that they should use a containment spell so they could have a drink. Greasy sheriff, as Scrungle had started to call him, said that with the cutbacks and new management, they only had one, and he was keeping it for later. The hobgoblins continued complaining until the greasy sheriff said they would be docked half their pay if they didn't shut up.

The river crossing was still abandoned, so Scrungle was forced to pull the rope for the ferry, as he had done on the way there. The only thing that happened was that it started to rain. Wet and dejected, they continued until night fell.

Listening to the talk between the hobgoblins, Scrungle overheard that someone was going to meet them further along on the road. Someone by all accounts, very important.

Down a short track leading off from the King's Road, an abandoned old crofter's house, was used for that night's camp. It was open to the elements as a large section of the roof was gone. Most of the hobgoblins went inside to find a little bit of shelter from the rain and set a fire in the old grate, settling themselves down to start drinking beer.

The captured duo were taken around the back which was penned in by a dry stone wall.

Their hoods were taken off, and Scrungle could see a hobgoblin holding a burning torch that spit when it caught a raindrop. The sheriff was handed a package. On the side was written, delivered by Amazing Shine. The sheriff unzipped the anti-tamper ribbon, taking out the contents: a leather pouch and parchment. Reading the instructions, the greasy little man mouthed the words as his slow mind worked. He nodded to himself and gave a little smile when he understood a tricky word, like 'open', 'spread', or 'chant'.

Picking up a short stick, the sheriff drew a circle in the dirt, leaving a gap to push Scrungle and Peetles into. The he put the hoods back on his prisoners before he closed the circle. Chanting while emptying the pouch of dust into the little grove he had made.

When the circle was complete without a break, the sheriff took the torch off the hobgoblin and set it to the powder. The rain-soaked ground did not affect the powder, which caught fire immediately and burned with an even red flame.

"If you haven't seen one," the sheriff was panting through his words, wiping rain and sweat from his face. He looked at the two-hooded prisoners.

"Well, you're not going to see this one either." The sheriff took a moment to calm his heart rate. "It's a ring of containment, and it's not one of those cheap ones either." He said, still panting.

"This is wrong; we are innocent." Scrungle trying one last time to get the sheriff to listen.

"I don't care. So get comfortable because you're going with the high sheriff and dignitary Dinjay Flat. Well, when they get here, Don't touch the flame; it can't be doused by water, and it can't be broken from the inside either."

Now sounding exceedingly tired, as the spell had taken a lot out of him. The sheriff headed into the unused croft to dry and lie down. The hobgoblin, who had been picking his nose throughout the proceedings, followed in after him.

Scrungle listened for a while to make sure the sheriff had left, then tentatively shuffled around a little, feeling with the stumps of his legs until he bumped into Peetles. The little creature jumped at the touch. Scrungle could feel the spikey, bobbly skin of his friend against his leg. He knelt as far as possible, so he was closer to Peetles.

"How are you, Peetles? Can you get out of your hood?" Said Scrungle who was keeping his voice low and concentrated on Peetles. Peetles shuffled around a little but stayed silent.

"You can talk Peetles they have gone inside out of the rain. I do believe we need to escape and very soon."

Scrungle was concerned about Peetles and what was to come of the pair if they didn't get away from the sheriff and the hobgoblins.

"I'm out." Said Peetles in a voice so low that Scrungle nearly missed it.

"Can you pull my hood off?" Scrungle bent down low, then he felt the hood to the side of his head being tugged and the sound of Peetles huffing and puffing, then a tearing sound, and the hood was off.

Scrungle felt warm air on his face. Looking down, he could see Peetles in the dim light thrown by the circle of fire and the curtain less windows of the crofter's house. Peetle's little body was covered in bruises. Their left eye was swollen shut, which looked worse with the bumpy lumps that would manifest when the little creature became agitated. His heart melted for his little friend as both of them stood, soaked through from the rain.

"Oh, my dear, dear Peetles, look how they have hurt you."

Limping a little, Peetles waddled over to his friend.

"I'm scared. Scrungle, how are we going to escape?"

"Hmm, if I could reach my pockets and empty them, maybe there will be something that may help."

Scrungle couldn't remember what he had packed; it had been an odd assortment, but he felt sick to his stomach at the thought of spending any more time as prisoners. It was the only thing he could think of as a plan; any plan was better than no plan.

Peetles sniffled a little but didn't cry. Scrungle felt a certain relief, hearing his little friend upset wounded him deeply. Shouts and sounds of laughter from the crofters ruined house-made Peetles shrink into Scrungle.

"If they see us without the hoods, they will hurt us," Peetles said in a whisper.

Then the sound of something smashing followed by laughter came from the open windows. The smell of stale beer drifted out to them.

Looking over Scrungle heard a door bang loudly, and shadows flickered in the light. The sheriff started shouting that the next one of the hobgoblins to make a sound would be thrown into the dungeon. Both Scrungle and Peetles recoiled when they heard the sheriff command the hobgoblins to set a watch. Then the door banged again, and Scrungle assumed it was the sheriff going back to sleep.

Peetles, fearing the worst clung to Scrungle for dear life. Half murmurs could be heard, and a few raised voices said,

'Am not ganin outside it's your turn, man." and 'It's pissin doon.'

The bickering went on for a little while before subsiding into murmurs. Not long after, snoring and the occasional night fart.

The rain didn't let up, leaving them feeling thoroughly miserable. Scrungle would never have believed he could feel this tired, scared, and hungry. All because he had wanted to replace some magic mushrooms so he could get in and out of his tree house. For reasons that beg belief, he was now a wanted terrorist.

He was about to ask Peetles if they could try and undo the rope securing his hands when something in the shadows at the side of the crofter's house shifted. A cloaked figure moved closer to the circle of red flame that held the captives.

The stranger was wearing fine leather boots heavy with mud, leather trousers, and a canvas shirt that looked travel-stained but expensive. Hanging from the hooded figure's belt was a sword. The hilt caught the light as they walked. Scrungle noticed the crest stitched on the cloak was the same as the royal crest they had seen on the banners flying from the castle walls. Scrungle couldn't be sure, but his nose picked up the sweet scent of Midnight Fantasy by Brittony Spears and he understood he had met this person before at the Gumptrude rally. She had been shouting that Gumptrude was a turd.

"No questions; I'm here to help." Whispered the hooded figure, the bottom half of their face hidden by a scarf.

"Who are you?" Said Scrungle, tuning his telepathy to the unknown figure. The figure put a finger to their hidden lips to shush him. The pair stood silent as the stranger moved around the circle of fire, looking for a weak spot.

"Have you tried getting out?"

"They said we couldn't," replied Scrungle.

The stranger inclined their head with their hands on their hips at the same time. Scrungle understood immediately that the stranger was a tad peeved they hadn't tried. With his hands still tied behind him, he shuffled forward towards the ring of fire. With each step, the enchanted flame leaped up higher and, at the same time, started to get hot. Only inches away, the heat was intense shrivelling Scrungles skin.

As close as he could get, he tried flicking some dirt over the flame, but the dirt bounced back, repelled by an unseen barrier.

"I don't think I can. It's too hot." Said Scrungle and stepped back. As he did so, the enchanted flame fell back to where it had been.

"I'm going to try something." Then the hooded figure walked up to the ring of fire, but the flame stayed low and constant. Drawing the long sword from the scabbard, the stranger pushed some of the wet dirt onto the circle of flame. It sputtered out, leaving a small opening.

"Well, that's a bit crap. Who thought of this? You'd think it would need a magic word or something." Within moments, the stranger had put the enchantment out with absolutely no problem. All the while keeping half an eye on the crofter's hut. Scrungle told Peetles to keep close as they shuffled slowly forward out of the circle. Peetles shook in fear and cold as their saviour cut their bonds.

Trying to get a closer look, all Scrungle could see were clear blue eyes, eyeliner, sensual eye shadow, and perfect lashes.

"Who are you?" Said Scrungle, although he had an idea who the mysterious figure was.

"No time to explain; we have to go."

The hooded figure turned and hurried around the side of the building towards the King's Road. The pair followed, then stopped when they saw the tricycle in the moonlight tied up against the gate.

"We can't go; they have the tricycle." Said Peetles.

The hooded figure was nearly on the road.

"We'll just be a moment." Said Scrungle. Not waiting for an answer and putting Peetles safely on his head, he walked with the utmost caution to retrieve the tricycle. A hand gripped his stick-thin arms.

"What are you doing? We really have to go." trying to drag Scrungle up towards the road.

"It was a gift from a dear friend." Said Scrungle.

"Yes, and we can go really fast on it. It's yellow." Added Peetles.

The hooded figure let out a breath as their eyes searched the night. After a moment, nodded, then followed Scrungle. The yellow marvel of the tricycle didn't look any worse for wear. Mounting it slowly so as not to make a sound, Scrungle placed Peetles into the basket, which took a long time since Peetles was still bumpy and nervous. Releasing the parking brake, Scrungle pedalled forward with the utmost care toward the King's Road.

Just when they thought that they were free and clear, the door opened up behind them, and a hobgoblin stumbled out, unbuttoning his denim pants. Swaying slightly and humming, he braced a hand against the wall while the other held his shrivelled member. Looking over his shoulder, he registered that something was wrong but not why it was wrong.

Understanding the alarm would be raised at any moment, the hooded figure drew their sword. Before the hobgoblin could register what was happening, the hooded figure plunged the weapon into the throat of the urinating creature.

The only sound in the night was the gargling and choking of the hobgoblin as it suffocated on its blood, starving its tiny brain of oxygen. Scrungle and Peetles watched in horror as its hands clawed at its neck and the sword that was causing the trauma.

The blood, black in the moonlight, splattered across the stone of the house as the hooded figure pulled the blade back out with a twist to open the wound up, rendering it beyond repair.

Peetles squealed at the carnage as Scrungle cried out at the horrendous attack.

The hooded figure panting with excitement turned.

"It had to be done. Now we must run."

Scrungle pedalled onto the King's Road his thoughts not on the pursuit, their treatment at the hands of their captures, or the savage murder of the hobgoblin but on the rhyming sounds of run and done. Their saviour bent down and scooped up a one-wheeled contraption that they must have left by the side of the verge. In one deft movement, they mounted it and pedalled away at speed. Scrungle's mind stopped musing over the sound of run and done and now documented the fact the hobgoblin killer was fleeing on a one-wheeled wheely thing at speed. He knew he couldn't call it a bicycle, as a bicycle had two wheels. He then had a rerun of the blood splattering across the walls of the croft in his mind. Then countered this with the thought of a tricycle; their tricycle had three wheels, so it wasn't a tricycle. He now saw the sword twist once more in the neck of the hobgoblin, splitting sinew and arteries. Changing tack his thoughts landed on a one-cycle. He just kept mulling over what the single-wheeled contraption could be called because if he registered what had just happened, he would still be screaming. From behind them came the cries of the drunken hobgoblins and the sheriff. None of the fleeing three looked back.

## Twenty-Four

# *Monocycle or Unicycle?*

What was left of the moon's light was bright enough to see the King's Road. As far as Scrungle could remember, it was flat for the most part until Dangle's Inn. Since the sheriff and hobgoblins were on foot, he had no reason to think they would catch up to them anytime soon.

He kept calling for their sociopathic bloodthirsty saviour to stop and explain who they were and why they were helping, but the monocyclist just kept telling them to shut up, urging them forward.

The light of dawn began to wash the night away, and with it, the rain. After what felt like miles the figure dismounted as they came to a stop. Looking around they motioned for Scrungle and Peetles to follow them a little way off the road.

Dropping the scarf and pulling back the hood, Scrungle realised he had seen the likeness on the wanted posters plastered all over Plombree and everywhere else he and Peetles had travelled. His stomach did a little flip when he noticed the dried blood on the leather gloves she was wearing.

"OK, You'll probably know who I am." The Princess made a circular motion with her finger around her face.

"Princess Isobella." Scrungle managed to utter still in shock from what had happened.

"It's OK you don't need to bow."

Peetles was fidgeting in the basket and pointing down the road.

"Scrungle if we keep going we can get to Dangle and he will help us."

"We can't stay at the inn; it's too dangerous," said the Princess, cutting Peetles off. Scrungle went to interject, but the Princess held up a finger, dropping the smile and adding a head wobble, which stopped the large gentle fungivore in his tracks.

"I have been trying to catch up with you two for ages. Now we're going to go to the forest of Reachingout, I have a place we can hide and I will explain everything."

"We're not terror wrists." Said Scrungle.

"I know." Said the Princess as if it was obvious.

She then pulled the designer scarf back over her face and lifted the hood over her head.

"I know you could speed off as the unicycle isn't as fast as you but we need each other. Trust me, I don't think you will get far without me."

Cautious of being observed. The Princess took a look up and down the King's Road. Seeing nothing, she pushed off, and then after a moment, Scrungle and Peetles followed.

Scrungle was still none the wiser as to why he and Peetles were being helped, but he had gained a little bit of knowledge on the correct term for a one-wheeled bike.

Adrenaline-fuelled, they sped along the road for hours. At the crossroads, they flew past Dangle's Inn and turned, taking the harbour road.

After another fifteen minutes, the Princess pedalled off the stone road and onto a rough track. It cut a path through the meadow towards the apple orchards further on.

Following the path the carts and wagons had made laden with fruit, it stayed level, bordered by red poppies nodding as they pedalled passed. The trio did not stop, passing by the long stone wall that fenced in the rows of apple trees and then into the woodland beyond.

Scrungle had to stop when the track narrowed, blocked by a forest of spruce and pines.

He wanted to rest, but the Princess would not have any of it. She pulled a compass out of the inner pocket of her tunic, consulted it, then collapsed the unicycle down and slung it over her shoulder. Scrungle dismounted and Peetles climbed out of the basket.

"I think you'll have to leave the tricycle here. It's too far to carry it." Said the Princess.

"Oh, Scrungle has big pockets." Said Peetles. The Princess was about to reply when Scrungle's magic pockets manifested themselves, and he defied all the laws of physics by putting the tricycle into them.

"Wow," said the Princess, her eyes wide at the spectacle. "That is some powerful magic."

"Oh, is it?" Scrungle had no idea if it was or wasn't. The Princess smiled at this and started away from the rough dirt track. Scrungle with Peetles in front followed the Princess into the denser part of the woods. It was the first time since setting out from the Chana tree that Scrungle felt heavy. He had never carried so many items in his pockets before, and maybe there was a limit. He felt bloated in the way that you feel after a Christmas dinner. His thoughts tumbled over each other. There were questions, lots of questions, but the Princess was moving fast, and every time he tried to ask something, he would get a look from the Princess and a waggle of the finger. After a while, he started to call it the wag look and just elected not to bother her.

"How are you, Peetles?" Said Scrungle.

"I'm alright." Said his little friend.

But to Scrungle, Peetles didn't sound alright at all. Peetles was bruised and hurt, Scrungle was worried that the hurt was more on the inside.

By midday, the trio found themselves walking along a riverbank. The dark waters, fast-flowing, the large boulders and jagged rocks created foaming eddies and whirlpools. Onwards they went, continuously climbing upwards, It was quite beautiful which helped the pair emotionally. Looking at the dazzling mini rainbows created by waterfalls falling down the mountain slopes. The Princess would stop at times, shushing Scrungle and Peetles, listen intently, eventually relax and move on. Higher and higher they climbed until Scrungle, ignoring the Princess's protest, called a halt to rest and for Peetles to have a drink from a pool by a small waterfall. It was at this time that the Princess realised that Scrungle didn't have a mouth.

"Is it really small, hiding behind your nose?" Scrungle lifted his white appendage while the Princess looked.

"How can I hear you?"

"I don't know, really. I just talk inside myself, and most things can understand." Said Scrungle.

"Most things, does that mean you can talk to birds and creatures and make them understand you? Can you read minds?" Said the Princess, who looked worried.

"No, just sort of put my words so you can understand them, I think. Then I can understand things when they talk back."

Intrigued by Scrungle's ability but not wanting to tarry, the Princess pushed them onwards. Leaving the trees behind they started to climb the rocky face of the mountain. Scrungle put Peetles on his head as the little creature was finding it difficult to keep up. Unable to ascend any higher, the Princess took off her gloves and, putting two fingers in her mouth, blew a warbling whistle. To Scrungle and Peetles ears, it could have been mistaken for a bird call. Without delay, a rope ladder tumbled down the rock face from above. Pulling at it hard, checking that it was secure, the Princess began her climb.

With Peetles perched atop his head, Scrungle painstakingly climbed, thinking about the Chana tree and how far away from home he was. Scrungle appreciated the ladder's roughly shaped rungs, realising he wouldn't have managed the climb without them.

Pausing periodically because of Peetles agitation and shifting centre of gravity, the gradual, precarious climb reaffirmed that a ladder into the Chana tree would be a mistake. Pulling themselves over the lip of the summit, they were confronted by the Princess standing on a spacious rock platform, looking at a panoramic view of the forest. Nestled at the base of the platform was an entrance to a cave that could be hidden by a grey tarpaulin when necessary. At the moment, it was tied back on either side.

Out of the darkness of the interior, a penguin waddled, holding a tray of refreshments that spilt everywhere. The Princess sighed.

"Wait here."

Disappearing into the cave, her footsteps echoing off the cavernous walls, then eventually silence. Scrungle had never felt so exhausted. He was tired, dirty, and altogether at his wit's end. Still, not forgetting his manners, he said hello to the penguin. It stared impassively at the pair. When no reply was forthcoming and neither decided to take the offered refreshment, it turned, losing two of the cups to gravity as it waddled back into the cave.

Drained and wanting to sit down, Scrungle pulled the tricycle out of his pocket. Putting it into park, he was going to put Peetles in the basket, but his little friend clung to him, so they both sat together in the high-backed chair, and Scrungle cradled the little creature in his lap.

"Let us sit awhile, Peetles, and catch our breath. Now we are safe for the time being." It was peaceful here, looking out to see the rolling woodlands and mountains. The wind was warm, and it didn't take long for Scrungle to do an imaginary yawn as he and Peetles fell fast asleep. A rumble of thunder in the far distance woke him late in the evening. Peetles was still asleep. Dark clouds were gathering, ready to unleash the rain onto the land below. He gently roused Peetles.

"I was having a lovely dream, Scrungle. We were in a tree, and you were showing me all your books."

"I would love to be home, Peetles. I find the world very confusing and petty. I don't want anything more to do with it. But we still need to find the magic mushrooms to return to the Chana tree."

The penguin waddled out of the cave entrance so they dismounted the tricycle and said hello again. The creature ignored them, walking to the cliff edge and watching the forest below.

"Maybe it can't talk." Peetles offered in a way of explanation.

The Princess had told them to stay where they were, so they did. The mountain rose steeply on either side of the little plateau they stood on. Only the hardiest of plants were growing on its cracked sheer surface. Their only way down was the rope ladder or gravity. To Scrungle it looked like the weather front was still a way off, suggesting maybe this was a good time to inventory his pockets. Peetles agreed it was a good idea to pass the time until the Princess reappeared.

It didn't take long before on one side of the entrance they had built a pile of extraneous items such as the hair dryer, toothbrush, a bag of conkers, a portrait of his great-grandfather, and other non-essential things. The larger items—the bookcase, fire surround, portable shower, and dinghy—were on the other side. The only thing that he kept in his magical pockets was the moon-dial. All in all, he did feel lighter, which was a bonus. When it came to food, the hamper that the family Morris had provided stood next to Peetles. It still had a decent selection of mushrooms wrapped in paper, and Peetles water bottle was half full.

Scrungle sat back on the tricycle, his legs up on the handlebars. Peetles straddled them using them as a bench, and Scrungle ate mushrooms that tasted of dandelion and burdock with a hint of dill, while Peetles drank what was left of the water from the bottle.

Sitting as they were Scrungle could see Peetles face still bruised but now with a more familiar smile on it. The nightmare of their capture had receded a little into the back of their minds now they had eaten. It had only been a day ago, but Scrungle marvelled at how quickly one can recover.

"What's a terrorist?" Peetles had a thoughtful look.

"I don't know for sure, but I have read about creatures with scary arms; maybe they have wrists of terror or terror wrist." Speculated Scrungle.

"What about creepy fingers? I bet you can get them."

"Probably," Scrungle said, looking at his hands. "I always thought mine were rather stick-like."

"I don't think I have wrists." Peetles was looking from one stubby arm to the other. "Do you think the Princess has scary arms or terror wrists?"

"Definitely has stabby stabby hands." Scrungle then shuddered, thinking about the sounds of choking and the desperate eyes of the hobgoblin's final moments at the abandoned croft.

They sat a little bit longer until they felt the wind change and the temperature begin to drop. Scrungle put the things back in his pocket that had come in useful so far, leaving the daft items out. If he hadn't used them yet, he probably never would.

"Where is she?" said Peetles, helping Scrungle put the fire surround back into his pockets. As if on cue, the Princess appeared at the cave entrance. She had cleaned up, changed clothes, and looked absolutely stunning.

Isobella walked over to the edge of the cliff and pulled out a short cylindrical brass tube, which she extended, bringing it to her left eye. Scanning the woods for signs of movement.

"What's that?" Peetles had waddled over to take a closer look at the strange instrument. The Princess smiled at Peetles.

"It's called a monocular; you can use it to see things far away." She handed it to Peetles, who took it with a certain amount of reverence as if it were an unexploded bomb.

"Just be careful with it." said the Princess, not unkindly, then as the thought hit her in an excited voice. "Scrungle, can you talk to Sergio, my retainer?"

She had dropped to her knees, grabbing the penguin called Sergio.

"We tried, but Sergio can't seem to say anything," Scrungle said with a shrug.

The Princess looked at Sergio with a sad smile on her face.

"Come on inside so we can talk."

The mouth of the cave was cramped, which was deceiving as it was really quite spacious as they followed her to the back. Hidden by the natural features of the rock, the Princess turned and followed a fissure in the rough surface. It was tall enough for the Princess, but Scrungle had to duck. It wound back and forth, going down until it opened up to a larger cavern. Here, the Princess had made a hideaway.

With high ceilings, the sound of water dripping from stalagmites echoed all around them. Dotted around the interior candles flickered, their light bouncing off the stone walls. A pool of deep water was so clear that they could see to the bottom. It was hard to make out, but the floor had been flattened either by tools or the constant passage of people over time.

The furnishings as such, and there weren't many, were an eclectic mix; the bedding was furs stitched together. Lying around was an obscene amount of scatter cushions and pillows with the royal crest stitched into them. There was an exquisite dressing table with figurative features, carved inlays and layered in gold leaf; its accompanying chair was a tree stump. In a small stone circle, a lit fire heated a pan of stew. The smoke spiralled upward, escaping through unseen cavities above. The Princess sat down on a floor cushion that had been hand-made and roughly sewn together.

"Welcome. Make yourselves comfortable. No need to bow."

Scrungle sat on a rock with Peetles holding the monocular next to him, still enchanted by it, looking at everything they could.

"Thank you for saving us."

Scrungle put on his top hat and went through the usual ritual.

"My pleasure, I've been trying to catch up to you since I saw the witch Waynex."

"You met the witch?" Said Scrungle at a loss as to why.

"Known her forever."

Scrungle then understood what the Sphinx had meant about the witch's last visitor when they returned to the library with Doris. Scrungle admitted to the Princess he didn't get out much, and this was the first time in a long time he had ventured anywhere other than the Chana tree, in all honesty, he was still at a loss as to what was happening with the Princess, Gumptrude, Plombree, and the Kingdom.

The Princess in the half-light of the cave, stopped Scrungle from listing anything more and spent the rest of the evening informing Scrungle and Peetles about her life, the King, how she would love to be a knight but it was forbidden, and how they both needed to find the island of the Huba mushroom.

"The kingdom had been a good place to live for many years. Fair and just with low interest rates, a decent education system, drainage, and a proper pension at a reasonable retirement age. For the people, by the people." Said the Princess.

Scrungle and Peetles had no real idea what a socialist democratic dictatorship was, so they nodded along, with the odd

"I see." at what they deemed the right moment.

Bad times arrived with the Baroness Bakeasy. She had come to the castle under the guise of a high-end pastry chef to head up the cake section of the royal kitchen. There were a few in court who found it just a little bit coincidental that the Baroness, who hailed from Flan, should come to work in the King's kitchen at Plombree just after the trade negotiation with Flan had fallen through. Leaving Flan with losses in their exports of curry sauce, scatter cushions, and paper.

It didn't take long for her to encourage rumours that she was also a lifestyle coach with a flare for costume design. Isobella's father, who had shown little interest in anyone after the loss of the queen, fell for her, beguiled by her knowledge of rustic bed throws, occasional tables, paper apparel, and feng shui. Not to mention her long dancer's legs and knock-out pair of tits.

"I see," Peetles said. Although they didn't, it just felt like the right moment.

The Princess paused, taking a drink from a gold chalice with the royal crest and her initials. They could hear the rain outside; a low rumble of thunder growled through the cave. It was late, but the Princess was on a roll, so she just kept going.

She watched as the Baroness whispered in the King's ear about the need for an heir to the throne and that Isobella spent far too much time hanging around the knights of Colour. The next thing Isobella knew, she was pushed into courting Prince Whackerknacker.

After a screaming argument, shouting that it was either her or Bakeasy, she ran away. Captured and brought back, she found her father changed; his health had declined not only in his body but also in his mind. The people at court put this down to his high-end, sugar-rich diet of baked food, the stress of running the kingdom, and a cleavage that would kill an ordinary man.

Isobella wasn't stupid and knew something else was at the heart of her father's failing health. It was then that she began keeping a close eye on the Baroness. One day she sneaked in and hid in the kitchen, witnessing the Baroness put something other than syrup on her father's flapjacks.

She confronted the Baroness, who just denied everything, saying it was Isobella, and her wilful refusal to marry Prince Whackerknacker and ignoring her father's wishes that were making the poor man ill. It was then that they got into an extreme and bitter argument about patriarchal society—the selling off of the kingdom's assets to the already rich. Also, how stupid it was to think that a closed system that only dealt with the perpetuation of wealth for the wealthy could generate choice, and then they swayed into the debate on the emancipation of women.

"I mean, we bear the children, then manage their mistakes; the vast majority of the housework and the men—what do they do? Off to watch the jousting trails on the weekend and say we're the weaker sex. Bloody systems rigged."

"I see." Said Scrungle and Peetles. Scrungle knew the pair could have said the walls could do with a coat of paint, and the Princess would have just nodded, not listening, only wanting to protest the bombast and frustration that plagued the kingdom and a woman's life in general.

The Baroness kept saying a woman's place was at a man's side. Isobella said she should give herself a good shake. Most of the kitchen staff who had come to see what the shouting was about stood dumbfounded. Wondering what women's liberation was and where they could go to get one. It was only when Isobella threw a rather lovely red velvet cake at her head that the Baroness's personal guard intervened. Roughly handling Isobella, taking her up to the tower to cool off.

Putting hands on the Princess at any other time would have been the loss of one's head. Now it didn't even rank as a me-too moment, as everyone, when questioned, said they were filling out a half-price flyer for the SCS.

After that, Isobella had tried to rally support from her father's advisors; anyone who came to her defence was either imprisoned, bought off, or disappeared. The Baroness was livid at the wasted cake, so she struck back in a cunning move to manipulate the town criers, poster makers and gossips. Most of the messages posted on the notice board in the courtyard of the castle were about Isobella and how the king's ill health had pushed her into a state of mental breakdown.

"I see." Said Scrungle. He did think about the look of rage that crossed the Princess's face when she skewered the hobgoblin and thought maybe they had a case.

Whenever these rumours were followed to their origin, it invariably ended up that Gumptrude was the main proponent. At that time he was just a highly disliked tax clerk but soon became Bakeasy's main advocate.

With her father more or less on continual bed rest, it was easy for Bakeasy and Gumptrude to take control, manipulating the court, king's council, and supporters. Isobella was put under watch night and day, escorted everywhere by the Baroness's personal guard, supposedly for her own safety. Then one day, by happenstance, the princes saw on the notice board, below a new exposé of the cake incident by a long-time friend of one of the scullery personnel, an advertisement that the SCS was having a half-price sale and a two-for-one in crystal ball predictions by the witch Waynex.

Isobella had been friendly with the witch and her sisters when she was young. They had been regulars at the court with their predictions, potions, and a rather risqué party trick of firing a ping pong ball into a flagon with a dragon by squeezing a certain set of muscles together. After the queen's death, she disappeared from court. Now she might be able to help Isobella Baroness and hopefully put an end to the terrible flatulence she was having at the time.

Isobella, with the help of Sergio, her retainer, slipped out of the castle unnoticed and made her way to the SCS building. She eventually found the witch Waynex after being pressured into buying salad tongues, a flannel, and two sets of welding gloves. She confided to the witch Waynex that she was positive the King was being poisoned. Waynex told Isobella about the Huba mushroom and that it was a known antidote to all known enchantments, maladies, and beguiling mammary glands, as an afterthought the witch said it would probably help with the flatulence. However, the chosen one who could find the island of the Huba mushroom was still to arrive.

Before they could come up with a plan, the guards found them. The Princess was taken back to the castle and a close watch put on them both. The Princess described how the next morning there was a proclamation by the King saying that, by royal command, she was being forced to get married to Prince Whackerknacker.

"It's just not like Dad at all. It'll be Bakeasy and Gumptrude. They're up to something." The Princess was now punching her fist into the soft belly of a stuffed toy.

"I see." Said Peetles, but was thinking about how long it takes custard to set.

She and Sergio had managed to escape for the last time, using some whipped cream, an elastic band, a mirror, and a small pretend-hand made from pasta shells. Leaving a false trail, she hid in the woods until she could make it back to the SCS and wait for the Scrungle to turn up.

"I see." They both said this together.

"I was the last one to see her. She said you had come. You and Peetles had gone to find the moon-dial. Then she was arrested and taken away. We need to work together. I need to save my Father, the kingdom, and get rid of the Baroness and Gumptrude."

"They called us terror wrists." Peetles chipped in as if being woken from a dream.

"We are all being hunted." Isobella stood and paced the floor of the cave. Her feet barely made a sound. Scrungle looked around.

"How did you find this cave?"

"The Gold Knight told me about it. I remembered it when I first ran away. There had been a number of highway robberies at the crossroads several years ago. Gold and Silver chased the gang here, eventually taking them prisoner. I thought it might be a good place to hide out, as it hasn't been used in years." The Princess sat down again and yawned. The sound of the storm echoed through the cave as they sat with their thoughts.

"Why does it have some of your furniture here?"

The Princess pulled a face that was both embarrassed and surprised.

"It's how I got caught the first time; nicking stuff from home to decorate it out."

"It is nice that you have Sergio as a valet; I don't know many penguins holding down royal jobs." Said Peetles.

The Princess remembered that the creature was still standing on duty and jumped to her feet.

"Bugger I forgot he's still keeping watch."

"I'll go." Peetles volunteered and waddled out to the cave entrance to tell the penguin to come inside. The Princess sat back down and looked at the impassive Scrungle.

"Sergio was hexed by accident. It was a trap meant for me."

"I see." Said Scrungle.

He did think that the Princess could talk the hind legs off Kevin, but now that she was talked out, Scrungle sat quietly, digesting all this new information. Remembering the tricycle, Scrungle stood, but Peetles came back into the cave with Sergio. They were both soaked through, water pooling at their feet. Peetles and Sergio said they had put the tricycle in the cave out of the rain and closed up the front with the tarpaulin.

"Before we retire for the evening, can I see the moon-dial?"
Princess Isobella moved over and sat next to Scrungle.

Searching around in his pockets, his stick-like fingers ran over its surface. A sudden reluctance welled up inside him, not wanting to show the Princess. It was his and Peetle's prize. They had suffered to get it, and they could have lost their lives to the Cheeseman.

Not only that, they were now branded terrorists, beaten and kicked, fugitives from the law, and their only crime was wanting to get back into the Chana tree.

He looked into the Princess's eyes, and she smiled, showing she regularly brushed her teeth, and he felt ashamed for thinking such uncharitable thoughts. Smiling an imagined smile back, he presented the moon-dial, which shone a blue light into the cave.

"Oh, that is cool. Do you know how it works?"
Scrungle, with Peetles adding bits to the story, instructed the Princess on how they had found it and worked out how to use it. The Princess's eyes looked less troubled; it was as if a heavy weight had been lifted from her shoulders.

"I'm very tired, and we still have a lot to do. Tomorrow, we will discuss options and set off to find the Huba mushroom island. Do you know how long it takes to get there?"

Scrungle shook his head.
"We must work together if we are to save the kingdom and clear your names."

Sergio stood guard all night while Scrungle and Peetles slept in the little dinghy turned upside down to give it a bit of a mattressy feel and away from the rock floor.

A clean breeze blew the next morning as they sat outside on the rock plateau. Most of the things Scrungle had left out of his pockets had been taken by the storm. He was a little sad about this, as he had toyed with the notion of just leaving them here and picking them back up at a later date. Isobella paced back and forth, talking constantly about strategy and what to do next, deciding that they would travel by night but leave now and get to the edge of the woods as soon as possible.

They ate a light breakfast, and Scrungle and Peetles agreed to tell Isobella about the overheard conversation on the castle tour. There was no reason to keep this a secret now. It sent the Princess off on an angry rant for the better part of half an hour. Neither of the pair had heard so many expletives in such a short time. When the Princess had calmed down, Scrungle plucked up the courage to ask.

"What did the Baroness mean by plan A and plan B?"

"Hmm, my best guess is A. I'm forced to marry Prince WhackerKnacker, who is one. That would mean King Archy WhackerKnacker would rule Plom and Flan, and I bet the Baroness is friendly with old Archy. I'd be pushed out or something worse. Or plan B. She's playing everyone." Pacing back and forth the Princess now and then would kick a stone off the ledge in temper.

"We could tell the knights; I think they would listen." Scrungle offered, hoping the idea might align with the Princess's thoughts. The thought of the knights and their protection while they travelled was comforting.

"I wish we could, but they are duty and honour-bound to follow the King's law. They might..... No, I know they want to help me; they just can't." The Princess turned and looked out into the forest below.

"Come on time to go." She said after a while.

They checked the moon-dial for directions and showed the Princess the map that the witch Waynex had given them.

"Well, it's sending us off Northeast; there are fishing villages all along the coast."

Her eyes shone, thinking over the options available. The Princess was happy that she had a plan of action and was moving in the right direction. Before going down the cliff face, Isobella used the monocular, making sure as best she could that they weren't being watched. Sergio the penguin was lowered down first on ropes, then Peetles, Isobella, and Scrungle followed using the rope ladder.

At the base of the mountain, Peetles elected to walk; the possibility of being knocked off Scrungles head by a tree branch wasn't what he wanted to start the day with. Scrungle asked how they hid the ladder, but without Sergio at the cave entrance to pull it up, it had to stay where it was.

"Don't worry, it's hard to see from a distance." Then the Princess struck off at a pace down the mountain towards the forest.

## Twenty-Five

# *Mushroom City*

Gnarled roots twisted across the ground, searching for nourishment. Pine needles, wet from last night's storm, scented their footsteps. Picking the best route she could find, the princess led the way with seamless surety of foot, following the compass bearing from the moon-dial. They were now headed in the opposite direction from their approach to the hideout,

Packed close together, greedy for the sun, the evergreen trees left little in the way of light to penetrate the ground below. Sergio found travelling the hardest as his short webbed feet had evolved for different terrain. Heading away from the King's Road, it was a reasonable assumption that they were putting more distance between themselves and their would-be pursuers. Isobella assured them that the woods would thin out soon.

Peetles thought the woods were called Reaching Out. Isobella said they were. Peetles asked why she had just called it woods wood. After a fruitless ten minutes of total misunderstanding between the pair, Isobella getting a little snippy, said the woods were called Reaching

Out, and told Peetles to leave it at that.

The forest of pines skirted the base of the mountain range, which in turn led to the coastal peninsula. If anything or anyone lived in the forest, they gave the company a wide berth, as nothing crossed their path all day.

Scrungle was delighted by the forest, finding mushrooms of all shapes and sizes every few yards. He didn't stop to eat; just picked as many as he could, filling the hamper. When it was full to the brim, he began filling the tin he had found the chocolate cake in that he had fed the wolves, The memory felt like a lifetime ago.

"Are you not hungry?" Scrungle asked the princess after hearing her stomach rumble loudly.

"I'm on a calorie deficit." The princess replied, talking through gritted teeth.

Scrungle didn't ask anything more. It was some form of primal instinct that stopped him from talking about a woman and her diet unless one had a certain death wish. As the princess predicted, the pine trees began to thin. Now they could see green fields ahead, peppered with bushes ripe with berries, wildflowers, and the odd oak tree. A small flowing stream cut the field in two and beyond that, more meadows spread across low hills. To their left, the mountains stayed a constant fixture as far as the eye could see.

Before they had left, Scrungle had packed as much as he could into his magic pockets for the princess. Most of it was food. Finding a suitable place to wait until nightfall, Sergio the penguin set up a small campfire and started heating a pan of water.

"Be alert; many will be hunting us for the reward money."

The princess said this after they had eaten, ever vigilant, she walked off to find a good vantage point for the first watch. Scrungle, Peetles, and Sergio settled down, filling the time as best they could, playing cards until they could move on.

Scrungle started to think about what had happened in such a short period. Swept along at a furious speed by fate and circumstance. He had never lived at this pace before, and his outlook had changed dramatically. It was a world that made absolutely no sense, and he now knew all he wanted was to be left alone to hide away in the Chana tree. Let them make Plombree great again; let them build roads for no apparent reason. Let them fight Plombreean against Plombreean. He wanted no part in the madness and rhetoric.

This was just wishful thinking, as the options for an easy life had now dwindled to naught. There was no way back unless he cleared his name. If he didn't do that what then? Scrungle shuddered to think, always on the run from the sheriffs or bounty hunters. Never calling anywhere home, or worse, he and Peetles would be caught, sentenced to life in the dungeon, or executed.

Scrungle looked over at the little creature, knowing full well that Peetles was now his responsibility, no matter what the future held. It saddened Scrungle to think that Peetles, with their big, untainted heart, had little in the way of a wider world-view, not understanding that sometimes people and creatures would hurt you for no other reason than they could.

By dusk, they were ready to move on. A yellow moon shone down, beginning to cycle into its next quarter. Consulting the moon-dial and finding the compass bearing, they set off at a slow and steady pace, heading towards the coast. Avoiding holdfasts, farms, or any signs of people they stayed close to the mountains. Neither lighting a torch nor a lantern, just using the moon or stars to see the way ahead.

On the second day, they came upon a road long overgrown with weeds. It was hard to tell in the night but seemed solid as if made from one long piece of blasted rock or put down in one continuous roll. Following the road, it took them up the mountain and then to an old ruined city.

Drawing closer, they could see it had been magnificent in its past. The buildings and outlying structures had a distinct mushroom shape with overhanging caps. Mottled stone in a variety of shades of grey in the light of the moon looked smooth to the touch without seams or lines in the stonework. Eerily quiet, its abandonment felt like a physical thing lying heavy in the air. There were no signs of life, and even the weeds were reluctant to grow there. It was beautiful in a sad and lonely way, thought Scrungle.

It wasn't until morning that they saw that the high towers and roofs had been brightly painted a long time ago. Now they were bleached by the sun and dimmed by time.

"Mushroom City." The princess explained.

"Once a long time ago, it was a great city; no one knows who lived here or what happened for it to become abandoned."

Birds flew from the high-rounded towers sprouting from the larger structures that had a definite cantilever-turret feel. The little company made camp, sitting in a bulbous building with high windows, waiting the day out.

"Why don't we use the tricycle Scrungle." Peetles enquired, looking out through the open, rounded doorway at the road.

"Yes, the road looks even and true, but I think the princess wants us to be able to hide quickly. Hard to do if you are on a bike." This settled Peetles, as the last thing they wanted was to be a prisoner ever again.

After four more nights, the company eventually came to the sea just as the sun was beginning to rise. The glint of the light bouncing off the water captured Scrungle and Peetle's souls immediately. Walking to the edge of the rocky cliff, looking upon the sea for the first time, they were robbed of anything to say.

Yellow sand on a long beach invited the waves to dance in and out, curling and rolling into a white foam, breaking their form with each greeting. Seagulls circled the air, crying the restless tide of being, while terns scampered across the sand, searching for signs of life.

Neither he nor Peetles had seen the sea before. Blue-grey water stretching out to the horizon. Cutting a definite line between what was sky and what was world. The majesty of the view was to Scrungle, the same as gazing up into the night sky. It made them both feel, without saying a single word, utterly small and insignificant.

The troubles that they had been carrying were soothed away for the time being, like footprints on the shore. Such a delight it was to breathe in the sea air, listening to the waves rhythmic cycle clearing the mind and settling the heart.

Further along the beach, the headland climbed up as the land then turned in on itself, making the long coastline that would eventually lead to the town of Harbour. Nestled amongst the slopes were the wooden and stone houses of a modest-sized fishing town.

Some of the gardens had nets up on lines, being repaired. Putting the monocular to her eye, the princess scanned the town. She caught the sign at the top of the climb.

**'Welcome to WetWang.'**

Then she followed the main road as it wound down into the town, passing a trading post, a shop front with hats for all occasions, and a fishing tackle shop, then a tavern on the docks. The swing board on the side said it was called **'The Squidney.'** in the front window was a sign saying rooms to let.

Moored at the dock were several fishing boats and a decent-sized sailboat with a covered wheelhouse. Dropping the monocular from her eye, she addressed Scrungle, Peetles, and Sergio.

"So here's the plan. I'm going into town to do a bit of scouting. I was thinking we should steal a boat, but if we can get a charter with an experienced captain, all the better. Plus, we'll need provisions, as the witch hasn't given any instructions as to how long it'll take to find the island."

Isobella handed the spyglass to Peetles so they could have a look at the town and docks. Peetles was immediately distracted by a ladybird on the ground next to them and started zooming in on that instead.

"We don't have any money."

The necessity of expenses for the expedition had not occurred to Scrungle, and the need for money never crossed his mind that much, if at all.

The princess patted her chest, which rattled with unseen coins. She winked at Scrungle, then pulled on her hood and scarf and discarded the sword, keeping with her a small blade in her tunic.

"Be careful," Scrungle said as the princess walked off into town. Scrungle, wanting to be alone, thought it best to get a light bite in. Peetles was in a world of their own, looking and behaving like Peetles once again. Sergio stood as still as stone, watching the princess depart. So he wandered off to find some fungi.

After searching the hillside nooks and a little scattering of bushes, he found a fair selection. Absorbing them, they tasted of many different things, but none of them had a taste of the sea. The closest he got was a brown-shaded mushroom growing next to a damp rock that tasted like fried fish with salt and vinegar.

From nowhere, a sudden longing to be home in the Chana tree came upon him. He sat on the stump of a tree and put his head in his stick-like hands.

"You seem a bit down."

The voice Scrungle could hear sounded as if it had come from a clump of grass in his peripheral vision. After a moment, it moved, and on closer inspection, Scrungle thought it was the witch Waynex dressed in green. Then he saw the eyes, and the illusion was gone.

"Hello. I'm Scrungle Bungus."

"Hello, Scrungle Bungus I'm the witch Waysup." Covered in grass, moss, and bits of bark the witches pointed hat was now unmistakable.

"Do you have a sister the witch Waynex?"

"Is that what's making you sad? She does have that effect on things and people."

The witch shuffled over getting closer to Scrungle. She was a wee thing; a walking landscape of sorts. Scrungle thought about it for a moment and in a way realised that it was all the unanswered questions that troubled him.

"What's the matter you look as if you could do with a good cry." The witch put a grassy arm around his sloping shoulders. "Come on tell me everything,"

Scrungle told the witch Waysup as much as he could.

"What happens if we just keep sailing and sailing and the island's not there?" He said it at last. The witch sat looking into the middle distance. Scrungle thought she smelt a bit twiggy with a kind of light mildew aftertaste. Pulling out a short, stubby pipe, she filled it with cherry tobacco, lit it, and blew out smoke, which shaped itself into a no-entry sign.

"Oh, just like sis to give you half the information. Loves her prophecies and the intrigue. She can be a right tit. Got this thing about secret plans and wanting to be exotic so people think she's interesting. Gets on my bloody nerves."

The witch Waysup took a long inhale from the pipe and then blew out smoke that coalesced into what looked to be a parrot trying to figure out the wrapping on a curly wurly.

"You'll have to sail out for about a week. Then you have to wait for a full moon. The moon-dial will start spinning; you can't see the island without it. Just wait until it comes out of the sea at the last light of the day. Get the mushrooms and get off before it sinks back into the ocean. Otherwise, it'll take you with it."

Scrungle was dumbfounded. "Why didn't she tell me all this."

The witch gave a long sigh.

"She has it in her head that you have to work for these things and loves all the drama. I think it's all the cigarettes, it's not just tobacco she sticks in them."

"Would you come with us," Scrungle asked inspired that having the witch with them would help immensely.

"Oh love I wish I could but I have to wait in for an Amazing Shine delivery. Last time they left it next to the bin and some bugger nicked it."

"How did you know I would be here." It was too much of a coincidence that just when he needed help, there was always someone there. The witch tapped the pipe, cleaning it out.

"I keep an eye on the gossip lines. Had a feeling you'd be turning up; birds talk you know, Twitter. Malcolm says hello."

The witch started to waddle away, and before he had a chance to ask anything more, she dissolved into the very grass that surrounded them. Scrungle stood looking at the space where the witch had been, then mumbled,

"Thank you." Feeling better than he had felt in a long time, Scrungle walked back to the camp.

The princess was in high spirits. Peetles and Sergio were standing next to her, investigating a large bundle of items she had brought back. After having a look around, the princess had gone into the tavern and ordered a cheese scone with camomile tea. The owner had said good luck with that, as they only served squid broth and rum. Not wanting to draw attention to herself, she had opted for fish sticks and a beer and was told yet again all they did was squid broth and rum.

"I struck up a conversation with the owner. There is chatter about us but everyone in these parts believes we are miles away at Harbour or captured. I got the name of a fisherman who may be willing to take us out: Sad Wally the Whaler. I told the owner to have him meet us at dusk on the dock, ready to leave. I said I'm from the fisheries commission studying the effects of pollution on the economy in the community."

"Is the sea being poisoned? What about all the creatures and things." Peetles worried that the fish may become ill.

"I have no idea I know nothing about fishing."

"You said you were."

"It was a lie."

"You didn't." Peetles took a step back, shocked that the princess had fibbed.

The princess looked at Scrungle for help, so he changed the topic and told her about the encounter with the witch Waysup.

"Excellent, excellent." She smiled such a stunning smile that Scrungle understood why the knights had held her beauty in such high regard.

"So if my reckoning is correct we have a week before the next full moon." Scrungle nodded, being a student of the heavens. Peetles agreed because Scrungle had, and Sergio just stared on impassively. Isobella had more to say; although Peetles looked distrustful and kept glancing sideways at her, brows furrowed.

It was apparent that this little coastal town didn't get many visitors. A few of the knights had passed through, but that had been weeks ago. By all accounts, it was Gold and Silver. Now the main talking point was that a boat carrying trolls without papers had landed, and the captain of the Coast Guard was called. Being a refugee was now a criminal offence in Plom, so they were taken straight to a detention centre on the outskirts of the town of Harbour. This ruling had only just been introduced by Chancellor Gumptrude.

"What about getting onto the boat? Won't it raise suspicion? We promised to keep the island's location secret. What happens when it comes out of the sea?"

Scrungle stroked his long white nose, which he did when he was deep in thought or a little nervous.

"All good points, but I have an idea." The princess knelt to huddle, beckoning Scrungle, Peetles, and Sergio the penguin to follow. Sergio tried but couldn't kneel, being a cursed penguin, and just inclined his body a little. The princess looked side to side as if the very air was listening and started talking in a low voice. Now and then, pointing at the bundle she had brought back.

## Twenty-Six

# *The Slippery Bastard*

They all walked into the little seaport at dusk. A few town folks gave them a curious glance, but it was late in the day, and most of the inhabitants of WetWang wanted to get home and relax. The harbour master, a grizzled-looking centaur, just nodded as they walked past. He seemed preoccupied with counting several crates that had been unloaded earlier. The crates were full of dead chickens, which smelt heavily of chlorine.

Scrungle was dressed in second-hand clothes the Princess had haggled for at the trading post. To cover his body, a very long brown leather fisherman's wet weather coat, roughened by use. The seams had gone in places under the arms, and it was missing two buttons in the middle. It trailed the ground as Scrungle walked, so whoever or whatever had owned it must have been huge. To obscure Scrungle's face, the Princess turned the high collar up, glueing it with egg paste to the back of Scrungle's head. He wore striped red and blue trousers and boots to hide his legs, fastened to his non-existent calves with string. They had come free almost immediately and lolled around, pointing randomly in different directions as he lifted his piano-shaped legs to walk.

On his head, he wore a large rain-proof black hat with a pointed brim at the front. Sergio and Peetles had fashioned a beard out of grey wool and pipe cleaner wire. Then, using her cosmetics, the Princess gave Scrungle a complexion and eyebrows that made him look like he had argued with a hyperactive face painter.

Scrungle was pushing a small cart with provisions for the voyage and under the blanket hid Peetles and Sergio. The wheels of the little barrow bumped over the bleached, uneven boards of the small dock, squeaking rhythmically in need of oiling.

The sun hovered on the horizon, bouncing sparkling jewels of light across the ocean. Gulls swooped and dove toward the water, while others sat buoyant on the surface as if done for the day. A single figure stood on the dock, looking out at the tranquil scene.

Next to the lone figure was a dilapidated fishing boat. It was the larger one Isobella had seen earlier. Its sails were different colours, patched in places with what looked to be old clothes and bedding. Brown rust tails from the metal fixings didn't help. Planks had been hammered over broken sections, and at the stern was a hasty mend with what looked to be an old chest of draws. It could have done with a coat of paint, if not several. A glass coffee table would have looked more seaworthy.

The figure waiting for them was Sad Wally, who, for unknown reasons and best left for Sad Wally to explain, was dressed as an apprentice baker in black chequered pants and double-buttoned whites. A chef's hat was on his head, and on his lone foot was a wooden clog.

Sad Wally looked weather-battered and slightly vacant. He had a patch over his right eye, and on closer inspection, his left eye was made of wood but painted to look real, although the iris was a slit and sideways. A scar running across his right cheek and up to his forehead was ancient, puckered, and lighter in contrast to his neutral complexion. Long, white shaggy hair poked out from under the chef's hat and was as thick as sea foam; it followed the contours of his jaw to a point at his chin.

His age was hard to determine; neither young nor old, as if his face had been sanded down for a royal visit. Scrungle noticed his left ear sooner than the right, which was to be expected since the right one was missing. Dangling from the remaining ear was a large, round earring. Through his nose was another gold piercing, and when he smiled, Scrungle saw two gold front teeth.

To keep himself upright he leaned on a crutch tucked under his arm. His left leg was missing from the knee. It had been replaced by an ornately carved chair leg of solid mahogany. When he moved, it thumped on the wooden planks of the dock. Finishing off his look, a multi-tool accessory had replaced his missing hand, and at the moment the pliers were out.

"Are you Sad Wally?"

The Princess asked when they were close enough. Scrungle thought this silly as the owner of The Squidney had given her a full description, which she had relayed to the rest of the party.

"Aye, lad, that I be." Said Sad Wally in the general direction of the Princess.

"I'll get straight to the point. I need to hire your boat for two weeks."

"Aye, lad. That I know."

"I have my own crew." Said Isobella trying to look Sad Wally in his wooden eye.

"Aye, lad. That'll be fine."

"I'm a woman," said Isobella, irritated by the wrong gender identifier.

"No, lad, she's called the Slippery Bastard. I'm a Woman, was me other boat. It sank. Went down with all hands and one of me legs."

Sad Wally paused as if reliving the moment. He was looking over the Princess's shoulder. It made the Princess nervous, and she turned, looking around for unseen foes.

"How much will it cost?"

"Five taploons a day."

The price was extortionate but the Princess was constantly aware of the need for speed to save her father the king. Every day she was on the run the closer to the end he would be drawing. It had spurred her on at a ferocious pace.

"Deal," she said with a nod. Sad Wally stuck out a weather-worn gnarly hand that wasn't clutching the crutch. It was missing the index and ring finger. Because Sad Wally was blind he hadn't orientated himself properly to Scrungle or the Princess. Neither of the pair was sure which one should shake, after a few attempts and a,

"No, no after you." The Princess grabbed what was left of the hand and shook.

"Normally there's a bit of haggling; you're not wanted for something. On the run." Sad Wally said this with a hearty chuckle. The remark left Scrungle feeling suddenly exposed and looking around the dock for the sheriffs. The Princess, however, had started counting coins onto Sad Wally's palm.

"Don't be silly. We have been travelling for ages. Just want to get started, so can we set off now." Wally transferred the coins into his empty purse.

"You seem in an awful hurry, Normally we settle the deal with a jug at Squidney."

The Princess being a Princess was still used to getting her way. Biting down on her temper, keeping her voice even.

"I'm already behind my schedule. If you don't want the charter hand the coins back over."

Sad Wally's bottom jaw dropped a little. He knew when he was getting told off no matter if he couldn't see.

"Aye lad," Sad Wally pocketed the coins, then held up his good hand for a high five. In Sad Wally's case, it was more of a sad three and a tricky move while leaning on a crutch. Scrungle and the Princess exchanged a glance and a shrug. Sad Wally let his hand drop.

"It's a new thing the nippers are doing. Slap hands in the air. Come on then me hearty; last one on board's a barnacle."

With that said, Sad Wally turned to walk up the gangplank behind him which was slightly to his right. Taking a step, he fell head-forward off the dock and, with a splash, landed in the sea. Thrashing around, trying to guess where the dock was, Wally shouted up.

"Missed me footing; I haven't found me land leg yet. Chuck us a rope; there's a good boson's mate."

Isobella blew out a very long sigh and then looked to the heavens for support. Scrungle picked up a coiled rope and threw it for Sad Wally to catch. Not thinking about the fact that he had a patch on one eye and was blind in the other, the rope just hit him square in the face. They hauled Sad Wally back onto the dock while fishing out his crutch and then guided him onto the boat.

With everyone on board, they cast off. It took a while to get out of the port. Everyone kept slipping, and no one knew any of the terms. Sad Wally was shouting down from the wheelhouse; since the captain was blind in both eyes, the Princess had to take the wheel to steer. After a few minor mishaps and a scrape along a buoy, they were in open water, with the little fishing village and timber dock disappearing behind them. The Princess called Scrungle up to the wheelhouse. A large brass compass took pride of place next to the wheel. Sea charts and a sextant were on a table, and on the wall was a beautiful ornate barometer.

Sad Wally was now at the helm, navigating the open water, while

Isobella made silent communication to Scrungle to get the bearing from the moon-dial.

"I have our direction captain." Said Isobella.

"Aye lad, do you see the pointer above the compass? " Isobella nodded then remembered he couldn't see.

"Yes."

"Set it to the bearing we want to be heading in."

The Princess did as requested, and Sad Wally turned the helm, hearing the spokes of the wheel clack as they hit the multi-tool accessories. A bell chimed when he levelled it off to the new heading. If the course drifted, the bell would chime once for starboard and twice for port.

"May as well just get Sergio and Peetles out of the cart." The Princess said quietly to Scrungle when she was certain Sad Wally was heading in the right direction.

"It's pointless them hiding; Wally's not only as mad as a bat he's also as blind as one."

In the hold, Scrungle lifted Peetles out of the cart, and then Sergio. Once he had explained to them about Sad Wally and his ocular deficiency, they went up onto the deck, slipping a little as they headed straight to the bow, watching the waves breaking against the front of the ship in the last light of the day. Scrungle abandoned his disguise, storing it in his magic pockets.

Peetles was a little bit lumpy, but as the fishing boat didn't seem to have any immediate plans to sink the little creature's anxiety began to subside.

The sun gave one last flash of brilliance then sank under the horizon. Until their eyes adjusted the surrounding darkness felt infinite then slowly they could see the moonlight making little diamonds on the surface of the water.

“Light the masthead and stern lanterns.” Shouted Sad Wally from the open window in the wheelhouse. Scrungle after a moment of thought called back.

“I’m sorry, but what’s a masthead?”

“What’s a stern?” Added Peetles.

“You have a strange voice, sounds different every time you talk. The masthead light’s above the gunnel. Stern light above the transom.”

Sad Wally then started to mutter to himself about millennials and having a nip of rum.

“Is he making the words up, Scrungle?” Peetles looked a bit agitated as they had no idea what was being asked of them.

“I suppose all words have been made up at some point. Let’s just go to the front, and if we see a lantern, we will light it. Then we work our way back from there.”

Scrungle and Peetles set off in the near dark to complete the task slipping constantly on the deck. When the ship was as bright as the opening of a new casino, they headed down into the ship’s sleeping quarters for the night. Sad Wally said he was content to be in the wheelhouse cabin and take the watch.

They were all up early the next day, excited to be at sea, heading towards the island of the Huba mushroom, not only for Scrungle but also to save the kingdom.

Providence held the wind steady, pushing them forward towards their destination. Scrungle introduced Peetles and Sergio the penguin to Sad Wally, who didn’t seem that interested. Only asked Peetles if he could find him his bottle of rum. Isobella effortlessly took command; being royalty, she was used to telling others what to do.

Sergio and Peetles were in charge of the galley, food, and water. Scrungle sails and rigging. Sad Wally would shout instructions down to him; Scrungle had no idea what went where, but between the two of them they managed to keep the sails straight. Isobella took over from Sad Wally at the helm, who went to eat and catch up on some sleep. For all of them, it was a sharp learning curve, not only for the hard work involved but also for the many new terms their captain introduced them to and the fact he was as mad as a March hare.

For the next few days, they sailed on into the unknown. Which for Sad Wally was always the case. The Princess studied the charts and maps that lay around the wheelhouse. Plotting their course into the uncharted waters. Most of the maps were blank, but others bore warnings such as 'here be dragons', 'sewage run-off', and 'no swimming'.

It was during this time that Scrungle and Peetles started to feel more like themselves again. Happy to be travelling, the nightmare of their capture receding. The Princess was also in high spirits, knowing that her quest was close to fruition.

It was at night when they began to see the moon-dial change. The heading was steady, but it glowed a deeper and brighter blue. On the third night, Scrungle noticed the rings of the moon-dial were turning, agonisingly slow at first, getting steadily faster as if counting down the closer they got to the submerged Huba island.

In the darkness, with Wally at the helm, the little company would talk about what to expect when they got to the island and what to say to Wally. Trying to plan for contingencies, using what little information they had. Scrungle showed the Princess the amphora jar. The Princess was still amazed at the magic and the amount his pockets could carry.

In the lower hold, Peetles found barrel upon barrel full to the brim of a dark pungent liquid; curious, the little creature asked Sad Wally what it was.

"Can't go on a trip without me, rum, lad. Wouldn't be right. It's also the ballast." Turning the wheel after hearing a correction chime.

"There is a lot of it," said Peetles, standing next to Scrungle, who was examining a sextant trying to figure out if it had something to do with slicing ham.

"Aye, well, I got it cheap from a fella I know in Flan." Sad Wally sounded evasive, so neither of the pair pursued the matter, but Scrungle couldn't hold out any longer and asked Sad Wally why he was dressed as a baker.

"What do you mean lad? I'm dressed as a baker?."

Scrungle described what Sad Wally was wearing, who on hearing this felt around himself. His fingers travelled over the double-breasted buttons on the white top and rounded collar. Then the chef's hat. He patted down his legs and touched the wooden clogs on his feet.

"Well, stick a nook in me cranny. Thought I had been getting a bit too wet lately, and me wellies were stiff. Now I know why people were asking for a steak and kidney pie every time I was in The Squidney and laughing."

"I met a man in Plombree City an apprentice baker who was dressed as a sailor. All yellow raincoat and black wellies."

Sad Wally slapped his forehead letting out a little cry of pain. It was his multi-tool hand and the small hacksaw attachment was sticking out.

"Wrong hand." Wally rubbed the red lump that was forming with what was left of his good hand. "Plombree city aye. Heard the SCS was having a sale, went to get a new wooden leg. Stayed at a place, Horseshoe and Bucket it was called. Dry cleaning service included with the room. That'd be where I'd been mixed up."

Sad Wally asked Scrungle to take the wheel so he could try and find something a bit more fitting for a captain to wear. With his hands outstretched feeling the way and a little bit of guidance from Peetles, he made his way to the lower deck.

Holding the spoked wheel and a little nervous at the start, Scrungle soon found steadying and keeping the ship on a straight course somewhat exhilarating. The prow rose and fell with the swell. He could see the Princess and Sergio slipping and falling, pulling rigging ropes while setting the main sail and turning it into the wind. The Princess turned, seeing Scrungle at the wheel. She waved.

The thump of Sad Wally's wooden leg announced his presence as he came back into the wheelhouse dressed in a long striped woollen jumper and red pants that would have looked good on a circus clown. On his head was a beaver pelt in the style of a wilderness hunter.

"Is this any better?" Sad Wally stood with his arm in a half-T pose. Scrungle didn't know what to say, and Peetles just blinked.

"You don't look like an apprentice baker anymore."

"That'll do then, lad." Sad Wally made his way over using the familiar layout of the cabin and took the helm from Scrungle.

"It's good isn't it lad. Feeling her move in your hands and the whole world to explore." Scrungle did feel good, but after relinquishing control and listening to Sad Wally, he knew he wasn't a sea Scrungle. His home was hundreds of miles away, in a peaceful and calm tree. He was only here because he needed to find an island, and that island was the only place where the Huba mushroom grew, which, somehow, was the only way he could clear his name of crimes he and Peetles had not committed and help Princess Isobella save her father. Scrungle still couldn't get his head around how any of this had happened. Before they left the wheelhouse, Scrungle asked Sad Wally if he needed anything.

"Thank ya, lad; I'm fine. Got me whittling to do, and I've got me rum." Sad Wally lifted a bit of flotsam from the wheelhouse table.

"What do you think of me mermaid? Nearly finished." Said Sad Wally. The flotsam was a completely round and smooth ball. Scrungle and Peetles thought it was impressive but looked nothing like a mermaid.

"It's very nice." Said Peetles.

They left the wheelhouse a little confused leaving Sad Wally to whittle his globe mermaid and steer the Slippery Bastard.

* * *

On the evening of the seventh day after leaving WetWang the sea had become restless, rolling the Slippery Bastard in the choppy waves that had been steadily building throughout.

Scrungle had put the moon-dial on a large, heavy barrel of tar in the middle of the deck after feeling the inner rings of the device getting steadily faster in his pocket. Now as the sun began to set, they crowded around it watching it glow a brighter blue with every passing moment.

Peetles did a little gasp when one of the rings clicked into place, coming to a halt, then another until the spinning concentric sections stopped, and the beam of light from the gnomon just pulsed.

"Does that mean we are here?" The Princess said, looking at Scrungle whose stick-like hand stroked his long white nose.

"What time is it?" Peeltes asked in a small voice.

"The witch said the last rays of the day." Said Scrungle.

They all looked at the setting sun and the full pale moon in the sky. The Princess shouted to Sad Wally that they were going to drop anchor. He didn't acknowledge. Assuming he was asleep at the wheel again, they just went ahead, pulling the main sail and tying the boat down.

Dark clouds of the storm that had been brewing all day were coming in fast, flecks of rain had started just as the wind picked up. With the last light of the day they all heard a low deep gong chime, then the moon-dial stopped glowing and collapsed into itself as if ready to be inserted back into a Farny.

It must have woken Sad Wally as he shouted down to them if anyone was there if they heard something strange, and if anyone had made food.

Then to Scrungle's ears came a deep and powerful rumble of the sea and earth-changing places, a convulsion in the bowls of the ocean. Air bubbles rose to the surface, off the starboard bow in the rolling chop of the water, spreading out wider and wider.

Scrungle lifted Peetles onto his head so he could see. The water spasmed, and the foaming turbulence bubbled outwards as if boiling. With a tremendous lurch and a deep echoing boom, the island of the Huba mushroom appeared from the depths of the sea. The splashback sent the boat listing to port, and they all fell sliding across the deck, soaked to the skin. The boat rocked and then settled itself as they picked themselves up.

"What there be happening." Sad Wally shouted down from the bridge cabin.

"We have bumped into a whale." Said the Princess.

"Aye. lad. Well just stay still and slowly back away. No sudden movements or it'll have you. Said Sad Wally.

"That's for bulls you mad tit." the Princess said under her breath. The island hadn't finished growing in size as it emerged from the ocean's depths.

"I'll get me harpoon." Shouted Sad Wally disappearing from view.

"Lift the anchor or it'll ground us." Shouted the Princess. Scrungle and Peetles ran to the winch and between them, as best they could pulled the anchor back onto the Slippery Bastard.

In preparation, they had already lit the hurricane lanterns, so Isobella, Scrungle, and Peetles grabbed one each. The little dinghy that had travelled with Scrungle all the way from the Chana tree was tied to the rails of the ship, ready for them to scuttle across to the island. In the falling light, they could see the island rocky and barren. It had stopped its upward thrust and now sat still in the rain.

"Time to go." Said Isobella

They hauled the dinghy over the side, slipping as they did so, knowing full well why the captain had named the ship as he had. Although the boat was rocking heavily in the wind and the rain, making the going treacherous, they made it over the side and into the now cramped dinghy. It was a short distance, but it felt like an age too long to paddle across in the high waves.

The Princess jumped out, pulling the dinghy up the shoreline as Scrungle, Peetles, and Sergio disembarked.

Standing on the island, it felt like they were in the eye of the storm. All could feel its magic, vibrating through them like a tuning fork, a thrill of static electricity. Even though the storm was beginning to get louder and stronger, the four companions paused, in awe that they had made it here.

As if by magic, for that is what it was, the storm clouds broke apart and the moonlight washed the island in silver light. No one moved as if the act would break the spell that was now changing the island's surface.

Mushrooms of different sizes and varieties started to push through. Long, elegant white ones twice the height of Scrungle, luminous orange fungus. Others lemon and blue, red-capped fungi, shell-shaped, and button-shaped—long, tall fungi with the scent of orange. Horned, bullet-capped, rounded, and cone, but the dominant fungi they could see had rounded heads, purple with flecks of white as if coated with candy sprinkles. The stems were purple, and a black line went down to the base. With such speed, they raced up to the pale light and crowded each other for space.

"Are these the Huba mushrooms?" Peetles asked, pointing to one of the telltale fungi. Scrungle was nervous, incredibly nervous. In his heart, it had taken a lifetime to get here. Now, at this moment, it began to sink in that he was actually at the end of his journey.

Stooping, he picked one of the smaller Huba mushrooms. With slow, deliberate movements, snapped it in two and threw it over himself with practised ease.

The fungi exploded into confetti and mini fireworks. A familiar sensation washed over him and he floated two feet off the ground. The Princess rushed over pulling Scrungle down, then grabbing Peetles and Sergio. The four awkwardly danced in a circle laughing and whooping in joy until Scrungle slowly descended.

The minute he touched the island again, clouds covered the moon, extinguishing its light and opening up the storm's fury, the wind, and torrential rain.

"The witch Waynex said all known ailments." The Princess raised her voice to be heard over the wind. She picked a Huba mushroom, snapping it in two just as Scrungle had done, then threw it over Sergio's head. It exploded into mini sparkles, blown by the wind, most landing on Sergio's penguin head and sloped shoulders. Holding their collective breaths, they watched as absolutely nothing happened. The princes screamed into the storm, which replied to her frustration with a loud rumble of thunder.

"Maybe it only works for you."

The princes had plucked another Huba mushroom and pushed it into Scrungles stick thin fingers. Without another word, he snapped the Huba mushroom in two and threw it over Sergio. The outcome was the same.

"No, no I will not have this. I will not." A look of mad desperation was on her face. The same frenzy she had when rescuing the pair from the hobgoblins and sheriff. The Princess plucked another Huba mushroom and knelt in front of Sergio.

"You might have to eat it. I don't know. We can wait until we get back and find the witch and ask her or."

The Princess let the sentence hang, leaving Sergio to make the choice. If it worked on Sergio, then there was a good chance it would help her father, the king. No matter how much she loved her father, it would not be right for her to make the cursed retainer ingest the fungi. Sergio normally tacet, nodded his penguin head up and down while making clicking sounds from his beak.

They looked deep into each other's eyes, then the Princess nodded. Sergio the cursed penguin opened his beak, as she placed the Huba mushroom into his mouth. Sergio tilted his head back and swallowed it down.

The reaction was almost immediate. The penguin started to shake, his flipper feet tapping rhythmically on the ground. Lighting flashed across the turbulent sky, and the flippers that had once been wings on either side of Sergio started to ripple, changing form. The penguin's body began to elongate and sprout up as the webbed flippers became legs, stretching out like cheese on a pizza. Sergio the valet, in no time at all, was standing in front of the Princess, stark naked, tackle out, steam rising from his skin. Screaming about icebergs, polar bears, and a nun stuck in a corridor with a javelin through her neck. All the while the storm raged around them.

He stopped abruptly and fell forward onto his hands and knees, shaking like leg day at the gym. They had come prepared, and Scrungle was ready with a blanket and the coat he had worn as a disguise. Wrapping Sergio up and pulling out other garments for him to wear.

"Go on, Scrungle, I have this." Said the Princess, turning her attention to Sergio, tending to him, helping him dress, and offering comforting words.

Having no idea how long they had and the storm getting stronger. Scrungle pulled out the amphora jar and he and Peetles set about gathering as many of the Huba mushrooms as possible.

"Remember Peetles, one at a time. As two together can explode."

They collected as many as they could. Scrungle would stop and lift Peetles whenever the little creature had picked a mushroom so they could throw it into the jar. The rain pelted down soaking everyone as the time ticked away.

Sergio had recovered some of himself, and he and the Princess started to collect and fill the jar. It was hazardous work; the island's surface was slippery, and the wind pushed and pulled, trying hard to throw them into the sea. Peetles was now going further and further into the island, hidden by the larger fungi, losing sight of Scrungle and the Princess.

A sudden gust caught them all, and Scrungle was thrown off his feet, losing his grip on the lantern. It tumbled through the air and smashed open as it hit the ground. The rain snuffed the light out immediately. He then watched Peetles being blown across the island's surface, only stopping when the little creature hit a large mushroom.

It was getting to a point where they wouldn't be able to stand. They were all shouting to be heard above the roar of the storm. The Princess and Sergio, walking against the wind in small steps, got close enough to Scrungle.

"We have to go." Shouted the Princess as the rain lashed against her face. Scrungle turned to search for Peetles who had disappeared from view. He was just about to shout when the island lurched alarmingly. Scrungle pocketed a Huba mushroom he had been holding without thinking, then the island lurched again; this time the amphora jar was upended and started rolling down the incline toward the sea, throwing out mushrooms from the open top.

"Scrungle the jar." Shouted Sergio.

At the same moment, Peetles still clutching a mushroom, was blown past them all and into the sea.

"Peetles!" Shouted Scrungle. Without hesitation, he ran as best he could towards Peetles, who was floundering in the high waves. The

Princess ran after the jar that was moments away from the water.

"We need a rope." Said Sergio, grabbing Scrungle. The Princess had caught up with the jar and was trying hard to keep it from being taken by the sea, but the waves were too strong. They could all feel the island begin to descend once again into the ocean depths.

"Peetles. Peetles" Shouted Scrungle torn between helping save his friend and the Huba mushrooms. The storm adding insult to injury sent a bolt of lightning down, hitting the Slippery Bastard. The main jib arm shattered, flying into pieces and knocking an oil-filled lantern; it crashed onto the deck, setting the main beam ablaze. In no time at all, the upper deck from the bow to midship was a golden hue of yellow flame.

Scrungle could just see Peetles in the rolling water. Sergio grabbed the Princess, as the weight of the stone jar was too much, and rolled into the sea. Isobella fell to her knees in tears that mixed with the rain.

"No." She screamed into the night. Sergio lifted her under the arm and carried the Princess towards the dinghy.

"Scrungle, come on we need a rope." Shouted Sergio over his shoulder. The island lurched again, and the sea rose to greet it. Scrungle scrambled onto the dinghy as the island began to slide back down into the ocean's depths.

"Hold on Peetles!" Scrungle shouted; he could just make out his friend being swept away between the cresting waves. Paddling in desperation against the swell, they headed towards Peetles. Scrungle grabbed the rope line that had tethered them to Sad Wally's boat. Pulling it loose, he emptied and then attached the lemon-coloured water bottle. Overarm, Scrungle threw it with all his strength toward Peetles.

Another lightning strike hit the Slippery Bastard, and the rum exploded.

# Twenty-Seven

## *Bollocks*

Day 1:

When Scrungle woke, it was still raining; the swell was still high, but the worst of the storm had moved on. In the dull grey light, he saw Sergio scooping water out of the dinghy using one of his boots. Next to him was the Princess curled up like a child. The designer cloak wrapped around her was soaked through. Her eyes were open but not seeing. Scrungle sat up, trying to remember what had happened.

Then the storm, the island, and the night came flooding back. He tried to stand, but the dinghy in the open water shifted his body, and he sat back down.

"Peetles, where is Peetles?" Scrungle shouted.

Sergio looked at Scrungle, then lowered his eyes and busied himself with his boot in a futile attempt to get rid of the rainwater.

"Peetles."

Scrungle did make it to his feet this time. Turning around and calling out in every direction, crying out for his friend. Scrungle's desperation rose, his frantic movements in danger of flipping them all into the water.

Rousing herself as if from the grave, the Princess stood and stumbled over to Scrungle, grabbing the big, gentle fungivore and hugging him tight. He resisted, not wanting to succumb to the Princess's embrace, as it would be an admission that Peetles was gone.

"Oh, Scrungle, I am sorry." Said the Princess.

Scrungle dropped his large white head as she held him, rocking back and forth, adrift in the ocean as the rain came down.

"Come sit with me Scrungle. Come sit down we need to stay together for warmth." Scrungle sat with the Princess who still held him. Sergio, tired beyond measure, was still doing his best to scoop water out of the dinghy. Huddled together as they were the Princess tried to give comfort, even though her heart was broken by the loss of the jar filled with Huba mushrooms.

"I'm so sorry about Peetles." Her eyes had filled with tears. Scrungle just felt numb, worse than numb; he was devoid of hope. The last thing he could remember was the Slippery Bastard exploding which had thrown him out of the dinghy and

waves urgent in their need to pull him into the depths, to follow his friend into the cold unforgiving water. He must have lost consciousness as he could not remember being saved or how he had gotten back into the dinghy. A rush of feeling went through Scrungle, black and dark, his despair a weight upon him. No tears came. All that held him was a terrible numbness, empty and dead.

"Sad Wally?" Scrungle asked but already knowing the answer. The Princess shook her head.

"We have lost everything." She added and then started to help Sergio bail the water from the dinghy stopping almost immediately.

"What's the point?" It was as if she had fallen inwards. Sergio put his arm around the Princess, but she tried to shrug it off, the loss too great. No comfort wanted, just a wish now for the tale to end. Sergio defied her and held her tight. Isobella eventually turned, letting go and crying hard.

As is Scrungles nature even in the throes of his loss he wanted to help. Feeling around in the magic pockets remembering the single mushroom he had put in his pocket.

"Not everything." Holding the solitary mushroom out to Isobella. It was a strange moment, from the grief of loss to hope rekindled.

"Oh Scrungle, you wonderful thing." The Princess, delighted and crying, hugged Scrungle and wouldn't let go. It was little comfort though. His one and only friend had been taken by the sea. The shock was the only thing that stopped Scrungle from screaming himself mad.

"Can you help? I'm exhausted." Sergio was struggling with the water in the dinghy as the rain pelted them all continuously. Scrungle searched in his pockets once more and produced the shower curtain and the trusty hat stand. Between them, they managed to secure it to the dinghy's sides with the stand as a centre pole. Scrungle also produced the cake tin for Sergio to use, which was far more effective than his boot.

It was the tin that had the chocolate cake in when he had met the wolves and Peetles. The memory was too much for Scrungle, who then sat with his head bowed as the rain came down on the makeshift roof and the little yellow oasis was lifted and tossed by a cruel sea.

Day 2:

The rain lasted through the night; nothing of merit was said; they were all in shock from what had happened. Eventually, the sun came up as the rain moved on, and they dismantled the shower curtain to dry out. The Princess had spent a large part of the journey studying the maps and charts Sad Wally had on his boat. Pulling out her compass, she found her bearing.

"We need to head in that direction if we have any chance of finding land." Pointing her hand in the Southwest direction. Her exuberance had been rekindled with the single Huba mushroom that Scrungle had saved.

"How? We have no paddles or anything," Sergio said rather bleakly. Scrungle pulled out the hammock.

"This might work as a sail." He said handing it over to Sergio. Isobella, with a gentle smile, looked at Scrungle, and then she and Sergio set about fashioning a rudimentary sail along with the hat stand as a makeshift mast. It was not in the slightest way elegant but oddly effective. Soon they were heading along against the current towards what they hoped was the coast of Plomb.

Scrungle was on a constant lookout for Peetles, and sometimes his mind would play games and see something in the water or hear the cry of his friend. It was never true, and his hopes would then fade a little more when it was nothing but a trick of the eye or the call of a sea. These moments would chip away at his hope for a miracle, giving more weight to the feeling that he would never see his friend again. The true horror of what had transpired was still far away in his mind, but he knew, or more rightly felt, that the longer the time went on, it would burst forth, and he would break in two with the grief.

Isobella was trying her hardest to keep his spirits up, talking about the royal court, also outlining the plan once they were back on land. Scrungle needed the distraction, as sitting here on the ocean thinking about Peetle's last moments was such a cruel thing.

Day 3:

It rained on the following day; they were glad that it did, as they didn't have any fresh water. Sergio filled the cake tin up after cutting a section of the shower curtain to make it watertight. Drinking their fill as it came down, the three were still terribly hungry, Scrungle searched his magic pockets several times but had exhausted all the provisions. There was small good fortune as the wind changed its direction, pushing the makeshift sail towards land. The sky cleared in the night, starlight and the waning moon lit the ocean.

Day 4:

The sun had been out for a good hour when Sergio saw the sails on the horizon.

"Isobella, look."

He grabbed the Princess and pointed towards the approaching vessel. A scream of delight, then she kissed him hard on the lips. Scrungle sat motionless and soulless.

"We are saved, Scrungle." Said the Princess. Scrungle didn't reply, and the Princess turned back to the ship and started to wave. Scrungle had retreated within himself. He couldn't take his mind off Peetles. Why was this world such a cruel place? He had never fostered anything other than curiosity about the world. For the most part, wanting to be at peace with the places and creatures he had come across. He had his little life, a world that never encroached upon anyone else.

Scrungle now couldn't find it in himself to care about the Chana tree or why he had set out on this journey to start with. All he felt were the beginnings of anger towards Gumptrude and the hobgoblins who had, in Scrungles mind, caused this misfortune to happen. It was better to feel something other than the emptiness and the abysmal bleak void of longing.

"Scrungle, do you have any of your disguise left?"

Scrungle just shook his head. Sergio and the Princess whispered together; Scrungle didn't care. The Princess knelt in the cramped dinghy and held Scrungles hands. She was weather-worn, lips blistered, skin and scalp dry.

"Scrungle, I know Peetles was your friend, but I need you." Her eyes held Scrungles filled with compassion and love.

"The kingdom needs you. Please, can you help me save my father? We will get justice for Peetles."

Saving the king would hopefully mean the hobgoblins and Gumptrude would get their comeuppance; it was all he had left.

"Yes." He said at length. "What do you need me to do?"

Isobella handed the only remaining Huba mushroom back to Scrungle.

"Keep this safe, hide it."

"What will happen now?" Scrungle asked.

"Well, I will be taken straight back to Plombree and married off, but before that happens I will save my father. I will try my hardest to keep you free, but it depends on whether the captain is pro-Gumptrude or Dad." Isobella pulled a face and bit down on her bottom lip.

"What if we wrap Scrungle in the hammock and pretend that he is dead," Sergio said.

"Have Scrungle taken back to the Plombree as a fallen hero who saved the Princess."

"That could work." Said Isobella.

Scrungle looked from Isobella to Sergio.

"I think that I will just take things as they happen. I am not a wrist error, and I have nothing to lie about. The truth will out, as my mother used to say."

Sergio and the Princess didn't say anything, thinking it was rather naive of Scrungle to believe this.

It was mid-day before the ship saw the dinghy. As it drew closer, Sergio identified it as a warship of Plom most likely on patrol.

Scrungle put the hat stand and makeshift sail away safely in his pockets. As it drew alongside, they could see the captain with a spyglass on the poop deck. Not long after, a bell rang on the warship. Shouts and commands as the crew was mustered together.

"I think the captain knows who you are, Princess." Said Sergio, watching the approaching ship.

Once on board, the captain knelt, saluting the Princess with a thumbs up, the emblem of Plom.

"Your Highness, the kingdom is glad you are safe. The crew of the Weetinkle is at your command."

"Rise captain, what is your name."

"Captain Black, your Highness."

Before the Princess could continue an official in purple, who was standing next to a griffin in almost identical attire, took a step forward to intercept Scrungle. His huge stomach overflowing his waistband, similar to dough in an oven, wobbled with malicious intent.

"Take the creature into custody. It is wanted by the state for acts of terror against the high chancellor Gumptrude and the Baroness Bakeasy." His voice was strangely whiny, high-pitched, and very annoying. His sad yellow thin hair swept up into a pompadour seemed to be glued into place. Before the Princess could say anything, a parrot in a cage hanging from a hook attached to the main mast shouted.

"Who's an ugly tit then?"

The crew standing to attention behind the captain laughed, and the urine-yellow-haired man blushed red.

"Put a cover on that bird," said the captain, stifling his mirth. This was hastily done, and the Princess addressed the whiny, high-pitched man.

"Who are you?" Demanded the Princess.

"I am inspector Dinjay Flat from the council of Gumptrude. Naval

and merchant vessels inspector."
The Princess came within inches of Dinjay Flat's face.

"Well, mister inspector. It is customary to bow before a Princess of royal birth. If I remember rightly the vessel you are inspecting is under the command of the King, and by extension me. The charges against my loyal servant Scrungle Bungus are hearsay and completely wrong; Scrungle Bungus is a hero. So if you so much as look at him the wrong way, I will have you hung from the yardarm. I am tired, hungry, and in need of rest. Now get out of my sight."

The vessel inspector gulped and looked around to see the crew staring back with a certain look of satisfaction and desire to stab the whiny shit. He had been on the ship assessing the crew for Gumptrude. A new income-related tax was to be introduced for seafarers, and the crew had also heard rumours of privatisation as well as redundancies.

Dinjay Flat, knowing he had no authority, bowed and then slunk off to hide somewhere on the ship. Isobella gave the slightest of nods.

"Please show me to my quarters."
The captain relayed instructions to the first mate, who then barked commands to the crew to make fast and set course for Harbour Town. The first mate was a man with a dog's head. It had been royal policy for many years to include badly cursed individuals in the armed forces.

The captain had given up his quarters for the Princess. The low ceiling meant Scrungle was bent double to get in the room. In the centre was a desk and table for the officers to eat at. Off to one side through a small doorway was a bed. Scrungle sat down in one of the carved chairs gilded in gold leaf next to the table. The Princess and Sergio sat opposite while the captain stood to attention.

"I hope my quarters will suffice until we land your Highness."

"It is more than generous, Speak freely, captain. How is my father the king? What have you heard? And please sit." Said the Princess.

The captain sat behind his desk, noticing the picture of his wife and children placed it face down, then on second thoughts hid it in a drawer.

"Please Captain leave your things the way they are." Said the Princess smiling.

"I would rather not your Highness, they're rather ugly children and the wife no oil painting."

This threw the Princess for a moment, but the captain was looking between Sergio and Scrungle, trying to make up his mind.

"Whatever you have heard is probably a lie. Scrungle and Sergio saved me. They are loyal to the King and Plom. Who was that man on deck with the piss-yellow hair? More importantly, what news of my father?" said Isobella.

Captain Black nodded, making up his mind.

"He has been sent by the high chancellor, Gumptrude. Overseeing the royal fleet and if I am to speak freely; I do not trust him." Captain Black paused to gather himself. "I am truly sorry, Your Highness. The last news before we left port was the King was close to the end. Rumours abound, Your Highness, that he will not see the celebrations."

The Princess's eyes filled with tears.

"What celebrations?" Asked Sergio

"The Baroness has announced a baking festival with a cake bake-off, to celebrate Chancellor Gumptrude's appointment as high chancellor and her marriage to your father. I think they hope it will quell the unrest."

Scrungle watched the face of the Princess as she stumbled through her emotions at hearing this news.

"What!" Said Isobella "That lousy trollop. Married! When did this happen?"

"Just after the vote came in. By all accounts, your father wanted to make things official. Well, that's what the town criers were saying."

Said Captain Black who didn't look that convinced it was the truth.

" When do we reach port." Asked the Princess

"Two days with this wind." Said the captain.

"Thank you, captain."

"I will have food and water sent directly."

Isobella stood up, bumped her head on a beam, and shouted out in anger. The captain rose as well.

"Your Highness." Said Captain Black

"Yes."

"There is a lot of unrest in the kingdom. When we left port, a large number of hobgoblins and sheriffs had come to the town. Here to supposedly keep the peace and to search for the terrorists and yourself."

The Princess was still rubbing her head.

"I have nothing to fear. The knights will take me back."

Now Captain Black came around the table and stood in front of the Princess.

"Your Highness, most of the knights gave up their colours when Gumptrude won. The ones that are left are at the castle."

"Oh my," said Isobella.

"Highness, I am loyal to the crown, but I fear for your safety outside of this ship. Things are happening which are beyond my control or understanding."

A light knocking on the door stopped any more talk.

"Enter." Said Captain Black.

"Sir, you're needed on the bridge. The first mate has had another episode with bananas and the quartermaster." Said the young master at arms.

"Follow the master at arms here, and he will have the boson assign you your hammocks." Then the captain bowed to the Princess and left.

Sergio and Scrungle followed the master at arms, who took them through the length of the lower deck to a small, four-sided galley serving food.

The boson was sharpening a knife on a stone. He had a grizzled look and didn't say much except grunt at Sergio, pointing with his knife at a hammock, then did the same for Scrungle. A small curtain was the only thing to afford them any privacy. Scrungle clambered onto the hammock and fell into a troubled sleep. It was late when Sergio woke him.

"Scrungle come."

Deftly alighting the hammock, Scrungle squeezed past the crew. The night shift was taking over, so the day crew now stood in line for food. Scrungle could feel eyes on him, a known fugitive roaming freely on the ship. He followed Sergio as he went up the narrow steps and onto the deck.

The Princess was at the prow, looking out towards the horizon. The sun was behind them now. Scrungle took a moment as he had seen the dinghy off to one side of the messin' hatch. With a quick check to ensure he wasn't being observed put it back into his pocket.

Isobella had washed and changed, borrowing a tunic and other clothes, boots from the captain, as well as some clean underwear from the short order cook, who liked to do drag when on shore leave. Isobella looked careworn by everything that had happened. There wasn't much of a swell, and the ship cut an even line through the water. Looking around, Scrungle saw that the crew gave the trio a wide birth as if being too close to royalty would hurt.

"How are you?" Said Isobella.

"Very sad," said Scrungle as honestly as he could. The Princess nodded and then took one of Scrungle's stick-like hands.

"I will not forget everything you and Peetles have done. But I fear for our safety when we reach port."

"Why do you fear my lady?" Sergio said, "Once we are in port you will be escorted back to Plombree. Once inside the castle, insist you see your father and just give him the Huba mushroom."

Isobella lifted Sergio's hands to her face and kissed them.

"My dear Sergio, several things are happening, and all the pieces are moving. Gumptrude is a puppet, It is the Baroness who is the puppet master. Her plan for me to marry Prince Terry Whackerknacker, and eventually rule both kingdoms has now, I fear, been abandoned. They forged the marriage to my father. She is queen. I believe anything could happen between leaving the port and reaching Plombree and the castle." The Princess looked tired and angry in equal measure.

"We must rally the Knights to our cause and get to your father as soon as possible," Sergio said defiant against the odds.

"The captain told me the griffin flew off, letting Gumptrude know that I am here." Said Isobella.

"How can we get a message to the Knights? How do we find them." Sergio asked.

"Well, if we could see Malcolm, he might be able to find them," Scrungle said.

"Who's Malcolm?" Said the Princess and Sergio together.

"Oh, he's the falcon that scouts for the Knights," explained Scrungle.

"Didn't know he had a name. I watched the yellow Knight train him. But we have as much chance of spotting the falcon as we have of getting any help from the job centre or universal credit." Said the Princess. There was a moment's pause, and then Scrungle heard the parrot over the sound of the ship in open water.

"I might be able to help." Said Scrungle and walked off to see if he could strike up a conversation with the parrot that had shouted at the vessel inspector. As he approached, he realised the red, blue, and green parrot was singing quietly to itself in its native tongue, punctuating the song with blows on a small harmonica lashed with string to the bird cage.

"Nobody knows the trouble I've seen. Nobody knows my sorrow. Nobody knows the trouble I've seen. Someone give me a cracker."

"Hello, I'm Scrungle Bungus. What's your name?"

"Who's an ugly tit then?" Squawked the parrot, looking at Scrungle then going back to the song. Scrungle a bit thrown by the comment kept his composure.

"That's a sad song you're singing." Trying harder to get on the parrot's good side. The parrot which had been blowing hard on the mouth organ stopped abruptly, mid-solo.

"You heard that?" Said the parrot.

"Yes, it made me sad and think about a friend."

"Never met anyone who could talk real parrot before. Sorry about the 'who's an ugly tit' remark. It's what the tourists expect. Good to meet you, Mr Bungus." The parrot's lilting deep voice would have been excellent for sports commentary.

"Call me Scrungle everybody does. I know we have just met but If I was to ask you for help in getting a message to a friend of mine would you be receptive." Scrungle said getting straight to the point.

"If you got me out of this cage I would kiss your feet." The parrot looked down to Scrungle's feet which didn't exist then looked back at Scrungle.

"Sorry about that."

"Oh, it's fine. Never had them never missed them. I need to talk to my friends for a moment." Said Scrungle then turned back to the parrot. "Sorry, I didn't catch your name."

"Ababacus Blue Wind, but these idiots call me Bill."

The Princess and Sergio had moved away towards the narrow of the prow and were in deep conversation in hushed voices. Sergio was very animated until he saw Scrungle then stopped. The Princess beckoned Scrungle forward.

"Princess, if we can write a message and attach it to Ababacus also known as Bill we might be able to get a message to the Knights." Scrungle indicated the parrot in the cage.

"Oh, Scrungle you give me hope." Said the Princess.

Sergio headed off to find writing implements. Scrungle went back to Ababacus also known as Bill and talked about what they needed the parrot to do. It wasn't long before they had a message written and a little piece of string to keep the message attached to the leg of the parrot.

"Ababacus. Can I put this message on your leg?"

Scrungle held up the little bit of parchment. The Princess and Sergio listened to the one-way dialogue. Ababacus also known as Bill lifted a leg ready. Scrungle opened the cage and attached the message. The parrot stood on the edge of the metal rung.

"So that I've got this right I get this message to Malcolm the Falcon or any Knight of colour. Also, spread the word to any other birds to find Malcolm the falcon who works for the Knights to get the Knights to go to harbour town."

"Yes, that's right." Said Scrungle.

"You do know falcons attack other birds right?" Ababacus said getting animated.

"Just say Scrungle sent you you'll be fine," Scrungle said trying to reassure the parrot but when he thought about it, Abacus had a point.

"What's he saying Scrungle." Asked Sergio

"He says he will help." Said Scrungle.

With that, the parrot took flight, circled the ship a few times to get his bearings then headed in the opposite direction to land. The Princess, Sergio, and Scrungle dropped their heads, despondent.

## Twenty-Eight

# *Not Again*

News had already reached the Town of Harbour which was a harbour. The port was thronged with people and creatures eager to see the Princess and the terrorist Scrungle Bungus. It was deemed necessary to hide Scrungle in the hold until the Princess had disembarked. Then hopefully all the attention would follow the Princess along with the town's local scribes who were jostling each other and security guards for the best position on the dock.

A press release was scheduled later in the day for the town criers to call out. Scrungle sat bored but relatively safe on the ship with Captain Black. He watched through the port-hole window as the Princess and Sergio left and walked down the gangplank. On the dock lounging around was a detachment of sheriffs and a host of hobgoblins as her escort.

He watched as Isobella became angry at the sheriffs pointing and shouting at the hobgoblins, but eventually placated by the captain, she boarded a carriage and drew the curtains to hide from the onlookers.

Watching all this, Scrungle saw the fat vessel inspector follow the entourage and chat closely with one of the sheriffs.

Scrungle was kept on the ship until night fell. In the darkness, he was given the uniform of one of the ship's soldiers, which didn't fit at all, and then taken along to the back entrance of the governor's house where the Princess was staying. Captain Black and two soldiers from the ship were his escort. Scrungle was shown into the house through the servant's entrance then hidden in the storeroom full of food.

"I will beg your leave, Mr. Bungus. The Princess Isobella told me to say she will come and see you soon."

Before Scrungle could say 'Just call me Scrungle', the captain had gone. He waited in the storeroom and, for the first time in his many years, felt a terrible loneliness, missing Peetles happy disposition. Eventually, there was a light knock, then the Princess poked her head around the door.

"Hello." Said Scrungle.

"Oh, Scrungle I am so sorry for this, after everything that has happened. You should be honoured."

With Sergio behind her, she came into the room and sat down on a large bag of flour. Isobella was wearing a regal gown of light pink with bows and frills. Scrungle had never seen her in a dress or all girly-looking. It was quite the difference, and he was suddenly aware she was a rather beautiful woman. Sergio dressed in formal wear looked handsome standing next to her.

"We are to leave in the small hours of the morning. I am in a bind... Scrungle I have to get home to Dad as soon as possible, but I fear the sheriffs and hobgoblins are up to something. The council member for Gumptrude insists that we all travel together." Scrungle wasn't getting the point as such and stroked his long nose for comfort.

"I'm not sure I understand. So am I not being sent to jail?"

"For now, you are safe with me. Once my father is awake, this madness will end. I felt safe with the captain, but he can't leave his soldiers with us."

"Oh." Said Scrungle

"I just hope the parrot delivered our message. It won't be long before we leave, be ready."

Standing on tiptoes, she kissed Scrungles cheek and left the storeroom with Sergio. With little to do and feeling abandoned, Scrungle decided to count the different foods stored on the shelves. Walking between two high shelving compartments, he came across punnet after punnet of mushrooms.

"Well, take comfort when one can." He said out loud in his head. Scrungle was not sure if he was a wanted felon or a hero; either way, he wasn't going to be hungry. Finding a comfortable place to sit, he absorbed a whole punnet, which tasted of roast chicken and rosemary. For safekeeping, he put a punnet or two in his pockets. After finishing the last mushroom, there was a knock at the door; it was Sergio; behind him were two hobgoblins and a pasty-looking sheriff.

"Scrungle time to go."

It was well past midnight and they went out the servant's entrance to the side of the three-story governor's house. where the carriage the Princess and Sergio had come in and wagons to carry all the hobgoblins waited. The sheriffs were on horseback. Scrungle could hear sniggers of laughter and a few calls.

"Look at the walking parsnip."

He clambered into the carriage and sat opposite Sergio and the Princess, and they set off under the cover of darkness. Heading out of the Harbour along the King's Road. A couple of speed sketch artists were out prowling for a good likeness to sell, but the carriage curtains were closed and the sheriffs wouldn't let them get close.

The Princess and Sergio were dressed for the night's cold, but no one in the carriage could sleep. Tension filled the air; something bad was going to happen.

The road was smooth but slow, and the Princess was certain that if they kept this pace up, they wouldn't be at the crossroads for two days, and she was desperate they should travel faster. Scrungle wondered about the tricycle, which was still in his magic pockets. Could they all cling onto it and dash for the castle together?

The morning light filtered through the curtains, then came a knock on the carriage door. The Princess pulled the sash. Outside Dinjay Flat was looking in. She shielded her eyes from the morning sun, flooding into the carriage.

"Sorry to disturb the Royal Highness but we have stopped for food and a bit stretch of the legs. Would Your Highness like to have a moment." Said Gumptrude's vessel inspector in a voice so irritating, Scrungle, Sergio and Isobella wished they were deaf. The Princess didn't reply, just let the curtain drop. She looked at Sergio and Scrungle.

"Keep your wits about you. They may be up to something. And don't eat anything."

They got out of the carriage. The sheriffs which numbered six were sitting at a fold-out table on the grass verge by the side of the road. Some hobgoblins were poking a grass snake with a stick while others were lounging around. A bunch were in a circle flexing their braces to see who was the most intimidating. All eyes fell on the trio as they got out of the carriage.

Scrungle had been searching for a word to describe Dinjay Flat and eventually, he found the word smarmy.

"We have put up a table for Your Highness." With a slight bow while extending his arm to lead the way for the Princess. Isobella dressed in the flowing gown walked over to the table that had a little pagoda erected around it

Isobella remarked to Scrungle quietly that it displayed no banners of the royal house and sat down. Scrungle and Sergio sat on smaller seats beside her. The food was chicken, ham, bread as well as several sweet cakes and a Victoria sponge cake which had a slice or two missing from it. It all looked enticing but Isobella didn't make a move for any of it.

"Would your Highness like some wine?" Dinjay was hosting but the Princess shook her head.

"No Thank you. You may go." Said Isobella.

Dinjay bowed and walked backwards for a little way smiling a smarmy smile before rejoining the sheriffs. All the while they watched and talked amongst themselves taking sideways glances at the royal table. Sergio leaned forward to break some bread when the Princess hissed for him not to eat anything. Sergio retracted his hand looking deflated all the while his stomach grumbled. Scrungle pulled out of his pockets the mushrooms he had kept from the store room and shared them with the Princess and Sergio.

It was the Princess who noticed and then nudged Scrungle to look over to where three of the hobgoblins were lying asleep or what looked to be asleep. Two of them had half-eaten cake in their hands the other had strawberry jam around his mouth.

"I think the cakes off." Said Sergio.

When the Princess showed no signs of eating anything on the table the hobgoblins hastily put the food into the bin.

Scrungle was half aware that he was looking at the sky. Subconsciously checking for Malcolm. A column of carriages passed on the King's road headed for the Plombree. They could smell sugar, cake mix, and strawberry essence. Isobella insisted on having them back in the coach and on the road. Scrungle took note that the excuses from Dinjay stopped when the column of carriages had disappeared. The coach rocked back and forwards as they set off again. It was crawling along.

"We must escape." Said Sergio keeping his voice low.

"I feel the same." The Princess leaned close bringing the three of them together.

"I think we should make a run for it."

"I can pedal faster than I can run." Said Scrungle.

"Sorry, what do you mean." Asked the Princess.

Scrungle pulled the handlebar out of the top of his magic pockets.

"Yes of course." Said Isobella in a loud voice then looked around conscious of being overheard. The three huddled close together and then discussed how they could all get on the tricycle and away.

The night came and they felt the terrain change as they were bounced around in the coach.

"We aren't on Dad's road anymore. What are they up to?" Said the Princess.

Sergio pulled the curtains aside but it was too dark to see. He tried to turn the latch but it had been fastened together with a leather strip on the outside. With one swift movement, he was halfway out of the window trying to climb onto the carriage roof but was hit with a billy club and forced back in.

"How dare you do this. Stop this carriage this instant." Shouted Isobella.

"Shut up ya silly bint." Shouted a hobgoblin and his mates joined in laughing. Branches snapped on the roof of the carriage and scrapped along the side. Then stopped and the door handle on the inside rattled as the leather restraint was untied. Moments later it swung open.

Sheriffs stood there brandishing swords, Dinjay Flat was astride his horse, while behind them stood hobgoblins holding flaming torches.

"Out."

Sergio went first then Scrungle, then the Princess.

"Hands up."

"What are you doing? How dare you." Said Isobella trying her hardest to intimidate with the royal lineage angle.

"Will someone gag that annoying cow?" Said Dinjay Flat.

"You'll never get away with this." Shouted Isobella.

"Of course, we will. The terrorist escapes and kills the Princess, then we kill the terrorist. I've even got the press release ready." Dinjay Flat held up a scroll tied in the middle with a ribbon.

Two of the sheriffs came forward to hold and gag the Princess but Sergio was in there first. Swinging a spinning back kick into the lead sheriff's face he flattened him, out cold.

Scrungle was very impressed for many reasons. The first was that there wasn't a lot of light being thrown from the torches the hobgoblins were holding in which to accomplish the manoeuvre, then the fact they were in a little copse of trees and the ground was very uneven, slippery, damp, and carpeted with rotting leaves. Also, he had never seen Sergio practicing any kind of self-defence—limber up or stretch for that matter—despite the fact the sheriff he had sent to bed early was over six feet. In all due consideration, Scrungle had to stop himself from applauding.

The Princess not to be outdone employed a more direct approach and with a swift kick to the short and curly's had the other one down. The hobgoblins just stood and watched. Scrungle pulled out the hat stand and threw it at the other sheriffs who automatically grabbed it between them.

"It's an heirloom." Said Scrungle.

The sheriffs expecting some form of combat looked at each other as Scrungle started to tell them the hat stands back story. Sergio picked up a sword from the prone sheriff and charged the hobgoblins who scattered.

"Run." Shouted Isobella grabbing Scrungles hand propelling him towards the King's Road.

"A bag of gold to the man or hob, that brings them down." Shouted Dinjay Flat.

Scrungle forgot how fast he could run until the right motivation came along. Then his nose swung and slapped his face reminding him why he didn't.

"Oh my, Oh my." He said unaware he was saying anything. Running through the uneven grass and tufts of sod Scrungle held on to the Princess dragging her at speed towards the King's Road.

When they reached the flagstones he stopped to pull out the tricycle, which was no mean feat considering its size. He slid onto the seat, and the Princess, as planned, grabbed onto the back of it, bracing her feet on the back bar. Sergio, who had been bringing up the rear and should have jumped onto the front handlebars, turned and stood his ground, facing the hobgoblins.

"Go," he shouted then started into the throng of little shits who for the most part fell back. Then one of them threw a stone hitting Sergio in the face.

"No." Screamed Isobella but Scrungle was pushing down hard and building up a little bit of speed. Sergio fell to one knee and the hobgoblins jumped him hitting him with the clubs. Scrungle pushed harder at the pedals but the sound of the mounted sheriffs could be heard as they galloped across the grass towards them.

Their swords drawn, horseshoe on stone they caught up with the fleeing tricycle. Scrungle braked hard and ducked. They flew past, the sword thrust missing its target by inches.

"I am sorry Princess, I think we are at an end."

The sheriffs reined in their horses and turned back towards the tricycle. Knowing they had caught their prey they didn't hurry. From behind they heard another horse and turned to see Dinjay Flat coming towards them holding a torch. The Princess buried her head into Scrungle from behind.

"Enough of this silliness now, there's a good Princess." Dinjay Flats' whining voice sounded even more irritating in the darkness.

"I am sorry for everything." Said the Princess.

They sat waiting for the killing blow when out of the darkness a horn was blown. Then a call from above.

"Scrungle we got the message mate." Looking up he saw Malcolm the falcon and Bill the parrot circling the tricycle and out of the night came the cry.

"Charge."

With lances in their hands and shields at their sides came the Knights of Colour. Smashing into the sheriffs with such fury the sound would ring in Scrungles ears for what felt like the rest of the night. Charging on the knights cut down Dinjay Flat and the hobgoblins as hot piss in snow. Scrungle pedalled back and the Princess jumped down and ran to Sergio lying beaten and unconscious but alive. Torches were lit and the knights dismounted, kneeling at the feet of the Princess.

"Your Highness." From the colour of their helmets and plumage Scrungle could see that the Gold, Green, Yellow, and Grey knights had come to their rescue. Isobella grabbed the Gold Knight, pulled her to her feet, and hugged her tight.

## Twenty-Nine

# *What's the Plan*

The Gold Knight, who had a head for tactics, made them pull the carriage back onto the King's Road. The bodies were put back into the wagons and left in the woods for the crows. Scrungle made sure he picked up the trusty hat stand. He never thought it would come in this useful especially since he rarely wore a hat.

Now at high speed, they pushed on for the rest of the night. Sergio was in the carriage with the Princess and the Yellow Knight, doing what they could for his injuries. Scrungle at the front of the column illuminated the way with the tricycle lantern. His eyes wandered to the empty basket on the front, a constant reminder of his fallen friend. Just before the break of dawn, the company reached Dangles Inn. Stabling the horses and waking the faun, they took over the common room. There weren't many guests, and Dangle told the ones who were curious that there was a last-minute booking for a surprise wedding and no one was allowed in.

Now in the light of day, Scrungle could see the knight's armour wasn't the same as when he had first met them. Only the breastplate and helm had colour; it was only later that he found out it was the knight's practice armour, and the only thing you could keep when you handed in your colours was the helm.

Dangle had some experience with broken bones and took over from the Yellow Knight to administer to Sergio. He bound his ribs as best he could, and then, with the help of his staff, they took Sergio upstairs to lie down.

Food was set out in a buffet-style arrangement, but Dangle didn't provide plates because, in his mind, this prevented customers from overeating.

They assembled the tables in the common room into a rough circle. Smoke from the candles lazily wound up towards the dark beams of the ceiling. On his return, Dangle was told by Isobella to sit at the table with them all, next to the parrot and Malcolm the falcon, perched on the backrest of the wooden seat.

Isobella looked around at the faces at the table. In her eyes was nothing but love for the people and creatures sitting there.

"My wonderful knights. I can't put into words how much I thank you."

Isobella started to fill up, then controlled herself. Scrungle absorbed a mushroom from the buffet. It tasted like whipped cream. The Gold Knight stood; she resembled Isobella in appearance. Her straight, jet-black hair was shoulder-length. Brown eyes and high cheekbones. The knight was a good two inches taller than the Princess, but many in the city had mistaken them for each other.

"What is your command, your highness? It was luck, I think, that we were at the inn when the message came to us." Lady Gold nodded to the birds.

"I am sure the other knights will join us once they have word."

"I'm not sure about that. Black and White are too concerned about their endorsements and losing sponsorship deals and Sir Blue just follows White around like a puppy." Said Lady Green.

"Sir Red will come."

"Lady Orange will join us." Said Lady Yellow.

"What about the Lady Silver." Said Isobella. The Gold Knight looked at her compatriots.

"She has a thing for the Black Knight. I'm not sure."

The Green Knight stood up, flushed with excitement.

"To war, we must go; this treachery cannot go unpunished. We will move through the towns and gather an army. Smash Gumptrude and Bakeasy into the ground and free your friend Scrungle. Then equal pay for all.."

It was a passionate outburst by the Green Knight but she had swayed into another agenda at the end of the speech. Scrungle had only been half-listening and suddenly took note.

"Sorry, what did you say." Said Scrungle.

"Equal pay for all."

"No before that bit."

"Your friend, The orange creature Petals is a prisoner of Easybakes." Said the Green Knight. Isobella raised her hand.

"Peetles was lost at sea there was a storm."

"Beg your forgiveness Your Highness but this Peetles was washed up on the shore, The harbour master recognised them from the wanted poster, and they were taken to the capitol by a griffin. It was all the news."

Scrungle stood up knocking the chair over as he did so. He felt like he had fallen out of the Chana tree onto his head.

"Peetles is alive?"

The knights nodded. Scrungle couldn't contain his joy, whooped and danced around the room. The Princess laughed at the good news, and the knights joined in cheering along with Scrungle's jubilation.

"Peetles is alive. Peetles is alive." Scrungle slowly calmed, elated; he felt so light in his heart he could have floated up to the Chana tree without the Huba mushroom magic. The Princess, smiling, happy that Peetles was alive, motioned for Scrungle to sit.

"That is good news." Said Isobella then the Princess stood and the Green and Gold Knights sat down.

"Well, that makes things different again. I want revenge but I will not start a civil war. Bakeasy, no matter how contentious, is by law the queen. I don't want people to die or split the country in two. We have the cure for the King thanks to Scrungle Bungus. Scrungle, please show us."

Scrungle's magic pockets manifested themselves, and he slowly pulled out the last Huba mushroom and held it out for all to see.

"Go faster stripe I see." Said the Grey Knight.

"We need stealth and cunning to save my Father. Once awake, can set things in order again. When are the celebrations going to start?" Said Isobella.

"They have started already. But the main event and bake-off are in two days. Here I have a pamphlet. Picked it up when I handed in my colours."

The Grey Knight choked up a little; it had hurt him deeply, and saying it out loud made it all the more real that he had forsaken his colours and the vows of chivalry. He laid out the fan-fold parchment on the table in front of him so the rest of the ensemble could see it. In the centre was a drawing depicting the inside of the castle for the festival, rides, confectionery stands, dancers, and the main stage for the bake-off competition.

The whole festival was sponsored by the SCS and Amazing Shine. Scrungle put the Huba mushroom away for safekeeping and watched as everyone crowded around the little map. He could hear little bits of conversation but was unable to concentrate after hearing Peetles was alive. Isobella and the Gold Knight were starting to formulate an idea, and Scrungle was ready to do anything the Princess asked of him. Isobella stood back from the map.

"We have a rough plan and time is of the essence. Make ready to leave."

With that, Isobella left to talk to Sergio. They all stood, bowed and then made their way outside to the stables. The parrot Bill hopped onto the Grey Knight's shoulder who looked well at ease with him and Malcolm landed on the Yellow Knight's pauldron.

Torpid was outside assembling the horses and the carriage. Scrungle said hello and asked how she was, as he had not been afforded the chance the night before. Torpid looked like she had just been caught having a sly pie. Nobody ever said hello or asked how she was. After tripping over her words a few times, she eventually spluttered out that she was fine.

Malcolm bid Scrungle farewell as he was being sent to scout and find the other Knights with Bill the parrot who joined the cause for the company and the crack.

Dangle handed over provisions for the rest of the journey with an itemised bill for the company's tab. He gave it to Scrungle with a

"Be a good fellow hand it to the Princess when you get a chance."

Before Scrungle could think they were back on the road. The tricycle kept pace with the horses easily. Isobella, now dressed in leather trousers and a cotton shirt, was on her horse travelling with everyone else. Occupying the carriage were the Yellow and Grey Knights who were working on something to do with the plan.

With the Princess and the Gold Knight at the head of the company, they galloped at pace, only occasionally slowing long enough for the horses to catch their breath. Scrungle could hear the horses complain while the ones pulling the carriage kept saying they had it easy.

When they slowed Isobella drew close to Scrungle and filled in the key elements of the plan. They would reach Plombree on the day of the competition. The Gold Knight would then disguise herself as the Princess and Isobella as the Knight. Once through the gates, they would be escorted up to the castle. Isobella would, at the right time, slip away. She knew a few secret ways in and out of the castle and would get to her father.

"What about Peetles?" Said Scrungle worried his little friend would be forgotten.

"Once Dad is better Peetles will be free. I need you by my side. If I am taken or captured or whatever I want the cure safe. Nothing safer than magic pockets. And Scrungle, you'll be in disguise." She said this and smiled at Scrungle.

"What's the disguise," Scrungle asked raising a non-existent eye-brow.

"Sir Grey and Lady Yellow are working on it now. They're the best at sewing and needlepoint."

The company passed others on the King's Road making their way to the capitol for the final of the bake-off. It was a heady mixture of creatures and people. Most recognised the Princess and stopped to bow or cheer.

When they passed through **Illecclefeckenhaveyoumate** the Green Knight and Scrungle looked for the miller's family but the windmill was locked, stationary, and the home was shuttered. Scrungle hoped that nothing bad had happened and they had gone to the festival as a family. On the notice board of the town, they saw posters and graffiti exclaiming

**'Gumptrude is a tool'** and **'Not my queen.'**

It warmed the Princess's heart. At a passing point, the company stopped and took a light meal. Scrungle inquired about the costume and the Grey and Yellow Knights showed him what they had been making. It was a colourful jester's top and baggy red pants. A hat with three horns and a felt mask.

"What do you think." Said Lady Yellow a half smile.

"Yes very nice." Said Scrungle without much conviction. Then walked back to the tricycle thinking he should have stayed at Dangles Inn.

* * *

Scrungle had been at the head of the column with the light of the tricycle lantern leading the way. His newfound focus to save Peetles had kept him going this far, but now he was flagging and needed sleep.

The Princess called a halt, and Scrungle fell into the arms of Morpheus almost immediately, sitting up on the tricycle seat wrapped in the strawberry duvet.

Hours had passed, but it felt like moments when he was woken by a raised voice. Sitting upright, he could see a figure in the darkness just outside of the light of a single torch. The Grey Knight had drawn his sword and stood in a fighting stance.

"Last chance to identify yourself." The Grey Knight's voice was calm, serene even.

"What you going to do you big loaf. You'll probably trip over your own feet."

Scrungle thought he knew the voice. Then the Grey Knight sheathed his sword and ran into the darkness. Scrungle could hear a clang as metal hit metal, a sloppy kiss, and then the Grey and the Red Knight, holding hands, walked into the light.

The talk had also woken the other knights. Who, on seeing the Red Knight, ran towards him excited at their compatriots' return. Trying hard to keep their voices low and let the Princess rest.

They all huddled together next to the embers of the campfire. The

Red Knight said he had been heading south towards the harbour wanting to find employment as a lighthouse keeper when he had received the message from Malcolm the Falcon.

Before the light of dawn, they set off. Isobella was delighted when she saw the Red Knight, chiding him about his moustache, saying he looked like he frightened children for a living. The Red Knight was in uncommonly good cheer and kept looking at the Grey Knight and smiling.

Early on the morning of the next day, the company could just see the outer walls of the city in the distance. The road wound through the valley of '**Non-dom statues**' before climbing a little through wheat fields and the run-down estate to the north gate of the city. The Princess halted the company. Two riders were coming fast towards them. Cloaked and armoured, it was hard to make out if they were friend or foe.

"Make ready." Shouted the Gold Knight, drawing her sword. The others followed suit, and without thinking, the Green and Yellow Knights flanked Scrungle. The Red and Grey Knights did the same for Isobella.

Galloping towards them, then stopping, all the knights cried out when the strangers dropped their hoods. It was Lady Orange and Lady Silver, the colours of their helmets unmistakable. The two knights had been travelling through the mountains when they were found by Malcolm. At once they dismounted, taking their helmets off they knelt before the Princess.

"Your Highness," they said in unison. Isobella, disregarding formality, jumped from her horse and hugged the knights.

"Have you heard anything about my Father?" Isobella searched their faces. The Silver Knight looked at her metal-clad feet.

"They say he will not last the night."

"Then there is no time to waste." As planned, Isobella swapped clothes with the Gold Knight, who wore Isobella's pink dress and now rode in the carriage, while the Yellow Knight explained to the Silver and Orange Knights what the plan was.

"There's a lot of unrest in the city. It would take nothing to have the people behind us," said Lady Orange.

"The plan is solid. We can restore everything without any violence." Said Isobella.

* * *

It was evening by the time they reached the gates leading into the city, A waiting queue was being processed, and a levy for entry was being taken. Anyone with the wrong papers or not enough money was sent off down a small dirt track by the side of the outer wall and corralled to be processed in five months.

"Make way for the Princess." Shouted the Silver Knight. The queue moved off the road as the carriage made its way to the front. Dismounting his horse, the Red Knight told them to lift the barrier as the Princess had arrived.

The customs official in new regalia dressed in purples and black had the 'Gump Security' logo over the breastplate.

"I don't recognise any of you, lot." Said the Red Knight.

"Staffing of the gates has been taken over by Gumptrude security group. You'll have to wait here until head office is informed that the Princess has been found. Need the correct paperwork mate."

Scrungle, dressed as a jester, was sitting on the back of Torpids cart, which transported the knight's weapons and lances. Torpid moved closer in case she was needed to squire.

The Gold Knight posing as the Princess alighted the carriage, tripping on the dress that was far too small for her. Regaining her composure, she walked to the guards. They didn't kneel. Still on horseback, the other knights crowded the Gumptrude guards.

"Kneel before the Princess." Said the Red Knight.

"It's been abolished. We only kneel in the presence of the Queen or High Chancellor Gumptrude." Said the querulous guard. Other security men had come out of the guard house in a show of strength. Most had some form of baked goods in their hands or mouths and outnumbered the knights two to one. The watching Scrungle had a bad feeling about the next few moments.

"Look I know you are just following orders. So just lift the gate and we will escort the Princess to the castle." Said the Grey Knight dismounting his horse.

"Look, mate, you've got no authority to tell anybody anything; everyone knows you lot handed your colours in, you're not a knight anymore, you're just a commoner, like…"

Whatever the guard was about to say was cut short as the Red Knight punched him hard in the face. His head hit the ground long before his teeth did. About ten other guards of the private security firm watched and then launched themselves at the Red Knight.

Scrungle sitting in the ringside seat watched in fascination as the Gold Knight, pretending to be the Princess in her long pink gown disarmed three of the on-rushing guards with such ease it looked like they had just fallen over when they got close enough. The Grey, Red, and Yellow Knights had drawn swords but had been forbidden by the Princess to kill anyone unless in dire need. Moving with speed and agility, they concussed the rest of the guards. A groaning huddle of Gumptrude Security lay on the grass and mud in less than a minute.

The on-looking queue gave a cheer.

"Come on, we still have the element of surprise." Shouted the Princess dressed in the Gold Knights armour. Then a horn sounded from further along the wall. The knights recognised it as the call for reinforcements.

"Bugger," said the Princess.

Between them, they lifted the barrier and headed along the main road that led to the castle. All manner of creatures and people thronged the streets. Stalls and barrows lined the pavement with sellers of baked goods, penny magic, and fireworks. Lights and bunting criss-crossed overhead. The sound of musicians and buskers filled the air.

Amongst the celebrations were knots of protestors shouting that the festival was in bad taste since the King was on his deathbed. Banners and parchments were being handed out detailing how the country was being duped as well as announcing a discount code for the SCS. In some places, little scuffles would break out between pro-Gumptrude and Royalists. As the company moved forward, word rippled through the crowd that the Princess and the knights had returned.

Following the main road, they came to the intersection. One road led towards the plaza and the other to the castle. At the top of the hill, a detachment of Gumptrude security guards was heading down towards them. Behind the guards were hobgoblins pushing small children down and kicking the elderly. Stopping in the middle of the highway, Isobella turned to the company.

"OK plan's went to shit." The Princess's searching look scanned the night as if trying to work out the word on a conundrum that was all vowels.

"Scrungle and Lady Green, you're with me. Sir Red and Grey and Lady Orange, head to the plaza. Cause as much mayhem as possible. Draw the sheriffs and hobgoblins to you. Lady Gold, Lady Yellow, and Torpid take the carriage on a tour of Plombree. Make yourself visible, Torpid; it's your job to shout that the Princess is back, as loud as possible. Lady Silver, find the Blue, Black, and White Knights and tell them what's happening. If they won't join us, make sure they won't side against us. And don't kill anyone."

The crowd was parting or being pushed out of the way by the

Gumptrude security men.

"We should stay with you. It is our duty." Said the Gold Knight in a dress that was too small for her, especially across the shoulders.

"Not the time to argue. It's a royal command and, my brave knights, be careful. I want to see you all again when this is over." With that said the Princess jumped down from her horse. The Green Knight and Scrungle followed as she ran up a small lane towards the castle. Stopping when she heard Sir Red, Sir Grey and Lady Orange shouting

'Come and have a go if you think you're hard enough.' Then watched as they galloped off towards the plaza and the carriage went in the opposite direction. Torpid was at the reins, shouting that the Princess was in the carriage and was being attacked by Gumptrude security. Isobella wiped a tear from her eye and ran.

As they climbed the streets leading to the castle, they passed many residents of Plombree in fancy dress. Scrungle blended in easily. The Princess, avoiding the larger crowds, took them through the smaller thoroughfares and alleyways, continuously leading them up until they climbed the steps of a steep bank, slowing to catch their breath at the top where the outer wall met the entertainer's green. Looking down, Scrungle could see the carriage moving at speed below. Men on horseback chasing while following behind were the hobgobblins.

Word had spread fast that the knights and the Princess were in the city, Hobgobblins and Gumptrude security were stopping anyone who looked remotely like a threat, walked funny, or didn't like cake. The Princess and the Green Knight discarded as much of the armour as they could to avoid drawing attention.

"Best lose the swords as well." Said Isobella.

"Please your highness, I can't protect you." Said the Green Knight. It was her favourite sword. Well balanced with a cream leather grip on the handle.

"If we carry swords in the castle we'll be stopped immediately. We have to get to Dad through stealth." Said Isobella.

The Green Knight gave up the sword, hiding it behind a stack of empty apple boxes with the rest of the armour. Grumbling all the while that it better be there when she came back for it. Then onward they climbed up towards the festival.

The castle looked resplendent in the dark of the evening, lit up with torches and enchantments glowing in the colours of Gumptrude, Pushing through the crowds as well as protestors, the Princess took them on a route that was parallel to the main wall and away from the drawbridge entrance. Cheers and the general hubbub of a great festival could be heard drifting over the ramparts. Looking up, Scrungle saw the banners of Plom still flew but were outnumbered by the colours of Gumptrude.

It became less and less inhabited the further they skirted the castle walls, heading towards the back thrust of the mountains. Now the terrain was mainly thorn bushes and stunted trees. The Princess looked around and then dropped to one knee, grabbing the cover that hid the entrance to the sewer. Between the three, they lifted it and headed into the smell. The tunnel was cramped, and they walked hunched up; combined with the stench, it did nothing for the tempers of the trio by the time they emerged. It took the Green Knight a bit of pushing, but eventually, she managed to topple the lid, and with a quick look around, saw that they were in a service hut under the interior wall walkway.

Once outside, they could see the castle was packed with the most affluent of Plombree. The ticket prices for the festival were so ridiculously high that only the most well-off could attend. A huge tent had been erected in the inner circle of the keep and had **'Sponsored by SCS and Amazing Shine'** across the length of the proscenium arch. They could just make out the stage where contestants at three tables were making huge, three-layered wedding cakes. Stage left, the judges sat on high back chairs; from the angle they were at, no one in the trio could make out who they were. It was apparent the stage had been bewitched to magnify the voice, as even from where they were they could hear the commentary. It had taken three wizards and a witch two days to enchant.

The enchantment still wasn't right, as now and then it would cut out, and the consensus of the crowd was that it was bass-heavy. An apprentice wizard had been left to fix the sound-mix whilst the senior wizards and the witch had wandered off to the beer tent. The apprentice wizard was getting a lot of complaints while trying to figure out the incantation for the bass cut and stop the slap-back delay.

Gumptrude guards were everywhere checking for the right parchment pass for the seating closest to the front and escorting anyone without it to the cells. The single bridge was choked with people trying to get closer to the stage and watch the final. Isobella couldn't see a single royal guard she recognised just men with the Gumptrude logo and apparel.

"He's privatised the castle, the little shit." Said an angry Isobella.

"How do we get to your father?" Asked Scrungle.

The Princess looked across the interior moat up to the royal building and the tallest tower.

"Do you see the tallest tower on the left?" Said the Princess

"Yes." Said the Green Knight and Scrungle.

"Well, follow it across to the right side and the three gargoyles on the side of that arch. Can you see the one light at the window?"

"Yes." They said together.

"Do you see the building opposite with the heavy iron bars on the window and the slanted stonework?"

"Yes." Said Scrungle and the Green Knight once again.

"He could be in any one of them." Said the Princess.

Scrungle and the Green Knight exchanged a look.

"Come on only one way to find out." Said the Princess.

The three headed into the throng of people and creatures. Everywhere cakes and delicacies caught the eye or nose. Vendors at stalls were shouting they had the best baked goods in the land. A large troll stood in the middle of the courtyard with a full sample tray of different salted loaves and other baked goods. His blank stare fixed on the middle distance. Because he was so tall, no one could see or reach what he was selling.

Around the outer bailey of the castle were, jugglers, jesters, stilt walkers, acrobats, people on pogo sticks fighting with wooden swords, and a group of chartered accountants balancing on barrels all the while filling in tax returns. It had been the firm's CEO's idea to drum up business and advertise the wonders of accounting and that it wasn't one of the dark arts.

Staying close together, they headed to the bridge, the only way to get into the inner circle of towers. After every other step, someone or some creature was thrusting a sample of baked goods into their hands: sausage rolls, quiche, eccles cake, cherry bakewells, pasties—everything was available.

Scrungle just took what was offered and put it into his pockets. Half hoping he would come across someone giving away watermelon so he could give it to Peetles once he was freed. It was in the middle of the bridge where Scrungle was accosted by a young child who demanded that he do something funny or juggle. He said he couldn't and wasn't part of the entertainment.

The child's father, dressed in the same attire as the council of Gumptrude, made it known he was a personal friend of the high chancellor and said that he shouldn't be parading if he couldn't entertain. It became fractious, and he grabbed at Scrungles mask, demanding to know who he was. Scrungle looked to the Princess and the Green Knight for help, but they had pushed on, lost in the crowd. The councillor managed to snag the mask and pull it free.

"Oh, my word." Said the jumped-up bag of shit. "It's you. He's over here, rebel, terrorist." To several people, it sounded like 'tourist', and they wondered what he had against visitors. The man abruptly stopped shouting when a slice of Victoria sponge was shoved into his face, then he was slapped across the cheek with a peach melba, which sent him to his knees dazed. The Green Knight had come back to rescue Scrungle. Some of the cream from the peach melba splattered onto a woman in a paper dress.

"You clumsy cow," said the woman.

The Green Knight took a moment to absorb the comment, nodded, and then slapped her hard across the face. The woman stumbled towards the bridge's handrail, missed it, and fell into the water. There was a scream from her friend, and guards were soon heading towards them to see what the problem was.

Flailing around in the water, the woman's dress fell apart instantly; wads of paper and globs of cardboard floated away into the moat. The little boy, whose father had swooned at the assault of pastry and cream, kicked the Green Knight, who then pushed the spoilt little shit into the water with the woman.

Scrungle, caught on the bridge, was being shouted at by anyone who saw him as a wanted terrorist. The Green Knight pushed through the crowd, dragging Scrungle with her. She expertly dove under the sword thrust of a charging guard, rising, she grabbed their blade hand and delivered a headbutt. The guard landed on his back and she now stood with his sword in her hands as a wide circle formed, waiting for the rest of the guards to charge.

Scrungle now behind the Green Knight watched out of the corner of his eye as the Princess, with the guards distracted, climbed over the barriers, clambered up, and ran to centre stage.

"Listen to me; I am Princess Isobella." Her voice boomed out across the courtyard and beyond; it was the best it had sounded all day. The apprentice wizard, mixing for the first time, looked pleased. The crowd became silent, except for the accountants, but no one had paid them much attention anyway.

"Bakeasy has been poisoning the King and Gumptrude has been hiding the truth." Shouted Isobella. No one moved, although there was a smattering of applause. On stage, shocked, sitting on the raised dais overlooking the bake-off, as judges sat Bakeasy, Gumptrude, Lord Sebastian Bigglesworth and the Griffin who had been with Dinjay Flat.

Bakeasy was the first to react. She got up from her high back seat, walked to the front of the stage, and addressed the crowd.

"My child we are so glad you have come back. You have not been the same since my beloved king became ill. Come to me, my child."

Bakeasy strode towards Isobella with her arms ready to embrace. Her face was the image of benevolent forgiveness, and her breasts the image of two bald men fighting in a sack.

Isobella's shoulders dropped, and her lip curled as if she were ready to cry. There was the sound of an 'arr' from the crowd moved by the moment then Isobella picked up the top section of the wedding cake and threw it straight into Bakeasy's face. Inertia gripped the guards, silence gripped the crowd, and gravity gripped the barrel-balancing accountants. As fate would have it, the gates of the castle smashed open, and the carriage that had the Gold Knight pretending to be the Princess flew into the grounds. With it came the rest of the Knights of Colour and residents of Plombree who couldn't get tickets and just fancied a riot. Time stopped. No one moved, no one breathed, then the Green Knight screamed.

"Cake fight."

Scrungle didn't hesitate and launched a chocolate éclair at the nearest guard, and all hell broke loose. Ducking down and rolling, the Green Knight snatched a pasty from a young centaur and threw it with tremendous force at a guard. The guard flipped backwards, landing hard. Within a heartbeat, the air was filled with lemon drizzle cake, jam tarts, cherry bakwells, flapjacks, swiss rolls, and mini battenbergs.

The working-class party crashers singled out the Gumptrude guards. Grabbing anything pastry-related, they launched into the fray. Puff pastry, cream, jam-filled rolls, and custard splattered everywhere. A guard loading a crossbow was hit with a pie on the side of the face. Its filling of hot apple exploded against bare skin; the scream cut through the night. Onlookers turned away from the carnage. Only the surface of the sun is hotter than apple pie filling.

A captain of the guards rallied the men into formation, using shields to block the onslaught of delicacies. As a unit, they started to push the crowd back.

On stage Bakeasy, wiping cream from her face, had watched Scrungle throw the éclair, then the torrent of cakes and savoury baked goods that followed.

Her first instinct was to flee, but then she watched Isobella run off stage and head towards the tower. Dodging the cream and flaky pastry as best she could, she grabbed the griffin and shouted a command into his face.

"What are we going to do?" Said Gumptrude, who was now by Bakeasy's side his skin decidedly on the blue end of the colour spectrum.

"You can always use your really big brain to get us out of this." Snapped Bakeasy.

Gumptrude looked blank, and Bakeasy turned, striding off to the back of the stage. After a moment, Gumptrude followed.

# Thirty

## *Lots of Steps*

The Green Knight and Scrungle were slowly being pushed back towards the bridge. He had thrown everything at the guards, and all the large fungivore had left was a deceptively sharp cornflake cluster when the Princess stayed his stick-like hand.

"Now Scrungle, follow me."

The Green Knight knocked a guard to the floor using a pogo stick and a slice of chocolate gateau.

"Go with the Princess." She shouted at Scrungle.

Isobella pulled Scrungle along towards the towers and the living quarters of the royal family. The crowd had thrown every cake they could find at the guards, now the ground was covered in cream, flaky pastry, and assorted fillings. Skirting around what was left of the Gumptrude Security Detail, who slipped and fell on the slick stones of the courtyard, they ran along to the left of the towers into a small arched recess in the stonework. Down a short flight of stone steps to a service door. Isobella felt around the brickwork until she rattled a loose stone in the wall.

Pulling at the edges, she dislodged the stone and plucked a key from the hole behind. There was a grating squeal as she turned the key in the lock and pulled the door open. Inside was the polishing room full of shoes and boots.

Torchlight outlined the seams of the door at the far end. They stumbled and bumped into furniture and through the door into the basement corridor facing a flight of stairs leading up.

"Have I told you how much I hate stairs?" said Isobella.

"No, you have never mentioned it. When did it first start this hatred?" Said Scrungle in genuine curiosity. It made the Princess smile.

"To the top, we must go," said Isobella.

Following, Isobella Scrungle had time to think how terrified and, at the same time, exhilarated he was. This was not how he had envisioned his little journey to find the magic fungus was going to pan out. He had found his best friend, lost them, then found them again. There was a huge fight involving cakes and various pastries happening below him as they took the stone stairs two at a time. He was dressed as a jester racing to force a mushroom into her dad's mouth, who was also the king. Even more bizarre were the little bells on the horns of the jester's hat catching the side of the stone walls as they climbed.

Scrungle, and the Princess panted. Well, the Princess was panting. Scrungle was panting in the imaginary sense, passing level after level until it stopped at the top where a wide circular anti-chamber opened up before them. At the far end was a set of double oak doors intricately carved with the coat of arms and black metal inlays. One door stood ajar, and candlelight spilled out onto the floor.

"One moment please." Said Scrungle. He started to take off the disguise.

"Scrungle come on there's no time for this." implored the Princess.

"I would prefer not to be introduced to your father, the King dressed like this." He threw the jacket, pants, and jester's hat to one side.

The Princess ran with Scrungle into the King's large and sumptuous chambers, The stone floor was carpeted in a deep brown shagpile. Drapes of gold adorned the four posts of the bed, and tapestries hung from the walls. Paintings of the castle from different angles caught Scrungles eyes. One of the watercolours made Scrungle shudder and he made a secret bet with himself it was probably one of Kevin's. Against the far wall under the duvet of the king-sized bed, a figure lay prone. Extracts from the castle tour floated into Scrungle's head, remembering that the bed had been commissioned by the King's great-great-grandfather with a handy drinks tray and extra individual cushioned springs.

Bakeasy stood at one side in the dimly lit room. The drapes and shutters blocked any outside light. Next to Bakeasy was Gumptrude, several of the Gumptrude security guards, and the griffin.

Bakeasy, in one hand, was clutching something, holding it up towards her hefty chest; in her other hand was the flash of steel.

"Father," cried Isobella, moving towards her dad.

"Stop there." Said Bakeasy, moving out of the shadows. Slumped in Bakeasy's clutches was Peetles. The little creature hung limp in Bakeasy's hand as if asleep. Peetles normal healthy colour of orange was now a lacklustre grey. Bakeasy pointed the knife at the Princess.

"Peetles." Cried Scrungle taking a step towards his friend.

"Stop. Just bloody well stop there." Screamed Bakeasy, stamping her foot in a petulant rebuke at not getting her way. Scrungle did as he was told; Bakeasy had put the knife to Peetles head.

"It's over you, silly tart." Said Isobella.

"Oh no, it isn't," said Bakeasy.

"Oh yes, it is," retorted the Princess.

"Oh no, it isn't," said Bakeasy.

"Oh yes, it is," replied the Princess, inching closer to the king or dad.

"Stop it, this isn't bloody panto." Squealed Bakeasy.

"Oh yes, it is." Said Isobella winding Bakeasy up.

"Give me the cure and your little friend lives." Bakeasy was talking to Scrungle.

"I know you have it or you wouldn't be here. This creature and the witch Waynex told me everything." She added as if the plan had been foiled from the start.

"Peetles." Said Scrungle. The little creature lifted their head. Peetles was neither bobbly nor lumpy, and to Scrungle, this was a bad sign.

"I don't feel very well, Scrungle." Said Peetles, their breath rasping and laboured. Out of the shadows, a lemon-coloured water bottle was thrown at Scrungles feet.

"Your friend is very sick. The dungeons are very cold," said Bakeasy.

"Don't listen to her Scrungle. It's a lie. She doesn't mean anything she says." Isobella implored Scrungle, her face a mask of anguish.

"Oh, I do. Cure your friend, and you can both walk away free. The Princess will marry Whackerknacker as planned. I have no problem with that. You know it makes sense."

Bakeasy had moved closer to Scrungle a beguiling smile played on her face. Then Gumptrude moved out of the shadows.

"Town criers and the proclamations and anyone to believe anything. We can take this any way that's what is needed; I have a very big brain. Ask anyone. Everything is fake news." His sentence structure and linguistics were the same as those of a four-year-old dog with epilepsy, but Scrungle understood: save the king or save his friend.

Scrungle's magic pocket materialised, and he put his hand in, bringing out the one and only Huba mushroom. Peetles breathing was becoming steadily worse. He looked to the Princess, then to Peetles, then to the king on the bed.

"I'm stuck," Scrungle said as if to himself.

"Give me the mushroom." Shouted Bakeasy, pushing the knife into Peetles, who moaned a little but didn't have enough strength to cry out. Later, when Scrungle thought the moment over, he could never be sure if he dropped the mushroom on purpose, if it just fell out of his stick-like fingers, or if something else took hold and made the decision for him.

The Huba mushroom fell and rolled to the middle of the floor between Bakeasy and the Princess.

Bakeasy looked at Isobella.

Isobella looked at Bakeasy.

Isobella launched herself forward and Bakeasy did the same throwing Peetles to one side as they grappled on the floor. Outside, the sound of feet on the stone steps and the clash of metal on metal.

"Don't let them in. Save me." Said Gumptrude pushing the security guards towards the bedroom doors.

On the floor, the two women scratched, bit, and punched each other. When one tried to grab the mushroom, the other would pull them away.

Scrungle picked Peetles up and away from the fighting women. Huddling down next to the four-poster bed. Peetles felt cold to the touch and Scrungle tried to warm the little creature holding them close.

Bakeasy wasn't much of a fighter and the Princess was getting the upper hand as the paper and cardboard dress disintegrated on the Baroness. Changing tactics and foregoing trying to grab the mushroom, the Princess put Bakeasy in a choke hold. Within seconds Bakeasy went limp.

Behind Scrungle, the doors burst open, and the Green and Red Knight, covered in raspberry, cream, and cake mix, charged into the room. Behind them, in different angles of unconsciousness lay the

Gumptrude security guards. The hand of the Red Knight went to the visor of his helm; it had a wicked-looking wedge of a samosa triangle stuck in it. In all the confusion the griffin had undone the latches that secured the shutters on the balcony, Opening them wide the lights from the illuminations bathed the room. Taking a little run it took to the sky and flew out of the tower.

"Had you beatch? I had you; who's the mama beatch?" Shouted Isobella.

The Red Knight pulled Isobella off Bakeasy.

"She's done you've won. Ease down, ease down."

Isobella turned on the Red Knight; the look on the Princess's face made him instantly let go. She brushed herself down and patted her hair to straighten it a little, then knelt picking up the mushroom. Peetles eyes fluttered open for a moment.

"Scrungle."

"Peetles."

"Can I have a drink, I'm very thirsty." Peetles breath gasping, eyes closed. Isobella watched Scrungle and Peetles. Scrungle looked up at the Princess.

"I have to I'm sorry." Said the Princess

She walked around the bed and lifted the King's head. The King was frail and barely alive. Only his tenacity of will and one last glimpse of Bakeasy's cleavage had kept him here. Isobella put the mushroom into his mouth and massaged his jaws so he could chew the cure. No one moved, the sounds of the cake fight drifted through the balcony window. Steps on the stone stairs echoed as if from far away.

Isobella lifted her father's cold hand and watched as the colour rose in the King's cheeks, his breathing became stronger, his fists flexed and his royal chest rose in and out. The King's eyes opened wide and he sat up straight as if shocked. Then looked to his daughter.

"What the bloody hell has been going on," he said in a heavy Welsh accent.

"Dada." Said Isobella wrapping her arms around him and crying. Scrungle didn't care; he was looking around for water for Peetles. He spied the lemon-coloured water bottle.

"Please." Said Scrungle pointing with his free hand at the water bottle at the Green Knight's feet

"It's Peetles." He said. Scrungle got up, cradling Peetles and sat on the edge of the royal bed. The Green Knight unscrewed the top holding it out for Scrungle.

"You are my bestest friend." Peetles little voice was barely above a whisper.

"You are my bestest friend too." Replied Scrungle. He tipped the water bottle and Peetles took the last few drops. Looking up at Scrungle, Peetles smiled, then with one last hitching breath, closed their eyes and passed away.

Scrungle rocked back and forth with Peetles in his arms, his heart had broken into pieces. Tears welled up and flooded down his face. He'd never cried, it was something he thought he could never do. Holding onto Isobella the King had gotten out of bed and came round to Scrungle and Peetles.

"I'm so sorry Scrungle." Said the Princess. Outside the sounds of fighting continued.

## Thirty-One

# *Well Then*

The silence in the King's chambers was an unbearable weight as Scrungle sat rocking Peetles in his arms. Shafts of moonlight from the open balcony mixed with the candle and torches washing the room in a soft glow, but to Scrungle it had never felt so dark. Something deep inside him had fallen, tumbling forever into the black endless abyss of loss and he would never be made whole again. Holding his friend, he didn't know what to do; He tried to tell himself Peetles was just sleeping. Words he wished were true but deep inside where it counts Scrungle knew it was a lie. From far away he watched someone else stroking a stick-like hand over his little friend's soft features. Trying to find the words to tell his friend he missed them. He thought about how many times Peetles had saved the day by accident, or just by being such an innocent soul, It was not fair that his friend now lay still and cold, Peetles would never see the Chana tree or go fishing for house bricks. Scrungle would forgo all the mushrooms in the world to have his friend again, even for one day. The journey to find the magic mushrooms had been what he wanted, but he had found something so much more along the way, and they now lay still in his arms. His bestiest friend as Peetles would have said. From far away Scrungle could hear words but couldn't understand what was being said.

"Scrungle, let me take Peetles; lay him down to rest." It was the Princess she stood at Scrungle shoulder, tears in her eyes. Scrungle just stared at Isobella and then shook his large white head. He couldn't and wouldn't let go.

Then something strange began as wind-chimes gently played on the air, soothing a troubled heart. Scrungle lifted his head, looking for the source. A flutter at first, then a wind blew the heavy drapes at the balcony window. It was fresh, like the first morning of spring, heralding the rebirth from winter's slumber. It grew stronger ruffling hair, swirling around the room as if searching for something. The torches and candles that lit the chamber blew out with a hiss. Through his tears, Scrungle watched as the lemon-coloured water bottle deep within its centre began to glow. Framed by their silhouettes the light spread outwards glowing in intensity and shining as brightly as a hundred candles. Scrungle felt Peetles little body pull in his hands wanting to rise. Scrungle reluctant, let go as Peetles floated in front of them all. The familiar orange of Peetle's skin started returning as their little round body slowly spun in the air. Then gently landed on the carpeted floor. The water bottle stopped glowing as Peetles eyes snapped open. The torches and candles lit with a pop.

"Scrungle I have a Huba mushroom. I put it in the water bottle to keep it safe."

"Peetles, you're alive." Shouted Scrungle jumping off the bed, picking Peetles up, and hugging his friend so tight Peetles was sure he would be crushed.

"Peetles, you're alive." Shouted Scrungle again and again in his delight.

* * *

Scrungle and Peetles now sat in the quarters reserved for visiting dignitaries and honoured guests of the realm. Eating a meal of mushrooms, melon and berry-infused water, reflecting on what had happened.

When Peetles had spoken, the King had moved into action. Gumptrude, who had hidden behind a chest of draws when the knights had come into the room, was dragged out by the Red Knight and pushed in front of the King.

The Baroness was still lying unconscious on the floor as Gumptrude had started to cry and blubber; it was all Bakeasy's idea. His face had turned blue, protesting his innocence, when the King had punched him hard in the stomach and he had fallen over, winded.

"Where's my bloody crown?" The King had shouted. Isobella, one step ahead, had already picked it up from the dressing table.

"Right, Lady Green, you stay here; I don't want these two toerags going anywhere."

The King had said this while adjusting his crown to what he thought was a jaunty but still serious angle. To clarify, the Green Knight pointed to Gumptrude and Bakeasy on the floor as Peetles had gone a bit lumpy, thinking the King meant them. Then he strode through the doors in his regal pyjamas to go down into the courtyard and put things back to normal.

Isobella had kissed Scrungles cheek, and then she and the Red Knight had followed after him. It hadn't taken long before the Yellow and Silver Knights had come to help and escort Bakeasy and Gumptrude down to the dungeons until things settled themselves. The Green Knight took the elated Scrungle and confused Peetles to the rooms they were now in, saying she would be back but to keep the door locked from the inside until she did.

Peetles sat on an expensive hand-carved oak chair, boosted by yellow and red cushions so they could reach the table. Swinging their little legs as they drank from the infused water.

"I am so glad you are here, Peetles. I was terribly sad when I thought you had gone." Scrungle said.

Peetles smiled. "I was scared in the storm, but when you threw the water bottle, it kept me up. I had a Huba mushroom, so I put it in the water bottle so I didn't lose it. I'm a bit forgetful at times. I floated and got colder and colder, it felt very dreamy. I thought it must be really hard to sharpen a pencil with a hammer. Then I felt claws, and I was flying, and then I was here at the castle in the dungeon."

Scrungle thought about the claws and then realised Peetles was referring to the griffin.

"Are we terror wrists still?" Said Peetles getting a little bit spikey and lumpy.

"No, I think we might be heroes." Said Scrungle.

Outside there was a knock on the door; upon opening it, Scrungle was greeted by the Princess, who had changed and looked a lot more Princessy but with a strong hint of steampunk in pink, black, and grey. Scrungle felt obliged to bow with everything that had happened, but she swept him up in an embrace. Pulling Scrungle into the room, they picked Peetles up and swung him around as they laughed and giggled together. Sitting down, she put Peetles next to her on the sofa. The space next to her she patted with her hand for Scrungle to take.

"Oh, Scrungle Bungus, everything is well. The minute the people saw dad, they cheered so loudly. He is out in the courtroom sorting out who needs a smacked arse and who doesn't. The Knights have all taken back their colours and are chasing the hobgoblins out of Plombree." Princess Isobella was flush with excitement. "Dad would like you to stay and have our story recounted to the scribes; you are part of Plom history. The Knights drew straws to see who could stand guard for you tonight."

"Who won?" Scrungle asked.

"The Red Knight," said Isobella, and with a smile, she stood and hugged them both and said "We won Scrungle," as she left the room.

* * *

The days in Plombree flew by as Scrungle and Peetles testified against Bakeasy and Gumptrude. At the end of the trial, Gumptrude was stripped of all his assets and banished from the Kingdom, and Bakeasy, being a resident of Flan, was deported in a political move to secure the release of spies captured there. Lord Sebastian Bigglesworth was put under investigation for embezzlement and being a stuck-up twat.

One of the first places they visited was the home of the family Morris, who had been imprisoned within days of Scrungle and Peetles leaving, they were released immediately after Gumptrude was arrested.

Mr Morris, his family, and Doris were glad to see them both. Scrungle and Peetles kept apologising, but the crown had handsomely reimbursed the family for wrongful imprisonment. They also coined it from the local news parchments and town criers for exclusive rights to their story. Mr Morris said the Knights of Colour liaison staff had come to see him with a contract to be the main smith for the knights' armour. It was early days, but the Princess was starting to overhaul the whole endorsement system, so it was even for both male and female knights, and everything had to go through the new ministry for the crown.

Scrungle and Peetles, who had rooms at the palace, were one afternoon escorted by the Yellow Knight to a vaulted, arched meeting room. A familiar cough greeted them. Sitting at the far end on a very comfy sofa was the witch Waynex. The day's sunlight streamed through the long slit windows, and they could see her properly for the first time. She was still dressed in wool, but it had been washed and pressed so the curry stains weren't as vibrant.

The pair sat opposite the witch and recounted their journey, apologising for not getting all the items on the list and pulling out the bits they had collected.

"Not to worry. It was only if you had the chance. But you never know when you might get a chance to pick the other bits up." Said the witch, which Scrungle thought was a little cryptic, but he had a more pressing thought on his mind.

"Sorry about the moon-dial. It went down with Sad Wally." Said Scrungle.

"Ah, things have a habit of washing up." Said the witch, looking at Peetles, then she coughed. Scrungle had been itching to see the witch and ask one simple question.

"Why did the water in the bottle work for Peetles?" He thought he knew but wanted validation from the witch. Her mesmerising eyes read his thoughts.

"Yes, I think you guessed it." She rasped and pulled a drag on a hand-rolled cigarette. It was a 'No Smoking' castle but the witch Waynex didn't seem to care.

"Chuck it over."

She proffered a bony hand towards Peetles. The little creature let go of the water bottle, and Scrungle passed it across. Witch Waynex sniffed it, then much to Peetles and Scrungles chagrin gave it a long lick. Her eyes rolled back in her head, and she chanted strange words in between coughs. Then sprinkled a mixture of herbs over it. To Scrungle and Peetles, nothing seemed to be happening.

"Well, as far as I can tell. The Huba mushroom dissolved into the very essence of the water bottle." The witch Waynex leaned in. "Don't tell another living soul, but I believe that if you both sip the water, you will feel a little lighter."

"I will be able to get back into my home." Said Scrungle delighted. "Peetles, would you like to come and be my best friend and live in the Chana tree with me."

"Yes, Oh yes I would." Said a very happy Peetles.

Scrungle was also happy that the end of the sentence with 'tree and me' rhymed, he hugged the mass of wool that was the witch Waynex.

* * *

As required, Scrungle and Peetles talked long with the scribes and historians, recounting their tale. When complete, they were given a formal audience with the King.

It was now part of the records of Plom that Scrungle Bungus and Peetles were to be given the order of the thumbs up and the keys to the city. Never having to stand in line at customs, free dental care, and a state pension if they wanted it. The King also granted the land around the Chana tree to be Scrungle's for time immemorial or until the crown needed to exploit the area for natural resources.

It was Peetles who asked if the wolves could be given honours, but the best the King could do was to say that no wolf in the land of Badly Designed Signs could be hunted.

They spent their free time walking or pedalling around Plombree. Often greeted as heroes and on numerous occasions asked to stand for a speed sketch selfie. The mood in the city had changed and almost immediately paper apparel was abandoned as the inhabitants of the city went back to more conventional dress that held up in wet weather. The pair did notice that there were a lot more tricycles around.

In the evening, the pair would spend time in the palace gardens, talking with the Princess, who was often in the company of Sergio. Different knights would join them and inform them of what was happening in Plombree. Then they would play 'Where did I put my finger last?' or 'What made it wet?' and 'Is it heavy?' It was the best of times.

Announcements and proclamations were made that the castle would be opened up for celebrations honouring Scrungle, Peetles, and the Knights of Colour. It was an open-air event, and everyone who was anyone attended.

Reserved tickets for family Morris, Doris, and Gladis, who was extremely excited and couldn't wait to get back to her little village and tell her neighbours. Maximus, Windy and the children were also in attendance and played with the Morris children, which turned into a long-time friendship between the families. It was decided by Scrungle and Peetles that they would say nothing to Windy about her grandfather unless they were asked. The pair felt the family had suffered enough.

Scrungle wanted to make sure Kevin the donkey had a ticket, but Gladis said he was quite the famous artist now and would have no problem securing entry.

At the top of the table next to the King sat the witch Waynex and her sister, the witch Waysup. The evening started with the winning poem from the open competition to catalogue the recent events and the heroes who had saved the King. It had been won by an anonymous entry from Scrungle's neck of the woods. The judges were impressed with the writer's ability to describe Peetles and find a rhyme for orange.

The king took the stage, his voice had been enchanted so everyone could hear. It was the same apprentice wizard from the bake-off battle and he seemed to have a handle on the spell now.

"Well, it is time to honour true friends of the crown. Without their diligence and sacrifice, I would not be standing here today. Their journey was arduous and their challenges immense. Please stand my daughter, Scrungle and Peetles."

The crowd cheered as they were ushered onto the small stage where Peetles was given a box to stand on. The banners of Plombree flew high behind them. The King hung medals around Scrungle's sort of neck, over Peetles head, and then his daughter. The King kissed Isobella on the forehead and she blushed a deep red. Turning to the crowd the King motioned for silence.

"It has also come to my attention that a young man in the service of the crown has something to ask my daughter. Come forward, Sergio Leon."

Scrungle and Peetles moved to one side as they had been told what was about to happen. Sergio walked up onto the stage and then dropped to one knee.

"Princess Isobella, you are my world, I am your humble servant. Your father has given permission that I may ask. Will you marry me?

Isobella squealed, then jumped on Sergio straddling him, and saying yes between kisses. The crowd cheered then the king pointed to the band and the party started.

One by one, in between dance numbers, the knights in their formal dress came to pay their respects to the duo. Scrungle handed the bill Dangle had given him over to the Yellow Knight, saying he didn't know what to do with it. The Yellow Knight laughed and said she would get it sorted.

Torpid dressed in the latest fashion approached the duo, her head was down and without looking at Scrungle handed him a rolled-up parchment. After undoing the ribbon he was amazed and thrilled to see a picture of himself and Peetles on stage with the King from moments earlier. It was a speed sketch and utterly brilliant. Scrungle hugged Torpid who panicked, giggled and smiling ran back to her table. This wasn't the only gift the pair were given. A harpy representing SCS and Amazing Shine gave the pair new hats and goggles as well as a year's half-price voucher.

As the days passed it was fine to be in Plombree but Scrungle was starting to feel the pull of home. Asking leave of the King if it was all right to travel back to the Chana tree. The King granted the wish although sad to see them leave.

The whole city lined the way on the day of their departure. Scrungle and Peetles waved from the tricycle as ticker tape, paper, and flowers rained down on them.

All the Knights of Colour were their honour guard with the Princess next to them as they moved along the highway. Isobella would journey with them as she wanted to see where Scrungle lived and visit the borders of the realm.

From above they heard a call. Malcolm the falcon and Abacus Blue Wind flew overhead. Scrungle and Peetles waved hoping the birds could see them.

They travelled the Kings Road which was now free of cones or any signs of road works. the Princess told Scrungle and Peetles that the trolls had been given a decent severance and left to go back to hiding under bridges and it was no longer mandatory for liability insurance for trolls. The King had rescinded all bridge inspection certifications. This would be until he had found someone with a decent knowledge of bridges to inspect them.

At the city limits, the Gold and White knights bade their farewells as they didn't want to leave the King unprotected. Saluting Scrungle and Peetles, they handed them a shield made of all the colours of the order; in the middle was the thumbs-up emblem of the kingdom.

The yellow tricycle, smooth on the road, took them easily up into the mountain pass. It was a pleasant journey in such regal company, and they laughed, joked, and talked as they travelled. Malcolm and Abacus would land on their respective knights, confirm nothing to report then fly off when they had rested. Abacus said he was now employed by the crown, sounding rather pleased with himself.

One day in the mountain pass, they stopped by an old watch tower. Scrungle and Peetles admired the view, watching the fish jump in the river.

"I'm sad we didn't get to see the wolves one last time." Said Peetles.

"Yes, I do too, they did help us with the Cheese man and the riddles." Said Scrungle picking up a stick thinking he might keep it.

"One day maybe we could go and visit," said Peetles rather hopeful.

"Yes, that sounds like a good pie." Said Scrungle, his world-view was different now he had had an adventure and the idea of a holiday to see the wolves was a welcome thought for the future.

At the bridge, Steve'o was still standing guard and looked terrified at the approaching entourage. Scrungle and Peetles cycled down the hill and talked to him about the new change in the law. They told him that he could go back to hiding under the bridge. He was pleased but gave the Red Knight a wide berth as they passed.

The autumn leaves were falling, covering the king's road. The princes said it would be a priority to change all the flags pretending to be stones because it was a bloody nightmare for the horses. The mornings had started to turn cold with a hint of frost. On their last day together, he and Peetles pointed to where they had come out after meeting each other in the woods, then they passed the picnic area where Scrungle had met the knights for the first time.

It was midday when Scrungle could see the top of the Chana tree poking above the little rise. A sense of excitement rushed through him like the wind in the wheat field. The company stopped where Scrungle had put his wedge-like feet on the King's road and started his journey. Dismounting the tricycle, Scrungle's magic pockets materialised, and he put it away. The princess got down from her horse and stood with the pair.

Looking down into the little valley, they could all see the tall, wide, beautiful Chana tree, appreciating the cantilever turrets. Its leaves rustled in the breeze, and the scent of shoe polish filled the air.

Isobella picked Peetles up and kissed the little creature on the forehead. Peetles giggled feeling self-conscious. Then she stood on tip-toe and kissed Scrungle on the cheek.

"Please visit the city and me. It is a royal command. I will miss you both."

Scrungle and Peetles bowed as best they could.

"You have earned your home. Go and enjoy it."

The friends walked off down the dirt track, turning halfway to look back at the Kings road. Tall and resplendent in their colours, the knights with the Princess in the middle, one by one drew their swords, holding them aloft to salute the heroes of Plom.

At the base of the Chana tree, they looked back one last time, but the road was clear and the knights and the Princess had gone. Scrungle looked up into the canopy of his nest-like home and arches.

"Can you see that big branch Peetles?" Scrungle pointed upwards, and Peetles followed his friend's finger with his eyes.

"Is it the branch that looks like a branch?" Said Peetles, concentrating hard.

"Yes, the branch that looks like a branch." Said Scrungle, an imaginary smile on his face.

Peetles slid the lemon-coloured water bottle off and handed it to his tall friend.

Scrungle looked at Peetle's innocent and radiant smile, then took a sip, handing it back for Peetles to do the same. Shouldering the water bottle that had been given as a gift. A light floating feeling washed over the pair.

Scrungle bent and held Peetles stumpy appendage as the sound of wind-chimes light and delicate filled the air, then together they flexed at the knees, bounced and floated up into the Chana tree and home.

# About the Author

A strange and complicated individual, Lambert can usually be found on a Wednesday outside the council's main office for traffic management, shouting at passing strangers about unpaid parking fines, potholes, orange cones, and wasps. During the summer months, he enjoys hanging upside down, pretending he is in Australia. Lambert was once caught agitating a ferret with an empty toilet roll; the charges were eventually dropped after pleading he lost all grip on reality after listening to a Nigel Farage podcast.

**You can connect with me on:**

http://www.scrunglebungus.com

Milton Keynes UK
Ingram Content Group UK Ltd.
UKHW020911291124
451807UK00013B/852

9 798227 993793